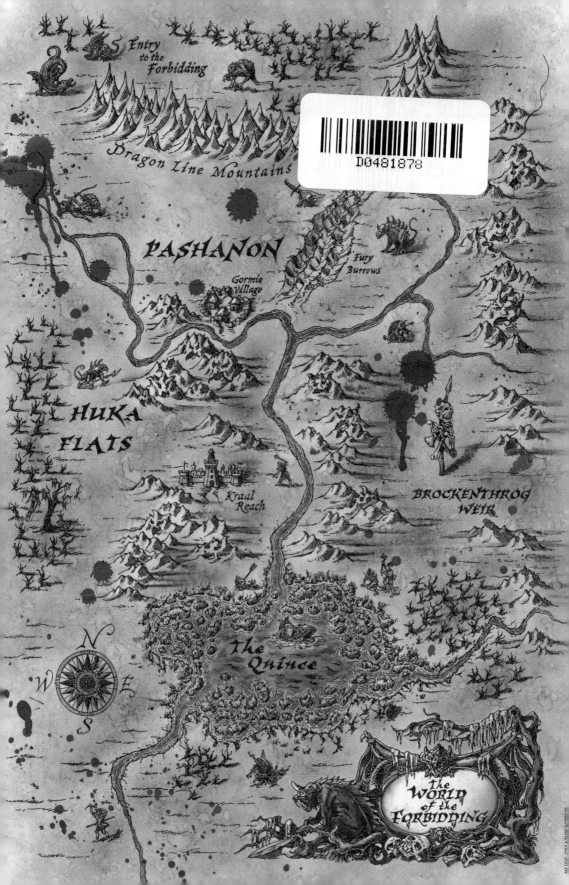

By Terry Brooks

Shannara
FIRST KING OF SHANNARA
THE SWORD OF SHANNARA
THE ELFSTONES OF SHANNARA
THE WISHSONG OF SHANNARA

The Heritage of Shannara
THE SCIONS OF SHANNARA
THE DRUID OF SHANNARA
THE ELF QUEEN OF SHANNARA
THE TALISMANS OF SHANNARA

The Voyage of the *Jerle Shannara*
ILSE WITCH
ANTRAX
MORGAWR

High Druid of Shannara
JARKA RUUS
TANEQUIL

THE WORLD OF SHANNARA

The Magic Kingdom of Landover
MAGIC KINGDOM FOR SALE—SOLD!
THE BLACK UNICORN
WIZARD AT LARGE
THE TANGLE BOX
WITCHES' BREW

Word and Void
RUNNING WITH THE DEMON
A KNIGHT OF THE WORD
ANGEL FIRE EAST

HIGH DRUID OF SHANNARA

STRAKEN

BALLANTINE BOOKS • NEW YORK

HIGH DRUID
OF
SHANNARA

STRAKEN

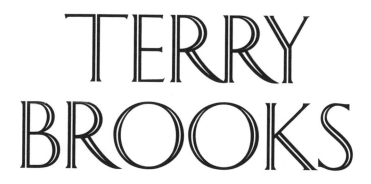

TERRY
BROOKS

Copyright © 2005 by Terry Brooks

Published in the United States by Del Rey Books, an imprint of The Random House Publishing Group, a division of Random House, Inc., New York.

Del Rey is a registered trademark and the Del Rey colophon is a trademark of Random House, Inc.

ISBN 0-345-45112-0

Endpaper maps by Russ Charpentier

Printed in the United States of America on acid-free paper

www.delreybooks.com

2 4 6 8 9 7 5 3 1

First Edition

In memory of Christina Michelle George and Caleb Alexander Delp
and
in celebration of readers like them everywhere

HIGH DRUID OF SHANNARA

STRAKEN

"Pen Ohmsford!" The black-cloaked figure called out to him from across the chasm that separated the island of the tanequil from the rest of the world. "We have been waiting for you!"

A male Druid. He came forward a few steps, pulling back his hood to reveal the strong, dark features of his face. Pen had never seen him before.

"Come across the bridge so that we can talk," the Druid said.

The firelight threw his shadow across the stone archway in a dark stain that spilled into the chasm, and the portent it foreshadowed was unmistakable. Pen wished he hadn't rushed into the light so quickly, that he had been more careful. But he had thought himself past the worst of it. He had survived his encounter with the tanequil and received the gift of the darkwand, the talisman that would give him access into the Forbidding. He had lost two fingers in doing so, but he had come to believe that they were a small price to pay. Losing Cinnaminson was a much larger price, but he had accepted that there was nothing he could do about it until after his aunt was safely returned, promising himself he would try to come back for her then. Finally, he had escaped the monster that had pursued them all the way from Anatcherae and knew it to be dead at last, pulled down into the chasm and crushed.

But now this.

His fingers tightened possessively around the darkwand, and he scanned the faces of the captive Trolls. All there, he saw. No one missing. No one even appeared hurt. They must have been caught completely by surprise not to have put up any fight. He wondered vaguely how that could have happened, how the Druids had found them at all, for that matter, but he guessed it was a pointless exercise.

A few of the Trolls were looking up now, Kermadec among them. The anger and disappointment on his face were unmistakable. He had failed Pen. They all had. The boy saw Tagwen there as well, almost hidden behind the massive bodies of his companions.

There was no sign of Khyber.

"Cross the bridge, Pen," the Druid repeated, not unkindly. "Don't make this any harder on yourself."

"I think I should stay where I am," Pen answered.

The Druid nodded, as if understanding him perfectly. "Well, you can do that, if you choose. I've read the warning on the stone, and I know better than to try to come across after you." He paused. "Tell me. If the danger is real, how did you manage to get over there without being harmed?"

Pen said nothing.

"What are you doing here, anyway? Trying to help your aunt? Did you think you might find her here?"

Pen stared back at him silently.

"We have your friends. All of them. You can see for yourself. We have your parents, as well, locked away at Paranor." His voice was patient, calm. "It doesn't do you any good to stay over there when those you care about are all over here. You can't help them by refusing to face up to your responsibilities."

My responsibilities, Pen repeated silently. What would this man know of his responsibilities? Why would he even care, save that he thought he could stop Pen from carrying them out?

A second Druid appeared beside the first, coming out of the darkness and into the light. This one was slender and small, a ferret-faced Gnome of particularly cunning looks, his eyes shifting swiftly from the first Druid to Pen and then back again. He muttered something, and the first Druid gave him a quick, angry look.

"How do I know you aren't lying about my parents?" Pen asked suddenly; it wasn't the first time he had heard the claim. He still didn't want to believe it.

The first Druid turned back to him. "Well, you don't. I can tell you that they were flying in a ship called *Swift Sure* when we brought them into the Keep. They helped us find you. Your father was worried about the disappearance of his sister, but more worried about you. That is how we found you, Pen."

Gone cold to the bone, the boy stared at him. The explanation made perfect sense. His father would have aided them without realizing what he was doing, thinking it was the right thing, that they were as concerned about his aunt as he was. The King of the Silver River was supposed to have warned his parents of the Druids, but perhaps he had failed. If so, his father wouldn't have known of their treachery. How could he?

Pen brushed back his tangled red hair while trying to think what to do.

"Let me put this to you another way," the taller Druid went on, moving slightly in front of the other. "My companion is less patient than I am, although he isn't volunteering to cross the bridge, either. But when morning comes, we will bring one of the airships across, and then we will have you, one way or the other. There are only so many places you can hide. This is all a big waste of time, given the way things eventually have to turn out."

Pen suspected that was true. But his freedom, however temporary, was the only bargaining chip he possessed. "Will you set my friends free, if I agree to come over?"

The Druid nodded. "My word on it. All of them. We have no use for them beyond persuading you to come with us. Once you cross over, they are free to go."

"What about my parents?"

The Druid nodded. "Once you are back at Paranor, they can go, too. In fact, once you've told us what we want to know, what your purpose is in coming here, you can go, too."

He was lying. He made it sound believable, exuding just the right amount of sincerity and reasonableness through his choice of words and tone of voice, but Pen knew the truth of things at once. The Druid would have done better to tell him something less soothing, but he supposed the man saw him as a boy and thought he would respond better to a lie than to the truth.

He paused to consider what he should do next. He had asked the questions that needed asking and gotten the answers he expected. It reconfirmed his suspicions about what would happen if he crossed the bridge to surrender to them. On the other hand, if he stayed where he was, they would capture him sooner or later, even if he went back down into the chasm, something he did not think he could do. Worse, he would be doing nothing to help his family and friends. If he was as concerned about responsibility as he liked to think, he would have to do more than go off and hide.

The decision was easier to make than he would have thought. He had to go to Paranor anyway if he was to use the darkwand to reach his aunt. Rescuing the Ard Rhys was what he had set out to do, and he couldn't do that if he didn't get inside the Druid's Keep. The Druids who had come for him were offering him a chance to do just that. He would have preferred going about it in a different way, but it all ended the same. The trick would be finding a way to keep the darkwand in his possession until he could get inside the chamber of the Ard Rhys.

He had no idea how he was going to do that.

"I want to speak with Tagwen," he called out. "Send him to the head of the bridge and move back so I can come across safely."

The Druids exchanged an uncertain glance. "When you surrender yourself, then we will let you talk with Tagwen," the taller one said.

Pen shook his head. "If you want me to surrender, you have to let me talk with Tagwen first. I want to hear from him what he thinks about your promises. I want to hear from him how good he thinks your word is. If you don't let me talk to him, I'm staying right here."

He watched their dark faces bend close and heard them confer in inaudible whispers. He could tell they didn't like the request and were trying to come up with a way to refuse it.

"If you think I will be so easy to find over here come morning, perhaps you should wait to try it and find out for yourselves," he said suddenly. "It might not be as easy as you think. That spider creature you sent to hunt me down? Or was it supposed to kill me? You did send it, didn't you?"

He asked the questions on impulse, not knowing how they

would answer, but suspecting. He was not disappointed. Both Druids stared at him in surprise. The one who did all the talking folded his arms into his cloak. "We didn't send him. But we know who did. We thought he was dead, killed in the Slags."

Pen shook his head, his eyes shifting to Tagwen, who was watching him alertly now, knowing he was up to something, anxious to find out what it was. "*He?* Not *it?*"

"Aphasia Wye. A man, but I grant you he looks more an insect than a human. Are you saying he isn't dead? Where is he?"

"No, he's dead. But he didn't die in the Slags. He tracked us all the way here. Last night, he crossed the bridge. Just as you want to do. Except that he found a way. Then he found me, but something else, too, and it killed him. If you want to see what that something is, fly your airship on over. I'll wait for you."

It was a bluff, but it was a bluff worth trying. Aphasia Wye was a predator of the first order—they might be hesitant to go up against something that had dispatched him. It cast Pen in a different light, giving him a more dangerous aspect, since he was alive and his hunter wasn't. He had to make them stop and think about whether it was worthwhile to refuse his request.

The taller Druid finished conferring with his companion and looked over. "All right, Pen. We'll let you speak with Tagwen. But no tricks, please. Anything that suggests you are acting in bad faith will put your Troll friends and your parents at risk. Don't test our limits. Have your talk, and then do what you know you have to do and surrender yourself to us."

Pen didn't know if he would do that or not, but it would help if he could talk with Tagwen about it first. He watched the Dwarf rise on the taller Druid's command and walk to the head of the bridge. He watched the Druids move back, signaling the Gnome Hunters to do the same. Pen waited until the area in front of the bridge was clear of everyone but the Dwarf, then stepped out onto the stone arch and walked across. He used the darkwand like a walking staff, leaning on it as if he were injured, pretending that was its purpose. Maybe they would let him keep it if they thought he had need of it to walk. Maybe pigs would learn to fly. He kept his eyes open for any unexpected movement, for shadows that didn't belong or sounds that were out of place. He used his small magic to test for warnings that might alert him to dangers he couldn't see. But nothing revealed itself. He crossed unimpeded, captives and captors staying back, behind the fire, deeper into the gardens, away from the ravine's edge.

When he was at the far side, he dropped down into a crouch, using the bridge abutments as shelter. He didn't think they intended to kill him, but he couldn't be certain.

Tagwen moved close. "They caught us with our pants down, young Pen. We thought we were watching out for you, but we were looking too hard in the wrong direction." His bluff face wrinkled with distaste. "They had us under spear and arrow before we could mount a defense. Anything we might have done would have gotten us all killed. I'm sorry."

Pen put his hand on the Dwarf's stout shoulder. "You did the best you could, Tagwen. We've all done the best we could."

"Perhaps." He didn't sound convinced. His eyes searched the boy's face. "Are you all right? Were you telling the truth about that thing that was tracking us? Was it really over there with you? I thought we'd lost it once and for all when we entered the mountains. Is it finally dead?"

Pen nodded. "The tanequil killed it. It's a long story. But anything that crosses this bridge is in real danger. I'm alive because of this."

He nodded down at the darkwand, which was resting next to him on the bridge, flat against the stone, tucked into the shadows.

The Dwarf peered at it, then caught sight of Pen's damaged hand and looked up again quickly. "What happened to your fingers?"

"The tree took them in exchange for the staff. Blood for sap, flesh for bark, bones for wood. It was necessary. Don't think on it."

"Don't think on it?" Tagwen was appalled. He glanced quickly over Pen's shoulder into the darkness of the tanequil's island. "Where is Cinnaminson?"

Pen hesitated. "Staying behind. Safe, for now. Tagwen, listen to me. I have to do what they want. I have to go with them to Paranor."

Tagwen stared. "No, Penderrin. You won't come out of there alive. They don't intend to let you go. Nor your parents, either. You're being taken to Shadea a'Ru. She's behind what's happened to the Ard Rhys, and once she's questioned you about what you are doing and you tell her—which you will, make no mistake—you and your parents are finished. Don't doubt me on this."

Pen nodded. "I don't, Tagwen. But look at how things stand.

We're trapped here, all of us. Even without the Druids to deal with, we're stranded in these ruins, surrounded by Urdas. I have to get out if I'm to help my aunt, and the quicker the better. It's already been too long. If I don't get to Paranor and use the darkwand soon, it will be too late. And now I have a way. The Druids will take me faster than I could get there on my own. I know it's dangerous. I know what they intend for me. And for my parents. But I have to risk it."

"You're risking too much!" the Dwarf snapped. "You'll get there quick enough, all right. And then what? They won't let you into the chamber of the Ard Rhys. They won't let you make use of that talisman. Shadea will see you for the threat you are and do away with you before you have a chance to do anything!"

"Maybe. Maybe not." He looked off into the gardens, into the pale, shifting patterns of color and the dappled shadows cast by the Druids and Gnome Hunters in the firelight's glow. "In any case, it's the only choice that makes sense." He turned back to Tagwen. "If I agree to go with them, will that tall Druid keep his word and let you go? Is his word any good? Is he any better than the rest of them?"

Tagwen thought about it a moment. "Traunt Rowan. He's not as bad as the other one, Pyson Wence, and certainly not as bad as Shadea. But he joined them in the plot against your aunt." He shook his head. "She always thought he was principled, if misguided in his antipathy toward her. He might keep his word."

Pen nodded. "I'll have to chance it."

The Dwarf reached for him with both strong hands and gripped his shoulders. "Don't do this, Penderrin," he whispered.

Pen held his gaze. "If you were in my shoes, Tagwen, wouldn't you? To save her from the Forbidding, to give her a chance, wouldn't you do just what I'm doing?" Tagwen stared at him in silence. He gave the Dwarf a quick smile. "Of course you would. Don't say anything more. I've already said it to myself. We knew from the beginning that we would do whatever was necessary to reach her, no matter the risk. We knew it, even if we didn't talk about it. Nothing has changed. I have to go to Paranor. Then into the Forbidding."

He closed his eyes against the sudden panic that the words roused in him. The enormity of what he was going to attempt was overwhelming. He was just a boy. He wasn't gifted or skilled or anything useful. He was mostly just there when no one else was.

He took a deep breath. "Will you come after me? In case I don't find a way to get through? In case I get locked away in the dungeons and don't get my parents out? Will you try to do something about it?" He exhaled sharply. "Even if I do get through and find her, the Druids will be waiting for us when we get back. We'll need help, Tagwen."

The Dwarf tightened his grip. "We'll come for you. No matter how long it takes us, no matter where you are. We'll find a way to reach you. We'll be there for you when you need us."

Pen put his hands over those of the Dwarf's, pressing them down into his shoulders. "Get out of here any way you can, Tagwen. Don't stop for anything." He hesitated. "Don't try to reach Cinnaminson. She has to wait for me. She can't leave until I come back for her." He shook his head quickly, fighting back tears. "Don't ask me to explain. Just tell me you'll do what I've asked. All right?"

The Dwarf nodded. "All right."

"I can do this," Pen whispered, swallowing hard. "I know I can."

Tagwen's fingers tightened. "I know it, too. You've done everything else. Everything anyone could have asked of you."

"I'll find a way. Once I'm there, I'll find a way."

"There are some still loyal to your aunt," Tagwen said. "Keep an eye out. One of them might come to your aid."

Pen glanced down again at the darkwand. "What can I do about the staff? It's too big to hide, but I have to take it with me. I know they won't let me keep it, if they see it. But I can't afford to give it over to them, either."

From back in the shadows, the taller of the two Druids called out, "You should have said everything you intended to say by now, Pen. You should be finished and ready to honor your promise. Tell Tagwen to step back, and then you come forward to us!"

Pen stared toward the firelight, to the cluster of Troll prisoners huddled together, to the shadowy forms of the Gnome Hunters surrounding them, to the cloaked forms of the Druids. It had the look of another world, of a place and time he could barely imagine. He was still enmeshed in the world of the tanequil, of orange-tipped leaves and mottled bark, of massive limbs and roots, of a sentient being older than Man. His memories of the past two days were still so painfully fresh that they dominated his present and threatened to overwhelm his fragile determination.

He despaired.

"That's a pretty piece of work," Tagwen said suddenly, nodding down at the darkwand. "It might help if it wasn't so shiny."

He eased back on his heels and reached behind him for a handful of damp earth, then rubbed it along the length of the staff, clotting the runes, dulling the surface. He worked in the shadows, shielding his movements.

"If they take it away from you," he said, finishing up, "tell them you found it in the ruins. Tell them you don't know what it is. If they think it was given to you to help the Ard Rhys, you'll never see it again. You might keep it long enough to use it if they don't suspect what it's for."

Pen nodded. He stood up, one hand gripping the staff. He leaned on it once more, as if he needed its support. "Go back to them. Tell Kermadec to be ready. Khyber is still out there, somewhere. I saw her while coming back to you. She should have been here by now. She might be watching all this, and I don't know what she will do."

The Dwarf took a quick look around, as if thinking he might see her in the darkness, then nodded and rose, as well. Saying nothing, he returned to the Gnome Hunters and the encircled Rock Trolls, his head lowered. The Trolls watched him come, but did not rise to greet him. Pen waited until he was seated among them again, then looked over at the Druids, who were standing to one side.

"Do you promise my friends will not be harmed?" he asked again.

"Not by us or those who travel with us," the taller Druid replied, coming forward a step. "We'll leave them here when we depart. What happens to them after that is up to them."

It was the best Pen could hope for. He would have liked to have found a way to get them back to Taupo Rough, but he couldn't chance trying to make that happen. Kermadec was resourceful. He would find a way.

Pen glanced down at the darkwand. The dirt and mud that coated its length mostly hid its runes. Its smooth surface was dull. If he was lucky, they would not pay close attention to it. If they took it, he would have to find a way to get it back later.

His gaze shifted to the island of the tanequil, to the dark silent wall of the forest that concealed the sentient tree. He was leaving things unfinished here, he knew, and he might never have a chance to come back and set them right. The urge to act immediately threatened to overpower him, to turn him from his path to the Ard Rhys. He knew her so little, and Cinnaminson so well.

He took another deep, steadying breath and looked back at the waiting Druids. "I'm ready," he called out in what he hoped was a brave voice.

Then, using the staff as a crutch, he began to walk toward them.

T W O

From deep in the shadows at the edge of the gardens, Khyber Elessedil watched the drama unfold with a mix of anger and indecision.

"Oh, no, Pen," she whispered.

She had returned before him, seen the Druid airships hanging over the gardens like spiders from an invisible web, the Gnome Hunters ringing the captive members of her little company, the Druids watching the bridge, and she had determined that she must do something to warn the boy.

But she was too late. He appeared abruptly, incautiously revealing himself before he could think better of it and before she could stop him. She held back then to see what would happen, thinking that she must not act too hastily, that she did not know yet what to do. She could save one—the boy or the rest of the company—but not both, not without a great deal of luck she could not depend upon. Two Druids were more than she was able to handle on her own; her skills were too rudimentary, her knowledge too shallow. She would catch them unawares, but that would not give her enough of an edge to guarantee success.

No, she must wait.

She must bide her time.

And so she did, listening to the conversation that ensued between Pen and Traunt Rowan. She could divine the nature of their maneuverings, of their hidden intentions, from what they said and how they moved. She understood what was at stake, but not how the matter would be resolved. Desperately trying to concoct a plan that would allow her to act, knowing that sooner or later she must, she waited them out. When Tagwen was allowed to confer with Pen in private, she thought that then was the time to do whatever she could, but she was unable to make herself do so. Everything she considered promised to end badly. Everything depended on help that wasn't available. She prevaricated and waffled. Indecision froze her.

Until, finally, it was too late. Pen was coming down from the bridge to give himself up, counting on Traunt Rowan to honor his word about Tagwen and the Trolls, giving himself over to a fate he had already determined he must embrace. Anything to get to Paranor, he was thinking. She knew it without having to be told.

She watched him limp forward, leaning on his staff, his young face etched with lines of determination. He was sacrificing himself. For the Ard Rhys. For Tagwen. For Kermadec and his Rock Trolls. Even for her. He did not know where she was, only that she was out there somewhere, still free, perhaps still able to do something to help. But he wasn't looking for that help just then. His intention was to get to Paranor and hope that help could be found there.

The staff drew her attention. She had seen it before, when he was scurrying through the woods on the island of the tanequil. But then it had looked much brighter and better kept. She had thought it was the darkwand, the talisman he had come to find. The tree would have given it to him, persuaded in a way that only he knew, a way that the King of the Silver River said he would find when it was time. If it was the talisman, in fact. If . . .

But it was, of course. He had muddied the surface and was using it as a crutch to disguise what it really was. He was taking a desperate chance that neither of the Druids would think it anything more than a length of old wood. He could not go to Paranor without it, and go to Paranor he must, of course. That was his intention in giving himself up.

She saw it all clearly, a conclusion about which she felt so certain that she never questioned it. Brave Pen.

Seconds later, she was moving, sliding along the edge of the trees, making her way toward the closest of the airships. She must do what she could to help him, and to help him she must go where he was going. She must get aboard the airship, travel hidden to Paranor, then disembark in secret and find him before they discovered his intentions and put an end to them. Because they would, she knew. He was not clever or strong enough to fool them all. One of them would see through him.

Within the circle of light cast by the fire, the Druids had moved forward to intercept Pen. He did not resist them as Traunt Rowan took Pen's arm and guided him toward the *Athabasca*. Rowan's actions were almost paternal. He spoke softly to the boy, walking beside him in a way that suggested good intentions. He had not bothered yet with the staff, did not seem to care much about it at all. Pen was still limping, perhaps causing the Druid to think he was indeed injured and in need of support. The other one, his sly eyes fixed on them, trailed purposefully, and Khyber did not trust anything about him. If he had been the one to make the promise to release Tagwen and the Trolls, she would have acted at once, she told herself. There would have been no hesitation.

She reached the rope ladder that dangled from the airship she had chosen—not the one Pen was boarding, unfortunately—and went up it in a rush, not bothering to look back until she was aboard. There were Gnome Hunters forward against the railing, but their attentions were occupied with the events taking place below, and they took no notice of her. She slipped into the shadow of the mainmast, then over to the shelter of a rail sling set in place to port. From there, she could see Pen being led to the ladder of the other ship, the Druids shadowing him watchfully. She watched the Gnome Hunters drift through the light toward their ships like wraiths to their haunts. She saw Tagwen's rough features, sad and desperate, peer upward as Pen climbed the ladder. She saw Kermadec's strong hands knot together in a promise of certain action.

She could still stop it, she told herself. She could fling Druid Fire or elemental winds all through those Gnome Hunters and knock them sprawling. She could separate Pen from those Druids, burn away the ladder from below where he climbed, and give him a chance to flee. But it would not be settled then and there, and the consequences for those Trolls too slow to reach the shadows or the weapons of which they had been stripped would be ugly.

Remember. Pen is not trying to escape. He is trying to reach Paranor. He has made up his mind.

She pictured him anew as she had seen him from across the chasm not two hours earlier. She saw the monster Traunt Rowan had named Aphasia Wye. She saw Pen prepare to do what he could to stop it, even when there appeared there was nothing he could do. Facing what must have seemed to be certain death, he had not tried to flee or hide. He had stood there to meet it.

And would have, had she not been there to give him aid.

Perhaps he was relying on her now.

Perhaps he knew she would not abandon him; that because she had saved him once, his life was her responsibility. Old legends said that this was so. She had never believed it.

But somehow, at that moment, she did.

"Are you injured?" Traunt Rowan asked pleasantly, supporting Pen under his free arm, not looking at him as he talked, moving him steadily along toward the *Athabasca*.

Pen shrugged. "Nothing serious."

"Aphasia Wye?"

"I hurt it trying to get away from him."

"But no broken bones?"

Pen shook his head.

"You're lucky. If you hadn't gotten away from him, broken bones would have been the least of your problems."

The second Druid, the one Tagwen had named Pyson Wence, moved up suddenly on Pen's other side. "How *did* you get away from him?"

"I don't want to talk about it." He risked a quick look at Traunt Rowan, seemingly the friendlier of the two. "Not until we're away."

Pyson Wence seized his arm, the blunt fingers squeezing so hard he flinched. "I don't like your tone of voice, little man," he hissed. "What you want in this matter is of no concern to us."

Pen shrank from him. "I want to know my friends are safe before I tell you anything."

"Let him go, Pyson," the taller one whispered. "Unfriendly eyes are watching. We can wait."

The one called Pyson let him go. Pen tore away from Traunt Rowan and rubbed his injured arm. He kept his head down and his eyes averted. He didn't want to do anything to aggravate them until the airships were aloft and his friends free. He didn't know what to expect then, but he would have a story in place to tell them that might buy him some time.

They reached the ladder, and as he made an attempt to climb it while still holding the darkwand, Pyson Wence snatched it away and cast it aside. "You won't be needing any crutches from here on," he said.

Pen froze, hands on the ladder, one foot on the first rung. He couldn't leave the talisman behind.

Then Traunt Rowan walked over and picked it up. "He might have need of it, Pyson. I'll carry it up for him. Go on, Pen."

Pen exhaled sharply and began to climb, taking care to favor his supposedly injured leg as he went. He did not look down at the Druids. He did not slow until he was aboard the airship, when he turned to wait for them. They were aboard quickly, dark faces shadowed and unreadable in the faint diffusion of the now distant firelight. Below, the Gnome Hunters were moving to follow, all but those who ringed the prisoners.

Traunt Rowan moved over to Pen and handed him back his staff. "You wouldn't consider trying to use this as a weapon, would you?" he asked with an edgy smile.

Pen shook his head.

"Good. Now let's go below and get you settled in."

Instantly, Pen moved over to the railing, away from everyone. "Not until I see that my friends are going to be all right," he said. "I want to watch what happens next."

Pyson Wence's Gnomic features were dark with anger, but Traunt Rowan merely shrugged. "Stay where you are then."

He turned to Wence and nodded, and the latter issued orders to the Hunters who crewed the airships. The Hunters began scurrying about the decks and up the rigging, preparing the three ships to sail. With a last, dark look at Pen, Pyson Wence moved into the pilot box to stand next to the *Athabasca*'s Captain, his face turned away from the boy.

Now only the few Gnomes guarding Tagwen and the Trolls remained, and one by one, weapons held at the ready, eyes fixed on the prisoners, they began to drift back toward the airships as well. Pen's companions sat quietly and watched their captors withdraw, making no attempt to stop them. Atalan was staring up at Pen, a strange look on his fierce face, one that suggested he couldn't quite believe what he was seeing. Tagwen was whispering to Kermadec, his head bent close to that of the Troll, their faces dark and intense.

Pen scanned the grounds at the edges of the firelight, where the walls caught the last of the flickering yellow glow, where the shadows encroached from the woods beyond. No sign of Khyber. But she had to be there. She had to be watching.

Then the *Athabasca* was lifting away, the other two airships following close behind, and the ruins of Stridegate were shrinking into the darkness. His former companions came to their feet and stood close together, looking after him. Quickly, their faces turned small and indistinct, and then disappeared. The ruins faded, as well, until all that remained was the tiny dot of the fire's heart.

When that disappeared and the island of the tanequil was nothing more than a dark lump silhouetted by starlight against the horizon, Traunt Rowan appeared at his side to take him below.

On the deck of the ship flying to starboard, Khyber Elessedil sat quietly in the concealing shadow of the aft port rail sling, watching the *Athabasca*. Pen had gone down the main hatchway and was no longer in view. The ruins of Stridegate had disappeared into the distance, and her companions with them. The glow of the fire had faded, and the position of the stars told her they were flying south along the edge of the Klu toward the Upper Anar, the vast sprawl of the Inkrim a dark lake below.

There was nothing she could do but wait.

When she was twelve, she had run away for the third time. On that occasion, intent on escaping her family and their dictatorial ways, she had stowed away aboard an airship flying to Callahorn. It wasn't that she didn't love them. It was that she didn't love what they had planned for her. Her brother and her father before him had very definite ideas about the ways in which an Elessedil Princess should conduct herself, and Khyber had trouble even seeing herself as a Princess. Her station in life was an accident of birth, and she could never quite bring herself to accept it as her due. She was always more comfortable with being someone and something else. Her family didn't like that. Her family let her know that rebelliousness would not be tolerated.

Her response had been to run away. She started at eight. At twelve, after two failed attempts, she had determined that this time she would succeed, that she would put herself permanently beyond their reach. Callahorn was Free-born land, and people of all Races were welcomed and accepted no matter who they were or where they came from. Everyone was treated the same. Royalty had been gone from the Borderlands for hundreds of years and wasn't likely to be coming back anytime soon. If she could get that far, she could disappear into the mix and never be found. At least, that was the way she saw it at twelve.

She got as far as her destination, but she was discovered by the Captain before she could disembark and was hauled back kicking and screaming yet again to her family. It was not a pleasant reunion. But she learned something valuable from that effort. She learned how to hide in plain sight. She learned that if you looked enough like you belonged, you stood a pretty good chance of being accepted. On that outing, she took on the look of a cabin boy or a very young crewmember, and to her surprise the crew never stopped to consider that she might be something else. Admittedly, she kept her exposure to a minimum, staying out of sight most of the time. But when she did surface, for food and water or just to breathe fresh air, she was able to move about without being stopped or questioned.

Aboard the Druid airship, she resolved to put this knowledge to good use. She had already appropriated one of the short cloaks worn by the Gnome Hunters who served as crew, using its hood to conceal her face. At night and in the absence of close scrutiny, she looked like one of them. She had already determined that by day, she would hide below, somewhere out of the way, somewhere the crew didn't often go. There were no Druids aboard the ship, so she had only the Gnomes to worry about. She knew airships well, and the configuration of the one she was on was familiar to her. Because the *Athabasca* was a warship, she offered plenty of hiding places. Because she was a Druid ship, everyone was trained to do their job and not ask questions.

Sitting by the rail sling as the ship flew into the night, pretending at inspecting its mechanism as the Gnome Hunter crewmen went impassively about their business, she considered her resources. She had the use of her Druid magic, although she possessed only a small arsenal and was largely unskilled in its use. She had the Elfstones, too. But, although powerful, they were of limited use. Mostly she had her wits and her determination, and she thought that those would probably end up serving her best.

Around her, things were settling down. The ship's course was set, her sails aloft, her rigging in place. Night enfolded all three vessels, rendering them starlit silhouettes against the horizon. She wished she were aboard Pen's ship so that she might reach him long enough to let him know he was not alone. But she knew that she was not likely to see him again before they reached Paranor. Even then, getting to him would be problematic. He would be celled and guarded, and he would be taken before Shadea a'Ru quickly once she knew he was there.

She leaned back against the rail sling. She realized she would have to reach Pen quickly once they landed or it might not be worth trying to reach him at all. The Druids would discover what he was up to, what he had come north to accomplish, and it would all be over quickly.

If he lived that long. Traunt Rowan and the other Druid might decide to dispatch him while they were returning. They might even have orders to that end.

She could not bear to think about it. Anyway, there was nothing she could do just yet. She could only wait. And hope.

She moved over to the provision hold, dropped through the hatchway quickly, found a shadowed place of concealment back among the spare light sheaths, and waited for sleep.

THREE

They took Pen Ohmsford to a storeroom that had been converted on one side into a sleeping space and told him that he was to stay there during the flight back to Paranor. His half of the room was furnished with a hammock, a clothes chest, a bench, a small table, and a lamp. The other half was piled high with coils of radian draws, spare light sheaths, casks of water and biscuits, and several crates of tools and caulking.

"Sorry we can't do better, but this is a warship and there isn't much in the way of accommodations," Traunt Rowan said.

They had sent three such airships to find him, Pen thought in response, which said more about their intentions for him than did the supposed dearth of decent accommodations. But he nodded because there wasn't much to be gained by doing anything else. He was their prisoner whether they said so or not.

They left him then, disappearing back through the doorway into the hallway beyond and closing the heavy storeroom door behind them. Pen heard the dull *snick* of the lock, further proof of his status. He waited until their footfalls had receded into silence, then sat down on the bench to think things through.

They had not taken away the darkwand, an oversight that surprised him. Having had it snatched away once already by Pyson Wence, he had been expecting to lose it again. But neither Druid had shown any further interest in the staff. He promised he would make them regret their carelessness, but then warned himself against making threats—even to himself—that he was in no position to carry out.

After giving it some consideration, he decided against trying to hide the staff. He could tuck it away amid all the stores, but they would notice it was missing the first time he limped about the room without it—and he would have to limp, at least for a day or two, to keep up the pretense that he was injured. No, hiding it would only call attention to it. They would find it quickly enough anyway, if they decided to look for it. It was better to just leave it lying out in plain sight and hope they paid no further attention.

He stuck it under the bench in a careless fashion and forced himself to pretend it didn't matter.

After a time, one of the Gnome Hunters brought him a plate of food and a cup of ale. He consumed both hungrily, realizing he was starved. It had been more than a day since he had eaten, and the rush of events was all that had kept him going. He needed sleep, too. After finishing the meal, he lay down to nap and was asleep in seconds.

He woke to the sound of the lock releasing, and another tray of food was brought inside and deposited on the floor. The Gnome Hunter barely looked at him as he backed out the door and locked it. Pen peered through the cracks of the shutters securing the single window opening into the storeroom. The sky was brilliant with either a sunrise or a sunset, depending on direction. He decided, after a moment's consideration, that it was a sunset. He had slept through an entire day.

He sat down and consumed his meal, thinking for the first time since he had been locked away of his friends back in the ruins of Stridegate. At least they were safe. Or safe from the Druids. They were still trapped by the Urdas and miles from any help. Kermadec would get them free, of course. Or Khyber, using her elemental magic to aid their efforts. But even after that it would take them a week to walk out and longer still to reach Paranor. Tagwen had meant well in promising they would come for him, but Pen knew that he couldn't depend on it. He had given them a chance at life by agreeing to leave with the Druids, but he had not given himself much hope in return. No matter what Tagwen had promised, Pen knew he was on his own.

He thought about what that meant. Barring unexpected help

from Druids still loyal to the Ard Rhys, he had to reach his aunt's chamber with the darkwand in hand and employ it quickly. That presupposed a lot of things that shouldn't be presupposed, the foremost of which was that he would be able to figure out how to use the talisman. He had no idea how it worked. He had no way of knowing what he had to do to summon its magic. Did he need to do *anything*? Or could he just stand there and wait to be whisked away?

The enormity of what he was hoping for left him momentarily shaken, and before he could pull himself together sufficiently to feel at least somewhat reassured that he would find a way out of his dilemma, the storeroom door opened, and his Druid captors reappeared.

He sat on his bench and stared at them, searching their faces for some indication of what to expect. Traunt Rowan seemed tense. Pyson Wence just looked angry. They moved into the room with an unmistakable air of authority, and Pen knew that the time for procrastination was over. Taking a deep breath, forcing himself not to look down at the darkwand where it lay on the floor beneath the bench, he came to his feet.

"I'm ready to tell you what you want to know," he said.

Best not to wait on the inevitable, he decided, and saw that his words had an instant calming effect on both, although the Gnome's brow remained dark and his eyes skeptical. "What is it that you think we want to know, little man?" he asked softly.

"You want to know what I'm doing out here. You want to know why I made such a long journey. You want to know if it has something to do with my aunt. Isn't that right?"

Pyson Wence started to answer, but Traunt Rowan held up one hand to silence him. His eyes fastened on Pen. "I think you prefer not to play games with us, young Pen, so I won't play games with you. The fact that you gave yourself up to save your friends tells me something about your character. I respect that. I won't waste any more time trying to convince you that everything in your life is going to be all right when this is over. As it happens, that isn't my decision. But you could help yourself—and your parents—considerably by doing just exactly what you propose. Tell us what we want to know, and I will see what I can do to help you. I have some influence in this matter. Shadea a'Ru is our leader, but Pyson and I are strong in our own right."

"Stronger than she thinks," the Gnome added, scowling at nothing, his eyes sweeping the room as if he was worried that someone might be listening.

"Let me repeat again that we didn't send Aphasia Wye to hunt you," Traunt Rowan continued. "We happen to agree with you. He was a monster. We're glad he's dead. But you need to understand that we think your aunt is a monster, too. A monster of another sort." He paused. "Do you know what we did with her?"

Pen nodded. "You sent her into the Forbidding."

He saw the surprise in both men's eyes. He knew more than they had thought he knew. "How do you know that?"

"She told me so," he said. "She came to me in a dream and told me she was being held prisoner by Druids. She asked me to help her. I didn't know what to think, but then Tagwen came to Patch Run and told me she had disappeared, so I decided to do what she had asked."

"Which was?"

"To travel to the ruins of Stridegate. To seek help that could only be found there."

Pyson Wence scowled. "What sort of help? Why would she ask help of you and not her brother?"

Pen's thoughts raced. "I don't know. Or, at least, I didn't know at first. I didn't think it was real. But I was afraid to ignore it, too."

"So you just decided to set out on your own?"

He took a deep breath. "Tagwen came to ask my father to help him find the Ard Rhys. Tagwen thought that my father could use his magic to discover where she had gone. But my father and mother were traveling, and I was the only one home. Then that other Druid appeared, the Dwarf, on the *Galaphile*, so we ran. He chased us all the way into the Black Oaks before we lost him. Then we flew my skiff to the Westland to ask Ahren Elessedil for help, and he got us a larger airship and took us north to Anatcherae. But the *Galaphile* found us again, and tracked us across the Lazareen and into the Slags, and there was a fight, and the *Galaphile* exploded and Ahren and the Dwarf were both killed."

He paused, trying to gauge their reaction. Did they believe any of this? He was trying to stay as close to the truth as possible without giving anything vital away.

"Terek Molt was always impatient," Pyson Wence growled, waving his hand dismissively. "This time it cost him more than he expected."

"What did you do after that, Pen?" Traunt Rowan asked.

"We continued north out of the Slags. We still had the airship. We flew all the way to Taupo Rough. We met Kermadec, and he agreed to guide us to Stridegate. Then you appeared and we started running again."

There was a long silence as the two men stared at him, weighing the truth in his story. Pen faced them squarely, meeting their eyes, willing them to believe.

"And all this time Aphasia Wye was hunting you?" the Southlander asked quietly.

Pen shook his head. "I didn't know anything about him, at first. He appeared for the first time in Anatcherae, after we had gotten away from the Dwarf. He chased us along the docks to the ship. Then we didn't see him until we were in the country beyond the Slags. He caught up to us again there. But we lost him. Then he appeared in the ruins. No one saw him that time but me. He crossed over to the island somehow, looking for me."

He paused. "If you didn't send him to find me, who did?"

Traunt Rowan pursed his lips. "Your aunt has many enemies, Pen. Not all of them are Druids."

An answer that wasn't an answer to the question, Pen thought.

"This doesn't feel right," Pyson Wence announced suddenly. "Aphasia Wye tracks you all the way to Stridegate, but twice you escape him along the way, something no one else has ever done. Then you confront him on the other side of a bridge that you say no one but you can cross, and you are able to kill him? You? A boy? Do you think we are fools?"

Pen shook his head quickly. "I didn't kill him. The spirits did. The ones who live on the island. They are called aeriads. They tricked him, lured him to the edge of the chasm. In the dark, he was confused. He fell, and the fall killed him. It is a long way to the bottom of the chasm. There are lots of rocks and tangled roots."

Pyson Wence was on him in a second, snatching him up by the front of his shirt and holding him pinned against the bulkhead. "Aphasia Wye could see better in the dark than most cats," the Gnome spit. "He was a skilled hunter. Nothing would have confused him. Nothing would have distracted him once he had the scent. Certainly not the dark! You are lying to us, little man!"

The Gnome's fist was jammed so tightly against Pen's throat that the boy could barely breathe, let alone talk. "It was the magic!" he finally managed to gasp.

Pyson Wence dropped him to the floor and kicked him hard. "Magic? What magic? Magic from these spirits you talk about? What sort of magic would they have that would stop Aphasia Wye? You're making this up, boy!"

Pen was shaking his head as hard as he could in denial, both hands clutching at his injured throat. "No, it's the truth! I didn't know they were there when I went to Stridegate. I didn't know anything except what my aunt told me in the dream. I was to go there and find out what I could do to help. So I went. The spirits were her means of communicating with me from within the Forbidding. She came to me on the island through them and told me that there was still a chance for her to escape so long as some of the Druids believed in her. She said that belief formed a connection to her and would help her find a way back!"

Pyson Wence kicked him harder still. "Belief in her? That's going to get her out of the Forbidding? That's what she told you?" He kicked Pen again, then looked over at Traunt Rowan. "Let's kill him now and be done with it!"

The tall Southlander seemed to consider the idea, then shook his head. "I don't think so." He walked over, moved the smaller man out of the way, then reached down and helped Pen back to his feet. Steering him by his shoulders, he led the boy back to the bench and sat him down.

Kneeling, he looked Pen squarely in the eye. "He's right about one thing," he said softly. "You're lying to us. I thought we agreed that there weren't to be any games played in this business."

Pen felt his throat tighten and his stomach clench. He thought for a minute he was going to be sick, but he kept it from happening by refusing to give them the satisfaction. "I wasn't lying!"

Traunt Rowan shook his head in disappointment. "Your aunt summoned you all the way to Stridegate to tell you that belief would help free her? Why didn't she just tell you that in your dream, Pen? For that matter, why didn't she just tell your father, who might have been able to do something about it? Why choose to tell you, a boy with no way to do much of anything without help?"

Pen looked down at his clenched hands. "All right. There was something else. While I was on the island, I had to do something. I had to find this tree, a kind of tree I had never seen before. I had to find it and carve her name into its trunk. The tree bled sap into the letters, and there was a kind of magic released. It was what saved me from Aphasia Wye. It kept him from me, confused him, sent him off into the dark so that he fell into the ravine. The magic was a part of her, brought back from the Forbidding by the carving of her name. It wasn't her body or mind or anything you could touch. It was her spirit, I guess."

It was a plausible enough story, given the nature of magic and its workings, much of which was elemental and released through nature's children. It even bordered on the truth.

Traunt Rowan smiled. "Strange, though. Your father couldn't do all this? It had to be you. A boy not out of his teens, Pen?"

Pen nodded. "I have the use of a kind of magic my father doesn't. It isn't much. I can understand the thinking and intent of birds and plants and animals from their movements and sounds. It isn't communication exactly, but it's something like it. My aunt understood that I would know how to carve the letters in the tree in a way that wouldn't hurt it, that would allow it to permit her to reach through the Forbidding."

A total lie this time, but he was too deep in to back away and he needed to buttress his story with reasons for how things had come about. He felt his credibility was slipping away, and he threw up his hands in mock disgust.

"I don't understand it, either. You can believe me or not, I don't care! But I love my aunt, and I did what I had to do to help her. I'd do it again, if she asked me! She isn't a monster, no matter what you say." He glared at Traunt Rowan fiercely. "I've had enough of this! You don't believe anything I've told you! Fine! I don't have to tell you anything else!"

From the other side of the room, Pyson Wence snorted. Traunt Rowan remained where he was, studying Pen's face in a way that the boy found disturbing. The Druid could tell he was lying, he realized. He didn't know how he understood that, but he did.

"You might want to take those words back," the other said. "You heard Pyson. He thinks we should kill you and put the whole matter behind us. We already have your parents. It wouldn't be difficult to make them disappear as well. You can prevent this, but it doesn't seem as if you want to."

Pen shook his head. "Of course I want to! But I don't think I can prevent anything. You'll do what you want with all of us, no matter what I say! Besides, I've told you what I know."

"Everything you know?" Traunt Rowan pressed. "You've told us everything?"

Pen knew he was dead, sensed it in the way the other asked the question, could feel it right down to the soles of his feet. But there was nothing he could do to change things, not even if he wanted to.

He set his jaw. "Everything."

Traunt Rowan nodded slowly and started to rise. But as he did so he reached down for the muddied staff tucked under the bench beneath Pen's feet and pulled it free. "Well, then, it will come as something of a surprise to you to discover that this simple staff you have been using as a crutch for your injured leg is actually something more than it appears."

He held it out for Pen to inspect, keeping it just out of reach as he balanced it loosely in the palm of one hand. Pen felt all the strength go out of his body. He had thought the staff forgotten and his secret safe. He had thought the Druids fooled.

"You did think this just a simple staff, didn't you?" the other persisted.

Pyson Wence had come over to stand beside him now, his dark face furrowed in surprise. Apparently he had missed seeing what it was, even if Traunt Rowan had not. "What are you talking about?"

The Southlander ran his hands slowly up and down the length of wood, and as he did so the dried mud and dirt fell away and the surface turned bright and smooth, revealing the intricately carved network of runes hidden beneath. He blew gently to clean it of any remaining flecks of dust, then used one end of his sleeve to polish the wood.

"There," he said, smiling cheerfully at Pen. "You can see for yourself. What do you make of this? Pyson?" He glanced over at the other Druid. "Isn't this a surprise?"

Pyson Wence started for Pen, his face flushed with rage, but

Traunt Rowan held him back. "No, what are you doing? No need for that! You heard Pen; he didn't know what it was. He probably just picked it up while walking around the forest and kept it because he needed a crutch. Isn't that right, Pen?"

Pen said nothing, his eyes fixed on the other, watching him the way a mouse would a snake. Traunt Rowan had known all along. He had been leading Pen around by the nose, letting him fabricate whatever story he wished, because in the end he knew the one thing that counted—that what the boy was really hiding was the secret of the staff.

"Little man, I will see you hung from meat hooks and gutted before this matter is finished!" Pyson Wence hissed at him. His gaze shifted to Traunt Rowan. "What are we waiting for? Let me have him now, and we will know the truth of things quick enough!"

Traunt Rowan shook his head. "Not until Shadea is done with him. I don't want to have to explain to her why we failed to keep him alive long enough for her to question him." He smiled at Pen. "This isn't going to work out the way you wanted, Pen. Not for you or your parents. You shouldn't have tried to be so clever. You're only a boy, and boys always think themselves much more clever than they really are."

Pen was having trouble breathing. He knew he should say or do something, but he had no idea what it should be. It was all he could do to keep himself from falling apart completely.

Traunt Rowan watched him a moment longer, then shrugged. "Cat got your tongue?" He hefted the staff and tossed it to Pyson Wence. "What do you make of it, Pyson? Can you read the markings? Elfish, I think. Very old."

The Gnome studied the runes a moment, then shook his head impatiently. "Nothing I've ever seen. We might find something on it back at Paranor, in the books. What difference does it make?"

"I don't know. Pen, do you?" Traunt Rowan looked at him. "Anything about these markings look familiar? No?" He pursed his lips. "Maybe we should see if they're even real."

He took the staff out of Pyson's hands, dropped it carelessly to the floor, and pointed at it. Blue fire exploded from his fingers, engulfing the darkwand. Pen gasped in spite of himself, leapt to his feet, and tried to snatch the darkwand back. Almost casually, Traunt Rowan backhanded him into the wall so hard that he almost blacked out. On the floor, the darkwand jumped at the touch of the searing fire, but to his surprise refused to burn. The Druid tried again, the fire flashing from his fingers in a fresh wave, licking at and engulfing the wood. But again, nothing happened. When the fire ceased, the wood was left untouched.

Pyson Wence snatched up the darkwand and smashed it against the bulkhead, but the staff bounced away unmarked and unbroken.

"Magic, of a very powerful kind," Traunt Rowan declared softly, looking down at a dazed Pen. "Is this meant for the Ard Rhys, Pen? I have a feeling it is. A talisman of some sort, to be used to free her."

Pen tried to keep his expression blank, his feelings from showing on his face or reflecting in his eyes. He tried to pretend he didn't feel anything, that nothing that was happening mattered. But pain ratcheted through him as he slumped on the bench, his head throbbing with the blow he had taken, and his hopes for achieving anything of what he had set out to accomplish vanished.

"He doesn't want to talk now, but he will soon enough," Pyson Wence hissed. "Do you hear me, little man?"

Traunt Rowan stepped forward and yanked Pen off the bench, holding him up so that they were face-to-face. "He hears you, Pyson." He bent so close to the boy that their noses were almost touching. "Are you worried for your parents, Pen?" he whispered. "I worried for mine, too, but it wasn't enough to save them. You think Grianne Ohmsford is worth giving up your life for, but she isn't. She killed my parents, and in a way she will end up killing yours, as well, won't she? She is a monster, Pen. She always was and she always will be. Except that now she's where she belongs—with the other monsters."

He let go of the boy, shoving him back onto the bench. "You think about it while we fly to Paranor. You think about how much she really means to you."

He stepped back, flushed with the heat of his words. Then he turned and walked from the room, taking the staff and Pyson Wence with him.

In the ensuing silence, Pen was left alone to consider the fate that awaited him.

"What do you think you are doing?" a voice called out from behind Khyber, causing her to turn abruptly to face the speaker.

It was the sunset of the following day, and the light was weak and tinged with twilight, so she could not make him out clearly, other than to identify him as one of the Gnome crew. Of course, he couldn't make her out, either, so she was able to act before he could determine who she was. A quick movement of her fingers caused him to hear an unexpected noise, a sound he recognized as dangerous. When he was looking the other way, she brushed the air about her to create a screen of mist and walked away.

It was one of the small skills she had learned from Ahren Elessedil while aboard the *Skatelow* all those weeks ago. A lifetime ago, she thought. It made her sad, remembering. It made her wish she could change things, even though she knew she couldn't.

She glanced back at the Gnome Hunter, who was looking around in confusion, trying to figure out what had happened. It was the first time anyone had challenged her, but she had been prepared for the possibility. Still, she would have to be more careful. One sighting might go unreported. A second was more likely to draw attention.

They were flying south along the spine of the Charnals, come out of the Klu now and gone down below the Lazareen. Ahead, the bleak wasteland of the Skull Kingdom was a dark smudge against the extended green of the landscape stretching toward the southwest, where the light was a dim reddish gold band along the horizon. In another day, perhaps as early as the next evening, they would reach Paranor. The Druid warships were swift, and they flew unhindered and unconcerned through that dangerous country. Few enemies would dare to attack even a single Druid warship, let alone three.

She scanned the countryside below for a moment, then started for the starboard aft hatchway. The decks were mostly deserted, the crew below eating dinner, the night watch not yet come topside. Only the pilot and two crewmen were in view, and they were mostly passing time until they could eat and sleep.

She was at the hatchway when she saw the flash of light from the *Athabasca*, which was flying just ahead and to port. The light was sudden and intense, and it came from somewhere in the hold, below-decks, flaring out through cracks in the shutters, slivers of brilliance against the black. She recognized it as magic right away; it was too sharp-edged for firelight. She stared momentarily in shock, then watched it flash a second time.

But that was all. She waited, but it didn't come again. She listened for some indication of what had caused it, but heard nothing. She tried to read its origins using her own magic, probing the space between the vessels, but the air currents caused by the airships' movements swept away all traces.

Was it Pen?

She had no way of knowing. She wouldn't be able to tell anything until they landed at Paranor—perhaps not even then. She stared out at the dark bulk of the *Athabasca*. The ship was only a hundred yards away, but it might as well have been a hundred miles.

Disconsolate and frustrated, she dropped her gaze and slipped through the hatchway to try to get some sleep.

FOUR

Rue Meridian sat with her back against the cell's far wall, facing the locked door. Her prison, like Bek's, was deep beneath the walls and buildings of the Druid's Keep. There was only the single door. The door was solid metal, save for a flap at its bottom, which permitted her jailers to slide a tray of food inside without opening the door, and a series of slits at eye level, which let in slivers of torchlight from the hallway beyond. Within her cell were a wooden bed frame and mattress, a blanket, a slop bucket, and a broom. The broom was a mystery. Was she supposed to sweep up the cell when it got too dusty? Was she supposed to knock down cobwebs?

Since she had been shut away, she had not been allowed out. Not once, even for a moment. Nor had anyone come inside. She had heard the guards moving in the hallway, and she had looked out in an effort to see them once or twice. But the guards kept out of her line of sight and spoke in low enough tones that they were out of hearing, as well. They had not spoken to her through the door. Other than delivering her food and allowing her to slide the bucket out for emptying now and then, they had paid no attention to her at all. As far as she could determine, in the minds of her captors she had ceased to exist.

So she sat and waited for something to happen, all the while thinking of ways she might escape.

She thought constantly of her son, frantic for his safety. Her husband was resourceful and would be able to help himself. And she would be fine. But Pen lacked their experience and their skills; he would be at the mercy of whoever went to find him. She knew enough of Shadea a'Ru to appreciate how determined she was to eradicate the Ohmsfords. It wouldn't stop with Grianne, though she was the excuse for the purge. It would continue until the last Ohmsford was wiped from the face of the Four Lands.

Thinking of it left her furious. She had never trusted the Druids, never cared for their secretive ways and manipulative schemes. It had been bad enough when there was only one, and that one was Walker Boh. But now there were dozens of them, not only within the walls of Paranor, but scattered throughout the Four Lands, as well. She had always felt at risk, especially with Grianne as Ard Rhys. Her feelings for Bek's sister were unchanged. In her mind, Grianne would always be the Ilse Witch. Bek's assurances notwithstanding, she had never been convinced that Grianne's transformation from dark witch to white queen was real. Her attitude was not so different from that of many others. She could understand why some among the Druids were so eager to be rid of her.

But the real problem was her certainty that their connection with Grianne put them all in danger. It didn't matter that they were not close to the Ard Rhys and had nothing to do with the Druid order. It didn't matter that their lives were so different. Blood and history bound them inextricably. She had always known that the cauldron of mistrust and dislike Grianne stirred among those who were troubled by her position of power as Ard Rhys was in danger of spilling over onto the rest of them.

Her present circumstances seemed to bear that out.

She stared at the iron door and wished she had thought to stick a throwing knife into her boot. She wished she had any kind of weapon at all. She wished she had two minutes alone outside that door.

After a time, she dozed, drifting away on thoughts of her family and better times. In the near blackness of her prison, sleep was the only form of relief she could find.

She did not know how long she slept, only that it ended suddenly and unexpectedly. She awoke with a start, her sleep broken by an odd sound from beyond her cell. She blinked in confusion, sensing that what she had heard was the collapse of something. She sat up straight, listening for more.

Then a key twisted in the lock, metal scraping on metal, and the lock released with a sharp *snick.* She got to her feet quickly and took a deep breath to steady herself, to clear her sleep-fogged mind. She didn't know what to expect, didn't know how to prepare herself. She snatched up the broom, the only thing at hand that might serve as a weapon, and moved to stand close by the door.

The door opened, and a black-cloaked figure stepped through. One gloved hand came up quickly in warning as she started to move out of her crouch. "Wait!"

The hands rose to pull back the hood, and she found herself confronted by a young man with angular features and a quizzical expression. He blinked at her and smiled. "No need for that. I've come to help." He glanced over his shoulder into the hallway, his lank brown hair falling over his forehead and into his eyes. "Hurry. We haven't much time. They'll discover you've gone soon enough and they'll know where it is they must look."

Satisfied to be free, to have a chance at escaping the Keep, she went with him without questioning their destination. They slipped from the cell into the hallway, where she saw the collapsed form of the Gnome Hunter who had been keeping guard outside the door. There was no blood, no mark on him anywhere.

"A sleeping potion," whispered her rescuer, his young face brightening with pleasure. "Worked on the one at the top of the stairs, too. They have a warning system to prevent your escape that travels from the bottom up, but not from the top down. They expect any attempt at escape to come from you. They don't think you have any friends here."

"I didn't think so, either," she admitted, reaching down to snatch away the guard's dagger.

"Oh, yes," he replied quickly. "A few. Well, two of us, anyway. I am the one who slipped your husband that warning note when you first arrived. But I couldn't do more until now. Come, hurry!"

They moved silently down the shadowy corridor. Torchlight from brands set in wall brackets cast pools of yellowish light on the stone floor. She listened carefully for the sound of other movements as she went, but heard nothing. At the bottom of a circular ascent, her rescuer paused to peer upward into the dark hole of the stairwell. No light filtered down.

He glanced over. "I left the door closed against intrusion. No shift change is due for another hour, but you don't want to take chances."

He smiled his infectious smile again. "I'm Trefen Morys." He stuck out his hand, and she gave it a quick squeeze. "Bellizen and I are still loyal to the Ard Rhys. And to you and your husband, too."

"Where is Bek?" she asked quickly.

"Imprisoned, like you. I couldn't risk trying to reach him until you were free. They keep him closely watched, held in check by a warning that any attempt on his part to escape will result in your death. They are afraid of his magic. They think that if they keep him contained, you will not present a problem. So I freed you first, to take the pressure off while we break him free."

She nodded. "Sound reasoning, Trefen Morys."

He blushed. "I hope you will have a chance to tell that to my mistress." His brow furrowed. "When she disappeared, I knew that Shadea a'Ru and those who follow her had something to do with it, especially after they seized control of the order. Then Tagwen disappeared, and the word went out that they were looking for you and your son. It was all too clear that they meant to stop any effort at finding my mistress."

"Do you know where Pen is?" she asked quickly. "Have they found him? Have they brought him here?"

He shook his head. "There is no word of your son. I know he has not been brought here. I have been watching for him. We both have, Bellizen and I." He gripped her arm. "We have been waiting for the right time to set you free, but we could not chance it while Shadea and the others were all present at Paranor. But Shadea has gone south to meet with the Prime Minister of the Federation and will not return for several days. Her closest allies, Traunt Rowan and Pyson Wence, flew north days ago."

"In search of Pen?"

He nodded. "We will try to reach him first, once you are both free and we have control of your airship. Our usefulness here is ended. There is nothing more we can do to help my mistress. The order follows Shadea now, all but a handful. Already, they believe she is the leader the order requires and that my mistress was an unfortunate mistake. Whatever we can do to change their thinking, to find my mistress and stop Shadea, must happen elsewhere."

He pointed up the stairs. "We have to go. Follow me." He put a finger to his lips. "Quiet like a mouse, now."

They tiptoed up the stone risers, the young Druid leading the way. Rue had the Gnome dagger in her right hand, ready for use. She wished she had more than one, but the truth of the matter was that if they were discovered, a dozen daggers wouldn't be enough to save them. They must count on stealth and surprise to see them through.

At the top of the stairs, Trefen Morys eased open the iron-bound wooden door and peered through the crack. Glancing over his shoulder, he nodded and pushed through to the light beyond.

They were in a guardroom that served as a waypoint between the cellars and the rest of the Keep. Weapons and armor hung from racks on the walls, and open doors revealed storage closets filled with cloaks and boots. Torches burned in their racks, but the room was empty save for them.

Trefen Morys walked over to a pair of closed doors and opened them. A Gnome Hunter lay slumped on the floor. The young Druid nudged the Gnome with his boot, and when he didn't move closed the doors once more. Then he took one of the cloaks from its peg and handed it to Rue.

"Your husband is being held in another part of the Keep. They are taking no chances that one of you will have any chance of finding and rescuing the other. But I know where to go and how to get there. The trick will be in disposing of the Gnome Hunters who serve as guards. Make no mistake. They are Shadea a'Ru's men—mercenaries recruited and paid for by Pyson Wence to replace the Trolls. They have been ordered to kill both of you if there is any sort of escape attempt. So we have to keep them from finding out what has happened here until we reach your husband."

He paused. "One thing more you need to know. It is important that we do this now. Things are very bad here. Many Druids have been dismissed from the order and sent home. Others have simply disappeared, including some who were close to Shadea. Terek Molt has been gone for more than a month. Iridia Eleri disappeared two weeks ago. And right before Shadea left for Arishaig, her consort, Gerand Cera, was found dead. There wasn't a mark on him. No one says so, but we all think the same thing—she used him until he became expendable. It might be true of the others, as well."

He shook his head. "Yet most within the order still follow Shadea. However they feel about her secretly, they don't mistrust her in the same way they did the Ard Rhys. My mistress is shackled by her history as the Ilse Witch. She cannot escape it. Too many refuse to forgive her, even though she has changed. It doesn't matter that in the end, Shadea will prove a worse choice. They cannot see that she will destroy the order, that she will lead it to ruin because she lacks my mistress's passion for doing what is right."

"Isn't there a good chance that Grianne Ohmsford is already dead?" Rue asked. "Is there any reason to think she isn't?"

He shook his head vigorously. "If my mistress were dead, why would they work so hard at finding your son? What difference would it make to them where he had gone and what he was doing if she weren't still alive? No, they think he has found a way to reach her and if not stopped might well do so."

Rue heard the sound of footfalls in the corridor outside, and they both turned quickly. "Your cloak!" Trefen Morys hissed, pulling up his hood and tightening the folds.

But Rue knew it was too late for any sort of disguise. Stepping silently to one side of the entry as the steps approached, she waited for the door to open and the Gnome Hunter to step through, then brought the haft of the knife around in a powerful blow that caught the Gnome on his temple and dropped him like a stone.

"Help me," she said, kicking the door closed and taking the Gnome's arms.

Together they hauled the body to one of the closets, bound his arms and legs, gagged his mouth, and stuffed him inside. Without another word or more than a quick glance at each other, they went out through the door the Gnome had entered and down the corridor beyond, Trefen Morys leading the way. One corridor intersected with another, one set of stairs wound to a second, doors opened and closed into rooms, and so they made their way through the shadowy halls, pausing only to listen for voices or footsteps as they went. The minutes slipped away, and Rue was quickly lost. She didn't know that much about Paranor anyway, having visited only a handful of times and having never ventured much beyond the main halls that led to the council chambers and the rooms of the Ard Rhys. They were deep underground here, in a maze of passageways she had never seen and could never have navigated on her own. She could feel the cold permeating the rock. Even the central fires of the Keep's furnace, the fires that burned from deep underground at the earth's core, could not push back the chill.

Once or twice, Trefen Morys glanced back, and each time she nodded quickly for him to go on. She was thinking of Bek, just out of reach, but she was thinking about Penderrin, as well, much farther away and more vulnerable. She was thinking about her child and how she would never be able to live with herself if something were to happen to him.

Finally, Trefen Morys slowed, then stopped altogether, dropping into a crouch beneath the light of a torch burning in its wall bracket. Ahead, a door stood closed to whatever lay beyond.

"A pair of guards keeps watch there," he whispered, as she crouched next to him. "We have to silence them both. Beyond that room, stairs lead downward to a corridor of cells. Your husband is in one of them. A second pair of Gnome Hunters stands watch there— one at the bottom of the stairs, another in front of the cell that imprisons your husband. Any sort of warning will result in a swift response."

She nodded. "There won't be any warning."

"I was able to get another note to your husband several days ago, so that he would know that someone was looking to help him. He will know we are coming, and he will be ready, even if the Gnome Hunter at his cell door attempts to kill him. I don't know a great deal about his magic, but I gather it was a match for his sister's, so he will have a chance to survive this." He sighed. "I wish I could have done more."

She gave him a quick smile. "You have done all that could be expected of you, Trefen Morys. However this turns out, you can't be faulted for your efforts."

He took her arm as she started to rise. "Wait." He seemed suddenly nervous. "I have to tell you something. I am not a warrior Druid. I am not skilled in the use of weapons or magic as a substitute for weapons. I have magic, yes. But my studies are of rocks and soils."

She stared at him. "Rocks and soils?"

He nodded. "I have never killed anyone." He dropped his gaze. "I have never even hurt anyone. I don't know how to fight."

She took a deep breath. She had fought alone before and against great odds. But she had been much younger then, harder and more resilient, reckless about her safety in a way she no longer was. Not with the lives of her husband and son at stake as well as her own. She wished suddenly that her brother were there, that Redden Alt Mer were standing with her as he had on so many other occasions. Having Big Red with her would change the odds considerably. But she might just as well wish she could fly.

"You won't have to fight," she told Trefen Morys, reaching out to grip his arm reassuringly. She saw some of the tension drain from his young face. "Stay behind me and do what you can to protect yourself if you are threatened. I will dispose of the guards." Her grip tightened. "One thing you must promise me, though. If I fall, wounded or dead, you must continue on. You must do whatever you can to reach Bek. You must free him and then tell him what you have told me. He will know what to do. Will you do that?"

Trefen Morys nodded. "You have my word."

She looked down at the long knife she had taken from the Gnome Hunter and wished she had something more substantial with which to work. It had been twenty years since she had fought a battle like the one she was facing, and she knew she had lost the sharp edge of her survival instincts.

Could she do this?

A fierce resolution washed over her as she hefted the knife in her palm, watching the way the torchlight played across its polished surface. Some things you did because you had to.

"All right," she said, looking up at him. "I'm ready."

In a guarded crouch, they began to creep down the hall.

FIVE

R ue Meridian was leading the way, Trefen Morys hanging
back. She reached the door to the guardroom, hesitated,
glanced down at the latch, then back at the young Druid.
He saw her questioning look and he nodded, motioning her to go
ahead, indicating the door was not locked. She wasn't sure how he
could know that, but had to believe him.

Taking a deep breath, she placed her hand over the heavy iron
handle, twisted hard, and pushed.

Two Gnome Hunters looked up as she entered. One was at work
on the broken handle of a short sword. The second stood across
the room, leaning idly against the wall. Both hesitated, confused by
the presence of the Druid behind her.

She had just enough time to register the open door across the
room, and then the Gnome leaning against the wall made up his
mind about her and reached for a pike.

Flinging the long knife underhanded with such force that the
blade was buried in his chest all the way up to the hilt, she killed him
before his hand could close on the pike's wooden shaft. The Gnome
gave a sharp gasp and sank slowly down, hands clutching at the haft
of the knife. By then, she was across the room and on top of the
other one. He awkwardly struck at her with the broken sword, but
she caught the flat of the blade on her forearms and knocked it aside.

She jammed her fingers into his throat, silencing his voice, and then struck him repeatedly on the side of his head with her fist. His eyes rolled back, and he collapsed and lay still.

Neither Gnome was moving. She found no pulse on either. She snatched a pair of daggers from a rack and stuck them in her belt, hesitated, then added a long knife. She turned to an ashen-faced Trefen Morys, who clearly hadn't exaggerated when he said he wasn't a fighter. She placed a warning finger to her lips and moved close. "Are you all right?" she whispered.

He nodded, his eyes big.

"Listen, then. I want you to go down the stairs ahead of me. The Gnomes won't react so quickly to the sight of a Druid. They will think Shadea or one of her allies sent you. When you reach the first, get him turned around so that his back is to me. Can you do that?"

He nodded again, breathing hard through his mouth.

"Don't worry," she said. "We'll be all right."

She steered him toward the open door across the room. Beyond, a set of narrow stairs spiraled downward into near darkness. She had to hope that no sound of the struggle that had just taken place had reached the ears of the guards below. It had been quick enough; there had been no cries of alarm. She paused at the top of the stairs and listened carefully.

Nothing.

She nodded to Trefen Morys and motioned him ahead. He moved reluctantly, woodenly, and she seized his shoulder to make certain he wasn't going into shock. He gasped in pain and glanced quickly at her, then took a deep breath and nodded that he was ready. She released him with a gentle shove and watched him start down.

She waited until he was out of sight around the bend in the stairs, then followed, creeping on cat's paws along the rough expanse of the curved wall, one of the daggers out and resting loosely in her hand. Halfway there, she thought. But the second pair might pose more of a challenge. She would have to silence them one at a time, and that wouldn't be easy. Bek might be ready or he might not, but the suddenness of a rescue like this one could throw your thinking off, no matter how formidable your skills. Bek was brave, but he did not have her experience at close combat. Though he had grown considerably during their journey to Parkasia, that had been twenty years ago and she was willing to bet that he had already forgotten much of what he had learned. Nor had he practiced with the wishsong in the intervening years. He had disdained to use it, preferring to leave that part of his life behind him. In spite of her own dislike and mistrust of the magic, she wished he had not been so insistent on ignoring his gift.

Well, that was the way of things, she supposed. Hindsight always suggested how you might have been better prepared.

She edged forward as the light grew slightly stronger near the bottom of the steps. Ahead, she heard Trefen Morys's voice and the responding growl of the Gnome Hunter on watch. She slid around the curve in the wall so that she could see them. The Gnome had his back to her. So far, so good.

She came up behind him swiftly and killed him with a single thrust of the dagger.

At which point Trefen Morys threw up. The retching sound reverberated down the corridor and instantly brought a sharp query from the near darkness. Leaping past the young Druid, Rue raced ahead, sliding free the other dagger as she ran, no longer bothering with stealth; speed was all that mattered. Ahead, there was movement at the edge of the light, and she saw the final guard peering at her through the smoky torchlit gloom, crossbow at the ready. She threw herself flat as the weapon swung up and heard the whir of the bolt as it shot past her, ricocheted off the stone walls, and fell harmlessly to the floor farther on. She was up and running again, watching her adversary wind back the string and insert another bolt with quick, practiced movements. This one was well trained, dangerous.

The crossbow came up, and she threw herself down a second time. But this time the Gnome did not fire at her. Instead, as soon as she was down he wheeled toward the cell door in front of him, grappling to release the heavy locking bolt. Rue was on her feet instantly, realizing at once what he intended. His orders in this situation were clear. She heard the locking bolt slide free and the cell door swing open. The guard brought up the crossbow a second time. She was still too far away to stop him, so she screamed at him, then hurtled the dagger as hard as she could. There wasn't enough force behind the throw to injure him, but the heavy blade ripped through his leather tunic, causing him to jerk back.

Then Bek Ohmsford was hurtling through the open cell door and slamming into the Gnome. The crossbow released, the bolt flew into the ceiling and dropped harmlessly. The Southlander and the Gnome went down in a heap, tumbling across the floor, arms and legs entangled. Rue put on a burst of speed, drawing the long knife from her belt. Ahead of her, the flat surface of a blade caught the light as it swept down. Someone cried out, and then she was on top of the fighters, screaming in rage, burying her own blade deep into the Gnome Hunter's back, driving it all the way through him.

The Gnome Hunter fell away, dead before his hands released their grip. Rue threw the body aside and knelt next to her husband, already seeing the red stain spreading across his tunic front. "No!" she hissed, and began trying to sort through the tangle of his clothes for the wound.

"Stop it, Rue!" He pushed her hands away, shaking his head. There was pain and frustration in his voice. "There's no time. We have to get out of here." He was already struggling to his feet, clutching his midsection. "I'm all right. He only scraped my ribs."

"It's more than that!" she snapped back. "Look at the blood!"

Trefen Morys came pounding up, his black robes flying out behind him. He looked at Bek and turned white. "How bad is it?"

Bek shook his head. "Not now. Which way out? Can you get us to *Swift Sure*?"

The young Druid nodded. "Bellizen should already be there. She will have secured it for us. Can you walk?"

Rue was tearing her robe into long strips, using the dagger to cut the fabric. Without comment, she began wrapping it tightly about Bek's midsection. He leaned into her and whispered as she did so, "I love you."

Then they were running, all three of them, back down the corridor past the dead men and fallen weapons, past the blood and vomit, and up the stairs, gaining the guardroom and the corridors beyond.

It was still quiet in the Keep, no warning yet raised, no alarm given. Then Trefen Morys took them a different way, using a series of narrow back stairways to gain the higher floors. Rue tried to help Bek, who was beginning to falter. His blood speckled the floor behind him as he ran. They were still in great danger, their escape reliant on reaching *Swift Sure* before the rest of the Gnome guards discovered their comrades.

Or they had the misfortune of stumbling across someone who would give them away—which was exactly what happened.

They had just reached the upper levels, where tall windows opened to hazy gray light and heavy clouds, when a lone Gnome Hunter came out of a room right next to them. Everyone froze for an instant, and then the Gnome was crying out. Rue buried her dagger in his chest, knocking him back into the room, but the damage had been done. The cry was immediately taken up, and the pursuit they had feared was mobilizing.

They began to run again, Bek's arm about Rue's shoulders, her arm about his waist. She felt the thick dampness of his blood seeping into her own clothing.

"It's not far!" Trefen Morys called back to them, leading the way. "Just ahead, through those doors!"

A pair of heavy, ironbound oak doors stood closed at the end of the corridor. But the sound of boots reverberated on the stone flooring from just out of sight behind the fugitives. *We're not going to make it,* Rue thought.

Gnome Hunters burst into view, rounding a corner of the hallway perhaps a hundred feet back. Too many to stand and face. Too many to overcome with conventional weapons. Rue glanced at Bek. His eyes were slits in a face gone pale and sweaty. His breathing was shallow and ragged. He was failing rapidly and in no position to use his magic.

Then they were at the double doors, and Trefen Morys was wrenching them open. Rue and Bek stumbled through, and the young Druid shoved the doors closed behind them and stepped back. "Wait!"

He mumbled something, his hands weaving. The locks on the doors melted and fused into a knot of iron, sealed shut.

He turned back to them and grinned triumphantly. "I know a little magic."

They were in the airship courtyard and *Swift Sure* hovered just off the ground not a hundred yards ahead, straining at her anchor ropes, her light sheaths rippling in the breeze and her radian draws taut. She was rigged for flying and ready to lift off. From the pilot box, a solitary figure dressed in black Druid robes jumped up and started waving.

"Bellizen!" Trefen Morys shouted.

The girl shouted back, then darted out of the box and down to the decking. A moment later, one end of a rope ladder flew over the side.

But in the same instant a clutch of Gnome Hunters appeared on the Keep's battlements behind them. They howled in anger when they saw what was happening. Still supporting a wounded Bek, Rue lurched toward the safety of the airship. Trefen Morys darted ahead. Then, seeing how badly his companions were struggling, he raced back to help, taking Bek's other arm and slinging it over his shoulder.

"Hurry!" he urged.

Rue didn't need to be told. Arrows fired from Gnome bows were falling all around them, sharpened heads clattering and skipping across the stones. Rue realized suddenly that she had no weapons of her own, that none of them had, that they had left everything behind in their battle to escape the cells.

She glanced ahead at *Swift Sure,* caught sight of the starboard rail sling in place on the bow, and felt a flutter of hope. "Does Bellizen know how to use airship weapons?" she shouted at Trefen Morys above the cry of the attacking guards. "Do you?"

The young Druid shook his head. "Neither of us does! We aren't trained in the use of weapons!"

A bad oversight, she thought. She took a deep breath. "Stay with Bek!" she ordered.

She dropped her husband's arm and sprinted for the airship ladder. She knew what she was doing. She was trying to save him, but she was also leaving him to his fate, abandoning him to the Gnome Hunters. He would never reach the airship if she failed. Both he and Trefen Morys would die.

But there wasn't any other way.

A crossbow bolt caught her in the thigh, passing so deep into her flesh it jarred the bone. She cried out in pain, stumbled, righted herself and hobbled on. Arrows rained down all about her, but she was only nicked until one caught her in the shoulder and spun her all the way around. She continued to run, teeth clenched, hands knotted into fists.

Just a little farther.

She leapt onto the rope ladder and clambered up the rungs in a wash of razor-edged pain and suffocating heat that took her breath away. She reached the top and Bellizen grabbed her arm and pulled her past the railing and onto the deck. The Druid girl was no older than Trefen Morys—younger still, Rue guessed. Short-cropped blue-black hair formed a helmet about a face paler than Grianne Ohmsford's. Eyes as black as pools on a moonless night peered over. "What do you need me to do?"

Rue hesitated. Gnome missiles thudded into the airship decking, bristling from the planks and rails like quills. Impatient with the failure of their bowmen to bring her down and infuriated by the efforts of Trefen Morys, Gnome Hunters were rappelling down the Keep's walls on ropes. The young Druid had shown enough presence of mind to use his Druid magic to cause clouds of dust to swirl across the courtyard, hiding Bek and himself. It was a clever strategy. But once those descending the walls reached the ground, the pair would be found again quickly enough.

And the rail sling, with its slow-cranking winch and single bolt, wasn't going to be enough to stop them.

"Help me into the pilot box," she said, struggling to stand.

Bellizen was stronger than she looked, and she hauled Rue to her feet, practically carrying her across the deck and up the three steps into the pilot box. Fighting the waves of pain and nausea that threatened to undo her, Rue gripped the controls of the airship, unhooding the parse tubes to release the power stored in the diapson crystals and readying the thruster levers.

"Cut the aft and forward anchor ropes," she ordered the girl. "Then drop flat against the deck close by the rope ladder. But leave the ladder down!"

Bellizen saw what she intended, jumped down the steps out of the box, and raced off to cut the ropes. *Swift Sure* was already straining against the lines, responding to the fresh power Rue was feeding her. In the courtyard, the haze of dust still obscured Bek and Trefen Morys, but the Gnome Hunters who had rappelled from the battlements were almost upon them. She shouted again at Bellizen, feeling the ship swing about as the aft anchor rope was cut, then lurch forward moments later as the bow anchor rope followed.

Swift Sure shot forward as if catapulted from a sling. Too much power! They would run Bek and the young Druid down! Rue hauled back on the thruster levers, reversing the flow of power through the parse tubes. The airship bucked and slowed, and she was suddenly in the thick of the dust cloud, arrows and crossbow bolts flying everywhere as shouts rose from the Gnomes charging across the courtyard.

"Bek!" she screamed.

The big airship swung about, clearing a space in the dust cloud, and she saw her husband and his rescuer almost underneath the hull. Bellizen was on her feet, calling down to them, directing them toward the ladder. They reached it in seconds and began to climb, Bek in the lead, Trefen Morys helping to boost him up. But they were too slow, each step taking too long. Bek, weak from loss of blood and exhaustion, was barely hanging on.

Frantic, Rue leapt from the pilot box onto the decking and charged forward to the rail sling. Cranking back the winch furiously, she inserted a bolt, swung the weapon about, and fired it into the clutch of Gnome Hunters just emerging from the haze. Three or four of them were knocked backwards like rag dolls. The rest, caught by surprise and not exactly sure what had just happened, dropped flat against the courtyard stones, trying to shield themselves. That gave Bek and Trefen Morys just enough time to gain the airship railing, where Bellizen was waiting to pull them aboard.

Rue dropped the handle of the rail sling and raced back for the pilot box. Leaping inside, she threw the thrusters to the left parse tubes forward and yanked the thrusters to the right parse tubes all the way back. *Swift Sure* swung violently about, turning toward the outer walls and the Dragon's Teeth, and Rue shoved all the thruster levers forward and tilted the tube noses up to gain lift.

An instant later, the airship exploded out of the courtyard and rose into the midday sky, leaving Paranor, with its Druids and Gnome Hunters and dark memories, behind.

S I X

Dawn broke on the Prekkendorran, a brilliant flare of golden light sweeping out of the eastern horizon down the twisting, broken maze of ridges and gullies where Pied Sanderling crouched. The sky was a cloudless canopy of brightening blue, the air still and cool, the light knife-sharp, etching the contours and folds of the land. It was a day created for the witnessing of great things.

The Federation army, a steady wave of silver and black visible through gaps in the shadow-dappled draw, approached like a winding snake toward the rise where the Elves waited. The scrape of their boots against the hardpan, and the clash of metal armor and weapons, signaled their arrival long before they came into view. In two days of steady marching, they had encountered only remnants of the force that had withstood their efforts to gain the heights for almost thirty years. Clearly, they felt they would encounter no meaningful opposition now that they had broken the back of the Elven army.

Maybe they will pay for their arrogance and overconfidence before the day is over, Pied thought. Or maybe such arrogance was justified, and he was the one who should take better stock of the situation. What reason did he have to think his ragtag force of Elves could defeat an army of regulars? Yet he knew that the Elves were determined, driven by rage at the losses they had suffered and by a humiliating sense of impotence at having been made to flee like cattle.

"Drum," he called quietly to his aide.

Drumundoon scooted over, staying low on the crest of the rise to keep hidden, his young face intense. "Captain?"

"What is this place called?"

Unable to answer, Drum shook his head. He crab-walked away, speaking to a handful of the Elven Hunters before coming back again. "It doesn't have a name. There's never been a reason to give it one."

Indeed, Pied thought. *Look at it.* A barren wasteland in which no one would want to live, a nature-ravaged stretch of earth which humans and animals passed through quickly on their way to somewhere more inviting. But it needed a name. His sense of his own mortality was strong that morning, and if he was to die there, he wanted to do so knowing where it happened.

"We will call it Elven Rock," he said. He gripped Drum by his shoulder. "It is here that the Elves become a rock against which all enemies are smashed. Pass the word."

Drum gave him a strange look, then turned and hurried off to do as he had been ordered. Pied watched him go, watched him stop and speak with groups of soldiers as he worked his way down the line, watched some of those soldiers nod in agreement, watched fresh determination etch their brows. They would fight hard, those men and women. They would not break easily.

Within the draw, the sounds of the Federation's approach deepened. The army was almost through. In moments, it would begin to emerge onto the flats leading up to the rise and the Elves.

Pied took a final look around at the defenses he had set, taking their measure one last time.

He could see nothing of the Elven bowmen hidden in the rocks and crevices in the heights to either side, where the draw opened onto the flats. There were more than two hundred, and they would have an unobstructed view of the Federation soldiers as they emerged from the shadows. Longbows were the order of the day, the favorite weapon of Elven bowmen, who disdained use of the bulkier, heavier crossbows. Erris Crewer, a Third Lieutenant, the highest-ranking officer left among them, commanded.

From his slightly higher vantage point, Pied caught glimpses of the Elven Hunters hidden in the deep folds of the ravines to his right. Almost a quarter of his little army was concealed there, waiting for the summons that would bring it into battle on the Federation's left flank. The timing of that strike would determine the outcome of the battle. The soldier who was to call for that strike was a veteran Captain of the Home Guard who had served under Pied for many years. Ti Auberen could be depended on, and Pied Sanderling was depending on him heavily.

The bulk of the army, the Elven guards armed with swords and short spears, was gathered about Pied, grouped in makeshift units with newly designated commanders and lieutenants. Because they were formed of remnants of decimated units, few had fought together before. That was a considerable disadvantage in close quarters, where one's life often depended on the experience and quick thinking of those on either side. But most were familiar with the triangle formations Pied had chosen to employ, so the Captain of the Home Guard could only hope that in battle the men would remember to do what was needed to keep the units intact and the enemy from breaking through.

Pied glanced up and down the lines to either side, checking for readiness. He found it in the faces of most, and he knew that would have to suffice. There was no time left for anything but hope and trust. Alternating the advances of the triangles would give each unit a short respite between strikes and a rear guard to buttress points threatened with breakthrough. He had decided to hold two units in reserve, keeping them back for when they were needed most. With luck, they would not be needed at all, but he couldn't trust to luck in the face of what was at stake.

These were the best of what remained; they were still alive and they had not fled during the night. They had chosen to stay, to stand with him against an enemy that had already routed them once. That said something to him about their courage.

The first wave of the Federation attack force appeared from out of the draw, marching in loose formation, shields up but swords locked in place in the carry straps behind the shields. Their scouts ranged to either side, but were still well below the ravines and rocks in which the Elves hid. Had they chosen to come on ahead, doing what scouts were supposed to do, they would have been disposed of. Pied had no idea what the Federation commanders were thinking.

Perhaps that the Elves were too disorganized to make a stand. Perhaps that they would do so farther north. Perhaps that they were rallying with reinforcements in Callahorn.

Or perhaps they weren't thinking anything. Perhaps they were just moving ahead, surprised themselves that after so many years the stalemate was broken. Perhaps they were still coming to terms with what that might mean.

Pied glanced behind him at the veteran archer he had chosen to give the attack signal. The man's bow was strung and the whistle arrow notched. Meeting his commander's eye, he nodded that he was ready.

Pied took a deep breath. The sounds of the approaching army filled his ears. Their boots stirred the dust from the flats and filled the air with a light haze. Spear blades glinted in the sunlight, and coughs and shouts emptied out the last of dawn's silence.

Patience, he willed himself. His hands closed more tightly about his sword. *Another few seconds.*

He let the first ten rows of the Federation army clear the mouth of the draw before he gave the hand signal to the archer at his back. The archer dropped to one knee, drew back his bowstring, and released the signal arrow. Its shaft meticulously cored and its tip altered, the arrow caught the wind as it flew and made a shrieking sound that could be heard for hundreds of yards. In the silence of the early morning, it was deafening.

Instantly, the Elven bowmen released their arrows from both sides of the advancing Federation force. A deep whine like the buzzing of a thousand swarming bees replaced the shriek of the warning arrow, and Pied's heart lurched. Positioned to fire in three alternating waves, his bowmen sent wave after wave of steel-tipped arrows raining down on the unprotected men. Screams and cries rose on the morning air. Dozens of Federation soldiers were dead or injured before they could react. When those remaining realized what was happening, they turned in all directions at once, and dozens more fell. Caught in the open, they had no chance of escaping the assault. Even using armor and shields to ward off the deadly killing shafts, they were vulnerable. No matter where they turned or what they did, some missiles still managed to get through.

Finally, someone in the ranks took control, and the remnants of the stricken forward units formed up and charged the archers in small groups, reinforced by soldiers still coming out of the draw—hundreds of them, flooding the flats with silver-and-black uniforms.

"Elessedil!" Pied Sanderling shouted the Elven war cry, leaping from his hiding place and raising his arm.

In a solid line, the front ranks of the Elven Hunters surged from their hiding places behind the rise and charged the Federation command, taking up Pied's war cry. The Southlanders, split apart in their efforts to reach the archers on their flanks, were caught by surprise. To their credit, they swung into defensive formation with practiced smoothness, but their ranks were already decimated, and there were gaps that could not be filled quickly enough. The Elves hammered through the front lines to the center, bowling over Federation soldiers who tried to stop them, pushing back the entire command.

But the soldiers of the Federation were well trained, and they regrouped quickly, first slowing, then stopping the assault, bracing behind dozens of oncoming ranks, behind weapons and armor, front ranks dropping to one knee and bracing the butts of their spears against the hardpan, rear ranks lowering spears over their shoulders. The Elves slammed into the wall but failed to break it, tried a second time and failed again.

Pied, still standing on the rise with the bulk of the Elven forces, signaled his archer a second time. A pair of arrows shrieked a command as they arced above the combatants. Not all heard the shrieking sound, but those who did signaled their fellows to pull back. Swiftly, the Elves disengaged, retreating on the run to the topmost part of the rise, moving past the six fighting triangles into which the remainder of the Elven foot soldiers had been formed.

It took only minutes for the first wave to retreat, but even in that short time, hundreds more Federation soldiers poured through the gap onto the flats, joining their fellows. It was a much larger force than Pied had envisioned, much larger than his Elves were equipped to handle, but there was nothing he could do about that. Lifting his sword a second time, he called out the Elessedil battle cry and sent his triangles into battle.

The triangles advanced as one. Shields locked and spears lowered, they presented bristling walls of steel tips. The triangles were formed into two lines, three triangles of eighty men each in front and three behind, the latter offset slightly to the right of the former, so that the leading points of each triangle filled all the gaps. As the triangles bore down on the Federation, Erris Crewer had the archers on the slopes rake the enemy soldiers once more, forcing them to cover up with their shields as they scrambled to re-form their shattered lines. Federation archers responded with crossbows, but they could not see their targets and were forced to fire blindly.

The men of the Federation re-formed their ranks once more, but many of those in the front lines had been downed by the initial attack and the gaps were hastily filled with reinforcements. The result was a reconfiguration of ranks where the soldiers were unfamiliar with each other and slow to act in concert or to a common purpose; it was all they could do to make ready to engage the advancing Elves. Their commanders struggled to unify them, but the chaos was so complete that no one could be heard.

Fifty yards from the Federation lines, the Elves shifted hard to the left, drawing the Federation squares about to face them. As the Federation lines turned to face the Free-born advance, their rear left flank was exposed. Ti Auberen, still hidden in the rocks with his men and waiting for his opportunity, was quick to act. Just before the triangles reached the Federation ranks, he brought his own soldiers out of hiding and attacked in a rush. Once again, the unexpectedness of the assault caught the Federation off guard. Having survived the first ambush, the Southlanders were not looking for a second. Ti Auberen's forces caught their rear ranks unprepared and vulnerable, and they smashed through before the surprised soldiers could even bring their weapons about to defend themselves.

Caught in a classic pincer movement, the Federation lines collapsed into pockets of men fighting to survive. The triangles came at them in a series of thrusts, first one rank and then the second, jabbing at them repeatedly, forcing them back and apart from each other. The Federation defense held only minutes against the Elves, then fell apart. The attack turned into a rout, the men in the front lines who tried to flee piling up against those still coming through the draw. Screams and cries filled the air as soldiers fell beneath the crush, trampled. The ground grew cluttered with dead and wounded; the flats turned into a slaughterhouse. The destruction of the Federation force was so complete that it became difficult for the Elves to advance across the body-strewn ground.

Finally, the surviving Southlanders broke free of the charnel house and began to retreat into the draw, the rear ranks falling back so that those still alive in the front could follow. Most of the latter never made it. The memory of their defeat on the Prekkendorran was still fresh in the minds of the Elven Hunters, and they were consumed by a killing lust that would not allow them to stop fighting, even when almost no one was left alive to oppose them.

"Signal a retreat," Pied ordered the archer at his elbow, exchanging a quick glance with Drumundoon.

The archer did so, three arrows whistling through the midmorning air, their shrieks mingling with those of the dead and dying men below. The Elven Hunters, streaked with blood and wild-eyed with battle fever, fell back reluctantly, leaving behind a tangle of dead men and an earth turned slick and matted with blood.

In the shadows of the draw, the last of the retreating Federation soldiers disappeared from view.

Thirty minutes later, Pied stood at the head of the rise with Ti Auberen and Erris Crewer, watching the details move through the carnage below, extracting the Elven dead and wounded. The sun was high in the sky by then, midday approaching, and the air was hot and still and thick with the smell of blood and death. Flies swarmed in black clouds. The men on the rise were making a conscious effort to breathe through their mouths.

"It's not finished," he said.

"No," Ti Auberen agreed, looking off into the hills as if he might catch sight of the enemy. He was a big man, broad-shouldered and lean, wearing his dark hair long and tied back. "But they will come at us another way."

Pied nodded. "They will regroup, reinforce, and come looking for us again, but not through that draw. There are other trails through these hills, tough to navigate, but usable. They will find one and try to get around behind us."

"But they won't underestimate us next time," Auberen added.

Pied thought about that a moment, then turned to Drumundoon, who was standing off to one side. "Drum, see if we have someone in the command who knows this country well enough to talk to us about its passes and trails."

Eager to be doing something other than standing around trying not to watch the burial teams, Drumundoon hurried off. Pied would have been happy to go with him.

"What about that airship?" Erris Crewer asked quietly. His blocky form shifted. "The one that destroyed the fleet?"

Pied shook his head. "I don't know how badly we damaged her. If they can make her fly, we're in trouble. We have no defense against her from the ground, and little enough from the air. We have to hope they can't use her yet."

"They might already be using her against Vaden Wick and our Free-born allies," Auberen growled. "If I was them, that's what I would do. Break us where we still hold, chase us back into the hills and then hunt us at leisure."

Pied considered the possibility. Auberen might be right. It made sense to finish the effort to drive the Free-born completely off the heights, to smash their defenses and claim the Prekkendorran them- selves before worrying about the Elves, most of whom were already scattered to the four winds, his command notwithstanding. After all, how much trouble could his little force present in the larger scheme of things? Pied did not fool himself about their chances. They might have won this one battle, driven back one unit of the Federation. But the enemy forces were vast and close to home, where reinforcements were readily available. A sustained Federation effort at finding and engaging his Elves would eventually succeed, and when that hap- pened, they were finished.

He exhaled softly, frustrated. They couldn't win the war, not with the way things stood. The best they could do was to avoid the forces hunting them long enough to link up with their allies. As their leader, it was up to him to find a way to make that happen. It was a tall order, one he was not sure anyone would be able to carry out, let alone a Captain of the Home Guard whose primary duty until two days ago had been to safeguard one man.

Drumundoon had reappeared with a smallish, nervous-looking Elf with lean features and quick, sharp eyes that darted everywhere.

"Captain," his aide said, "this is Whyl. He has served on the front for more than a year, working as a scout on both sides of the line, much of the time aboard airships. He has seen more of the terrain than most. I think he can help."

Pied nodded. "Tell me what you know about the passes that run through the Prekkendorran to these hills. Are there many?"

The Elven Hunter hunched his shoulders and pursed his thin lips. "Dozens."

"How many that a large force could negotiate, coming south to north?"

"Three, maybe four." The eyes skipped across Pied's face to the faces of his companions and back again. "You think they'll come at us again, Captain?"

"Maybe. Could they, if they wanted to, do you think? How would they come?"

Whyl thought about it. "Other than through the draw they just retreated down, they have only one other good choice. There's another cut through the hills to the west. It's wide and flat and open. But it will take them two or three days to reach it and get through, then come up to where we are."

"To the west," Pied repeated, thinking. "Nothing east?"

The Elf shrugged. "One trail, through scrub, forests, low country. Pretty dangerous. Lots of bogs and sinkholes. Cuts pretty close at its south end to where the Dwarves and Bordermen hold the east plateau. It would be risky for them to try it."

For them, but maybe not for us, Pied thought. The beginnings of a plan were taking shape. He nodded to Whyl. "Your help is appreciated. You may go back to your unit. But keep what we've said to yourself for now. Don't speak of it to anyone."

The Elven Hunter nodded and hurried off across the grass with several anxious glances back. In spite of his promise, he would tell his friends what had been said. In particular, he would tell them that their commander was anticipating another attack, one that might not turn out as well for the Elves as this one had. Word would spread quickly. Panic, if not squelched, would as well.

Pied turned back to Ti Auberen and Erris Crewer. "Form up the wounded—everyone who can't fight another battle right away. Detail enough men to carry those who can't walk. Use as few as you can manage, but enough so that they can travel afoot for several days. I want them to make for the Rappahalladran, then for the villages in the Duln. They will find wagons there to complete the rest of the journey home. With luck, they will come across an airship to transport them. Form up everyone else and prepare to march. We'll move east toward that pass Whyl mentioned, the tougher one that leads to the defensive position of our allies. Our best choice now is to try to link up with Vaden Wick before the enemy finds us again. There's some cover along the way. It may help shield us from Federation airships."

"Captain, if they send airships after us, whether it's the one with that weapon or not, we won't be able to hide this many men," Erris Crewer pointed out quietly.

Pied met his gaze. "Get on with it, Lieutenant. I want all burials completed and the wounded dispatched north within the hour. I want the rest of us heading east. Wait, not all of us. Detail two dozen men to stay behind to watch the pass in case the Federation decides to send scouts through to see if we're still here. We don't want them to find out too quickly that we've gone. All we need is a presence to keep them guessing. The men can use the time to create false trails. I want them to hold the pass for one day, then catch up to us. Put a Tracker or two in the mix. And bring up Whyl again, as well. We'll need what he knows about the country."

When they were gone, he walked over to Drumundoon. His aide shifted his lanky body from foot to foot. He looked dusty and tired, but he smiled at Pied anyway. "Not much help for some things, is there, Captain?"

"Drum, I need you to do something," Pied replied, taking the other's arm and steering him away from everyone else. "Word has to be sent to Arborlon of what's happened. Maybe it's already been done, but we can't know. The Elven High Council has to be told that the King and his sons are dead. More to the point, they have to be told to send reinforcements. More airships, more men to fly them. We don't stand a chance without their support. I want you to do this. Travel on foot until you can find horses. Then ride until you can find an airship. Take two of the Home Guard with you, just in case. Leave at once."

Drumundoon looked at him. "Arling will be Queen now," he said. "It will be her decision."

He was saying that she might not be favorably disposed toward Pied's suggestion, no matter what the High Council said. Nor toward Pied, for that matter, once she learned that he had failed to keep her sons safe. But there was nothing Pied could do about it without speaking to her. He had to hope she would allow him the opportunity, that something of what he believed she had once felt for him would persuade her to do what was right.

"Do the best you can, Drum," he said quietly. He placed his hand on the other's shoulder. "But do it quickly."

"I don't like leaving you, Captain," his aide replied, shaking his head slowly, looking down at his feet.

"I don't like having you leave me. But we don't always get to choose in these matters. I have to send someone I can depend upon to do this. There isn't anyone I depend on more than you."

He thought he saw Drumundoon actually blush, but it was hard to tell beneath the layers of dirt and sweat. Drum rubbed his fringe of black beard and nodded. "I'll do my best."

He was, as usual, as good as his word. By the time the wounded were loaded on litters and their bearers and caregivers ready to depart, Drum was already gone. Pied found himself wishing he could have given his friend something more than encouragement, but at least he was sending him out of the fighting. Drum was a good man, but he wasn't meant to stand in the front lines on a battlefield.

Maybe I'm not meant for this, either, Pied thought. *But here I am.*

He slung his longbow across his shoulders, cinched his quiver a notch tighter, and went off to meet his fate.

Darkness had settled across the cities of the Southland, but it was nothing compared to the darkness that had found a home in Shadea a'Ru's heart. She stood at a floor-to-ceiling window in a reception room deep inside Sen Dunsidan's compound, staring out at the lights of Arishaig. She had not moved from that spot, had barely changed her position, in more than an hour. She had gone deep inside herself, escaping the disagreeableness of the present, a Druid trick she had taught herself early on in her time at Paranor, when she had no friends and no future. It had served her well then; it was less effective now.

Behind her, the Captain of her Gnome Hunters stood with two of his men and watched her uneasily. He could feel the heat radiate from her. He felt her anger as she quietly seethed. He did not want to be present when she reached the boiling point, but there was nowhere else for him to go.

It had been a long day in more ways than one. They had arrived aboard the *Bremen* the previous night, only to be told that Sen Dunsidan had not yet returned from the Prekkendorran, where he was personally overseeing the destruction of the Elves. Shadea had been willing to forgive his failure to adhere to their schedule; the defeat of the Elves was a major blow to the Free-born hopes, and the Prime Minister would want to make certain things did not go awry. She had heard of the defeat of the Elven fleet, of the burning of their airships, and of the deaths of Kellen Elessedil and his young sons. She had heard of the subsequent rout of the Elven army and its frantic retreat into the hills north. Sen Dunsidan had accomplished something important, and he had done it without her help. She would grant him his victory, even though it rankled her that he had deliberately gone behind her back to achieve it. She had gone to bed in the quarters provided for her with the expectation that their meeting would take place promptly the next day.

She had been wrong. A day of touring the ministries, of speaking before the Coalition Council, and of deliberate delays had left her convinced that something she knew nothing about was happening. She could feel it in the attitude of the Ministers with whom she met—men and women who were civil and indulgent, but clearly disdainful of her, as well. They extended courtesies because they would do so even to their worst enemy on such a visit, but there was no warmth or sincerity in the efforts.

By nightfall, she had lost her patience with Sen Dunsidan entirely. She had been advised of his return several hours earlier, but then he had asked that she wait while he freshened himself for their meeting. She had kept her composure mostly by telling herself that it would only weaken her position with him to reveal the depths of her irritation. If he thought he could undo her so easily, he would be much more difficult to manage. And she already knew from the news of his victory on the Prekkendorran and the nature of her reception here that he would be difficult in any case.

A knock sounded on the door to the reception room and a functionary cautiously stepped just inside the opening. Shadea came out of her shell instantly, but let him stand where he was for a moment, her eyes directed out the window toward the city. Then, drawing herself up, she turned to face him.

"My lady," he said, bowing to her. "The Prime Minister apologizes for the delay and begs your indulgence for just a few minutes more. He is almost ready to receive you and asks that you wait—"

"I have waited long enough," she said quietly, cutting off the rest of what he was about to say.

The words were edged in steel so sharp that the functionary winced visibly. He hesitated, then tried to speak again, but Shadea's hand had lifted, her fingers had pointed in his direction, and suddenly his voice had failed completely. He gasped and tried again and again, but nothing would come out.

She crossed the room and stood before him. "Captain?" she said to the leader of her Gnome escort. His hard, weathered face appeared at her elbow. "Ready the *Bremen* for departure. Take your men with you. I will be along in a few minutes."

Her Captain of the Guard frowned. "It is not safe for you here alone, Mistress."

"Safer for me than for some," she answered. "Do as I say."

He left without further comment, taking his men with him, leaving her alone in the reception room with the still-voiceless functionary.

"As for you, little man," she said to him, "I have other plans. Do you wish your voice back?" The functionary nodded eagerly. "I thought as much. What service do you think I require of you if I am to grant you this favor?"

He didn't need to ask. He led her out through the doorway and down the hall. They passed dozens of guards, all armed and at watch, but none tried to stop them. Shadea had drawn her Druid robes tight about her, but within their folds, concealed from view, the fingers of her right hand flexed in a series of intricate moves, calling up magic to within easy reach, readying herself for the unexpected. She did not think she would have to use her magic, but she knew enough to be prepared in case she did. She could not trust Sen Dunsidan, could not rely on him to act honorably toward her, even as a guest of state. One thing she had learned about the Prime Minister of the Federation—he would do whatever he felt was necessary to get what he wanted.

The hallway ended at a pair of ornately carved double doors that stood open to the light. The room within was candlelit but draped in its corners and along its edges by deepest shadow. She heard Sen Dunsidan's voice, smooth and persuasive, a hiss against the silence. A snake's voice, she thought. But she knew how to draw the poison from his fangs.

The functionary turned toward her questioningly as they reached the door, uncertain of what he was expected to do next. She solved the problem for him by fastening one hand about his neck and marching him into the room in front of her.

Sen Dunsidan was seated on a couch to one side, sipping wine and speaking with a shadowy figure seated in the corner of the room where it was darkest. Shadea did a quick search of the chamber, found only the two and no one else present, swept up to Sen Dunsidan in a rush of black robes, and threw his functionary at his feet.

"Ready to receive me now, Prime Minister?" she asked softly. She eyed the glass of wine he held poised midway to drinking and smiled. "Go ahead. Finish it."

He did so, watching her carefully, clearly surprised by her appearance, but not altogether unprepared. A man like him was never entirely unprepared. She gestured at the functionary, who coughed out a few startled words, climbed quickly to his feet, and ran from the room.

"I was just about to come for you," Sen Dunsidan said, putting down the glass of wine and rising. "But I wanted to make certain of what I would say before we met."

"You have had time enough to make certain of what you will say for the next year. What seems to be the problem? Are you at a loss for words? Do you find your oratorical skills have suddenly deserted you?" She paused. "Or are you simply worried about how I might perceive your duplicity in acting without my knowledge in the matter of the Prekkendorran?"

The Prime Minister's face darkened. "I do not need to apologize for that. I acted when the opportunity presented itself, just as you would have done in my place. Had I waited to consult with you, the opportunity would have been forever lost. Don't presume to lecture me on how to conduct myself as leader of the Federation. I do what I must."

"Yes," she acknowledged. "And you tell me of it in your own good time, it seems. I do not judge you for your decision in attacking the Free-born. I judge you for your failure to inform me of it. It smacks of an independence that verges on rebellion. Have we come to a point where you think you no longer have need of an alliance with me? Or with the Druid order? Does your success whisper to you that you are sufficiently strong that you need ally yourself with no one? Is that the course you have chosen?"

She turned toward the shadowy figure in the corner. "Or do you take your counsel from someone else these days, someone you think may advise you better?"

There was a long silence. Then the figure in the corner rose, a slow languid movement of limbs and torso. "He seeks the counsel of someone who has his best interests at heart, Shadea."

"Iridia."

She breathed the name like a curse. Iridia Eleri—or at least a pale imitation of the Elven sorceress—stepped into the light. Whatever Shadea might have thought she would find, it wasn't this. There was no reason for Iridia to be present, not as an ally to Sen Dunsidan, not as a creature in thrall to the Prime Minister of the Federation. Even more shocking was how her onetime ally looked—bloodless and drained of life, thin to the point of emaciation, and hard-eyed in a way she had never seemed before. There was something wrong with her, but Shadea could not decide what it was.

"Did you think you had seen the last of me?" Iridia asked, her voice as bloodless as her face. "Did you think me safely away from Paranor and your Druid schemes?"

Shadea stared, not knowing what she thought, except that it wasn't this.

"You drove me from Paranor," Iridia continued in her flat, lifeless monotone. "You refused me any chance to gain revenge over the man who had wronged me. You took away my power. You stripped me of my pride. So I came here, to give my services to one who would better appreciate them."

Shadea looked back at Sen Dunsidan. He shrugged. "She acts as my personal adviser now. Her help has been invaluable to me. I hope you don't intend to try to rob me of it out of jealousy or a misguided sense of prior claims."

She grimaced. "Please, Prime Minister, try not to sound as stupid as you act. I don't care whom you bring into your confidence. Even her. She speaks the truth. She was banished when she failed to live up to her pledge to serve the order. She would not be welcomed back now even if she sought to return voluntarily. I certainly have no intention of trying to make her return by force. But you might think about her failure to serve one master and ask yourself how likely it is that she will successfully serve another."

"I think I am the best judge of how well a person will serve me, Shadea." Sen Dunsidan shrugged. "After all, I was smart enough to ally myself with you, wasn't I?"

"An alliance that no longer seems to have much merit, given what I see of your present situation."

The Prime Minister moved over to his couch and sat down again, his earnest expression only barely concealing the satisfaction she was certain he was feeling at her discomfort. She would have liked to wipe it away with her fingernails, but she wanted to see where things were going first.

"Our alliance still has value," he said, motioning for her to sit. She remained where she was. "As I said, I acted as I did on the Prekkendorran because the opportunity presented itself. But the war is not over, and I still have need of your support. And the support of the Druid order. If I am to successfully conclude the war with the Free-born, I must press north and west to force a resolution. I cannot do this without at least the tacit support of the Druids. By the same token, I know that you need my support, as well. You lack any other alliances. The Dwarves, the Elves, the Trolls, and the Bordermen all refuse to give you the allegiance you seek. They have not yet accepted you as Ard Rhys. For that matter, some within your own order have not accepted you."

She said nothing, holding her temper, showing nothing of what she was feeling. When the time was right, she would squash him like a bug—assuming Iridia let him live that long. Shadea was convinced that the sorceress was making use of him for her own needs and would keep him around only so long as was necessary.

"I don't say that you won't find a way to deal with these trouble-makers, Shadea," the Prime Minister continued. "But you must agree that it will make things considerably easier for you if we maintain our alliance rather than cast it aside. And, of course, it will make things easier for me, as well."

"Especially if your armies suffer another defeat like the one they suffered in the passes north of the Prekkendorran two days ago." She smiled. "How many men did you lose? More than a thousand? At the hands of some ragtag Elven castoffs you had driven from the heights?"

She enjoyed the look of surprise that appeared on his face, a look he tried without success to conceal. He had not expected her to know of the army's defeat, a secret he had tried hard to conceal from everyone. But there were no secrets that he could conceal from her.

"You had them beaten, Sen Dunsidan. You had them scattered and disheartened, and you let them drive your pursuit force into the ground. In all the years I served in the Federation army, I never heard of such stupidity. How could you let something like that happen?"

"Enough, Shadea. You have had your fun with me. Now let it alone. I intend to rectify matters on the Prekkendorran within a few days. When I am finished, the entire Free-born army will be in tatters, and my armies will be deep within their homelands."

"If I decide to let you do so." She kept Sen Dunsidan's eyes locked on her own, chained by the steel of her gaze. "I am not certain now that I should."

She saw the rage in those eyes, his hatred for her burning in them. She did not look away. The silence between them lengthened.

"You presume a great deal, Shadea," Iridia Eleri said suddenly.

Her voice was as cold as winter midnight and empty of feeling. Shadea was taken aback in spite of herself. Something about Iridia Eleri was not right. Something about her was changed, something deep and abiding, invisible to the eye, but there all the same.

She broke eye contact with Sen Dunsidan and glanced over. "It worries me that I may have allied myself and my order's cause with fools. I will presume what I must to remedy such a mistake." She studied Iridia a moment longer, then turned back to Sen Dunsidan. "Tell me, Prime Minister—must I do so here?"

Sen Dunsidan sighed. "I don't want you for an enemy, Shadea. You must know that. I need the Druid order to give its blessing to my efforts. I need to know you will not interfere with my plans. Surely you can see this?"

Shadea walked over to the wine pitcher, poured herself a glass, and drank deeply. She watched Iridia casually as she did so, trying to read something of what it was about her that was so troubling. It was in her eyes, she thought. It was in the way she looked out at the world. The problem was there.

"You need me," she said, "but not enough to tell me of your plans until after they are executed."

"I have kept nothing back from you that you couldn't find out on your own, it seems."

"Your attack on the Elven fleet, your destruction of their army, your own army's subsequent setback, your alliance with Iridia—what other secrets do you keep from me?"

He sighed. "What secrets do you think I keep, Shadea?"

"I haven't heard any mention of your new weapon, the one that so effectively destroyed the Elven fleet. An oversight?"

The Prime Minister shrugged. "It is a fire launcher, a pressure feed that sends burning liquid from a nozzle mounted on our airships into others, setting them aflame. A conventional weapon, good over short distances when properly manned. It is hardly worth mentioning."

What a pathetic liar, Shadea thought. "Which must be why you failed to mention it. Or is there something about it I might find objectionable? A forbidden use of magic, perhaps?"

"Magic?" Sen Dunsidan laughed. "Where would I get magic? Oh, you think Iridia might have given me something from the Druid storehouse, do you? Wouldn't that be useful! But, no, the weapon was developed long before Iridia appeared with her offer of support. She brings nothing of her Druid lore or of Druid magic to our relationship. Nothing that isn't her own, anyway. There is no betrayal of the Druids involved in the building of this weapon, Shadea. What are you worried about? The power of the Druids is more than a match for anything I have at my command. I have only my armies and my airships."

It was difficult to judge how deep the lie went, but it went sufficiently deep that Shadea was certain the weapon was much more powerful than he was suggesting and that he intended it for more than simple warfare. At some point, he would seek to use it against the Druids, because in his heart he could never be at rest until he had destroyed everyone who might threaten him. That was the demon that had driven him since he had begun his ascent to power all those years ago. It was a demon with which she had a fair amount of personal experience.

"Your plan," she said, "is to use this weapon against the remaining Free-born ground forces on the Prekkendorran? On the Dwarves and Bordermen?"

He nodded. "And on the remnants of the Elves who ambushed my pursuit force. The Free-born have nothing with which to combat it. The best they have been able to do is damage the airship that transports it, and that was a fluke." He sipped at his wine. "The war on the Prekkendorran is over, Shadea, the moment my airship returns to the skies. All I require to proceed is your clear support for my efforts. For the Federation's efforts," he corrected.

She walked over to the window, brushing past Iridia Eleri as if she weren't there, but feeling something so dark and empty as she did so that she wished she had avoided the sorceress entirely. Pausing at the window, she shuddered a moment in spite of herself. Whatever had happened to Iridia wasn't anything for the better.

She looked out at the city, considering her options, giving herself sufficient space and time to choose wisely. She made several decisions in that moment, but she spoke only of one.

She turned back to Sen Dunsidan. "The Druid order will support your efforts, Prime Minister. I will announce that support on my return to Paranor. But there are two conditions. First, you will speak before the Coalition Council tomorrow in support of my ascendancy to the position of Ard Rhys. You will make your support complete and unequivocal. No half measures, no politician's word games. Second, you will fly to Paranor within the week to speak before the Druid order so that all may hear your justification for the invasion of the other lands. You are good at explanations, Sen Dunsidan. You should be able to come up with one."

The Federation leader studied her, thinking through the ramifications of accepting her offer, as she knew he would, then nodded. "Agreed."

She walked back across the room, her eyes never leaving his, coming to a stop when she reached him. "A final word. Do not even think about trying to use your new weapon against me. Your hunger for power is vast, Sen Dunsidan, so I know the thought has crossed your mind. Control the Druids, and you control the Four Lands. But you lack the skill and the experience to manage such a task—even with your new ally to advise you."

She glanced at Iridia. "She is good at what she does, and once she was great. But she is only one person and nowhere near strong enough to challenge me. So keep a tight rein on your ambitions and do not forget your place in the pecking order. The Druids wield the real power in the Four Lands, just as they always have."

She looked back at him, waiting for his response. "I won't forget," he said quietly. "I won't forget anything."

He was making a thinly veiled threat, but she would allow that. A threat was only words until it was backed up by something more substantial than anything Sen Dunsidan could command.

She moved close to him, placing herself squarely between Iridia and himself. "Watch your back, Sen Dunsidan," she whispered.

Then she strode from the room without looking at either of them again and made her way through the halls of the compound buildings to board her airship and fly home.

"She is too dangerous," Sen Dunsidan declared, once she was gone. He faced Iridia Eleri in challenge. "Too dangerous for either of us. You would not argue the point, would you?"

She floated across the room into the darkness from which she had come and sat down again, cloaked in shadows. "I wouldn't worry about Shadea a'Ru, Sen Dunsidan."

He didn't care for the way she said it. "Well, I do worry about her, Iridia. If you choose to pretend she isn't a threat, that is up to you. But I intend to do something about her."

"I can protect you," she said.

"Perhaps. But if Shadea is dead, I won't need your protection."

There was a long silence. "Killing her won't be easy," she said. "And if you fail, she will know who to come looking for. Besides, who will you send to eliminate her? Who can you trust to make certain she is dead?"

He hesitated, unable to answer those questions.

"And we have other concerns at the moment." Iridia sounded sleepy and bored. "Your airship is nearly ready to fly again. You need to do what I told you. You need to take it into the Westland and attack the Elven home city of Arborlon. You need to convince the Elves they are not safe anywhere so that they will agree to abandon their alliance with the Free-born."

"If I smash the Free-born army first, I won't need to worry about persuading the Elves to abandon their alliance. There won't be anyone left for them to ally themselves with."

"An ill-advised course of action." He felt displeasure radiating from her words. "A waste of time and effort. You might smash this army, but they will simply raise another. You think too small, Sen Dunsidan. You must think in larger terms. Winning the war on the Prekkendorran will not happen until you win the war in their homes. Strike at their capital cities, and they will seek your peace quickly enough. Start with Arborlon, then fly on to the others. Soon, all re-sistance will end."

Her argument made sense, as it had the first time she had made it, but something about it bothered him. It felt to him as if she was saying one thing, but meaning another—as if she had thought the situation through better than he had and knew something about it he didn't. Besides, he could not ignore the defeat he had suffered in the Borderlands at the hands of the Elves. His army, so certain of vic-tory after the destruction of the Elven airfleet, was stunned by the abrupt turnabout. He could not ignore what that meant to morale. If he didn't give the army a fresh reason to believe that the war was ending, it was hard to say what might happen.

"The best approach is still the one I settled on originally, Iridia. We attack the Free-born position on the east plateau of the Prekken-dorran, using the airship and her weapon to break their defensive lines. Once they are scattered and the position overrun, the Federa-tion will hold the entire Prekkendorran. Then I will do as you sug-gest and fly the *Dechtera* to Arborlon and attack the Elven home city."

She said nothing. She stared at him from out of the darkness, an all-but-invisible presence, faceless and silent. He waited for her to speak, but she didn't. Finally, he lost patience and rose. "I am going to bed. We can talk about this later. Think about what we can do to eliminate Shadea. I won't sleep soundly again until she's disposed of."

He walked quickly from the room, the weight of Iridia Eleri's eyes pressing against his exposed back.

Eight

A sudden lurch of the airship brought Khyber Elessedil awake, jarring her from sleep with such abruptness that for a moment she did not know where she was. Then her scattered thoughts came together, and she remembered. She was hiding in a locker in a forward storeroom that was filled with yards of light sheaths and coils of radian draws and heavy rigging. Rough voices sounded from somewhere outside the locker and she flinched anew. Gnome guards. She blinked uncertainly, listened as the voices drew nearer and the storeroom door banged open. She caught her breath as the Gnomes rummaged about, conversed in their guttural tongue, then departed once more.

She took a deep, steadying breath, squeezed free of the sail material into which she had wrapped herself, then opened the locker door cautiously and peered out.

Shadows draped the storeroom in heavy layers, the darkness broken by slender bands of moonlight spearing through cracks in the shutters that closed off the storeroom's solitary window. Reluctant to chance another encounter that might end less favorably, she had been hiding there since she had been discovered and almost caught the previous night. If she was discovered, she knew Pen would have no chance at all.

Not that he had much anyway. After watching the flare of magic explode from the hold of the *Athabasca* the previous night, she feared the worst had happened already.

She slipped from the locker and moved over to the shuttered opening, peering through its cracks into the night. The airship had landed inside a courtyard ringed by high walls and stark battlements interspersed with watchtowers. To one side, huge buildings rose against the moonlit sky like the squared-off sides of cliffs. They had landed and were inside Paranor. She glanced across the courtyard for the other airships, but at first saw only dark figures scurrying about the landing site, securing lines and fastening anchors. Lights appeared suddenly in windows in the buildings that formed the bulk of the Keep, and she heard locks release and a door open. Voices drifted on the night air, whispery and muffled. She needed to get out of the storeroom to find out what was going on, but she knew it was still too dangerous to do so.

Her patience ebbing swiftly, she forced herself to wait as the Gnome crew went about its business and finally disappeared altogether, save for a watch that patrolled the yard. That she knew because a Gnome Hunter strolled by the shuttered window, thickset and armed with a spear and short sword. There would be more stationed close by. Anchored farther down the length of the yard were other airships, their dark shapes barely identifiable in the shadow of the walls. Within the Keep, the lights remained aglow, bright squares framed by the windows through which they shone. She wondered how late it was, whether it was past midnight or not, whether it was approaching morning. She glanced at the sky, but could not tell from the position of the stars she could see.

When sufficient time had passed and her patience was exhausted, she opened the storeroom door and stepped out into the companionway. She stood listening for a long time, making certain she was alone. Satisfied at last that she was, she moved down the passageway and climbed on deck. Crouched in the shelter of the pilot box, just beyond the hatchway, she peered around the airship decking, then beyond to the courtyard. The *Athabasca* was anchored right next to her own ship, and the third ship was anchored just a little farther away. All appeared deserted.

But on the ground below, Gnome Hunters patrolled, slow-moving shadows in the night.

Khyber considered her situation. She could not get off the airship without alerting the watch. Yet she had to reach Pen. She assumed he had been taken inside the Keep, but could not know that for a fact without checking the *Athabasca* first. That would take time, however—time she felt she didn't have.

She studied the night sky, the position of the stars and moon, reading the time. It was after midnight and getting toward morning. The Druids would be asleep, but that would all change when it grew light. Any help she could offer Pen had to come soon.

But how could she reach him when she hadn't the faintest idea where he was? She had never been to Paranor; her time with Ahren was spent entirely in Emberen, his place of exile. He had deliberately chosen to stay away from the Druid's Keep and its politics. Since she had begun her studies with him, he had not gone back even once, and so she had never gone, either. It was something she had always meant to do, something she had assured herself would eventually happen.

Well, it had, but the circumstances were not what she would have hoped for.

She knew a little of the Keep's layout, having asked Ahren about it on several occasions, even persuading him once to draw her a rough map. But, in truth, she remembered little of the detail, and it was different being there, staring at its walls and buildings with no idea where to begin her search. She would need someone to help her find her way around, but she could not afford to ask for assistance because that would mean giving herself away.

The impossibility of her situation quickly became apparent. On starting out, she had thought that it would be easier, that a way to get to Pen would present itself. She had been wrong, and the boy was likely to pay the price for her presumption.

She shivered in response to her dark thoughts, and as her hands rubbed her arms and body to warm herself, they brushed against the small bulk of the Elfstones in her pocket.

She froze, her fingers closing over the talismans. She had forgotten about the Elfstones. Fresh hope warmed her chilly thoughts. She could use their magic to find Pen! The Stones would lead her straight to him!

And lead the Druids straight to her. Her hopes faded. Using the Elfstones would give her away instantly. Every Druid in the Keep was familiar with Elven magic. She would be detected in a heartbeat.

She released her grip on the Stones reluctantly and sank back against the pilothouse wall. The use of small magics was common-place within the Druid's Keep. Small magics would not be noticed. But the Elfstones were a large magic that no one could mistake for anything other than what it was. Nothing could disguise the extent of their power. Another way would have to be found.

Another way, she thought, that utilized her skills and training as an apprentice Druid. A way that relied upon the lessons she had been taught by her mentor and best friend before his death. It was all she had left to call upon. It was what she would have to employ if she was to have any chance at all of saving Pen.

She went still inside as she measured herself for the task she was about to undertake. She had studied hard the skills that Ahren felt she should master. He had given her so little; their time was too short for more. But what he had given her would have to be enough. Most of what she could call upon relied on her ability to concentrate and to center herself. She had worked hard during the voyage to Anatcherae to become accomplished at both. She would put it to the test.

Gathering her resolve, she rose, moved over to the side of the airship, and looked down. The yard directly below her was empty. She went over the side quickly, down the rope ladder and onto the ground, not bothering to hide her descent or even her presence. Subtlety would not serve her well just then. The key to her success lay in boldness. She stood at the bottom of the ladder, looking around for the Gnome guards. Still wrapped and hooded by the cloak she had stolen earlier, at a distance she could pass for one of them. It was her best chance.

She picked out the guards in the darkness, then started toward the window-lit walls of the Keep as if it made no difference to her whether they were there or not.

Darkness served her purpose well. She was shadowed for much of the way by the hulls of the airships and then the walls of the para-pets and buildings; she was just another solitary figure crossing the yard, no different in appearance from the others. One of the guards glanced her way as she advanced toward the doors she had spied ahead, but he made no attempt to challenge her. When another turned toward her in the making of his rounds, she released a quick

bit of magic to create an unexpected noise behind him, causing him
to turn back again. In the windows ahead, shadows passed through
the light, their appearance unexpected and startling. She felt her
throat tighten, but did not slow.

Keep going, she told herself.

She reached the doorway after what seemed an interminable
length of time, pulled down on the handle to release the latch, and
stepped inside.

A large anteroom, its ceiling cavernous and smoky with torch
burn, its walls hung with heraldic pennants, opened into three long
corridors that stretched away through pools of torchlight and layered shadows to lines of closed doors, high windows, and dark al-
coves. She started forward and stopped. A pair of Gnome Hunters
stood to either side of her, neither more than a dozen paces away,
armed and gimlet-eyed as they watched her freeze in place.

She had no time to think and only a moment to react.

She threw back the hood to her cloak and fastened the one on
the right with a dark glare. "Where have they taken him?"

The question was asked in Elfish, a language with which she did
not think he would be familiar. She was right. He stared blankly at
her, a hint of surprise shadowing his sharp features.

"The boy!" she snapped, speaking now in Callahorn's tongue, a
Southland dialect everyone in the Borderlands spoke, accommodat-
ing him in a way that would demonstrate her superiority "Where
is he?"

She shifted her gaze quickly from the first Gnome to the second,
her impatience evident, her sense of command clear. She radiated
what she hoped was Druid authority, giving clear indication that as a
member of the order, she was where she belonged and had a right to
ask the questions she was asking. There was no reason to doubt her.
All that was required was a quick, concise response.

Not surprisingly, the Gnomes had trouble supplying one. "The
cells, I think," the second Gnome told her in the Southland dialect.
He said something to the other in Gnomish, but his companion simply shrugged. "Yes, the cells. To be held until the Ard Rhys returns."

She nodded perfunctorily and marched past them down the central corridor, acting as if she knew exactly what she was doing, when
in fact she had no idea at all. The cells? Where were the cells? Below

ground somewhere? She couldn't ask that, not of these guards. Someone else, maybe. She was inside and she had a destination, and that was going to have to be enough.

A handful of doors farther down the corridor, she stepped into a deeply shadowed alcove and stood breathing hard with her back against the rough wall, her mind racing. Ahren would have known what to do next if he were there. She must try to think the way Ahren would. She squeezed her eyes shut against the pain that thinking of him cost her, then opened them quickly, determined not to give way. The mechanics were easy. She needed to find her way to the cells. To do that, she needed to find someone to tell her how.

She brushed at her short-cropped dark hair, squared her shoulders, then stepped back out into the corridor and began walking deeper into the Keep.

Empty of life, the passageway tunneled ahead, her footsteps soft echoes in the silence. She was aware that she still wore the Gnome hunting cloak and that it would eventually draw unwanted attention. Her first order of business was to replace it with a Druid robe. But that was easier said than done. It wasn't as if there were robes hanging on hooks all up and down the hallway, Druids wandering about from whom she might steal one.

But she got lucky. At a juncture of corridors much deeper inside the Keep, just as she was despairing that she might wander the halls of Paranor until sunrise, she came upon a study chamber with lights burning and Druids at work. She paused just outside the doorway, still within the corridor shadows, and peered inside. She could see three dark-cloaked forms, hoods thrown back, bodies hunched over books at tables, heads lowered in concentration.

She stood for a time, trying to decide what to do next. But she couldn't think of anything that didn't involve going into the room for a closer look around. That was too dangerous. She hesitated, undecided, and as she did so, she felt a finger tap her shoulder.

"Are you looking for someone?"

That she didn't jump out of her skin entirely was something of a miracle. She even managed to turn around. A Druid stood behind her, a questioning look on his scowling face. Bright green eyes peered out from under heavy, furrowed brows. A Southlander. She stared at him without speaking, her heart gone straight to her throat.

"Sorry," he said, not sounding sorry at all. "Didn't mean to frighten you. But you look like you don't know what you're doing here." He rubbed his smooth chin reflectively, then glanced at her robe and gave a disapproving frown. "Why are you wearing a Gnome Hunter's cloak? You know the rules."

She didn't, of course, but she nodded anyway. "I was working on the airships and wore the robe to keep from getting dirty. I forgot to take it off."

"Well, it's not allowed." He glanced past her into the study room. "Wait here."

He stepped inside, out of view, then returned a moment later and thrust a Druid robe into her hands. "Here, wear this until you can put on one of your own. The rules are clear."

She nodded her thanks, slipped off the Gnome cloak, and slipped on the proffered robe. "I've been away. I don't know all the new rules."

The Druid looked suddenly eager. "Did you come in one of those airships that just landed? Has something else happened?"

She hesitated. Something else? What was he talking about? "The airships brought in a boy," she said, deciding to measure his reaction.

"Ah, the Ohmsford boy." The Druid shook his head. "What a lot of bother. They've been looking for him for weeks. Nephew to the old Ard Rhys. They think the whole family is at risk, so they're bringing them here to keep them safe. Found the parents, but they couldn't find the boy. Until now."

"So the parents are here?" she tried.

"No, no, that's what I was talking about. They're gone. Disappeared with their ship two days ago. Flew off in something of a confrontation, I hear. Hard to say; the Gnomes won't talk about it with us. But there was a fight of some sort. No one knows. Shadea keeps such things secret from everyone but her closest advisers." He shrugged. "Typical."

Khyber took a deep breath. "Do you think she would be awake this late? I need to see her."

The Druid shook his head. "You don't know much about what's going on, do you? She isn't even here. She went to Arishaig and hasn't returned."

"As I said, I've been away," Khyber repeated. "All this is news to me." She had learned all she was going to learn and more than she had expected. She had to break this off. "Who would I speak to in her absence?"

The Druid frowned. "I don't know. Traunt Rowan or Pyson Wence, I suppose. Didn't you fly in with them? How did you get here?" The disapproving frown was back. "Where did you say you had been?"

But she was already moving away, giving him a perfunctory wave as she did so. She couldn't believe her luck. She knew now that the ringleader of the conspirators was away, so Pen would not be touched until she returned. That gave her a small measure of time in which to act. She also knew that Pen's parents were no longer prisoners in the Keep, so that the boy, if she could free him, would be able to go into the Forbidding without fear of reprisal against his captive family. But she had to find Pen quickly if he was to have his chance.

"Wait up! Stay where you are!"

She wheeled about, astonished to find the Druid she had thought left behind chasing after her down the corridor, black robes flying out behind him. One arm came up as if in challenge, a sense of urgency to the motion, his heavy brow furrowed more deeply than ever.

Having no choice but to deal with him, she stood her ground. "Who did you say you were?" he demanded, panting and out of breath as he reached her. "How is it you happen to have been aboard an airship bringing back the Ohmsford boy when . . ."

Khyber braced her feet, cocked her fist, and hit him so hard she knocked him backwards into the wall. She was on him instantly, hauling him up with one hand while putting a dagger to his throat with the other.

"Not another word," she hissed at him. "Not unless I tell you to speak. If you yell for help, I'll cut you chin-to-navel before you finish. Do you understand me?"

She had never seen such fear in another's eyes as she saw in his. His throat worked as he tried unsuccessfully to speak and finally settled for nodding.

"You don't know who I am and you don't want to," she told him softly, her eyes locking on his, making sure he did not misjudge her determination. "Behave yourself, do what you're told and you might stay alive. Now listen carefully. I want you to take me down to the cells where they keep the prisoners. Don't speak to anyone we pass on the way. Don't try signaling for help. Am I clear?"

She was only a girl, but the Druid she held pinned against the wall saw her as infinitely more dangerous than he was, and he nodded vigorously. "One thing more," she said to him. "I have the use of magic, just as you do. I understand its complexities. If you try to use your own, even secretly, I will know."

He found his voice again. "You've come for the Ohmsford boy."

She put her face inches from his own. "He means a lot to me. So much so that if something bad happens to him now, something much worse will happen to you. What I intend for him is safe passage out of here. If you interfere with me, I will kill you."

His face was bloodless, his eyes wide. "Don't hurt me."

"I won't if you don't make me. Now, which way?"

He pointed, his hand shaking. She pulled him away from the wall and marched him back down the cavernous hall, the dagger at his back, her free hand gripping his arm. They moved quickly, following the corridor to its end, turned into another, followed that for a time, then turned into a third. They passed no one on their way. They heard no movements or voices that would indicate the presence of others. What she was doing was madness, an impulsive act that could end badly for her, but at least she was getting to where she wanted to go. Someone would have had to tell her, and it might as well be someone under her control. Her eyes darted left and right as she walked, to every crevice and alcove, to every closed door. She kept waiting for her luck to run out. She kept waiting for things to go bad.

They reached a broad stairwell leading down and her prisoner hesitated.

"Keep moving," she whispered, nudging him with the tip of the dagger.

They descended carefully, Khyber watching the bend in the wall ahead for shadows cast by torchlight. None appeared. At the bottom of the stairwell, they reached an anteroom that served as a hub for five different corridors leading off like the spokes of a wheel.

A Gnome Hunter sat facing them from behind a table, his wizened face unreadable. Farther down the corridor at his back, torchlight cast the shadow of a second guard against the stone-block wall.

Keeping one hand firmly attached to her reluctant companion, Khyber moved over to the Gnome at the table. "We've been sent to speak with the boy," she said, again using the Callahorn dialect. "Where is he?"

The Gnome Hunter stared at her, clearly surprised by her demand. Then he shook his head. "No one sees him. I have my orders."

"Orders from Traunt Rowan," she snapped. "Who do you think sent us here? Now take us to the boy. Or do you want me to drag him down here to tell you for himself?"

The threat cut off whatever reply the Gnome was about to make, and he simply nodded. "Someone should tell me these things. I can't know them otherwise." He paused. "You just want to speak with the boy?"

She shrugged dismissively. "He won't be leaving his cell, if that's what you are asking."

He rose doubtfully, reached under the table to produce a ring of keys, and led them down the hallway. Khyber felt the beginnings of some resistance on the part of her reluctant companion and shoved him ahead.

"Don't," she whispered, the dagger digging into his back so hard he whimpered.

They passed the second guard on his way back. He glanced at Khyber and her companion without interest and moved on. She fought the urge to look over her shoulder at him when he was out of sight. Instead, she pulled the dagger away from the Druid and close to her body so that it was hidden in her robes, still keeping the fingers of her other hand tightly fastened to her prisoner's arm. She did not know how much longer she could hold him in check. Sooner or later, he was going to give way to his growing panic or to the temptation to run. If it happened now, while she was still out in the corridor with the Gnome Hunters, she was in trouble. Her plan to free Pen, born of opportunity and chance, was just beginning to take shape. She needed time to flesh it out, to think it through, to find a way to implement it fully. Getting to Pen was just the first step. The ones that followed would be much harder.

They reached the door of the cell, and the Gnome Hunter turned. "Do you want me to wait?"

She scowled. "I want you to go back to doing what you are paid to do and leave me to my work. I'll call you when I need you."

"I have to lock you in."

"Then do so. You are wasting my time."

The Gnome fiddled with the keys, slipped one clear of the others, inserted it into the lock, and turned it. The lock clicked, and the door opened with a squeal of metal fastenings.

As it did so, Khyber's prisoner wrenched free of her grip and ran screaming down the hall.

NINE

Khyber didn't stop to think, didn't do anything but respond to the disaster that was unfolding. She wheeled on the Gnome nearest, slammed the hilt of her dagger into his temple, and dropped him without a sound. As he collapsed, she turned back toward the fleeing Druid, her hands weaving, conjuring a magic with which she was familiar and on which she had depended before. In response to her summons, a sudden gust of wind exploded down the hallway, caught up her quarry before he had run a dozen yards, snatched him off his feet, and hurled him into the wall like a sack of wheat.

The remaining Gnome Hunter came racing toward her in response to the shouting and tumbling bodies, his weapons drawn. She used her magic again, picking him up off his feet and bearing him aloft as she had once done a simple leaf. Remembering to focus her efforts, she held him suspended in midair, kicking and squirming in a futile effort to break free. No failure of attention, no break in concentration. She was at her best in that moment, her uncle's attentive student in the way he had always wanted her to be. She reached the Gnome and dropped him to the floor in a ragged heap, kicking him so hard in the head that he did not move again.

Glancing back at the door to the cell, she called out. "Pen! Are you in there? Answer me!"

No response. Returning her attention to the bodies crumpled

about her, she used laces, bindings, and belts to secure them, then dragged them back up the hall and dropped them next to the Gnome with the keys. Peering inside the cell, she saw a bundled form lying at the back of the tiny room, trussed, gagged, and blindfolded.

"Shades!" she hissed under her breath.

She rushed into the room, bent to Pen Ohmsford, and began working to release his bonds. She freed his eyes first, looking to see if he was conscious. He blinked into the uncertain light and stared at her, wide-eyed. She grinned in response, then loosened the gag.

"I guess you didn't expect to see me again so soon, did you, Penderrin?"

"Khyber! How did you find me?"

The obvious relief mirrored in his boyish features made her smile broaden. "I saw what happened, slipped aboard one of the other airships, and flew into Paranor with you. Are you hurt?"

He shook his head. "Just get me free. I'll tell you everything."

She did so, using the dagger to cut through his bonds, then told him to wait while she hauled her three captives inside the cell and dumped them in a far corner. None of them moved even once while this was happening. "Let's see how *they* like being locked away in here," she muttered. "Come on, Pen."

"Help me walk, Khyber," he asked, struggling to rise.

They went out of the cell as quickly as his legs would permit, but his mobility was severely restricted by leg cramps and stiffness. He had been bound up in the airship for much of the flight back, then brought directly to the cell and left as he was. He had lost all the feeling in both legs and feet in that time, and it was slow to return.

"I thought I was finished," he admitted as he limped down the corridor, leaning heavily on her for support. "They caught me out, Khyber. I told them lies about what I was doing, but they saw through me and took the darkwand away. You saw that I had it, didn't you? From across the ravine? I took it with me from the tanequil's lair, kept it from that thing that tracked us from Anatcherae to Stridegate, kept it safe to use as I was instructed by the King of the Silver River, and they took it away!"

He was so distraught that he was practically crying. Khyber gave his shoulders a rough squeeze. "Then we'll just have to get it back, Pen."

They reached the end of the corridor, and she lowered the boy into the chair formerly occupied by the Gnome jailer, kneeling before him to rub some life back into his legs. "Now tell it all to me," she said.

He did, beginning with his crossing to the island of the tanequil with Cinnaminson and his efforts to communicate with the tree and hers to form a bond with the aeriads. He continued by describing his ordeal in gaining possession of the darkwand from Father Tanequil, Cinnaminson's seduction by the aeriads, his futile efforts to free her from the tree roots of Mother Tanequil, and his battle with the creature from Anatcherae. Finally, he explained how he had decided to surrender to the Druids both to help his captive friends and to reach Paranor, where he could use the darkwand at last to go into the Forbidding.

"I thought I could do it, Khyber. I thought they wouldn't know what the staff was, even if they took it from me. I was stupid. They knew it to be a talisman at once. They pretended ignorance, then mocked me for my foolishness."

"We will live to see them mocked for their own foolishness," she muttered, still rubbing his leg muscles. "Any better?"

He nodded. "I didn't know what had happened to you, except that I knew you were free. I thought you would be able to help Tagwen and Kermadec and the rest, even if the Druids took me. I never thought you would come after me."

"Let's hope the Druids were fooled, too. I don't think they know I'm here yet, but they will soon enough. Someone is bound to come looking to see how things stand. Or for a change of guards. We have to get moving right now. Can you stand?"

She helped him to his feet, where he took a moment to stretch his legs and stamp his feet. "That's better. The feeling's back." His face was drawn and weary, but determined, as well. "Traunt Rowan says Shadea will be back late tomorrow. I have time to get into the Forbidding before she does."

The Elven girl brushed back her short-cropped hair and grimaced. She had only been told by the Druid that Shadea was away. "There are a lot of others we have to worry about in her absence, though, so we don't want to get complacent. What is it you have to do, Pen?"

He moved close, then put his hand on her shoulder to steady himself. "Two things. I have to get the darkwand back from Traunt

Rowan, and then I must get inside the chamber of the Ard Rhys in order to enter the Forbidding. It shouldn't be too hard, except that I don't know how the magic of the darkwand works."

She exhaled heavily. "It sounds pretty hard to me. Which part do you view as being easy?"

"No, no, you don't understand. Now that I'm free, things are much easier. I can get to the darkwand and to the chamber of the Ard Rhys—I know I can do that much. Especially with you to help me." He grinned at the consternation that registered on her sharp features. "Really, I can. Listen a moment. Something happened in the shaping of the darkwand. Or maybe even before, when the tree broke off its limb and took my fingers, but certainly by the time I was done carving its runes into the wood. There was a joining of sorts, a binding of the staff to me. I didn't know about it, at first. I didn't realize what it was. But I do now. I am connected to the darkwand in the same way I am connected to the parts of my own body. I can feel its presence. I can feel its responses to my needs."

She shook her head. "I don't know about this, Pen. You're talking about a wooden staff—"

"I know where it is right now," he said, cutting her short. "I knew it as soon as they took it away from me and brought me down here. The runes are like a voice in my head, calling to me. They want me to find the staff. No matter where the Druids take it or how hard they try to hide it, the runes will tell me how to find it. I will always know where it is. All I have to do is follow its voice."

She wanted to say something about the reliability of voices in your head, but she forced herself to accept that what he was saying might be true. There had to be some kind of special connection between the boy and the staff or he wouldn't have been summoned to receive it in the first place.

"So you can go right to it, now that you're free?" she pressed.

"I can."

"And then take it to the chamber of the Ard Rhys, where she went into the Forbidding, and figure out how to go in after her?" Khyber gripped his face in both of her hands and squeezed. "This doesn't sound easy at all. We're inside Paranor, and every Druid in the Keep is looking for you—or will be soon. We have no friends here, Penderrin. We have no allies, only enemies and potential enemies. We have no magic that counts. I can use the Elfstones once we're backed into a corner and it doesn't matter anymore, but by then we're probably done for."

"We can do it, Khyber," he answered softly.

She stared into his eyes. "I think you believe that," she said. She shook her head and sighed. "In any case, what does it matter? We both know we're going to try. That is what we have been given to do and all we have left to do unless we try to go back to homes that aren't even ours anymore."

His enthusiasm faded suddenly. "My parents! What about my parents? The Druids still have them!"

"As a matter of fact, they don't. Your parents fled or escaped or whatever, but they're gone. I got that information from the Druid who brought me down here. So you don't have to worry about them."

His smile returned. "Then this is going to work. I know it."

She wanted to tell him that he was right, that it would. But it was a stretch to accept that all the steps he must take to reach Grianne Ohmsford and return with her would be the right ones and none missteps that would doom them both. He saw things in simple terms, in the terms of a boy who believed everything was still possible and no reach too great. She knew better. She had a stronger sense of the possible than he did, and that made her cautious of embracing rarefied hopes too warmly.

She took her hands away from his shoulders and tucked them into her robes. "Let's give it a try, Penderrin," she said.

Outfitted in Druids' robes, with weapons concealed and hoods pulled over their heads to shadow their faces, they went back up the stone stairwell to the upper corridors of Paranor. If Khyber had read the position of the stars correctly, it would be dawn in a few hours. She felt strongly that they had to complete their efforts by sunrise if they were to have any chance of succeeding. Once it grew light, they would have to hide. By the time it was dark again, everyone in the Keep would know that Pen was free and be looking for him. There would be little chance of succeeding after that.

Not that there was all that much chance of succeeding now.

She tried not to be negative in her thinking, but the odds against them were so enormous that she could not help herself. She re-minded herself that the odds had been enormous from the begin-ning, and yet the two of them were still moving ahead, however slowly, still working their way toward their goal. They had lost good friends and strong allies, but even that hadn't been enough to stop them. She must take heart from that. She had come a long way from her forbidden Druid studies with her uncle in Emberen—and a longer way still from her rarefied life as an Elessedil Princess in Ar-borlon. She could barely remember what the latter had been like. Her worries at the prospect of being married off on the whim of her father or brother seemed to belong to another person altogether. She was so far removed from that time, so distanced from it by the events of the past few weeks, that it might never have existed.

And might not ever exist again, given her present situation.

She felt a moment of panic and fought to contain it. Uncle Ahren would calm her if he were there. He would tell her not to think beyond the moment, but to confront what frightened her and bring it under control. She tried doing that, isolating the source of her fear and putting it aside. But it was hard to give it a name or even a shape. Her fear was for something too large and too amorphous to define, an overwhelming sense of smallness and weakness and inex-perience in the face of a tidal wave of power and dark intent. She might thrash and struggle. She might try whatever she could to break free of its grip. But in the end, it would have her anyway.

"We need to go farther up," Pen whispered suddenly, clutching at her arm, breaking the chains of the spell.

She gasped at his unexpected touch, caught her breath, then nodded quickly to conceal her shock. "Farther up," she repeated. She glanced around, surprised to discover that they had reached the top of the stairs. The corridor ahead stretched away into pools of torch-light and layered shadows, the silence as thick as cotton wadding. "Can you show me?"

He pointed diagonally upward into the darkness of the passage-way, then looked back at her expectantly, excitement dancing in his eyes. He was enjoying himself. He wasn't even thinking about the danger—or if he was, he was discounting it in favor of his strong ex-pectations for achieving the quest given him by the King of the Sil-ver River. The realization made her smile inwardly, although she kept her face expressionless as she motioned for him to lead the way.

They walked down the passageway swiftly and silently, listening for voices or footfalls but hearing neither. Khyber was back to worrying about how they would regain the darkwand if they encountered any resistance. She would use her small Druid magic if she was forced to, but stealth and secrecy were better allies for as long as they could call on them for help. If they could get as far as the chambers of the Ard Rhys without being discovered, they had a reasonable chance of getting Pen through to the Forbidding, whether or not he knew how to use the magic of the staff, because such magic would reveal itself when it was time. It was in the nature of most magic to do so, and there was no reason to think it would be any different now.

And plenty of reasons to hope it wouldn't.

The first corridor turned left into a second corridor, and Pen, leading the way, stopped suddenly. "Khyber!" he hissed.

A pair of Gnome Hunters was coming toward them from out of the mix of light and shadows, spears resting on their shoulders, heads lowered in conversation. Their attentions on each other, they had not yet seen the boy and the Elven girl.

"Keep moving," she whispered, giving Pen a push. "Don't say anything when we pass. Keep your head lowered."

They walked toward the Gnomes at a steady pace, Khyber moving over to place herself between Pen and the guards, shielding him. She looked right through the Gnomes as they passed, a Druid preoccupied with more important things. It had the desired effect. The Gnomes, in turn, looked right through her.

Seconds later, they were alone again.

Pen turned them onto a broad stairway that wound upward into the Keep, and they began to climb. As they did so, the sound of voices reached them for the first time, coming from somewhere above. Khyber took Pen's arm to keep him moving. Hesitation was the enemy. At the top of the stairs, the corridor divided, one branch continuing on, the other angling left. A pair of Druids stood conversing not a dozen yards away, heads bent close, sharing possession of a book that one held while the other slowly paged through. The two gave Pen and Khyber only a cursory glance, and Pen turned down the corridor that ran left.

"It's not far now," he whispered.

Khyber nodded, feeling a renewed sense of trepidation. This would not be as easy as it seemed. There would be guards, probably watching over the darkwand, but certainly warding the sleeping chambers of the Ard Rhys. They would have to get past those guards and do so without a fight. How would they manage that?

There wasn't time to think it through. They were down the corridor, around a corner, and moving toward several Gnome Hunters stationed at the foot of a narrow staircase leading up into the highest reaches of the Keep. For an instant, Khyber considered turning back, withdrawing to a place where they could talk this through and decide how best to proceed. But it was already too late for that; the Gnomes had seen them coming and were turning toward them.

"The darkwand is up those stairs," Pen said quietly, sealing their fate. "In the chamber of the Ard Rhys."

Two of the Gnome Hunters moved forward to intercept them, one holding up his hand to slow their approach. "No one is allowed in this part of the Keep," he rumbled, speaking to them in a fractured Southland dialect.

Khyber stopped in front of him. "Traunt Rowan sent for us."

The Gnome hesitated. "I wasn't told."

"Is he up there?" she asked, gesturing toward the stairs.

"He has gone to bed. Do the same and come back again tomorrow when he is here."

She shook her head. "I have to leave something for him." She pointed at the stairs. "Up there."

Another Gnome drifted over. The three of them were staring at her. The remaining Gnomes were clumped together on the far side of the hall, engaged in their own conversation and not paying much attention to the first group. It was time to act. They could break past these three, she thought. They could gain the stairs before the guards could stop them.

She took a deep breath and exhaled slowly. That kind of thinking could get them killed.

She gestured at the Gnome. "You can come with me, if you need to make certain of what I will do. Surely you can allow me that?"

The Gnome had shifted his gaze to Pen and was studying him closely. "I don't know you," he said. "You're just a boy, too young to be a Druid. Why do you wear a Druid robe?"

Pen straightened. "I am an apprentice in training. I am nephew to Traunt Rowan himself and not a boy." He folded his arms across his chest. "I will tell him what you said."

"Tell him what you like," the Gnome grunted. He looked back at Khyber. "You can't go up there. Not tonight. I have my orders."

She stared at him with an intensity that would have melted iron, knowing she had pushed matters as far as she could, that her only options now were to turn around and go back or try to fight her way through. She glanced at Pen, saw that he was set to fight, put a hand on his shoulder to calm him, and said, "Let's go."

She walked him back down the corridor without looking at him, silencing his protests with a quick squeeze of his shoulder, her mind racing. She wasn't about to give up, not with what was at stake. But she needed a better approach than a straightforward attack on six armed Gnome Hunters.

When she was around the corner and out of their sight, she wheeled on Pen. "Don't worry, we're going back. But we need a plan for this. It won't help if we're injured or killed—especially you. You'll have all you can do just to stay alive on the other side."

"I can manage," he said.

She gave him a long, hard look. "I have to say this before the time to say anything has run out. What you encounter inside the Forbidding will be much worse than what you've encountered here. You will be all alone, and I haven't any idea how you will protect yourself from the things imprisoned in there. I can help you. I'm not Ahren, but I do have training in the use of Druid magic, enough so that I can be of use. More important, I have the Elfstones. I think you should take me with you."

He shook his head. "You know I can't do that."

"I know you *think* you can't. I know you were told you couldn't. But maybe we need to test what you were told. The King of the Silver River has misled you more than once. You have already sacrificed yourself in ways that you weren't expecting. What might you be expected to sacrifice this time? Maybe I can keep that from happening."

"No, Khyber," he said firmly. His mouth tightened into a thin line. "If you come with me—if you even can—no one will ever know what has happened to either one of us if I fail. But if you stay behind, you might be able to change things without me. You might find a different way to help, a better way."

She snorted. "There is no other way. You know that."

"No, I don't. I don't know anything. Neither do you. We're still learning what's possible." He paused. "I do know this much. The staff and I are bonded in a way that makes it very clear to me that in this one instance, at least, the King of the Silver River was right. I have to go alone. No one else is going to be allowed to go with me."

She stared at him. "You are so stubborn, Penderrin."

"You should know, Khyber. Who is more stubborn than you?"

"I wish you would change your mind." She folded her arms and waited, then gave him a cryptic nod. "Just remember not to put yourself in danger needlessly. Remember to be patient when you come up against things you can't get past. Don't be reckless, Pen. You are, sometimes. But you can't be in there."

She waited on his response. "I know," he said.

"You say it, but I'm not sure you mean it."

His lips tightened. "I mean it. I know what it will be like. I know it will be bad. But I have to think I have a chance or the King of the Silver River wouldn't be sending me in the first place. Maybe the darkwand will help protect me. In any case, I promise to be careful, Khyber. You'd do better to worry about yourself. You won't be much better off than me."

He was right. She would be alone in the Druid's Keep with no way out. She would be in as much danger as he was.

She put the matter aside. There was nothing either of them could do about what lay ahead "Are you ready?"

"Are you?"

"I don't know."

"Do you have a plan, Khyber?"

"Just stick close."

With Pen at her shoulder, she moved back to the bend in the corridor and stopped just out of sight of the Gnome Hunters. She glanced both ways to be certain they were alone, then summoned magic in the form of a spark of light no larger than a firefly. It flared to life then danced in the palm of her hand. She held it for a moment, looked at Pen to be certain he was ready, then stepped out into the hallway and threw the spark at the Gnomes.

The spark flew down the corridor so quickly that it was on them before they knew what it was. One or two had just enough time to glance up before the spark exploded in a ball of fiery light that consumed them. But nothing burned. Instead, weapons, armor, iron stays, and clasps were turned to magnets that locked together instantly, becoming a clutch of metal pieces, pulling all six guards into a struggling heap.

"Now," Khyber hissed, yanking Pen out of the shadows.

They raced for the stairway, black robes flying out behind them, watching as the pile of hapless Gnome Hunters rolled and thrashed about the floor, trying to free themselves from one another. One or two saw the pair run by and yelled in warning, but could not do anything about it. Before even one of them had regained his feet, Khyber and Pen were past them and racing up the stairs.

By the time they reached the upper floor, Pen was leading the way, flying up the steps and across the floor as he turned down the hall. Rounding the corner of the stairwell, Khyber glanced back over her shoulder. No one was following, but the guards were cursing and screaming and the sporadic flash of her entangling magic revealed that it was still holding them fast. Help would arrive quickly, though. She ran after Pen, who was pulling futilely at the iron handles of a pair of wooden doors that were carved with intricate symbols.

"Locked!" he screamed in frustration.

Khyber pulled him aside, took a moment to study the locks, found the magic that bound them too much for her, and stepped back, motioning Pen behind her. Using a skill Ahren had taught her long ago, she attacked the fastenings on the hinges, where the securing magic was weakest, loosening the bolts that held them, ripping free the outer stays. In moments, the doors had collapsed in a thunderous crash, giving them access to the room beyond.

They rushed into the chamber, Pen wheeling left and right, desperately searching for the missing staff. "Khyber, I don't see it!"

"There," she said, pointing toward the ceiling.

The staff hung suspended from a hook, threaded through with ropes of magic, bound securely in place and out of reach.

"Can you get it down?" the boy pleaded.

She shook her head. She could feel her heart pounding as desperation flooded through her. "The magic is too strong for me, too complex. I'm not skilled enough to break it."

In frustration, he leapt for the staff, snatching at it with both hands. As he did so, the runes glowed like bits of fire, as if live coals were embedded in the polished wood. They were responding to his efforts to reach him, anxious for him to succeed.

"Pen, stop!" she exclaimed. "Let's try something."

She positioned herself beneath the darkwand, locked her hands together in front of her, palms-up, to form a cup, then said, "Step into my hands and I'll boost you up. Grab one end of the staff and whatever happens, don't let go."

He did as she asked, waiting until she had braced herself, then stepping into her locked fingers. He was much heavier than he looked, and it took all her strength to boost him up and then hold him in place as he groped for the staff.

"I have it!" he shouted after what seemed an endless amount of time.

She released him with a gasp and left him dangling from the ceiling, both hands holding on to the staff. The runes were burning so fiercely it looked as if the wood might spontaneously ignite. But Pen did not seem to feel any pain, and the threads that secured the staff were beginning to shimmer and lose their brightness.

"It's weakening, Pen! It's giving way!"

There was a flurry of movement and the sound of boots in the hallway beyond. She whirled, summoned her magic almost without thinking, and turned it on a rush of Gnome Hunters who suddenly appeared in the gap where the doors used to be. A burst of wind materialized right in front of them, a huge gust that caught them up and sent them tumbling back down the hallway in a jumble of grunts and cries.

Behind her, in the face of the talisman's need to serve Pen, the magic that chained the darkwand failed and the boy crashed to the floor. He scrambled up again almost at once.

"It worked, Khyber!" he exclaimed, beaming with excitement.

"Go," she told him, gesturing. "Do what you have to, but go now. They're coming."

She turned back to the doorway, stepped to the opening, and sent another gust of wind sweeping down the hall toward the Gnome Hunters and a single black-cloaked Druid who had joined them.

When she glanced over her shoulder, Pen was running his hands up and down the staff as the glowing runes radiated spears of brilliance that chased back the darkness in all directions and surrounded the boy in a halo of fire. "It's working, Khyber!" he shouted. "I can feel something pulling at me!"

She wasn't sure what he meant or even if he understood what was actually happening, but she couldn't do anything to help him in any case. Her attention reverted to the hallway, where something new was developing. A regrouping was taking place just out of her line of sight. She stepped to one side of the opening, trying to find shelter. She scanned the torchlit darkness beyond their refuge, searching for movement, readying herself for whatever was coming.

"Hurry, Penderrin!"

There was no response. When she glanced back to see what he was doing, he was gone.

"Good luck," she whispered.

In the next instant, something that might have been a huge fist slammed into her and sent her flying backwards through the last of the fading streaks of light from the darkwand's runes. All the breath went out of her as she struck the far wall and collapsed in a stunned heap.

Use the Elfstones, she thought, fumbling through her clothing for them.

Then the fist struck her again, exploding out of the darkness of the corridor through the gap in the wall, hammering her back a second time. She fell away from the blow like a rag doll, and all the light and sound went out of the world.

T E N

In a second, much darker world, in a stronger, more heavily warded Keep, in a place and time where life was measured by the thickness of sinew and iron and the durability of hope was as ephemeral as mist, another attempt at escape was hanging by a thread.

Grianne Ohmsford lay motionless on the floor of her cell, a ragged, broken creature, listening to the sounds of an approaching Goblin's heavy breathing. The guard it had come to relieve was dead, and in its place, sitting cloaked and hooded not ten feet from her cell door, was Weka Dart. Her would-be rescuer and the one creature in that wretched world who had demonstrated any compassion for her, he was also her betrayer and a liar of such monstrous proportions that it was impossible for her to know his intentions from one moment to the next.

Grianne Ohmsford, Ard Rhys of the Third Druid Order, had been reduced to a place in life where reliance on betrayers and liars was the best she could expect. How she had come to that end was still something of a mystery, although she knew the identities of those responsible. She knew, too, what was at stake, and it tethered her sanity and resourcefulness directly to a driving need to get clear of the dungeons and find her way back to her own world.

But once the Goblin caught sight of the poorly concealed Weka Dart—which it surely must—the alarm would be given and her last hope of ever escaping would be ended. She could not let that happen. Whatever her misgivings about the Ulk Bog, however uncertain his loyalty, he remained her one chance. Her expectations were reduced to little more than gambling on the mercurial nature of a creature she barely understood. It would have to be enough. Weka Dart would have to do.

She stirred, deliberately drawing the Goblin's attention. It turned toward her, hearing her scuffling sounds, her whimpers, her sudden gasps, watching her attempts to rise from the floor on which she had lain by then for the better part of three days. It grunted something at her, taking hold of the bars to the cell, leaning forward and peering in. She was an amusement that could keep it entertained during the long hours ahead, a curiosity to be enjoyed and, perhaps, even teased. She could see it in the Goblin's eyes. She could read it in the look on its face.

Then a shadow slipped behind the gnarled figure, swift as smoke on wind, and the Goblin inhaled sharply as a knife blade thrust through its throat and pinned it against the bars. Weka Dart held the Goblin in place until it was limp, then dropped it on the dungeon floor and kicked the body aside.

"They should all go the same way," the Ulk Bog hissed. There was a look in his eyes that Grianne hadn't seen before and wasn't sure she wanted to see again.

She pushed herself off the floor and limped over to the cell door. Her mouth was dry and her head was pounding. Her vision was blurred from too many days of no food and water and no real sleep. She was still impacted by her ordeal with the Furies, her impulses still governed by her need to be one with them, to mewl and spit and snarl. She fought those impulses, but the effort was debilitating.

"Open the door, Weka Dart!" she snapped at him. "Let me out! Hurry!"

She did not mean her words to sound so urgent, did not intend to appear so desperate. But her needs overpowered her intentions, and the truth escaped before she could contain it. She would do anything to escape. She would give anything to distance herself from the horror she had endured as the Straken Lord's prisoner.

But instead of opening the door, Weka Dart glanced sharply at her, an uncertain look in his yellow eyes.

"What are you waiting for?" she snapped. "Do you have a way to free me or not? Is our bargain still good? Will you honor it as you have said you would?"

"Our bargain is not complete," he growled. He reached into his pocket and produced an iron key, holding it up for her to see. "My end of the bargain is here—the key to your cell door. I can take off the conjure collar, as well. But what of your end of the bargain? What of the service I require of you?"

"Forgiveness? You already have that. I have told you that by telling me the truth, you have gained that forgiveness. I don't want revenge on you. I won't harm you when I'm free. You have my word!"

His strange, wizened face scrunched down farther on itself and the yellow eyes glittered. "Your forgiveness was the price for my truth. That bargain is made and done. This bargain is new, Grianne of the Straken Lord's jails. If I give you your freedom—from this cell and from the collar—you must give me what I need in turn."

She stared at him, realizing suddenly that he had failed to reveal as yet his reasons for coming back. Coming to her aid was not something the little Ulk Bog would do out of the kindness of his heart. He had abandoned her, cast her off as useless to him when she had refused to allow him to lead her where he wanted—which was right where she had ended up anyway. But he had lost his chance at reinstatement as Catcher with Tael Riverine, a loss that left him homeless and shunned. He had come back because he expected her to do something about it.

"I can't give you anything," she told him. "It isn't within my power to give you anything."

"Ah, Straken, you underestimate yourself. You are exactly the one who can help me, and it is for that reason that I will help you. A favor for a favor. I don't want much. I don't want anything more than what you want for yourself. Freedom. From these prisons and from this world. I want you to take me with you."

Take me with you. She stared at him. Take him out of the Forbidding, he meant. Take him back with her into her own world. Voluntarily release a creature that had been locked away by the Faerie world since before the dawn of Mankind.

"You want to come with me?" she asked him, still not certain she was hearing him right. "You want to leave the Forbidding and come back with me into my world?"

He licked his lips and nodded eagerly. "When you find a way to get free, you must free me, as well. I know that you were brought here against your wishes. I know that you are trapped. But I have seen what you can do. I think that you know a way back—or if you do not, that you will find one. I have seen how resourceful you are, much more so than any other Straken I have ever encountered. You may be a match for Tael Riverine himself!"

"I am a match for no one," she countered. "I don't know if I can help you. I don't know if I should."

He bristled at her words, stepping back from the cell door and hissing at her like a snake. "Then I don't know why I'm wasting my time! I don't know why I bothered coming here at all! You would rather stay in this cell than escape back into your own world? You would rather die here? Better that than help someone like me? Is that what you are saying? That I am not worthy of your efforts, that I don't deserve your help?"

He spit at her. "Free yourself, then!"

He wheeled and started to walk away. It took everything she had to refrain from calling out to him, from begging him to come back to her. But if he thought she needed him more than he needed her, she would be in his power, and that was a price she could not afford to pay.

He was halfway down the hall when he wheeled about, his face contorting in fury. "I came back for you!" he screamed so loudly that she jumped in spite of herself. "I risked everything to come back for you! I came to save you, and now you won't help me? One little thing I ask of you, Straken! One tiny, little thing!"

He came rushing back down the hall, sobbing uncontrollably, his shoulders shaking. "Nothing, for someone with your power! Nothing! Why won't you do it?"

She took a deep breath. "I can't be sure of my power here. I can't be sure of what it will do. What if taking you out of the Forbidding is more than I can manage?"

He shook his head slowly from side to side, as if her words made no sense. "Don't you understand, Grianne of the cat sounds? I was driven from my tribe for eating my children! They will never take me back! No Ulk Bog door will ever be open to me again! Losing the protection of Tael Riverine closed every other door, as well. Now all creatures are my enemies. I am shunned by everything that breathes.

I have nowhere to go and no one who will take me in. Better I was dead than to try to live like this!"

"But why bother with me, Weka Dart?" she pressed. "If you just wait, won't this demon that Tael Riverine has dispatched to my world break down the Forbidding and free you anyway?"

"Free me from what?" he screamed at her. "Free me from one prison so that I can go into another? Free me from one world in which I am outcast so that I can be outcast in another? I don't want the Straken Lord to succeed! I don't want the Forbidding destroyed! If your world becomes like the world of the Jarka Ruus, what difference will it make whether I escape into it or not!"

He pushed his face up against the bars. "You can help me, Straken. If I can help you, surely you can help me! How hard can it be for someone like you to give me what I want?"

In truth, she didn't know. What would it take to escape the Forbidding? Was the boy foreseen by the shade of the Warlock Lord real? Was he coming to set her free, or was the prophecy a cruel trick? She couldn't be certain, but it was the only hope she had. The shade of Brona had not lied about the truth behind the reason she had been sent into the world of the Jarka Ruus—Weka Dart had confirmed that. She was here so that a demon could be free, a demon that would destroy the wall of the Forbidding. If Brona's shade had told the truth about that, then it might well have been telling the truth about the mysterious boy.

So she must gamble on the words of a monster. She must accept the possibility that her only chance for escape was through the coming of a boy she didn't know. It didn't seem to her that Weka Dart's hopes for escape were any less realistic than her own. While she did not relish setting the Ulk Bog free in her world, it would be infinitely worse to refuse his bargain if it meant that she must stay imprisoned, as well.

"If you release me," she said, "I will try to find a way out of the world of the Jarka Ruus and back to my own world. If it is within my power to do so, I will take you with me. I can promise you nothing more."

"I have your word?"

"You do." She held up one cautionary finger. "But remember, I don't know yet that I can find a way back for either of us. I don't know that I can save us, even if you set me free. I don't know that I can find a way to stop the Moric from destroying the Forbidding. I don't know that."

He was already working the key to her cell into the lock. "You will find a way. I know you will."

He released her from the cell, then used a second, smaller key to unlatch the conjure collar. Stepping back, he handed her the collar, his wizened face bright with pleasure.

"I kept my keys to the cells and the collars from my days as Catcher," he said to her. "Tael Riverine never suspected I would dare to do such a thing."

"He has misjudged us both," she said. She cast the collar aside. She would never wear such a thing again or ever again be anyone's slave. "How do we get past all the guards and their demonwolves?" she asked as they stood facing each other in the empty hall.

He grinned, all his teeth showing. "We won't go that way. That way is death. We will go another way, a way I know that few others do. It is how I got into Kraal Reach to find you in the first place. I know secrets, little Straken. I know many secrets."

She didn't doubt him. But she refrained from saying anything, gesturing for him to lead the way. She was weak from her imprisonment and lack of nourishment, and she was already wondering how far she could go before her strength failed completely. She had no idea how long she had lain semicomatose in her delusional state in that cell, but it had to have been days. During that time, she had not eaten or drunk anything that she could remember. She had barely slept, suspended between sleeping and waking, beset by dreams and dark imaginings, still caught up in the subterfuge she had used to survive her ordeal in the arena of the Furies.

Some part of her was still there, she knew, amid the cat-things, unable to quite let go of the identity of the creature she had pretended so hard to be. Her magic was a powerful thing, and when it was employed as she had employed it in the arena, she could do or be anything. But the aftereffects were equally powerful and tended to cling to her psyche like the damp leavings of a sweat brought on by nightmares. She was Grianne Ohmsford again. She was Ard Rhys of the Third Druid Order once more. But she was also the Ilse Witch and the things the Ilse Witch could become. She had opened a door she had kept carefully closed for more than twenty years, and she was not sure what it would take to close it again.

They went down a corridor lined with doors that opened into cells like her own, some of them empty, some of them become containers for piles of bones and small lumps at which she chose not to look too closely. The corridor was silent and musty and empty of life. She heard Weka Dart's breathing and the scrape of his boots, but her own passage was soundless, a wraith's passage through darkest night.

The corridor ended at a set of narrow steps leading up, but Weka Dart took her into the shadows behind the stairs, where a rusted iron door was seated in the stone. He worked its ancient latch back and forth, a slow creaking in the deep silence, and at last the door opened into a wall of blackness.

"Very dark down here," the Ulk Bog announced solemnly.

He reached into the blackness to produce a torch, stuck its pitch-coated tip into the flames of one already lit in the corridor behind them, and caught it aflame. He gave the fire a moment to spread, then grinned at her once more and led the way forward.

She followed him down into the earth, down stairs eroded by centuries of footsteps and moisture, into depths so frigid that the cold cut right to the bone. The tunnels they traversed smelled of old damp and raw metal, and at times she saw what looked like frost on the rock but was, in fact, patches of lichen that glowed with a strange, bright radiance. Weka Dart's torch burned with smoky insistence, clogging the air with its distinctive smell, causing her to cough and finally forcing her to breathe through the sleeve of her tunic. There was no ventilation in the tunnels, and the smell of burning pitch trailed after them like a marker. If anyone thought to look for them down there, they would not have a hard time tracking them, she thought.

Weka Dart pressed on as if pursuit were not a concern, glancing back at her now and then to be certain she was keeping up, as if fearful he might lose her in the dark. Indeed, it wasn't an altogether unrealistic concern. She was already having trouble keeping up with him, even absent his tendency to roam as he had earlier in their travels. Her head ached from the cold and smoke, and her body was fatigued and shaky. She wished she had looked for something to eat or drink, but she had not even thought of that, so anxious had she been to get clear of the cells. In truth, she had not eaten or drunk in any reasonable way since she had come into the Forbidding, and the gradual erosion of her energy was finally making itself felt.

Time passed, more than she could keep track of, and the trek through the tunnels beneath Kraal Reach wore on. Clearly determined to take them through as swiftly as possible, Weka Dart did not stop or even slow. From time to time, he retrieved a fresh torch from a crevice she would have passed by without even seeing, lighting it from the old one so that they could continue. Their passage wound down crude steps cut into the stone, along narrow, twisting corridors in which they were forced to stoop, and through caves thick with stalactites dripping with mineral-rich water. After a time, the air warmed a bit, and Grianne stopped shivering. The floor of the tunnels began to rise; they were moving back toward the surface.

But still their journey continued with no end in sight.

Finally, as they were passing through yet another cavern, she stumbled and fell. She lay where she had fallen, her vision blurred and her muscles aching, too tired to rise.

"Are you hurt, Straken?" Weka Dart asked, trying in vain to pull her back to her feet.

"I am exhausted," she told him. "I have to rest."

He shook his head. "It is not safe here."

"I don't care. I have to rest."

She crawled along the floor of the cavern to an open space where she could stretch out. She was breathing so hard that the wheeze filled the silence of the cavern, frightening her with its intensity. Her head was spinning, and she felt as if all the strength had left her body.

"Do you have anything to eat?"

He produced a tuber of some sort, which she ate without questioning its strange taste, then accepted the water he produced from a gourd tucked in his clothing. She was beyond caring about the source of the offerings, beyond caring about anything but taking nourishment and going to sleep.

"I have traveled through these caverns often," he advised, glancing around at the darkness. He sat cross-legged before her and wedged the torch upright between two stones. "That's why I know where torches can be found to light the way. Most of them, I put there. I used these passages to leave the Keep undetected when I was Catcher for Tael Riverine. Sometimes secrecy was best."

He shrugged. "Of course, these tunnels are home to things you don't want to take chances with. That is why I said it is dangerous. We don't have to worry, though. I know what they are and how to avoid them. Mostly. Some are very large, some very small. Some have no eyes, they have been down here so long. Some are things no one but me has ever seen."

Her breathing had steadied enough that she could respond. "This whole world is filled with things I have never seen."

"I suppose that's so." He thought a moment, rubbing his fingers across his wrinkled features. "I will not be sad to leave this world," he said suddenly. "I will be happy to leave."

She nodded, saying nothing.

"I was never meant to be here." He shook his head emphatically. "I was born into this world, but it was a mistake. I should have been born into yours. If I had been, I would not have done the things I did. I would not have eaten my young. I would not have been a Catcher for Tael Riverine. I would have done something important."

He smiled, showing off a frightening display of teeth. "I will be much better when I am living in your world, Grianne of the kind and gentle heart. I will serve you. I will be your friend and helper. Whatever you need me to do, I will do it. I am good at many things. I can find anything. That is why I was such a good Catcher. That is why I was able to find you—both times. Nothing escapes me once I set my mind to finding it. It is a gift. I am lucky to have it."

"I have to sleep," she said.

"When I am in your world, I will not do bad things," he continued, apparently not hearing. "I will not eat things I shouldn't or hurt those I care about. I will work hard. I will become your most trusted companion because I know how important that is. I have never had anyone I could trust before. I have not even had a friend. In the world of the Jarka Ruus, friends are hard to find. Mostly, we have alliances with those we protect or who protect us. Everything hunts or is hunted. It is not safe to have friends."

She was stretched on the ground now, barely aware of what he was saying. She felt his hand touch her arm. "But you are my

friend, little Straken. We are friends, you and I. We shall always be
friends."

A moment later, she was asleep.

She dreamed of dark creatures and long chases, of being hunted
relentlessly, of each pursuit ending in a fall that segued into the next.
She never knew exactly where she was. She never knew what it was
that was after her. She caught shadowy glimpses of her surroundings
and of the things that hunted her, but both changed shape and size
so often that she could identify neither.

She woke groggy and out of sorts with Weka Dart shaking her.
"Wake up, little Straken!" he hissed. "Something's coming!"

She could hear the fear in his voice, and it brought her all the
way awake. "What is it?"

"A Graumth! A cave wyrm!" He glanced over his shoulder
quickly, then back at her. "There hasn't been one in these tunnels for
years. They live deeper underground; you don't see them ever here.
But this one scents us. It comes!"

She scrambled to her feet, still unsteady, still aching and worn.
She took a moment to gather her thoughts and test her balance.
"What should we do?"

His teeth showed in a glistening line. "Run from it! If it catches
us, we will be eaten. Have you ever seen a cave wyrm? Very big. Not
afraid of anything. I saw one destroy an entire company of Goblins
once. There was nothing left but their armor and their weapons
when it had finished feasting on them. Come!"

She didn't require any further urging. Weka Dart was already
moving away with the torch, and she hurried after him. They cleared
the cavern and plunged into a fresh set of tunnels. But they were
going back down into the earth again, and she realized that the Ulk
Bog had been forced to alter their escape route to avoid the Graumth.
She guessed there was nothing she could do about that, but she
wasn't sure how she would hold up if the detour proved lengthy. Her
headache and sense of disorientation had returned. The food, water,
and sleep had helped, but she was not yet herself.

Behind her, something huffed powerfully, like an angry bull or an
explosion of steam. Only much, much, louder.

"This thing is big?" she asked, panting.

"Very big."

"Then it can't get down into these smaller tunnels, can it? We should be safe!"

She saw the glint of his eyes in the torchlight as he glanced back at her. "Graumths can squeeze themselves down to a quarter of their size to get through small spaces. We are not safe anywhere, Straken."

They hurried on, not at running speed, but perhaps at half, which was dangerous enough under the circumstances. Even with the torchlight to guide them, the way was treacherous, strewn with knobs and depressions, spits in the rock floor, outcroppings, and occasional drops. Running was dangerous, but easier for the Ulk Bog than for her. She did not possess his agility or his strength. With her balance already uncertain, she soon found herself unable to keep up.

"Weka Dart!" she called to him. "Not so fast."

As if in response, the Graumth's huffing burst out of the darkness behind her in a wave so unexpectedly loud that she almost screamed. It was much nearer, rapidly closing the distance between them.

Weka Dart rushed back to her and seized her arm. "If it catches us, Grianne of the clever tricks, I have no weapons with which to fight it! Can you bring your Straken magic to bear?"

In truth, she didn't know. She hadn't tried to use her magic since the ordeal with the Furies, and she wasn't sure what part of it would respond in her present condition.

"Keep running!" she said, pushing him ahead.

They cleared the narrower tunnel and emerged into a broader one, its ceiling fully twenty feet high. Ahead, the walls opened wider still, the beginnings of another cavern. There was movement behind them now, a kind of sibilant scraping that suggested something heavy and slick. The huffing was all around them, the sound of breathing, heavy and anxious.

They ran on through the broader tunnel to the entrance to the cavern, and then she grabbed Weka Dart's arm and pulled him around.

"We'll make a stand here."

She was played out. She had nothing left. She pushed him behind her, then summoned her Druid magic. It would not come. It resisted her call, locked away deep down inside her where it refused to budge. She had not had that happen since she was little and in training with the Morgawr during the early years of her life as the Ilse Witch.

In the darkness of the tunnels they had just come through, the Graumth was moving rapidly, sensing their presence. For a moment, she panicked.

"Straken!" Weka Dart hissed suddenly, thrusting the torch at her. "Use this! It cannot see in the light! Graumths live in the dark and never see the sun! Perhaps this torch—"

"Keep it!" she snapped at him, furious with the interruption, her concentration completely broken. "Use it yourself if it gets past me!"

She resumed her efforts at summoning the magic, burrowing down inside herself, breaking down barriers one by one. It was her fear of becoming a Fury again that most resisted her efforts. That fear closed about her as she worked to reach her recalcitrant magic. It threatened to make her lose control completely. She understood its power. She would do anything to avoid becoming a Fury again, anything to escape the terrible madness that becoming one of the cat creatures would cause. If she was to do it again, she did not think she could reverse the effects. The madness would claim her, and she would be lost. That fear permeated everything about her need to call up the magic, and she could not seem to separate it out.

"Straken!" cried Weka Dart.

Writhing and twisting, the Graumth burst from the darkness of the smaller tunnel. It was a huge insectlike creature covered with bony plates that gleamed with an oily lubricant. Mandibles clicked at the center of its flat, featureless head, and short, spiky legs ended in huge claws that supported its narrow, reticulated body. It seemed to grow larger right before her eyes, and the forward part of its body lifted right off the cave floor, filling the tunnel with its bulk, undulating as it advanced on them.

As she fought to bring magic to bear, Weka Dart lost control. Whether from fear or impatience or out of desperation too overpowering to resist, he gave way. With a terrifying howl, he burst past her, waving the torch wildly at the Graumth, sparks flying from the flaming brand in long crimson streamers. The Ulk Bog went right at the monster, a bothersome gnat waiting to be crushed. The Graumth made the familiar huffing sound, then jerked back from its tiny attacker, clearly bothered by the presence of the light from the torch.

"No, don't!" Grianne screamed.

Weka Dart was right underneath the monster, rushing it and then backing quickly away, waving the torch as if it had magical powers, howling as if he were the magician who could make them come alive.

In that instant, driven by her fear for the little Ulk Bog and her rage at her own impotence, she broke down the last of her resistance to the summoning of her magic. She smashed through her hesitancy and her reticence, tore down her fears and doubts, wrenched the magic free, and brought it to bear. The wishsong, its blood heritage both a blessing and a curse to generations of her family, but to no one so much so as to herself, surfaced.

Like a tidal wave.

Release me!

Terrified by its unexpected force, by the immensity of it, she fought to contain it. The magic's powerful response was something new, entirely different. It roiled inside her like the winds of a storm, breaking down everything in its path, threatening massive destruction. She clutched at herself with both hands, trying to contain it, to keep it inside until she could control it. For she had no more control over this than she had over her Fury self. She was enveloped. She was consumed.

Release me!

She could not stop it. The magic exploded out of her. Responding instinctively to her needs, it swept through the dark and the damp like a hammer, slamming into the Graumth, striking it with such force that the creature was lifted off its crooked legs and thrown back against the rock of the tunnel walls. The result was instantaneous and devastating. The Graumth didn't merely collapse on impact; it shattered. Armor plates, legs, and body parts flew everywhere until all that remained were bits and pieces that twitched with slow jerking motions in the faint light of Weka Dart's flickering torch.

Then the magic simply faded until no trace of it remained.

Drained of her strength and stunned by her body's response to the magic's implacable surge, Grianne Ohmsford sank to her knees. The wishsong had come out of her with more power than she had ever experienced. It was as if she had been storing it away for weeks on end, had accumulated and hoarded it, waiting for just that moment to set it free. The wishsong had been put to the test countless times over the years, but she had never seen it respond that way.

What had happened to make it do so?

Weka Dart was standing before her, wizened face bright with unrestrained exultation and wild-eyed glee. Holding out the torch in a kind of salute, he bent his head in crude submission.

"Straken Queen," he whispered, the awe in his voice unmistakable. "Yours is the greatest power. Yours is the supreme magic. I bow to you. I salute you. You have no equal."

She closed her eyes against what she was feeling and made no response. She did not pretend to know if the extent of her power was as vast as it appeared. But she knew without question that it was strong enough to have revealed their presence to the Straken Lord, and that he would be there quickly enough to test it for himself.

ELEVEN

When the rune-carved length of the darkwand began to glow, Pen could sense a shift in place and time almost immediately. It was an odd feeling, a suggestion of movement that felt like a small tremor in the earth coupled with a subtle progression of light toward dark. He knew immediately that the magic was in play and the darkwand was responding to his silent plea for help. There was nothing earthshaking about it, nothing overtly dramatic or astounding, just a hint of things being altered.

He had time to glance once at Khyber, who faced the opening where the doors to the Ard Rhys's sleeping chamber had stood before she collapsed them, her body rigid with concentration, her arms lifted and her fingers extended to meet whatever challenge might appear. He regretted abandoning her to so many enemies—hated himself for it, after everything she had done for him—but there was no time or way to act on it. She had accepted the consequences of her fate by agreeing to bring him there, knowing what must happen. What he could do best for her was what he could do best for them both: cross over into the Forbidding, find the Ard Rhys, and bring her back into the Four Lands.

It happened quickly after that. The runes caught fire beneath his fingers and the staff turned bright with their glow. Then the glow was all around him, enveloping him, shutting him away from his surroundings. The room and Khyber disappeared. He closed his eyes, hands tightening on the staff, praying that he would be strong enough to do what was needed.

A giant fist clutched his body, and all the air disappeared from his lungs. He gasped in response, trying to breathe, fighting to keep from choking.

Then he was standing in a twilit clearing of wintry grasses and barren earth surrounded by sparse woods and a deeply clouded sky. Paranor was gone. The world of the Four Lands was gone. Nothing he was looking at reminded him of home. Except, perhaps, for the bleaker places he had visited, like the Slags or the Klu. He stared blankly for a moment, making the comparisons, measuring the differences in his head, looking slowly about as he did so.

What struck him first was how dark things were. It didn't seem to be nightfall, but the sun was nowhere to be seen, the brightness of the overcast sky like a pale reflection off clouded waters. The trees and grasses were washed of color, their greens muted and dulled. He peered into the distance. There wasn't much to see, the woods fading into shifting walls of mist; the sky and earth coming together miles away in a grayish haze; the mountains stark and barren; the woods skeletal and empty looking. He could not imagine what lived there. He had the feeling that whatever did spent most of the time hunkered down and watchful.

He had a feeling that here you were either pursuer or pursued, hunter or prey.

I hate this world already, he thought.

He was grasping the darkwand so tightly that his hands hurt. He loosened his grip on the staff and forced himself to take a few deep breaths to stay calm. He had made the crossing; the magic of the staff had done its job, bringing him out of the Four Lands and into the Forbidding. He could scarcely believe it, and in truth he might not have if everything did not look and feel exactly right for what the Forbidding should be. Despite the oppressiveness of his surroundings, he felt an odd sense of relief, as if the hardest part of the task given him by the King of the Silver River were finished. But he knew that wasn't so, that the hardest part lay ahead. He had accomplished much since he had left Patch Run. He had crossed half the Four Lands to find the darkwand and bring it back to Paranor. He had endured hardships and privations of a sort few survived. He had escaped his enemies time and again.

But just staying alive in this dark place would take all the strength he had and then some.

He finished scanning his surroundings, found nothing useful, stood for a moment longer, and then sat down to gather his thoughts. He wondered briefly about his parents. There was no way for them to know what had happened to him unless Khyber managed to reach them. At least they were free of Paranor and the Druids. They would not be tricked again by Shadea a'Ru and her minions. He was still bothered by the fact that the King of the Silver River had failed to warn them, as he had promised he would. Unless they had ignored that warning, of course, and had determined to help him no matter what the risk. His mother would think like that. His mother would brave anything for him.

As would any of his friends and companions on this journey, he thought. As all of them had. He found himself missing them desperately—steady Tagwen, brave Kermadec, resourceful Khyber, and even the truculent Atalan. But most of all he missed Cinnaminson. Just thinking of her made him ache in a way nothing else ever had. He tried to picture her as he remembered her best—free and alive, smiling at him on the decks of the *Skatelow*, reaching out to take his hand. He tried not to think of where she was and what had become of her. But he couldn't quite manage it.

He compressed his lips in a tight line and forced himself to think instead of other things. He was alone for the moment, at least until he found his aunt, and there was nothing he could do to change that. He hoped the others were all right, that they had found ways to escape their predicaments, but wondering if they had was just another dead end in his thinking.

What he must think about was finding his aunt, the Ard Rhys, and bringing her home safe.

He started as sudden heat flooded through his palms. The runes of the darkwand were glowing, turning the staff warm. He got to his feet quickly and looked around, wondering if the staff were warning him of hidden danger. But he sensed nothing. He stared down at the staff once more, but the runes had dimmed and the wood gone cool.

He frowned in confusion. Something had triggered the reaction, but what was it? He looked around. Nothing.

He looked back at the staff. Was it something inside him? Was the staff responding to him? He knew already that they were connected, sufficiently so that he had been able to find it when it was taken away by Traunt Rowan and had known instinctively how to trigger its magic when crossing from his world into this one.

The staff responded to his needs. Was it doing so here? Was it responding to his need to find Grianne Ohmsford?

Experimenting, he turned his thoughts to his aunt, asking himself where she was and how he could find her. At once, the runes turned fiery, pulsating beneath his hands, enveloping the entire staff in a red glow.

He grinned. Now he knew what the staff could do. But he still didn't know how to make practical use of it.

The grayness of the day was fading rapidly toward night, the sky darkening and shadows beginning to drape the world below. Pen glanced around, thinking that he did not want to be caught out in the open once night arrived. He needed to find shelter, but first he needed to determine which way he should go.

To do that, he needed to figure out how to use the darkwand.

He looked at it again, turning his thoughts away from his quest, watching the brightness of the runes fade. Maybe if he asked it to show him where his aunt was, it would do so. If he thought about a direction to take in the same way he thought about looking for her, perhaps the runes would show him something.

He gave it a try. He thought about his aunt, about his need to find her, watched the runes brighten anew, then started thinking about directions he might take, projecting himself going first one way and then another.

Nothing happened. The runes stayed bright, but did not respond in any way to his silent questions.

He shook his head in disgust. So much for that approach. Still, there had to be a way.

He decided to try something else. Keeping his thoughts focused on his aunt, he started walking toward the last of the light, a direction he assumed might be west, but the runes dimmed almost at once. He stopped and turned around to walk the other way, toward the encroaching darkness, which would be east. Again, the runes darkened. At least he was getting a clear response, he thought.

He turned south, toward the mountains that were closest to where he stood. Instantly, the runes turned fiery.

He felt a surge of elation. He would go that way.

He started walking, the staff held before him in both hands like a compass, the runes glowing brightly, providing him with both light and reassurance. All around, the shadows thickened and the world began to change. What had been indistinct before began to lose all shape and form, until most of what he could see was distinguished by little more than changes in color and brightness. He could still make out the peaks ahead of him, but little else. He would have to find shelter soon.

He was further persuaded of that when he noticed movement in the shadows, movement that hadn't been there earlier. He caught only glimpses of it, sudden dartings, like the scurrying of small furry animals except that there were no small furry animals living within the Forbidding—at least, not ones that were likely to be friendly. In any case, he didn't think he wanted to find out. Other than the dark-wand, all he carried for protection was a long knife he had taken from one of the guards. But he didn't think it would prove much of a weapon against the things that lived in the Forbidding—especially after dark.

He trudged on, keeping as much to the open as he could manage, following the dictates of the staff while keeping close watch on his surroundings. Once, something massive flew overhead, a great winged creature that, had it fallen on him, would have crushed him instantly. He froze when he saw it, distant and indistinct, and he did not move again until he was certain it was gone.

He saw other things, too. He saw catlike creatures leaping through the dead-limbed trees and lizard-things that slithered along the earth through the grasses and scrub. He started to hear hissing and snarling, the sounds of hunters at work. Once a shriek momentarily brought his heart to his throat. In the silence that followed, he could hear the rasp of his own frightened breathing.

I am alone here, he kept thinking. *I am alone, and I have no idea what lives here or how to defend myself.*

He swallowed hard. *I wish I weren't so afraid.*

Darkness was almost complete by then, and he had reached the lower slopes of the mountains that blocked the way forward. Clusters of boulders formed huge barriers that rose before him like sentries to challenge his passage. The bare limbs of trees rose against the sky like the finger bones of giants long dead. He saw that a trail led upward through the maze to a pass that in turn opened toward the mountains, to the land beyond. But the way forward was long and arduous. And with the fall of darkness, he would not get far before he couldn't see at all.

So he moved into the center of the tree trunks and boulder piles, found a shelter in the rocks where he was protected on three sides, and settled in. He quit thinking about his aunt, turned his thoughts away from his search, and watched the light of the runes fade. He had nothing to eat or drink, so he tried not to think about how hungry and thirsty he was. Beyond his shelter, the world was ink black, devoid of light from moon or stars, empty of sky. But there were sounds everywhere, sharp and piercing, low and rumbling, sudden and slow to build and die. There were sounds of every sort, but none of them familiar and none pleasant.

Pen wedged himself into one corner of his shelter, clasped his arms about the darkwand, and took out the long knife and placed it against his chest. He sat staring out into the darkness for a long time before he fell asleep.

When he woke, the dragon was staring at him. He didn't realize it was there at first. He woke slowly and lethargically, still half asleep as he opened his eyes to look around. He didn't know where he was. He was stretched out on the hard ground, his bones aching and his muscles sore. The world was dark and hazy; there was no sunshine, no bright color, and no welcoming warmth or birdsong to encourage his rising. The new day was cloaked in sullen stillness and a deep gray wash that made him want to go back to sleep.

He closed his eyes for a moment, then opened them again as his head cleared and he remembered that he was inside the Forbidding. He glanced down. The long knife was still in his hand, his fingers stiff from gripping it. The darkwand was clutched to his chest, its runes pulsating softly, come alive with the day.

He stared at the staff doubtfully. Why was it glowing? He couldn't remember thinking about his search for his aunt or anything that would have made it brighten.

Then his attention was drawn to a huge cluster of mottled boulders settled squarely in front of him. He didn't remember those boulders being there the night before and wasn't sure how he could have missed seeing them, even in the dark. It was like having a wall materialize out of nowhere, a great massive barrier that somehow didn't seem to quite belong.

He stared at them in confusion.

A window-size eye blinked, a lazy lowering and lifting of a scaly lid.

Pen caught his breath and held it. The cluster of rocks began to assume shape and take on definition. Limbs studded with spikes crooked awkwardly at the joints to end in claws that were each the size of his leg. Scales larger than blankets layered a body that would dwarf a small cottage. Bony ridges ran in parallel lines down a broad back and long, reticulated tail. A triangular head was tucked between its forelegs, encrusted snout and brow thick with armor and blunt horns.

"Shades," he whispered.

He had never seen a dragon, of course. No one in his lifetime had ever seen a dragon. Most types were extinct. Those that weren't were consigned to the Forbidding, like the one before him, or so deeply and thoroughly entrenched in mountain caverns and wilderness forests that no human had ever ventured in far enough to encounter them. But he knew what dragons were and what they looked like, and the creature facing him was clearly a dragon.

It was easily the biggest living creature that Pen had ever seen. It was bigger than he had imagined anything could be. Fascinated in spite of himself, he stared at it. He wondered what it was doing there. He wondered why it hadn't eaten him.

He wondered if it planned to.

He became aware all at once that it was looking at him. It was watching through half-closed lids with a sleepy, almost dreamy gaze. It seemed mesmerized, like a cat stretched out for a nap, lazy and content, drifting in and out of private reveries. Then it occurred to him, almost as an afterthought, that the dragon wasn't looking at him.

It was looking at the darkwand.

Or, more particularly, at the glow of its runes.

At first, he thought he must be mistaken. After all, why would the dragon be interested in the staff and its runes? Was the beast sentient? It certainly didn't look it. But maybe it understood something of magic and of talismans and recognized the darkwand for what it was.

He didn't think that was right, though. The way the dragon was watching the staff suggested that it was all but hypnotized, that its interest was one of almost primordial attraction. Pen glanced down, watching the way the light played across the runes, how it worked itself up and down the staff in ever-changing patterns, how it brightened and dimmed, pulsed and steadied, reinventing itself over and over. The dragon was watching, too, fascinated by the movement of the light as it danced from rune to rune.

Pen tried an experiment. Taking his cloak, he covered the top half of the staff, blocking the light.

Instantly, the great horn-encrusted head lifted, the triangular snout swung about, and its maw split wide in a hiss that sounded like an explosion. Rows of blackened teeth revealed themselves, some still clotted with bits of flesh, some with bones wedged between them. A gaping throat as black as damp ashes pulsed and shimmered, and the stench of carrion on its breath flattened the boy against the rock wall of his all-too-inadequate shelter. Pen gagged and nearly fainted, but he retained sufficient presence of mind to uncloak the darkwand at once. As the runes began anew their intricate play across the polished surface of the wood, the dragon slowly settled back into place, its maw closing, its eyelids drooping, content.

That was a really bad idea, Pen thought, taking great gulps of air to clear his head.

He remained where he was for a moment, sagging against the wall of his shelter, the darkwand held firmly in front of him, his talisman against a monster with breath that would melt iron. He hung his head for a time, thinking he was going to vomit, but when the nausea had passed, he straightened and looked out again at the dragon, trying to think what to do. He still wasn't certain what was happening with the darkwand, which until then he had assumed would respond only to his thoughts of the Ard Rhys. But it had apparently begun to glow even before he was awake and knew what was happening. How could that be?

He returned his attention to the dragon, saw how its eyes were fixed on the glowing runes, listened to how its breathing came slowly and evenly as it crouched there, waiting. Waiting on what? He didn't know. How long did dragons wait on things, anyway? He wondered suddenly if he was trapped. He hadn't thought of it before, but it might well be that just as the dragon wouldn't let him cover up the light, it wouldn't let him take it away, either. That would mean he was stuck in these rocks until the dragon tired of him and moved on.

Which might take a very long time, he realized. Time he didn't have to spare.

He took a moment to consider his options. He didn't have many to consider. He could stay where he was until the dragon grew bored and went away, or he could try leaving and hope the dragon didn't follow—or if it did follow, that it wouldn't follow for long. And that it wouldn't eat him.

He didn't like where his thinking was taking him, so he abandoned it in favor of trying to decide what else he might do to help himself. The long knife he carried was all but useless against something the size of the dragon, so there was no point in relying on that. Of course, any weapon was all but useless against a beast as big as that one. A whole army was probably useless.

He might try using his magic.

It was a reach. He didn't even know if his magic would work

in the Forbidding. But he didn't have anything else he could look to for help, and he had to do more than sit around waiting for the dragon to decide to eat him. His magic had worked with the moor cat they had encountered in the Slags, well enough that it had saved his life. It was conceivable that it might work here, as well.

But how should he try to use it?

He decided to find out first if it irritated the beast, because if it did, that was the end of the matter. He began by reaching out with his five senses, taking in everything he could discover about the creature, from the sound of its breathing to the baleful look in its sleepy eye. He scoured the monster from head to tail and back again, working at finding a connection, at trying to feel something of what the dragon felt. It was hard work, and in the end it yielded almost nothing.

Dragons, apparently, didn't give much away.

There was nothing for it but to try using the magic in the only way that seemed feasible—as a tool of communication. He had no idea how dragons communicated. All he had learned so far was how they breathed and how they reacted when irritated. Perhaps if he started there, a way might reveal itself. What made his efforts so difficult was that the dragon wasn't really interested in him at all; it was only interested in the darkwand. If it were the darkwand that was trying to communicate, he was certain that he would make better progress. But that wasn't possible, of course, so he would have to settle for using his own voice and hope the dragon gave something back.

He began with an imitation of the dragon's breathing, slow and heavy and raw. Enhancing his efforts with his magic, giving them life, it still took him a while to get it right. Eventually, he was sounding exactly like a miniature version of the larger thing. The dragon blinked—once, twice. When he began alternating the breathing with variations on the disgruntled hissing, the dragon lifted its head off its forefeet and looked at him. But it didn't seem inclined to do anything more than stare. Still, Pen kept at it, hoping for something more.

Nothing happened. Eventually, the dragon lost interest, lowered its head to its forefeet and went back to watching the dancing glow of the runes.

Pen sank back, exhausted. He was getting nowhere. Worse, he was growing weak from the effort. He had not eaten or drunk anything since arriving and could not remember when he had done so before that. It had been more than a day. His throat was parched, and he was feeling light-headed. If he didn't get away soon, he was going to pass out from lack of nourishment.

But what in the world was he supposed to do?

He spent several hours trying to figure that out. He used his small magic in every conceivable way to entice the dragon into communicating, but the beast simply ignored him. It lay there across the opening to his shelter, a great scaly lump that refused to move. With one eye fixed steadily on the darkwand and its intriguing runes, it dozed like a monstrous cat in front of a mouse hole, transfixed by the movement of the light. It barely stirred for the whole of the time it kept watch and then only to shift positions.

After a while, Pen dozed off. He wasn't sure how long he slept, as the gray light that marked daytime in the Forbidding was virtually unchanging from dawn to dusk. But when he awoke, he came to a decision. Rather than experiment further with the magic, he would simply try to leave. He had no idea if the dragon would permit it. But anything was better than doing nothing.

Holding the darkwand in front of him so as not to disturb or obscure the play of the light across its runes, he stood and gathered his strength. He was so weak by then that it took him a few minutes to do so. When he felt sufficiently ready, he took a single step out from his shelter.

The dragon blinked slowly.

He took another step. And then another.

The dragon's head came up, the horn-encrusted snout swung toward him, and a sharp hiss escaped through a pair of wide-flaring nostrils.

Pen stopped at once, held his ground, and waited. The dragon continued to watch him, head lifted, yellow eyes fixed. They stared at each other for long moments, each waiting to see what the other would do. Pen listened to the sound of the dragon's breathing and smelled its fetid stench. He forced himself to ignore the urge to gag. Instead, he focused on his determination to keep going.

When he felt he had waited long enough, he took another step.

This time the dragon slowly extended one great spiked foreleg in the manner of a cat toying with a mouse that had become its favorite plaything. It took its time, reaching out slowly and leisurely until the foreleg was stretched directly across the path Pen had intended to take, blocking it.

Pen stared at the dragon in dismay, then slowly backed into the rocks once more.

He spent the rest of the day hoping for a miracle. If only the dragon would grow bored. If only it would grow hungry. If only it would leave for just a few minutes. Didn't it have something else to do or somewhere else to go? Dragons must have lives like other creatures, habits and patterns of behavior that this one would be compelled to act on eventually. If he was just patient, if he could just wait it out, it would have to move on.

Daylight faded and night set in. It began to rain, a soft steady drizzle. Pen stuck his head far enough out of the shelter to catch a few drops in his open mouth, then used his cloak to gather a little more and sucked the water from the cloth. All the while, the dragon lay there, its scaly hide glistening, its eyes lidded, watching the darkwand and its glowing runes.

Eventually, Pen grew sleepy once more. He worried for a short while about what the staff would do when he closed his eyes, then dismissed the matter. Apparently, it would continue to glow, just as it must have done the previous night when the dragon was first attracted, just as it must have done while he was napping earlier. Otherwise, the dragon would have eaten him already. He wondered again how the staff could function independently of his thoughts when it had seemed before that it relied on them. He was missing something, wasn't picking up on what should have been obvious if he wasn't so hungry and exhausted. He wished he could think more clearly, that he could reason better.

He closed his eyes and dreamed about his home and his parents, about how things had been not two months earlier. He had been so anxious for an adventure, so willing for a change in his mundane existence. He had embraced the chance to go in search of the tanequil with Tagwen and the others. He had relished the excitement that would result.

He wished now that none of it had ever happened. He wished that things were back to the way they had been.

He fell asleep, and his wishes drifted away.

T W E L V E

Dreams, bits and pieces of incomplete thoughts and unfinished stories, came and went with the swiftness of shadows
and light in a cloud-swept forest. They were bright and
bold and filled with promise, and Bek Ohmsford rode them like a
bird across landscapes that stretched away forever. Sometimes he
was in motion for the duration of the dream without ever touching
the earth. Sometimes he felt the solid ground just long enough to be
reassured that it was still there before winging away again. Nothing
of what he saw was familiar to him. People came and went in the
course of his travels, but he did not know who they were or why they
were there. He had left his waking life behind; he had gone ahead of
those he once knew.

It could have been a time of peace and contentment, but the
dreams were interspersed with nightmares, and the nightmares were
horrifying. Some were memories of things in his past, of creatures
and events that he could never forget. Some were dark prophecies of
what lay ahead if he could not turn aside in time. All were populated
with predators that pursued him relentlessly, hunters of a sort that
lacked recognizable purpose or intent. They came at him in waves,
and no matter where he fled or tried to hide, they meant to have him.

Dreams and nightmares. There was no recognizable connection
between the one and the other, and he transitioned between light

and dark visions with distressing unpredictability. He slept, but his sleep was not sound or restful. The strange mix left him plagued with anxiety over which would appear next and how he would deal with it. He sought to combat them by gaining a measure of control, but his efforts fragmented and failed. He sought to wake, swimming upward through the waters of his sleep toward the bright surface of waking, but the distance was too great. Each time he felt himself getting close, the nightmares would come and drag him down again.

He did not know how long the ordeal continued, but it was a considerable time. At times, he came close to crying out his frustration at being unable to break the chains that bound him to a sleep from which there seemed to be no waking. Perhaps he did cry out. He couldn't be sure. But no one came to help. No one reached to take his hand and pull him clear. He struggled on alone, battling to keep the dark from overshadowing the light.

Then something changed. He did not know what it was or how it came to pass, but suddenly the dreams and the nightmares withdrew, fading like wind-blown dust. He was left wrapped in warm silence, in a quietude he had not experienced before. He found solace in his isolation. He was able to breathe normally, to ease down into a comforting sleep that allowed him to rest in the way he needed, deeply and peacefully.

For he had been injured, he knew. He had suffered damage of some sort, though he could not put a name to it. He slept because his body was trying to heal, but the injuries were severe enough that it was not certain yet that he could do so. He knew that without being able to say how. He knew it without being able to remember the specifics of what had happened to him. What he knew was he was fighting to survive and the battle had been going badly.

But the tide had turned and the storm had receded and his damaged body was healing. He dropped deep into a place in which a sense of calm prevailed and no dark things were allowed. He was so grateful for it that he wanted to cry in happiness and relief. The possibility that he had died occurred to him, but he dismissed it. His physical state did not feel like death, unless death was something very different than he had imagined. It felt like living, as if life had found him again.

Time passed, his sleep stretched away like a deep blue ocean, and the world about him began to take shape again. It assumed color and definition in the way a landscape is revealed by the lifting of a fog. As it did so, he found himself in the most beautiful gardens he had ever seen. The gardens were of varying sorts, different shapes and sizes and formations. Some were carefully cultivated beds, each given over to a flower and a theme. Some were hanging, vines and blankets of moss cascading off walls and trellises. Some were hillside and some meadow. There were flowering plants and bushes and grasses. Great ancient trees with broad leafy canopies shaded portions of the gardens while bright sunshine flooded the rest. The colors were vibrant and shimmering like the bands of a rainbow after a storm, blankets of one color and quilts of many. Amid the radiance rose the buzzing of bees as they pollinated flowers and the bright whistle and chirp of birds as they did all the things birds do. Wisps of cloud floated overhead, passing across the sun, casting strange, fleeting shadows on the earth.

It was a vision of paradise. Bek Ohmsford stood in the center of it and marveled. The gardens weren't real; they couldn't be. They were only dreamed. Yet in his sleep, he found them as real as the flesh of his own body.

"Welcome, Bek Ohmsford," a soft voice whispered from behind him.

He turned and found an old man staring at him, an ancient wearing a white robe and carrying a long, bleached wooden staff. White hair tumbled from his head to his shoulders and from chin to chest. His face was deeply lined and careworn in a way that suggested that he had been waging a long, hard fight. But his blue eyes were the eyes of a child, bright and interested and filled with expectation.

"This is my home," the old man said, a smile deepening the wrinkles of his face.

Bek looked around, confused. He was asleep; he was dreaming. But he felt as if he were awake. Was he?

"You have never been here," the old man continued, as if reading his mind. "But we have met before, a long time ago. Do you remember?"

Bek nodded slowly, realization dawning. "You are the King of the Silver River."

The old man nodded. "I am the last of my kind, the last of the Word's children. I am keeper of these gardens, guardian of the Silver River, and watcher over the Races. I am also friend to the Ohmsfords. Do you remember when I helped you?"

Bek did. He had been only a boy, dispatched on a quest he had barely understood to a land no one had ever visited before. He was called Bek Rowe then, and he did not yet know of his Ohmsford heritage. While his companions slept, the King of the Silver River had come to him to give him glimpses of the truth about himself and his sister, who was then the Ilse Witch and not yet Ard Rhys of the Third Druid Order. It was the beginning of a journey of discovery that would change the lives of brother and sister forever.

That had been a long time ago, in a different life.

"I have come to help you again," the old man said. "I do so because I promised your son that I would, although I am late in keeping that promise."

"Pen?" Bek asked in surprise.

"Penderrin, who has gone to find the Ard Rhys and bring her back to us. Penderrin, who is beyond our reach now." The seamed face dipped momentarily into shadow. "Walk with me."

Bek fell into step beside him, thinking again that what was happening wasn't real, that it was only a dream come to him in his sleep, but knowing instinctively that it was important nevertheless. He was being given a vision, a fever dream. In this vision, he might be shown truths that would help him find his son.

"Why is Pen beyond our reach?" he asked, impatient with waiting for the other to speak.

The aged head lifted slightly, one hand gesturing in a quick, dismissive motion. "It only matters that he is. It only matters that he must be. I would have told you sooner. I would have come to you. I promised him I would, weeks ago, when I first appeared to him in the Black Oaks, while he was fleeing from the Druids. He relied on me to tell you, to warn you of the danger. But I could not risk it. Had I told you, you would have gone in search of him. You would have promised me not to, but you would have gone anyway. Had you found him and rescued him, everything that must happen in its own time would have failed to happen at all."

Bek shook his head. "Are you saying you deliberately stopped me from helping Pen by not telling me what was happening to him?"

"I am saying that I stopped you from *thinking* you were helping him when in truth you would have been doing the opposite."

"I don't understand. Why are you telling me this now, since you chose not to before?"

The childlike eyes fixed on him. "Because now your help is needed. But it is needed in an entirely different way from before. And it will not be so easy to give."

They walked on, not speaking. Bek, floating within his vision, dreaming through his sleep, was a disembodied presence with thoughts and emotions, but a lack of substance. It left him feeling oddly removed from what was happening, even while participating. He experienced a need to grasp on to something hard and strong, something real and true. But the words of the King of the Silver River were all he had.

"This is what has happened, Bek Ohmsford," the old man said finally. "Druids within the order have conspired against the Ard Rhys. They found a way to banish her to a place from which she cannot return without help. Your son has gone to find her. He was asked to do so by me because I knew he was the only one who could make the journey and return. He did not think himself equal to the task, but I convinced him otherwise, and now he has convinced himself. He has crossed a barrier that no other may cross to reach the Ard Rhys. When he finds her, he will bring her back through that barrier, and they must both face their destinies."

He paused, looking over at Bek. The look seemed intended both to measure and to reassure. "Your son and your sister are inside the Forbidding."

Bek turned sharply toward the old man, but the heavy staff struck the earth hard enough that he could feel the blow through his feet. "Don't speak. Just listen. Shadea a'Ru and her minions believe they have orchestrated the imprisonment of the Ard Rhys through their own cleverness and skill, but they are mistaken. They have been tricked by one of the demons that dwell within the Forbidding. That demon is a warlock, a sorcerer of great power. Its goal was to exchange the Ard Rhys for another demon, bringing her into the Forbidding in order to free one of its own to come into this world. That exchange has taken place. The demon set free now seeks to destroy the Forbidding so that all those imprisoned since the time of Faerie will be freed. The demon must be stopped or the Four Lands are lost. You must stop it."

Bek shook his head. The charge weighed on him like a set of chains. "How?"

The old man slowed and turned to face him. The childlike eyes were kind and reassuring. "I did not come to you to tell you of your son or warn you of your own danger before this because Penderrin alone was needed to cross into the Forbidding, and you would have stopped him. Penderrin knows that he must find and rescue his aunt. He has the means and the will to accomplish this. I think he will succeed. But he does not know that when the Ard Rhys was sent into the Forbidding, a demon was sent into our world. He only knows that he must use the talisman he has been given to rescue your sister and bring her out again. He believes that is the extent of what is required of him. This was my decision, too. Telling him the rest would have crushed him."

He turned and began walking again, his steps careful and measured. Bek stayed at his side, waiting impatiently to hear more. All around them, breezes rippled the petals of the flowers and gave the impression that they walked upon the surface of a multihued sea.

"The talisman Pen carries is called a darkwand," the old man said. "Penderrin has already used it to cross into the Forbidding. Once he finds the Ard Rhys, he will use it to cross back again." He paused. "But there is one thing more he must do. What has been done must be undone—not in part, but in whole. In order for matters to be put right, everything that the combined magic of the demons and the Druids has brought to pass must be put back. Therefore, not only must the Ard Rhys be returned to this world, but the demon must be put back inside the Forbidding. The darkwand possesses the magic to do this, but only Pen has the power to wield it. He must find the demon and use the darkwand against it."

He looked at Bek. "You are the one who must see that he has the chance to do so."

"What am I supposed to do?"

The old man looked away again. "Two things. First, you must

find a way to protect your son when he crosses back through the For-bidding with the Ard Rhys. They must return to exactly the same place they went in—her sleeping chamber at Paranor."

"Where Shadea and the others will be waiting," Bek finished.

The old man nodded. "Second, you must find the demon. It will not look like a demon. It will look like something else. It is a changeling and takes the shapes of other creatures. This one is par-ticularly dangerous. It absorbs its victims and becomes them. You must find out which disguise it has assumed and unmask it."

Bek looked down at his feet. He couldn't see them. He didn't seem to have feet, even though he could feel himself walking.

"The darkwand will reveal the demon," the old man said. "The talisman will respond to its presence. It will tell you who or what the demon is. If you get close enough."

The scent of tuberoses filled Bek's nostrils, sweet and heady. He shook off the distraction. "The wishsong told me that Pen was at Taupo Rough in the Upper Anar."

"The wishsong did not lie. But now he is inside the Forbidding."

"So I must go back to Paranor to find my son?"

The King of the Silver River turned to face him. "The path that leads to your son does not begin at Paranor. It begins at Taupo Rough, with Penderrin's companions. The Dwarf, the Rock Troll, and the Elven girl will provide you with keys to the doors that you must open to reach him."

He paused. "It is not within the Forbidding that Penderrin faces his greatest danger; it is here. The Druids will know where he has gone and be waiting for him when he returns. If they reach him be-fore you do, they will kill him."

"Nothing will happen to my son while I am alive," Bek said at once.

He felt a subtle shift in his surroundings as he made that vow, a shimmering in the air, a ripple in the blankets and clusters of flowers, a whispering of breezes, and he knew he had committed himself in a way that could not be undone.

The old man nodded. "Do you feel the weight of your words, Bek Ohmsford? They have sealed your fate."

He stepped aside, an effortless movement that belonged to a much younger man. His ancient face lifted and changed. He was something else now, an old man no longer, another creature entirely, not human, not of this world. Bek backed away involuntarily, hands coming up to ward off the thing that stood before him.

The King of the Silver River had become a monster.

"See the future, human!" the monster rasped, teeth showing, eyes bright with hate. "Look upon it! When the Forbidding falls, your world becomes mine!"

Then the gardens withered before Bek's eyes, the flowers dying, their colors fading and their stalks wilting. The great shade trees lost their leaves, and their branches took on the look of bones blackened by fire. The grasses dried and cracked, and all sights and sounds of life disappeared. Overhead, the sky lost its brightness, its depthless blue becoming as gray as ashes, misted and empty.

Bek knew at once he was being given a glimpse of what his world would become if the demon set loose by the unthinking rebel Druids was successful in bringing down the Forbidding and setting free its denizens. When that happened, his world would become the world of the Forbidding. It would be the end of everything that mattered.

Do not fail.

The words echoed softly in the rapidly diminishing sweep of daylight, and Bek turned swiftly to seek the King of the Silver River, to protest that he would not, to give fresh voice to his promise to do as he had been asked, but found he was alone.

He woke with a gasp, jerked from his sleep by a sense of impending horror, his body racked by pain and fever and his mind roiling with wild, uncontrollable emotions that careened through him like tiny razors, jagged edges cutting. He tried to speak and could not. He tried to see, to discover where he was, but his surroundings were blurred and indistinct. He felt a slight rolling motion beneath him and heard the creak and groan of wood and metal fastenings, of lashings and the wind's steady rush. He was aboard a ship, but he couldn't understand how he had gotten there.

Penderrin is inside the Forbidding!

It was his first thought, and the realization all but stopped his heart. Pen, in that monstrous prison, where so much of what was evil in the world had been banished. That the King of the Silver River would send his son to such a place was impossible for him to understand. How could a mere boy have any chance at all of surviving?

How could he hope to find his aunt and bring her back again when everything he encountered would be looking to kill him?

But it is not inside the Forbidding that Penderrin faces his greatest danger.

"Bek, can you hear me?"

He took a deep, steadying breath and blinked against the haze that clouded his vision. A face swam into view, young and with skin ghostly pale, framed with a helmet of close-cropped black hair. A slender hand reached out to touch his cheek. "Can you hear me?"

He nodded, his mouth too dry to allow him to speak. Seeing his difficulty, she raised his head from the bedding on which he lay, brought a cup of water to his lips, and allowed him to sip.

Intense dark eyes peered into his. "Do you remember me?" she asked. "I'm Bellizen. I'm Trefen Morys's friend."

He nodded weakly, remembering nothing. "Where am I?"

"Aboard *Swift Sure*. You have been very sick, Bek. You were badly hurt. A knife wound deep in your side and an arrow through your shoulder. You have been delirious for two days, fighting off a fever. I think it has broken finally."

It all came back to him in a rush. His escape from Paranor with Rue, helped by the young Druid Trefen Morys, the battle to reach *Swift Sure* with the Gnome Hunters attacking from every quarter in an effort to stop them, his collapse moments after finally managing to reach the rope ladder, and then—nothing. This girl had been aboard the airship waiting for them. He remembered looking up into her face as they placed him on the deck and she bent to tend his wounds.

"You helped me," he said.

"Healing is my Druid skill," she replied, giving him a quick, reassuring smile. "Rue sails the airship, Trefen lends her a hand where it is needed, and I care for you. We each have our task. Mine seemed the harder for a time; I was afraid I was going to lose you."

He thought back to the dreams and nightmares of his sleep, already growing distant and vague in his memory. He thought back to the fever dream, to his vision of the King of the Silver River. He had turned the corner into recovery then, he believed. He had been near death, but the dream had brought him back to life. He shivered at the memory of what the dream had shown him, the images of a desiccated, demon-invaded world still fresh in his mind.

Bellizen gave him another few sips of water from the cup and then laid him back down again. "You still need to rest."

She started to rise, but he reached out for her arm. "Is everyone else all right?"

She turned back. "Rue was hurt, too, though not as badly as you. Several arrow wounds, but they were quick to begin healing once I cleaned them and applied the necessary salves. She moves slowly still, but she is able to sail the airship. Yours was the wound we were most worried about. I did not think we could save you unless we went to Storlock for help from the Healers, but Rue said that was the first place the Druids would look for you. I have some skill with infection and fevers. I worked the front on the Prekkendorran for a year in my early training. We decided not to chance going to Storlock."

She stopped, her face turning somber. "I am talking too much. You need to rest. I will tell Rue you are awake."

"Wait," he said again. He swallowed against the tightness in his throat, against the urgency he was feeling at needing to act on his dream. "How long have I been like this?"

"A little more than three days."

Three days. A lifetime. "Where are we?"

"Above the Streleheim, flying north along the western exposure of the Anar Mountains." She hesitated. "We stopped last night so that I could collect plants to treat your wound. And to allow you a chance to sleep on solid ground for one night. But Rue said we had to go on this morning, that we could not afford to delay longer. The Druids would be after us, and we needed to find your son before they did. That's where we are flying."

"To Taupo Rough?"

"To Taupo Rough. You told us just before you lost consciousness that this was where the scrye waters showed him to be."

But where he no longer was, Bek thought. Still, it was where they must begin their search for his companions, whose help the King of the Silver River had said they would need. Keys that would open doors to reach him—what did that mean?

"Rest now," Bellizen said, touching his arm as she rose.

He exhaled slowly and lay back, and she was gone before he could say anything more. He lay in the ensuing silence and stared up at the beams of his cabin, at the underside of the decking, at the windows through which the heavy streamers of daylight shone. It was all so familiar. But he had the feeling that the familiar was rapidly vanishing, and that what lay ahead would be as strange and new as the idea of Penderrin and Grianne inside the Forbidding.

He closed his eyes for a moment, to rest them, and immediately fell asleep.

THIRTEEN

When Bek Ohmsford woke, he was alone. He lay in his bed staring up at the same patch of the decking's underside that he had been looking at when he fell asleep—crossbeams, rough planking, wooden dowels, and iron nails all fitted into place. He felt the sway of the airship and knew she was still flying. Outside, the light was pale and washed of color. It was twilight, he guessed. Or the gray of a new dawn. He wondered how much time had passed. He wondered how far they had come.

For a while he lay without moving, allowing himself to come fully awake, taking time to test the limits of his strength. He found bound about his waist the compress that protected the knife wound, as well as the bandage to his shoulder. Both wounds ached, but no more than he might have expected them to. He moved his arms and legs without difficulty and even managed to lift himself up on one elbow, although the effort caused a sharp twinge in his injured side.

He lay back, feeling appreciably better than he had when he had first regained consciousness. Still, he accepted that he was not yet at full strength. He reached for the cup of water that Bellizen had left at his bedside and drank deeply. The water was sweet and cool, and it helped clear his head of sleep. He thought he might be able to get out of bed and up on deck if he took his time. But he would have to try standing and he would have to dress. It would not be easy.

He was working his way into a sitting position when the door to his cabin opened and Rue appeared.

"What do you think you're doing?" she snapped, rushing over and pushing him down again. Her face reflected a mix of concern and irritation, but it softened almost at once as she leaned down and kissed him. "Wait a bit. You're not ready yet."

"I feel better," he said.

"Apparently. But how you think you feel doesn't necessarily reflect how you really are." She sat down beside him. "Didn't Bellizen tell you how worried we were? You lied to me about that knife wound. It was much worse than you said."

"I just wanted to get out of there. I wasn't thinking about the wound."

"We almost lost you, Bek."

He smiled. "You can't lose me as easy as that."

"I hope not." She ran the tip of one finger across his cheek. "Losing you would be too much for me."

She kissed him again, and he kissed her back, holding her close, even though it hurt both his side and shoulder to do so. When she pulled away, she brushed back her short-cropped hair and shook her head in despair. "You risk too much, Bek Ohmsford. You take too many chances."

"I must have learned that from you," he answered, laughing. "Let's be honest for a moment. Who in the world ever took more chances than you?"

She nodded, conceding the point. "But you feel better, do you?" She held her hand against his forehead for a moment. "Your fever has broken; you're much cooler. Earlier, you were burning up. And delirious. Thrashing and talking about things none of us could understand. You were dreaming. Or having nightmares. Do you remember any of it?"

"I remember what matters," he said quietly.

Then he told her of his vision and of the words of the King of the Silver River. He was surprised to see her cry when she learned that Pen was inside the Forbidding. But immediately afterward she was angry and quick to blame Grianne. "If not for her, none of this would be happening." Their lives were caught up in hers, snared in her Druid machinations and political maneuverings, held prisoner by her web of intrigues and subterfuges. She might not be the Ilse Witch any longer, but as Ard Rhys she inspired the same hostility and enmity. Anyone connected with her, whether by blood or by alliance, suffered as a result. None of them would ever be free of her entanglements.

Bek tried to reason with her, but there was no doing so while her son was in such terrible danger and her anger so great because of it, so he quickly gave it up, instead turning the discussion a different way.

"You did the right thing by keeping us flying toward Taupo Rough. If the King of the Silver River is to be believed, our chance for helping Pen lies in first finding his companions."

She frowned at him. "*Are* we to believe him, Bek? Are we to believe any of those who harbor secrets? We know better than to trust the Druids. Should we trust a creature like the King of the Silver River any farther?"

Bek shrugged. "I think we have to. Pen trusted him."

"Which put our son inside the Forbidding. You make my point."

"But maybe we have to extend our trust a little farther in order to get him out again. After all, what other choice do we have? We haven't another way of reaching Pen."

"I hate this!" she snapped. "I hate that everything we do is dictated by these secret keepers, Faerie and Druid alike. Everything that has happened is their doing. We are just their pawns!"

He nodded. "I know what we are. But we are thinking pawns, and in the end we will make our own decisions. For now, we have to follow the path we have been put upon and hope that it leads us to where we want to go. That path takes us first to Taupo Rough."

She took a deep breath and exhaled slowly. "All right. Taupo Rough." She looked out the window at the graying light. "Dusk comes. You've been asleep for more than a day, but we traveled on while you slept. We should reach the village before dawn. You should go back to sleep while you can. Or would you like something to eat first?"

He chose to eat, and she sat with him while he did. He was heartened to find that her anger gradually lessened and her mood lightened, and he did not argue with her when she told him to go back to sleep afterward. She kissed him and told him she loved him, and he told her that he loved her, too. It was as much as they needed to say. It was enough to leave things at that.

He slept then, surprised to discover that sleep came again so quickly and easily. He was still sleeping when Rue reappeared to tell him that they were almost at their destination. She helped him sit up and then stand, and when he found he was strong enough to do more, she helped him dress and walked him up on deck. It was night still, but the first tinges of dawn were visible east along the crest of the mountains. The land they sailed through was stark and barren, a vast sweeping plain to the west that climbed into foothills east, which in turn rose to the jagged majesty of the Charnals. Small clumps of trees, tiny silver-web streams, and small lakes that reflected the moonlight brightened an otherwise rocky terrain. Bek knew that country. He had explored it with Rue once upon a time. But few expeditions went that way, and he had not been there in years.

Trefen Morys was at the helm and nodded to him as he climbed into the pilot box. "Good to see you looking well again," he said.

Bellizen came over from the port railing and joined them, her pale oval face shining with moonlight. "Are we close, Rue?"

Rue Meridian nodded, then said to Bek, "Tell them everything you told me. They need to hear it from you."

Bek did so, his words floating away from him as he spoke them in the soft rush of the wind, the night air swift and cool, the world vast and dark about their little circle. He covered everything, making certain to include the words of the King of the Silver River that suggested the Ard Rhys was alive and that Pen could reach her.

When he was finished, Bellizen spoke first. "It sounds so impossible. A boy is the only one who can bring the Ard Rhys back? A boy with no magic, no special skills?" She looked quickly at Rue. "I do not doubt his determination, but I do question the reason for the choosing of him."

"No more than I," Rue said. "But Bek keeps nothing from us; the secrets for which we seek answers belong to the King of the Silver River. If we wish to discover those answers, we will have to discover them another way. Pen might know some of them. The Ard Rhys might know the rest."

"We will seek those answers with you," Trefen Morys assured her quickly. "We will do whatever is necessary to find my mistress. If your son can lead us to her, then we will find him and help him as best we can. But first, it appears, we need to find his companions. Three were named. The Dwarf would be Tagwen. The Rock Troll would be Kermadec. Once, he was Captain of her Guard, and he remains her close friend. Taupo Rough is his home." He paused. "But who is the Elven girl?"

Bek shook his head. "I wish I knew."

He wished he knew as well why the King of the Silver River had made no mention of Ahren Elessedil. The Druids had said Tagwen had gone to him for help first before going to Penderrin. Shouldn't there also have been some reference to him?

But he said nothing of his worry to the others.

He stood at the railing and watched the ground sweep away as *Swift Sure* sped onward along the line of the mountains. Rue took several compass readings and directed Trefen Morys, whom she had allowed to keep the helm. She must have been working with him, Bek thought. The young Druid had no flying skills, no experience with weapons, and he had learned both in a very short time under less-than-ideal circumstances. But he was doing better than many would have.

The sky continued to brighten slowly, the darkness giving way to a silvery wash that gradually turned golden. Ahead, the buildings of a fortified settlement came into view, a village built back against a cliff wall. But there were no fires in the village and no signs of movement. Dark smears dotted the plains fronting the village walls, and the village itself had a ragged, neglected look. As they drew nearer, he saw that sections of the walls had been breached and the greater number of buildings were collapsed and blackened by fire.

"Are we in the right place?" he asked Rue.

She nodded, her face dark with concern. "This is Taupo Rough. Not what we expected, is it? Someone has been here before us."

Bek did not care to speculate on who that someone might have been. It was possible that the Druids had gotten to the village ahead of them, but the destruction did not look recent. There were no fires burning, no lingering curtains of smoke, no battle smells, nothing to suggest that anything had happened here for days.

They landed the airship at the edge of the walls, and while he stayed at the helm, the other three went down the rope ladder to have a look around. He hated being left behind, but as Rue sensibly pointed out, he was too weak to be making long treks. So he contented himself with watching their progress and trying to fit together in his own mind the story of what had happened here.

By the time the sun was fully up, white-hot in a cloudless sky, they were back, grim-faced and empty-handed.

"A battle was fought here perhaps two weeks ago," Rue reported. "At least one Druid warship was brought down in the fighting and burned. The remains lie out on the flats. So the battle was probably between the Rock Trolls of the village and the Druids. There are Gnome weapons and pieces of armor, so Gnomes probably fought in the service of the Druids. Hard to tell for certain what happened, but in the end the Trolls fled into the cliffs. There are caves in those cliffs, and I would imagine tunnels that connect to the far side of the mountains."

"This must have all happened because of Pen," Bek said. "This is Kermadec's home. Pen and the others would have come to him for help. The Druids tracked them here while we were imprisoned at Paranor and tried to take Pen prisoner. Kermadec refused to give him up. So the village was sacked."

Rue nodded, brushing back loose strands of her auburn hair. "But where did Pen and his protectors go from here? What route did they take?"

"They went in search of the darkwand," Bellizen answered her.

"Somewhere in these mountains," Trefen Morys added.

"Or somewhere beyond." Bellizen looked at Bek. "Can you track your son's passage from here as you did at Paranor?"

Bek shook his head doubtfully. The battle had happened days ago, and Pen had been gone from there a long time. He wasn't in the mountains anymore; he wasn't even on the same world. In any case, Bek's connection was with his son, not with those who had accompanied him. His magic might not allow him to track them as he had Pen.

But he knew he had to try.

"There's nothing here for us," he said. "Not unless we try tracking them through the tunnels. Why don't we fly to the other side of the cliffs and see if we can pick up a trail?"

They did so, Rue taking the helm, not trusting anyone else to navigate in a place where the winds could prove unpredictable and a moment's inattention could send an airship into the rocks. Keeping

Bek beside her in the pilot box, she sent the young Druids to the starboard and port forward draws to work the lines by hand in case of heavy turbulence. But they were lucky that day. The winds were mild and the way into the mountains clear. *Swift Sure* sailed through gaps in the jagged peaks unhindered and unchallenged, and by midday they had reached a valley that lay between the peaks of the Klu.

While the airship hovered midway across the valley, Bek used the wishsong to seek out some sign of Pen or his companions. He had learned the trick from his sister years earlier. As the Ilse Witch, she had used the wishsong to track him. Later, on the long voyage home, she had showed him how. He would see if it could be made to work the same way for him.

It was something of a gamble to do so. Any use of his magic would alert Shadea and her Druids to their presence and remove any doubt about where they were. On the other hand, she would know already where they were going and what they were trying to do, so he really wasn't giving all that much away. And if she had discovered that Pen was inside the Forbidding, she might have lost all interest in pursuing them anyway. Whatever the case, without the use of the wishsong they had no way of knowing where to go.

Eyes closed for better concentration, he sang the magic, slow and smooth, like a carpet being spread across the valley floor, searching for traces of passage. He found several, all of them more than a week old and none distinct enough to identify. Frustrated, he spread his net a little wider, reaching deeper into the peaks ahead, into the mountains of the Klu that fronted the huge forests of the Inkrim.

There, far beyond anywhere he could see, he found traces of his son, tiny beacons in the ether. But the traces were unlike anything he had ever come across before, and for a moment he didn't trust what the wishsong was telling him. Still, his certainty that it was Penderrin and not someone else was so strong that he could not ignore it.

He broke off his efforts, the wishsong dying into silence. His breathing quieted and his eyes opened once more.

"I found him," he said. "Traces of him, anyway. Deeper into the mountains ahead, east." He paused, looking now at Rue. "But something's wrong. What I found wasn't familiar to me; it wasn't what I know of Pen. What I found of his passing was tinged with magic."

She stared at him. "Magic? Whose magic?"

"His own."

She shook her head. "That isn't possible. He doesn't have any magic. He's never had any magic. We both know that."

He held her gaze. "Nevertheless."

"You must be mistaken. You have to be."

He could tell from the way she said it that she needed him to be wrong, that she was frightened at the prospect that the Ohmsford heritage might have been passed on to her son after all. He could discern her thinking. She had believed Pen safely removed from the wishsong's influence, the bloodline dying out with Bek. What if she had been mistaken? What if the magic had simply lain dormant? It had done so with Bek. Was it so strange that it should do so with his son, as well?

"I don't think we can decide about this until we talk to Pen," he said carefully. "What matters is that I feel certain I've found his route of passage. We can track him now."

"What if what you've found is his passage coming out, rather than going in?" Trefen Morys asked suddenly.

It was an uncomfortable thought. There was no way to determine the answer from where they stood. There might not be a way to determine the answer once they reached the source. It might be a long, dangerous journey to their destination, and the journey might well yield nothing.

But it was all they had to work with. It was the only lead they had been given.

"I think we have to try following it for a time, at least," Bek offered, looking to Rue for support.

His wife studied him, her fine, clear features masking what she was feeling, keeping hidden the wash of doubts and fears he knew she must be experiencing. She stayed silent for a long time, considering. Then she nodded. "Bek is right. We have to try."

They turned *Swift Sure's* bow toward the Klu and flew east for the remainder of the day into peaks wrapped in storm clouds and layers of mist, buffeted by heavy winds. *Swift Sure* was battered and tossed and her occupants thrown from side to side. Bek was sent below to help protect his wounds, and the other three strapped on safety harnesses while on deck. By the end of the day, all three were drenched and freezing, their bodies aching and their minds numb from the effort of holding course and staying aloft. Snow was flying all about them in thick gusts, threatening whiteouts at every turn, cloaking cliff walls and passages alike so that the way forward remained an ever-changing mystery.

As darkness approached, Rue Meridian began to despair. If they did not get clear of the mountains quickly, she would have to set down, and there was nowhere for her to do that. Flying blind at night could have only one result. She called Bek back up on deck and had him use the wishsong again, searching for a way to go. But the magic failed Bek this time, refusing to give up anything at all that would help, leaving them adrift and at risk.

Finally, when it seemed that no help was to be had from any quarter and the outcome of their efforts unavoidable, the storms subsided and the peaks ahead opened into the Valley of the Inkrim. Rue took *Swift Sure* through as the last of the day's light gave way to a scattering of stars and no visible moon, just a faint brightening that allowed her enough illumination to set down at the edge of the trees at the rim of the valley.

They slept then, exhausted from their efforts. All but Bek. Awake and awash in fresh doubts, he sat alone in the pilot box, wrapped in a blanket, thinking about what they were doing. He understood the need for it; he understood as well the reasons. What bothered him was the number of uncertainties. Trefen Morys had been right about tracking Pen's passage. It was probably impossible to determine which way the boy was going, absent some physical evidence. He told himself that if they could locate just one of his companions, they would have a way of finding his son.

But he was bothered most by something he had kept from Rue. The traces of Pen he had found had been infused with wishsong magic. Not just any magic, but wishsong magic. He hadn't thought Rue needed to know that just yet. She was distressed enough about the presence of any magic where their son was concerned and would have been beside herself to learn that the magic had its origins in the Ohmsford bloodline. But there was no mistaking its nature. He should have felt a measure of relief; if Pen had the use of the wishsong, he was in a better position to protect himself. But in fact Bek was as upset about the prospect as his wife. He didn't want Pen to have the burden of the wishsong any more than she did. Too many generations of Ohmsfords had struggled with it. Too many had seen their lives altered irrevocably as a result—and not always for the better. It had been so with him. He had hoped that his son might have an easier road.

He thought about it for a long time. He tried to picture Pen within the Forbidding and failed. How could anyone imagine what that must be like? He knew what sort of creatures the Forbidding contained, but no one knew what it would feel like to be a human trapped there. That Penderrin should have been sent to find and retrieve Grianne was still something he could not fathom. The King of the Silver River had given him no reason for the choice of his son as rescuer. There would be a reason, he knew. And the reason might have something to do with Pen's use of the wishsong. Yet if that was so, why hadn't the Faerie creature come to Bek, who had more experience and better command of the magic? Why had Pen been chosen?

It had to be something else—something about Pen that wasn't true of Bek.

He fell asleep at some point and woke to the sound of the others coming up on deck. He was stiff from sleeping upright, but overall he felt better than he had the day before. He felt stronger, more ready. He was mending; he was coming back to himself.

The day was clear and bright ahead of them, the storms of the Klu left behind. After they had eaten from their steadily dwindling stores, Bek used the wishsong to seek anew the traces of Pen he had found the other day. He found them with little trouble. They were stronger, and he was better able to read them. The magic that had infused them a day earlier was more diverse than he had believed, a mix of couplings that involved his son and someone or something else. The source of the traces lay ahead, deep within the Inkrim.

After checking the radian draws and light sheaths for breaks and tears and finding everything intact, Rue took *Swift Sure* off the ground, pointed her east across the sweep of the forested valley, and sailed in search of Bek's findings.

It was nearing midday when Trefen Morys, who had been keeping watch at the bow for the better part of an hour, called back, "There are ruins down there!"

Rue dropped *Swift Sure* into a slow descent toward the canopy of the trees, following the young Druid's shouted directions. Within minutes, the ruins were visible to them all. Remnants of buildings sprawled for miles, a jumble of broken walls, columns, and battlements. What little remained had been overgrown by trees and scrub, enveloped by the foliage of the jungle. In places, wildflowers formed bright patches amid the blanketing shadows.

"There are people down there!" Trefen Morys shouted suddenly.

Bek went forward at once, picking his way gingerly across the decking to where the Druid stood. They were only a hundred feet above the canopy by then and able to see the whole of the valley clearly. As Bek came up beside him, Trefen Morys pointed. Gnarled, string-thin forms darted about the rubble at the edges of the ruins, creatures similar to Gnomes but clearly something else.

"Urdas," Bek said aloud.

He recognized them from earlier expeditions he had made into the Charnals. He saw them look up as *Swift Sure* hove into view, repositioning themselves to meet the newly perceived threat, brandishing slings and bows and arrows.

"Keep us flying, Rue!" he shouted over his shoulder.

"What are they doing?" Trefen Morys asked him.

He shook his head. "I don't know. Keep your eyes open."

He went back to the pilot box and climbed up beside Rue and Bellizen, telling them what he had seen. "They've ringed the ruins. I think they're looking for something. Maybe the same thing we're looking for."

He decided to use the wishsong again, to seek anew the traces of Pen's passing he had sensed that morning. He found them immediately, strong and clear and just ahead in the ruins. The magic was diffuse and fading, days old and no longer clearly defined. But its use had been powerful and reflected both determination and clear intent. Pen had experienced an epiphany or confrontation of major proportions. If he had survived that, Bek thought, then there was some reason to believe he could survive the Forbidding.

"Ahead, five degrees east southeast," he told Rue, pointing for emphasis.

Swift Sure altered course slightly and flew on, Rue holding the airship's speed down so that they could scan the ruins below for other signs of life. They were flying along the southern perimeter, and there were Urdas scattered all along it. They seemed reluctant to go farther in. Bek remembered that the Urdas were superstitious about places they considered sacred; the ruins might well be one such place. But the Urdas were clearly there for a reason. If they could not enter, then they were waiting for something that had.

"Smoke," Rue said suddenly, pointing off to the right.

From just beyond the main body of the ruins, separated by a series of deep, wooded, rifts, a column of black smoke rose from a crumbling blockhouse and tower. The Urdas were all about it, three and four deep within the cover of trees and rocks, showering the fortifications with darts and arrows and spears.

"I'd say we've found something," Rue offered, giving Bek a quick glance.

But it was not something that tracked to the traces of Pen's passing that Bek had detected. It was something entirely apart. He hesitated, wondering how advisable it was to become distracted by something that might have nothing at all to do with what they were looking for.

"All right," he said finally, "let's have a look."

FOURTEEN

It was like flying into a hornet's nest.

Swift Sure descended in a long, slow spiral, drawing the attention of the band of Urdas below. Bek had hoped that their appearance alone would prove startling enough to these superstitious people to make them withdraw. But instead of bolting back into the trees and seeking cover, the Urdas immediately turned their weapons on the airship. Trefen Morys barely had time to shout a warning from the bow when a hail of spears and darts struck the underside of the vessel and a wash of arrows arced over the railing in a deadly sweep.

Everyone ducked behind the protective railings as Bek took *Swift Sure* back up again, out of reach of the attack. As he did so, Trefen Morys came running back.

"There are Rock Trolls down there in that tower!" he shouted up to Pen. "They were waving to us for help!"

Bek turned to Rue. "Load both the port and starboard rail slings. Maybe we can drive the Urdas far enough back into the trees to gain space to get a ladder down."

The starboard rail sling was still in place from their flight out of Paranor, and with help from Trefen Morys it took Rue only minutes to set up the port weapon and arm them both. Placing the young Druid on the former and herself on the latter, she sent Bellizen amidships to stand ready to lower the rope ladder, then signaled for Bek to take *Swift Sure* down again.

It was trickier going in the second time. The Urdas were waiting, neither awed nor frightened of the airship. Even from high up, Bek could tell that they were aggressively hostile. Whatever had incensed them had stirred their anger to such intensity that they were beyond caring what happened to them so long as they stopped any rescue attempt. They were clustered at every quarter of the tower walls, and as soon as *Swift Sure* came within range, they attacked. Bek kept his hold on the airship steady to give Rue and Trefen Morys a chance to chase them off, but even after both rail slings were emptied twice into the attackers, they held their ground, refusing to fall back. Gnarled, hairy forms swarmed through the wooded ravines, keeping the tower and its occupants besieged.

Bek took the airship out of range once more, trying to think what else they might try.

Rue returned from the railing and climbed into the pilot box. "Our weapons aren't going to work, Bek. If we want to get those Rock Trolls out of that tower, we have to take a different approach."

She leaned close so that only he could hear. "Could you use the wishsong to help?"

He stared at her in surprise. She hated his magic, hated the legacy that went with it—so much so that he had barely used it since coming back from Parkasia. The search for their son had marked his first serious attempt in several years. In truth, he wasn't even sure he knew after so long how to employ it in the way that would be necessary.

"I understand," she said, reading the look on his face. "But we don't have any choice."

She was saying that if they wanted to help Pen, this was what it was going to take. The wind shifted and blew across his face, unexpectedly chill and biting as it came down off the mountains. He held her gaze a moment longer, then nodded. "Take the helm."

He went down on deck to where the young Druids stood waiting and motioned them over to the rope ladder so that both could help with the rescue effort. Then he moved forward to the bow and looked down.

Urdas swarmed through the trees below, too many to count. Rue was right. Even a dozen rail slings wouldn't be enough to chase them off. A more effective weapon was needed, and there was nothing more effective than the wishsong when it was used in the right way. Grianne had taught him so years ago when she had tried to kill him. He thought it ironic that he would use that lesson now to try to save her.

"Take us back down!" he shouted to Rue, a sudden gust of wind nearly obscuring his words. It was heavy enough that it shook the airship from bow to stern. "Slowly!"

He glanced north to where huge storm clouds were beginning to build on the horizon, sifting down through the peaks toward the Inkrim. A change in the weather was coming, and it did not favor their efforts. If they failed to get a ladder down soon, given the nature of storms in that region, it might not be possible to try again for days.

He looked down again at the Urdas, trying to think how to force them to move back from the walls of the tower. He could do some things safely with the wishsong, but he did not want to risk trying too much after so many years of no practice. The magic was powerful and at times unpredictable. Using it the wrong way could prove disastrous. If it failed to respond as intended, it might send them all crashing down with the airship.

The wind gusted across his face again, and suddenly he remembered that the Druids favored using the elements as allies in their wielding of magic. Perhaps he could do the same here.

He brought up the wishsong in a soft hum, calling it to life, feeling it come awake and then flood through him with a slow, rising heat. He kept his gaze fixed on the scene below as he began to give the magic a shape and a form, a sense and a purpose. He found the wind currents that preceded the coming storm and stirred in the magic. The currents gained force and consistency, and as they gusted about him they began to take on a new intensity. What had begun as a series of uneven bursts now became a steady blow. Changes of pitch evened and slowly built into a howl that suggested the cresting of a tidal wave.

The Urdas began looking around in confusion and then in fear. A storm of that kind wasn't something they understood. They were unfamiliar with winds of such magnitude. They crouched lower, and then began to back away from the tower toward the deep woods, their superstitious nature warning them that the elements were spirit-driven.

Bek built on the power of his magic, adding fresh layers, giving the wind an extraordinary sound and feel, a roar that began to shake trees and earth alike. He did not look back at Rue, trusting her to continue *Swift Sure's* descent, to understand what he was doing and not be frightened by it. He didn't know what the Druids were thinking, but he couldn't spare time to worry about them. He had the wind tearing across the landscape by then, scattering the Urdas in all directions, their determination to stand fast shattered.

Then the treetops were right below them, and the outer walls of the tower became visible through the gaps. He risked a quick glance back at Trefen Morys and Bellizen and saw them dropping the rope ladder over the side of the railing, down to the besieged Trolls. Almost immediately bulky forms began to emerge, scrambling from their concealment, some helping others, all of them moving swiftly for the ladder. But then they ducked back again, unable to advance. Bek felt his strength beginning to fail, and forced himself to push harder to keep the wind in place. The Trolls had still not begun to climb the ladder, and the Urdas were beginning to reemerge from the trees. Rue was yelling something at him, but he couldn't hear what. He intensified the magic once more, feeling his hold on it slipping away.

Then Bellizen was beside him, frantic. "Your magic is too strong, Bek! The force of the wind is keeping the Trolls from climbing the ladder!"

He realized it was true, that his efforts at keeping the Urdas at bay were keeping the Trolls pinned down, as well. Rue must have been trying to tell him as much. He slowed his efforts, letting the wind diminish. Within the ruins of the tower, the Trolls recognized their opportunity and scrambled for the ladder. The Urdas, in response, rushed to stop them.

There was nothing more Bek could do to help. Any further use of the magic to intensify the wind would do as much damage as good. The Trolls would have to make it on their own. He kept the wind in place a few moments longer, tuning its sound to an earsplitting shriek in an effort to frighten the Urdas. But the Inkrim natives were no longer intimidated, having seen what was happening and become newly enraged at the thought of losing the intruders to an airship rescue. They came at the Trolls in waves, weapons loosing, the air filling with missiles. Two of the Trolls were struck, and one fell to his death. The others pressed on, climbing steadily through the hail of fire, helping each other as they did so. One of them, he saw, carried a smaller figure tucked under one arm, a squat blocky form that could only be a Dwarf.

Then the Trolls were over the side of the railing and on board the ship, and Rue was lifting away, taking them quickly out of range of their attackers. Bek broke off his efforts with the wishsong, now thoroughly spent, and hurried over to the newcomers. Seven Trolls and a Dwarf, he saw. The Dwarf wrestled free of the Troll who was carrying him and stood clinging to the rail, breathing hard.

"Tagwen?" Bek asked, coming up to him.

Tagwen looked over, his face ashen and his mouth a tight line. There was blood on his neck and right arm from wounds, and his clothing was torn and soiled.

He blinked rapidly at Bek. "I don't ever want to come to this place again!" he snapped. "Not ever!"

Then he fainted.

There was no time for an exchange of information or for anything but making a quick escape from the fast-approaching storm. If it caught up with them over the Inkrim, their efforts to get free of the Urdas might come to nothing. With Bek at the helm, Rue and Treten Morys worked the draws and light sheaths by hand to gain speed and maneuverability, heading south and west toward the relative safety of the mountain peaks below the clouds and winds building north. *Swift Sure* skated hard across the long stretch of the valley, buffeted and tossed as storm winds gusted ahead of rain and dark skies. Lightning began to flash in the heart of the encroaching dark, and thunder rumbled ominously across the heavens in long, crackling peals.

On the decks below the pilothouse, Bellizen worked on the injured Rock Trolls. Two of them were badly hurt, wounded by Urda weapons. According to Kermadec, who had managed to say a few words to Bek before *Swift Sure* set sail, his little company had tried to slip past the Urdas during the night, convinced that any attempt at fighting to get free was useless. By then, Pen had been gone for almost a day, and they were desperate to find a way to help him. But the Urdas, furious at what they perceived to be a deliberate violation of sacred ground, had been keeping close watch on the intruders and had no intention of letting them escape. They reacted swiftly to the attempt, catching them out in the open and killing two outright. The surviving Trolls and Tagwen had fled into the tower, where they had remained, trapped and under attack.

Rain struck *Swift Sure* a broadside blow that sent her scudding sideways across the roof of the forest. Bek righted her quickly, trying not to think about Pen and what had happened in the ruins days earlier, concentrating instead on getting them across the valley to the relative safety of the mountains. Inside the peaks, they could find protection from the storm and cross into the valleys beyond. But the rain descended in torrents, inundating the decks and those clustered on them, leaving the entire ship sodden and dripping. Visibility was dropping fast, and Bek turned the ship farther south in an effort to run before the storm and remain clear of its impenetrable shroud of rain and mist.

Then lightning struck the mainmast, dancing down its length and along the conductors to the hull, sparking and flashing in the near dark. The Trolls flattened themselves against the deck until Bellizen signaled for help to get the injured below. Staggering across the slick wood with their burdens, the Trolls did as she asked, and soon everyone had disappeared below, leaving Bek, Rue, and Trefen Morys to sail the airship.

They were flying dangerously low, trying to slip the stronger winds at the higher elevations. But radian draws, stays, and sails were all giving way, tearing loose or shredding, slowing eroding *Swift Sure's* maneuverability. Bek held the airship as steady as he could, relying on the power stored in the diapson crystals to keep her flying. When that was gone, they were finished. He could make out gaps in the mountain peaks ahead, dark passages to the valleys beyond, and he pointed toward them as the storm closed about.

The winds howled like a living thing. They slammed into *Swift Sure* with devastating impact, knocking her off course, forcing Bek to wrestle her back into line again. Rain descended in sheets, and visibility dropped to nothing. Even the dark gaps for which they were headed began to fade. The storm was sweeping the whole of the Inkrim now, a great roiling mass of wind, rain, and darkness.

Then abruptly the mountains ahead disappeared and the gaps toward which *Swift Sure* had been heading were gone.

We're not going to make it, Bek thought.

For heart-stopping minutes, they hung suspended in a gray, fathomless void, directionless and lost.

Then the curtain of rain lifted and the rock walls loomed out of the rain-soaked darkness once more, massive slabs of stone lifting thousands of feet into the mists. Bek caught sight of a gap between them and banked *Swift Sure* sharply toward its dark maw.

Seconds later, they were inside a craggy split that was as dark and still and windless as a subterranean passage.

"Savages!"

Atalan spit the word out as if to rid himself of its bitter taste. It was a word he had used three times in the last two sentences by Bek's reckoning. Apparently the bitterness had a tendency to linger.

"Killed four of us for no better reason than to punish us for coming into those ruins! A place of dead things! Nothing there but bones and rubble and monsters like that tree!" His blunt Troll features were unreadable, but his eyes were fierce. "We should come back here with the rest of our people and wipe them out!"

He was incensed, even now, hours later. They were seated at the bow—Atalan, Kermadec, Iagwen, the young Druids, Rue, and Bek. They made an odd-looking group. The Trolls were giants with skins of bark and flat, virtually featureless faces. The Druids were much smaller and impossibly young. The Dwarf was squat and solid, his thick beard like a mask. And Bek and Rue, fatigued and weak from the wounds they had received during their flight out of Paranor, had the look of the walking dead. *Swift Sure* hung anchored above a valley floor somewhere deep within the Klu, west almost to the Charnals. The Inkrim and the storm had been left behind. It was nightfall, and the Trolls who had been wounded were sleeping below. Everyone was exhausted.

Kermadec shifted his large frame and leaned back against the ship's railing. His rough face was impassive, his voice calm. "Let it be,

Atalan." He nodded at Bek and Rue. "So young Penderrin has found a way into the Forbidding, after all. Your son is nothing if not resourceful. He has kept his wits about him."

"He has his wits, but does he have the use of magic, as well?" Rue asked, reminded suddenly of what Bek had revealed of the traces of her son's passage.

Kermadec shrugged. "He has some. He has that ability to read the responses of living things. He can discern their thinking from that. Like the lichen. Like that moor cat." He glanced at Tagwen. "It's a magic I wouldn't mind having, Bristle Beard."

"He said it was a small magic," the Dwarf muttered. He scowled at Kermadec. "Having seen nothing to suggest otherwise, I am inclined to take him at his word. Penderrin is not given to exaggeration."

Tagwen had recovered from his faint, though he was still embarrassed about the collapse. Kermadec had spent a long time reassuring the Dwarf that it had nothing to do with his courage, but was a result of exhaustion and stress. Anyone might have suffered the same indignity, and it would not be mentioned again. Tagwen, however, did not appear convinced.

"There is the magic he generated during his encounter with the tanequil, as well," Trefen Morys pointed out. "To create a talisman of such power, a tremendous amount of magic would have to be released. Even if it didn't come from Pen, traces of it would cling to him. And he carries the darkwand with him. Any reading of magic attached to Pen would be influenced by that."

It was a reasonable explanation, and even Rue seemed to accept it. Only Bek knew that the reasoning was wrong. The readings given him by the wishsong had told him that the traces of his son's passage encompassed only magic that belonged to him. The blood connection between father and son was too strong for him to be mistaken. Pen had uncovered a form of magic that was still a mystery, possibly even to himself.

"I am very sorry to hear that Ahren Elessedil is dead," he said to Tagwen, changing the subject.

The Dwarf looked down at his hands and shook his shaggy head slowly. "He was a brave man, Bek Ohmsford. He gave his life so that the rest of us could go on. We would not have reached Kermadec and Taupo Rough, let alone Stridegate and the tanequil, if not for him."

"And the Elven girl is his niece?"

"Khyber Elessedil. Tough as old leather, that girl, though nearly as young as Penderrin. She has the Elfstones. Took them from the Elessedils and brought them to Ahren so that he would teach her how to use them. Turned out he had no choice. She used them in the Slags to sink the *Galaphile*, then again later to help us on our journey here. She had them with her when she disappeared in Stridegate."

"But you think that she boarded one of the Druid airships that took Pen to Paranor?" Rue asked.

Tagwen looked at Kermadec and came to some unspoken agreement. "Something might have happened to her in the ruins after she left us and went in search of Penderrin, but I don't think so," the Dwarf declared. He looked up. "She was very close to the boy and determined to help him reach the Ard Rhys. I think she found a way, and that's why he was able to get into the Forbidding after the Druids took him prisoner."

"Well, the fact that the King of the Silver River told Bek in his dream that an Elven girl is one of the three who will help us reach Pen suggests you are right. But where is she now?"

"She must be at Paranor," Kermadec answered with another shrug. "Waiting for us."

"Then we must go there to help them," Tagwen declared firmly. "It was the promise I made to young Penderrin before they took him, and I intend to fulfill it."

"As do I," Kermadec agreed.

"How, exactly, are you going to go about doing that?" Bellizen asked suddenly. Starlight reflected in her ink-black eyes. "Do you have a plan?"

Neither of them did, of course. No one did. There was a long silence as they pondered her question. They had been so consumed with reaching Paranor that none of them had given much thought to what they would do once they were there. It wasn't at all clear, they realized as they reflected on the possibilities, what their course of action should be.

"What are we up against at Paranor?" Bek asked finally, looking from Bellizen to Trefen Morys. "How much support does my sister have?"

Trefen Morys shook his head. "Very little, I'm afraid. There are a handful of Druids who openly support her and will stand with her when she returns, but most have been dismissed from the order. Those who remain support Shadea. It isn't that they believe so strongly in her; it's more that they mistrust your sister. She has never been able to shed her image as the Ilse Witch, not entirely."

"Some will stand with her when she returns," Bellizen added. "But only some, and I do not think we can count their numbers with any degree of certainty. Some will stand with her because, like us, they believe in her. Some will stand with her because they have seen how badly Shadea a'Ru has dealt with her power. But most will take no stand at all."

"That works both ways, of course," Kermadec pointed out. "They do not choose to stand with her, but will not stand with Shadea, either. That gives us a chance."

"Why do you support her?" Rue asked Bellizen, glancing at Trefen Morys, as well. "Why have you taken her side?"

Bellizen blushed. "It is not easy to explain. I do so in part because she was kind to me when others were not. She brought me to Paranor at the suggestion of another Druid, from a village in the Runne where my talents were considered abnormal and my safety threatened. I do not know how she found out about me, but she told me that I belonged with her. I believed that. She has never given me cause to think badly of her or to want her gone. I think she is the Ard Rhys we need. I think she understands the purposes of magic better than anyone."

"I came from a village close to Bellizen's," Trefen Morys added. "We did not know each other before Paranor, but have become friends since. I came to Paranor on my own, seeking a chance to study with the Druids. My mistress gave me that chance. She gave me responsibilities and taught me herself on more than one occasion."

"She is a great lady." Bellizen bit her lip, glancing quickly at her companion. "Those who follow her are mostly younger and never knew her as the Ilse Witch. The others, the older ones, cannot seem to forget. They think of her still as a dark creature, capable of reverting without warning. They do not know her as Trefen and I do. They are less forgiving because their lives are too deeply rooted in the past."

"They are not alone," Bek said quietly. "Perhaps that is just the way of things." He surveyed the faces of the others. "Very well. We know what we have to do. We have to find a way into the Keep and the sleeping chamber of the Ard Rhys. That is where Penderrin and Grianne will reappear when they return from the Forbidding."

He almost added, *if they can find a way back*, but he caught himself just in time. Rue didn't need to hear him saying anything about the odds. She understood them well enough.

"It is more complicated than that," Trefen Morys interjected quickly. "We have to find a way to be inside the sleeping chamber at just the right time. We have to devise a way of knowing exactly when Pen and my mistress will reappear. If we don't choose the right moment, Shadea and her allies will find us out."

The little company went silent, dismayed at the prospect of being stopped after they had come so far and endured so much. But the task the young Druid had just described seemed impossible.

Bek turned to Tagwen. "The King of the Silver River said that the keys to helping Pen were in the hands of his companions— Kermadec, Khyber Elessedil, and yourself. Maybe we should start there. Can you think what he might have been talking about? Is there some special kind of help that you can give us?"

Tagwen considered the question. "Well, there is one possibility," he said after a moment. "I know a way into Paranor using tunnels that run beneath the bluff to the furnace room and continue all through the walls of the Keep. The Ard Rhys showed them to me once, a maze of passages. She used magic to block those leading to her rooms, but perhaps your own magic can undo hers."

"So we can reach the sleeping chamber unseen if I can remove my sister's safeguards?" Bek asked.

The Dwarf nodded rather reluctantly. "Perhaps. If Shadea hasn't discovered the tunnels as well and set traps of her own."

"We'll have to risk it," Bek declared at once. "We've risked worse already to get where we are. Kermadec, what of you?"

The Rock Troll knotted his great hands and looked at Atalan. "Brother, I think the Trolls need to show the Four Lands where we stand in this business. Marching against the Urdas is a waste of time and purpose. We need to march on Paranor and the Druids instead. They attacked Taupo Rough and drove our people out. The attack was unprovoked. Dismissing the Troll guard while it was still in ser-

vice to the Ard Rhys is insult enough, although we could have endured it. But attacking our home is beyond acceptable. Perhaps we
should repay their visit with one of our own."

Atalan's response was a slow, wicked grin. "Let's pull down the
walls around their ears!"

"Or at least pull the wool over their eyes—a distraction to give
you time to get into place." Kermadec glanced at the others. "Several
thousand Rock Trolls gathered at the gates will be something that
not even the Druids can ignore. If we must, we will come through
those gates to your aid, but at the very least we will keep those
snakes pinned down within their own fortress for the time it takes for
our mistress to deal with them as she chooses."

"And deal with them she will, you may be sure," Tagwen grunted,
looking almost happy.

"That leaves Khyber Elessedil," Bellizen said. "What of her?"

"Her purpose seems easier to divine," Bek responded quickly.
"She carries the Elfstones given her by Ahren Elessedil. They are
seeking-stones, and I think finding the demon that has crossed over
from the Forbidding will be our first order of business after my sister
returns. The Elfstones will make that task much easier."

He looked from face to face in the darkness. "We have at least
the beginnings of a plan. I think that is the best we can hope for."

"What I don't understand," Rue declared suddenly, "is why the
King of the Silver River didn't make this business of the keys and the
companions clearer to you in your dream, Bek. He could have told
you what purpose Kermadec and Tagwen and Khyber Elessedil were
to serve. Why didn't he do that?"

"Faerie creatures and shades are secretive and seldom speak the
whole truth," Bellizen ventured.

But Bek shook his head. "I think it is something else. I think we
were given a starting point, but nothing more. The future remains
undecided. Things may change as events unfold, and we must be
ready to change with them. If the King of the Silver River had told
me in my dream exactly what the keys were, we might have become
too reliant on his words. As it is, we remain uncertain that we have it
right. He wants that. He wants us to find our own way. He wants us
to understand that the way is not yet determined."

There was a long silence as the others contemplated his words.
They knew where they must go and what they must do, but they still

did not know how they would accomplish it. The future was a mystery. It was the way the world had always worked. It was the way it would work here.

"We must leave at once," Tagwen declared. "We have no idea how much time remains before the Ard Rhys and young Penderrin cross back."

But Bek shook his head. "No, Tagwen, we need to rest first. We'll stay where we are until dawn, sleep while we can, and fly north tomorrow to Kermadec's people. Once the Trolls are safely delivered and can begin their preparations for a march on Paranor, the rest of us will go ahead to search for Khyber Elessedil."

"And to discover when my mistress and your son will reappear within the Keep," Bellizen added quietly.

It was a disturbing reminder of how difficult the days ahead were going to be.

One by one the members of the company rose and went off to sleep. Most had not slept in days and were exhausted. Bek was the exception. Better rested than the others, he went back up into the pilot box to keep watch.

He was surprised when he found that Rue was following him.

"You should go to sleep," he said, turning back to stop her, reaching out to touch her cheek. "You've slept less than anyone."

She nodded. "I'll sleep soon enough. But I have to say something to you first. Whatever else happens, Bek, I intend to make certain that once Penderrin gets free of the Forbidding, he is kept safe. I intend to protect him from Shadea a'Ru and the rest of those monsters. I don't care what it takes. I don't even care what happens to me."

She was almost in tears as she finished. He tried to hold her, but she pushed him away, refusing to be comforted, defiance on her features. "Promise me that you will do the same."

"You know you don't have to ask me this," he said. "You know I feel the same way you do."

Tight-lipped, she nodded. "I do know it. But I also know that your sister is involved, and that her interests may conflict with ours. Her plans for Pen may not be acceptable. So I need to hear you say it, just in case that happens. I need to hear you promise that if a choice is necessary, you will choose our son."

A sadness inside left him hollow and sick at heart. He knew he would never be able to resolve his wife's feelings—her mistrust and her suspicions—for his sister. He understood why, and he did not blame her. Had he been in her shoes, he would have felt the same.

He reached for her hands, and this time she did not back away. "I promise," he said. "Nothing bad will happen to Pen. No chances will be taken with his safety. His needs come before those of Grianne and the Druid order."

She came into his arms then, reaching to hold him close, her cheek placed against his, her mouth so close to his ear that he could hear her breathing.

"I'm sorry I had to ask that," she whispered.

"Don't be. Don't be sorry for anything."

"I wish Big Red were here."

"I wish Quentin were here."

But her brother was somewhere off the coast of the Blue Divide, flying his airship in service to whoever had paid him most recently, and Quentin Leah was dead two years, never fully recovered from the wounds he had received in Parkasia. Bek thought often of them both, and thinking of them made him wish he could turn time back far enough for them all to be together just once more. But life didn't give you second chances at such things. Life just swept you along and never took you back to where you had been.

"It will be all right," he whispered.

He had said that to her once before and had not been certain it was true. This time, for reasons he could not explain, he felt that it might be.

FIFTEEN

When he was finished speaking, Shadea a'Ru studied Pyson Wence as if studying an interesting insect, glanced momentarily at Traunt Rowan, and then turned her back to both of them and looked out the window into the fading afternoon light.

"Tell it to me again," she said softly.

She managed to keep the rage from her voice, but it radiated from her body like heat off sunbaked earth in midsummer. She sensed their trepidation, their uncertainty, but she let them live with it as the silence between them lengthened.

"I really don't see the point in going over it a second time," Pyson Wence replied.

She could picture his exchange of looks with Traunt Rowan, could picture as well the sullen, gimlet-eyed stare, the one that waffled between boredom and disdain, he was giving her back. She could picture the way his sharp Gnome features were tightening, eyes narrowing and mouth twisting into a crooked line. She had seen that look often enough to have it memorized. She knew when to expect it. Even thinking of it enraged her further.

"I just want to be sure I didn't miss anything," she said.

She remained turned away so that they couldn't see her face. The silence returned and lengthened slowly as she waited to see which of them would speak next. Until then, Pyson had done all the talking.

That was unusual, given the fact that it was Traunt Rowan who normally did the talking for them both. He was the one who stayed calm when there was bad news to deliver or an untenable position to defend. He was the steady one. Pyson was the weasel, the sly one, the manipulator, and perhaps they had decided that his skills were what would work best in their current predicament.

If they had possessed an ounce of sense between them, they would have realized that nothing would save them.

Pyson cleared his throat. "There is nothing to be gained from going over it all—"

"Tell it to me again!" she screamed, wheeling now to fix him with her white-hot glare.

Her tall, muscular body was taut and flexed, as if she might attack him. He blanched at her words, at her posture; he wilted under her glare. He turned small and insignificant. But he was quick-witted and adaptable, and he could return to form in a moment's time, so she gave him no hint of compassion, no suggestion that his lifeline would extend beyond the next moment.

"Cat got your tongue, Pyson?" she spit, taking a quick step toward him, causing him to take several back. "Is the task too difficult for you? Is repeating the words you just spoke too onerous, too demanding? I want to hear them again, Pyson. I want to hear you tell it all to me again! Now!"

"Let him be," Traunt Rowan said, speaking for the first time.

She shifted her angry gaze instantly. "Oh, so you would speak in his place, then? Do so, Traunt Rowan. Amuse me."

"No one is amused, Shadea. Your sarcasm is wasted. We are as angry as you are about what has happened. But it isn't anything we could have avoided. We thought the boy safely locked away."

"Yes, I'm sure you did!" she snapped. "Very much the way you thought his parents were safely locked away. But they escaped as well, didn't they? In fact, they escaped first! Odd. You were given some indication that your security was not all that tight, but that doesn't seem to have made any difference because you didn't change anything and so the boy escaped, too!"

Traunt Rowan shook his head. "The parents escaped because two of our number, misguided believers in the right of Grianne Ohmsford to be considered Ard Rhys even past all reasonable hope, helped them escape. Young Druids—Trefen Morys, whom we mistrusted already, and a girl about whom I know almost nothing. If not for them, the boy's parents would still be here, locked away. But we will get them back again."

She laughed at him. "You sent out word that you have their son, thinking that they will march right back to Paranor when they hear the news. You are deluded. They know what will happen if they return. Even to save their son, whom we don't, in fact, have anyway! You underestimated them once and you are doing so again! Besides, it makes no difference now whether we have them or not, does it?"

She stalked across the room to where the door to her sleeping chamber stood closed, flung it open, and knocked the Gnome guard who crouched with his ear to the door all the way across the hall and into the wall beyond, where he lay stunned and bleeding.

"Try to listen in on my conversations again, and I will cut your throat," she hissed, speaking to him in his own tongue, her voice thick and guttural in the Gnome way. "No one is to come near this door again until I open it!"

Without waiting for a response, she slammed the door shut, wheeling back on the other two. "They listen to everything, your trusted followers, Pyson. They listen and report to you, but that's going to stop right now."

Terror flickered in Pyson Wence's yellow eyes. She watched it shift into a hint of desperation and shook her head in disgust. "You are hopeless." She glanced disdainfully at Traunt Rowan. "Both of you."

She stalked across the room to the window and stared out into the coming night. She wished it would close around the Keep and swallow up everyone in it who had failed her. She wished it would swallow those traitors who had helped the Ohmsfords escape. She wished it would swallow up those fools who had taken sides against her in the matter, starting with Sen Dunsidan and Iridia Eleri.

She wheeled back around. "The parents escaped because you weren't smart enough to expect them to try!" she snapped at Traunt Rowan. "The boy escaped because you weren't smart enough to learn from the example of the parents! You took away the staff, you locked him in a cell, and you thought that was the end of it. *Wait for Shadea to return*, you thought. That was all that was necessary."

"I thought it sufficient, yes," Traunt Rowan replied tightly.

She gave him a withering glare. "It never occurred to you, I don't suppose, that you were bringing the boy to the one place he should never have been brought."

He frowned. "What do you mean?"

She stared at him without speaking, the weight of her gaze enough to crush another man. "You don't understand anything, do you? Neither of you understands what's happened."

Pyson Wence exhaled sharply. "We understand, Shadea. They've escaped, all of them. If you want to blame us, then do so. But we will get them back again."

"Will you?" she whispered.

She walked over to her writing desk and sat behind it, thinking that it might be time to put an end to them both. Why wait? With Terek Molt dead and Iridia turned traitor and perhaps something worse, these two were the last of those who had conspired with her to eliminate Grianne Ohmsford. Her grip on the Third Druid Order was strong enough now that she could afford to do away with them.

She considered the idea a moment longer before dismissing it. It was still too soon.

"You took a staff from the boy," she said to Traunt Rowan. "It had rune markings carved up and down its length. The boy tried to hide it from you, but you knew it was a talisman." She paused. "Do you know what it does?"

The tall man shook his head. "No."

"You took it away from him and you put it in this room?"

"I used magic to suspend it in a cradle so that it would wait undisturbed for your return."

"Except that the boy or this Elven girl who helped him escape found a way to undo your magic. So now the staff is gone as well as the boy. "

He stared at her wordlessly.

"Where, Traunt Rowan? Where do you think they went?"

He shook his head. "He was trapped in this room with the girl when we found them. The girl has the use of Druid magic. Rudimentary, but effective. She held us off long enough for him to find another way out. Perhaps out one of the windows or maybe into a secret passageway, like the one you used to get access to Grianne Ohmsford while she slept."

"But you searched?"

"Everywhere."

She rose from the desk and came out to stand in front of him. "Think back. That boy has been on a mission from the beginning. He has been searching for something that will help him find his missing aunt, his beloved aunt. Tagwen went with him, then Ahren Elessedil and Kermadec. They all went with him. That suggests they believed in him. What is it that they thought this boy could do? I'll tell you what. They thought he could find a way to get inside the Forbidding."

"That's ridiculous," Pyson Wence snapped.

"They didn't think so," she snapped back. "Ahren Elessedil gave his life to help that boy. We might assume that he had a good reason for doing so. We might even assume he thought the boy's life more important than his own. Why would he think that? Because the boy was the best hope any of them had of reaching Grianne Ohmsford inside the Forbidding! That being so, the one thing we didn't want to do was to bring him anywhere near the place where she went in! Especially after you caught him trying to hide a talisman of unknown origin and power!" She paused, looking from face to face. "But that was exactly what you did. Now both are gone, the boy and his staff, vanished into thin air in this very room."

She took a deep breath. "Take a moment and think it through carefully. Where do you think they are?"

Traunt Rowan's face had gone white. "That isn't possible," he whispered. "No one can get into the Forbidding."

She gave him a tight smile. "We did."

He stared at her, unable to put words to what he was thinking.

"There is one way to find out if I am right," she said softly. "You do still have the Elven girl locked away, don't you? She hasn't escaped with the others, has she?"

Traunt Rowan flushed. "We have her."

"Bring her to me."

He left at once, taking Pyson Wence with him. Eyes straight ahead as they stalked through the doorway, neither of them glanced at her on their way out.

Good, she thought. *Let them think about what they have done. Let them dwell on it a little and consider what might be in store for them if I am right.*

She stood alone in her chambers and despaired over how convoluted things had become. Their plan had been a simple one in the beginning—confine Grianne Ohmsford to the Forbidding and take control of the Druid order. Sen Dunsidan had given them the liquid night, and she had found a way to use it. The plan had worked exactly as it was supposed to work, but since then the situation had spiraled steadily out of control. It had begun with that boy, Penderrin Ohmsford. Why it had begun with him rather than with his more experienced and more deeply talented father, she still didn't know. Nor did she know even now exactly what it was that he had set out to do, even though she was pretty sure that he had found a way to do it. If this Elven girl confirmed her suspicions about where he was, she would have to take new measures to protect herself. She had come too far and suffered too much to think of giving up what she had gained. The rest of them could do as they wished, if she let them live long enough, but she had set her mind on her own course of action and did not intend to deviate from it.

Grianne Ohmsford was powerful, but she was also mortal. By now, she could be dead. By now, she *should* be.

But a nagging certainty whispered that she wasn't.

Better I die than that I concede anything to her. Or to that boy.

She imagined momentarily what she would do to Penderrin Ohmsford if she somehow managed to get her hands on him. The image that came to mind made her shiver.

When Traunt Rowan and Pyson Wence reappeared with the Elven girl, Shadea was surprised to see how small and vulnerable looking she was; she had imagined the girl larger and more imposing. The Gnome Hunter clothing she wore, obviously stolen to provide her with a disguise, was ill fitting, loose, and made her look smaller still. But when she saw Shadea, she displayed a look of such obvious defiance that it instantly infuriated the sorceress.

Little fool!

She walked up to the girl without a word, snatched her by her clothing so that she was off balance, and struck her hard across the face. The blow was delivered open-handed, so as not to break anything, but the sound of it caused Traunt Rowan to flinch. The force of the slap sent the girl sprawling. Without waiting for her to recover, Shadea stalked over to where she lay, grabbed another handful of clothing, and hauled her back to her feet.

Then she placed her face inches from the girl's. "That was to give you some small idea of how I feel about what you have done. It should also indicate what sort of trouble you are in."

The defiance was gone from the girl's face, replaced by a sullen acceptance of her fate. Shadea gave her a moment to recover, to let the words sink in, then struck her again, knocking her to the floor once more.

This time when she stood the girl up again, there were tears in her eyes. "It hurt more this time, didn't it?" Shadea asked softly. "But I haven't begun to hurt you yet. What is your name?"

When the girl didn't answer fast enough, Shadea struck her again, twice, the open-handed blows delivered first to one side of her face and then to the other. The girl's head snapped back and forth with the blows, and she gasped audibly with each one. Shadea gripped her clothing with her free hand so that she couldn't fall, kept her standing upright, sagging slightly from the attack.

"Your name, girl," she repeated. "You are an Elessedil or you are a thief because only one or the other would possess the Elfstones. Which is it?"

"Khyber Elessedil," the girl whispered. Her face was already beginning to redden and swell.

Shadea glanced at her companions, both of whom shook their heads. Neither recognized anything beyond the *Elessedil* part of the name.

"What are you to Kellen Elessedil?" Shadea snapped.

"He is my brother."

"Was," Shadea corrected. "He's dead. Killed on the Prekkendorran almost a week ago."

She watched the girl's gaze lift to meet hers and saw more tears fill her eyes. Good. She was already beginning to come apart. This wouldn't be so hard.

"You are all alone, Khyber Elessedil," she whispered, her voice flat and emotionless. "No one even knows you are here, save those you left stranded in the ruins of Stridegate and the boy you helped escape. I wouldn't expect any help from them, if I were you. Nor from any other source. You no longer possess the Elfstones; I have them safely tucked away. You have no real Druid magic to help you escape; you are a neophyte. Your fate is sealed. If you want to live, you will tell me exactly what I want to know. Are you listening to me?"

The girl nodded, but there was a hint of defiance still in her dark eyes. Shadea smiled. Foolish bravado.

She reached inside the girl's clothing, found a place where the flesh was soft and vulnerable, fastened her fingers like a vise, and twisted. The girl screamed with pain, her body jerking in an effort to get free. Shadea held her fast and twisted harder.

"Are you listening carefully?" she hissed.

The girl nodded, her eyes shut against the pain. "Then be quick to answer when I ask you a question." She withdrew her hand. "I can cause you a great deal more pain than a few slaps across the face and a little twisting of your tender parts. I can hurt you in places you haven't even begun to think about. I can make you beg for me to kill you. I learned how while I served with the Federation army on the Prekkendorran. I learned that and a good deal more that you don't want to know anything about!"

She paused. "Let's try it again. I ask a question, you give me an answer. Where did Penderrin Ohmsford go?"

The girl exhaled sharply, her head sagging. "Into the Forbidding. After the Ard Rhys."

Shadea glanced disdainfully at Traunt Rowan and Pyson Wence. *Hear that?* Her eyes challenged them to say otherwise. "How did he get into the Forbidding? No one can go there without magic. Was it the staff he carried out of Stridegate that let him do so?"

The girl nodded again and swallowed thickly.

"How did he find this staff?" She was furious at the idea of it, enraged that such a talisman even existed. "How did he know what it would do?" She reached down and yanked the girl's chin off her chest, pinching her jaws. "Speak to me, you little fool!"

The dark eyes opened, filled with hate. "The King of the Silver River told him."

Shadea stared at her wordlessly, then let her head drop down again. A Faerie creature was aiding the boy. No wonder he had found a way. She refused to look at her Druid allies, afraid of what she would see in their eyes after hearing that.

She snatched a handful of the girl's close-cropped hair and pulled her head back up again. "Why this boy?" she demanded. "Why him? Why not his father? His father is Bek Ohmsford, brother to Grianne. He is the one with real magic. What does this boy have that brought the King of the Silver River to him?"

The girl shook her head slowly. "I don't know. Something different. Something . . ."

"If he succeeds, if he finds Grianne Ohmsford, what happens then? How does he get back?"

"The staff."

"The staff? The staff what? What does it do?" She shook the girl until she could hear her bones crack. "What does the staff do, little Elven girl? How does it work?"

The girl shuddered. "Brings . . . them back . . . together. To the place . . . they went in."

She sagged heavily, and Shadea realized she had fainted. Too much pain, apparently. She wasn't as strong as she had tried to make herself appear. She looked frail, and she was. A poor ally to the boy. But then they were all poor allies, those who had sought to help him, the living and the dead. He had wasted himself relying on them. Whatever chance he had, it did not lie with the likes of this girl and Tagwen and Kermadec and his Rock Trolls.

She flung the girl to the floor and let her lie. Her mind raced. It didn't matter if the boy had crossed over into the Forbidding. It didn't matter if he had found a temporary ally in a spirit creature. What mattered was that his chances of surviving inside the Forbidding were much less than those of Grianne Ohmsford, and hers were poor. What mattered was that if he somehow got *out* of the Forbidding, she must reduce those chances to zero.

She exhaled sharply, her focus on what was needed sharp and clear. She understood the situation perfectly. If Grianne Ohmsford and the boy must return the same way they went in, then they must come back through the very chamber in which she now stood. That gave her a distinct advantage, and she intended to make use of it.

She turned toward her allies. If either had been startled by what they had heard, they had managed to recover their composure.

Pyson Wence wore his sly, cautious look. Traunt Rowan was steady-eyed and stone-faced against whatever she had to offer.

She surprised them. "What's done is done," she said quietly. "It was as much my fault as it was yours. I am the one who leads; I am the one who must bear responsibility for any failure. I should have taken better precautions before going south to Arishaig. I regret that, but there is nothing to be gained by dwelling on it. Let us consider instead what we must do to compensate."

She moved over to the window and beckoned for them to join her. They did so with a certain degree of hesitation. Neither was convinced that she had undergone a real change of heart.

"The boy is inside the Forbidding searching for his aunt. He might find her, if both can manage to stay alive long enough. He might even manage to bring her back again, through the wall of the Forbidding, using whatever magic it is that this staff gives him. I don't think it is likely or even possible, but I don't want to chance being wrong."

She spoke in a whisper, so that they were forced to bend close. She spoke as if she were in fear of being overheard. In truth, she simply wanted them to think she was taking them into her confidence. Which, in a way, she was. She just wasn't doing so for the reasons they thought.

"We know that the staff's magic will bring them to these chambers. We must be waiting for them if that happens. More to the point, we must find a way to make certain that they will be rendered helpless. Even if we are not here, personally, to intercept them, we must make certain that it doesn't matter, that they are caged and stripped of their power and made prisoners. They must be given no chance to use their magic—especially Grianne Ohmsford. They must be disarmed."

"You make this sound so easy, Shadea," Pyson Wence sneered. "As if disarming a Druid of Grianne Ohmsford's power were easily within our means. But it isn't, is it? Catching her off guard and vulnerable was our best chance. She won't be caught napping a second time. She will come back through that doorway like a whirlwind and we will all be swept away!"

Shadea gave him a pitying smile. "Such dramatics, Pyson. You would think she frightened you. Are you frightened of her?"

"We both have a healthy respect for what she will likely do to us if she gets the chance," Traunt Rowan answered for him. "As should you."

She gave him a quick shake of her head. "I don't respect anyone who misuses power as she has. I don't respect anyone with her history. She is an animal, and I will see her caged or put down."

"Brave words, Shadea." He looked less than convinced. "How do you intend to give them weight?"

She shrugged. "We'll create a triagenel," she said.

For the first time that afternoon, she saw agreement reflected in their eyes.

"First," she declared, when they had finished discussing how the triagenel would be achieved, "we have to dispose of the girl. She's told us what we want to know about the boy. She has no further use. Sooner or later, someone will come looking for her, and I don't want them to find her here."

Pyson Wence shrugged. "What do you want done with her?"

"Have your Gnome Hunters take her down to the furnaces and throw her in." She glanced at the girl, who still lay unconscious on the floor. "She won't be much trouble, but bind her anyway. Here, take these and throw them in, as well."

She handed the pouch with the Elfstones to Traunt Rowan. He stared at them in disbelief. "But, Shadea—"

"They're useless to us," she interrupted quickly. "Only Elves can make use of their magic. We're not Elves. If we can't make use of them, let's see to it that no one else can, either. Besides, they are markers. If anyone finds them on us or at Paranor, they will have found a link to the girl. We don't want that. No, throw them into the furnace and be done with it. Come back here when it is finished, and we will begin building the triagenel."

When they were gone, taking the girl and the Elfstones with them, she slipped from the room and went down through the corridors and stairwells of the Keep to a small guardroom that sat near the back of the north wall. *A triagenel is strong enough to hold even Grianne Ohmsford,* she was thinking as she moved along the passageways. Traunt Rowan and Pyson Wence recognized this and so were willing to offer their talents to form it. Three magics from three separate sources, combined in the right way, created a net that would contain and neutralize even the most powerful magic wielder. It took time and effort to build a triagenel, but she had never heard of anyone who was able to overcome one once caught in it. Stringing it about the perimeters of the room would assure them of snaring anyone who entered. There was no escaping a triagenel, once caught in it. Only its creators could undo it. Grianne Ohmsford and the boy would be snared like rabbits—or more like wolves—but snared nevertheless. By the time the triagenel was released, their lives would be over.

She considered the possibility that the triagenel would disintegrate before they were ready to attempt their return. It enjoyed only a limited lifetime, only a finite period of existence because the magic was so powerful that eventually it became unstable and collapsed. But another could be built. And another after that, should the need arise. At some point, it would be clear that her victims weren't coming back after all, and the effort to create further triagenels could be abandoned.

She was satisfied that her plan would work. She was confident that she could undo the damage that her inept allies had created.

She reached a heavy wooden door at the end of a darkened passageway set in the recesses of the northeast tower. She rapped sharply on it and heard a murmur of voices and a furtive scuffling from the room beyond. Then the lock released and a bearded face thrust into view. Eyes that were mean and piggish fixed on her, then looked quickly away. The man's head disappeared back inside the chamber.

"Gresheren!" he hissed.

She waited until a second man appeared, this one big and hulking, but with a sharper, more cunning look to him. He bowed to her immediately and stepped outside the room and into the hallway, closing the door behind him.

"Mistress," he greeted. "You have need of me?"

She took him away from the door and into the shadows. "I have a job for you. I want you to select four of your best men to dispose of someone. They will have the advantage of numbers and surprise, but that is likely all. They must strike quickly and surely. There will be no second chance. If they succeed and return alive, I will give them a year's pay for their efforts."

"Fair enough, Mistress," he rumbled. "More than fair. Who is it that you want killed?"

"A traitor, Gresheren," she told him. "A Druid traitor."

SIXTEEN

When Traunt Rowan threw her over his shoulder and carried her from the room, Khyber Elessedil was not unconscious. She was pretending to be, as she had pretended to be for most of the time after Shadea had thrown her down. But she was awake.

It was a trick of elemental magic she had learned from Ahren. If she was suffering too much pain, whatever the reason, she could distance herself from her anguish. She could quite literally go outside her body; she could disconnect her emotional self from her physical self. She couldn't do it for long, only a couple of minutes at a time. When the ruse worked, it gave her the appearance of being unconscious or asleep. In the past, the attempt was sometimes unsuccessful because her concentration failed. She had good reason not to let it fail here—the pain Shadea was inflicting on her was excruciating.

Once she appeared unconscious and Shadea lost interest in her, she slipped back inside her pain-racked body, hoping the Druids were preoccupied enough that they would let her be. She listened to what they had to say, though. She listened carefully. Some of it was inaudible to her, the words whispered too softly and from too far away to be heard clearly. But she heard enough to get the gist of what they were deciding, especially when it came to the part about disposing of her.

All she could think about after that was, *They're going to kill me.*

She had to do something to save herself—anything—but she had no idea what that might be. She was without weapons, including the Elfstones, and weak with pain and fear. The ordeal at Shadea's hands, while not breaking her, had left parts of her physically and emotionally drained. She had thought herself tougher than she was; Shadea had been right about that. It was a sobering experience to discover how badly mistaken she had been.

She lay limp over Traunt Rowan's shoulder, her eyes closed, but her mind racing. She heard the tall Druid's breathing as he carried her. She heard the sound of Pyson Wence walking next to them, his gait just different enough from his companion's to be distinctive. There were only the two of them; it was probably the best numerical odds she would get. But she knew that favorable odds alone weren't going to be enough to save her.

At that point, she didn't know what was going to be enough, and she was trying hard not to panic.

She had been confined to a cell in the depths of the Keep since they had broken into the chambers of the Ard Rhys two days earlier and overpowered her. Penderrin was gone into the Forbidding by then, swept away by the magic of the darkwand, and when they discovered she was alone, they tried to make her tell them where he was. She had feigned ignorance, as if his disappearance were as confusing to her as it was to them. She had suggested every false possibility she could think of, and they had seemed all too willing to accept that somewhere in the web of her deceptive explanations they would find the truth.

They had not tortured her or mistreated her in any way to discover if she lied, which had surprised her. She had come to understand why; they had saved her for Shadea a'Ru. They had saved her for someone who understood how to employ torture in the most effective way. Still racked with pain, still humiliated by her collapse, she knew that she would have told the sorceress anything.

In fact, she had told her more than enough. Shadea was now aware that Pen was inside the Forbidding, searching for the Ard Rhys. She knew that if the boy found his aunt, they would return with the aid of the darkwand to the chambers of the Ard Rhys. Shadea would be waiting for them. The damage to the chamber entry in the battle of two days earlier had been repaired. It would be an easy matter to seal off the room. Once that was done, Shadea could implement a triagenel.

Even an apprentice Druid like Khyber understood what a triagenel was. Every practitioner of magic in the Four Lands aspired to a level of excellence that would allow his or her participation in the creation of such a wonder. Triagenels were the most difficult form of magic to employ because they required the talents of not one, but three practitioners of equally advanced abilities. Druids were the only ones she had ever heard of who even thought about trying to create triagenels. Even then, under current Druid law, it could not be done without the authorization and supervision of the Ard Rhys. Few attempts at a triagenel had been made in her lifetime, and she did not know the details of any of them. Most such attempts were little more than forms of practice to give credence to the belief that a Druid had advanced far enough in his or her studies to combine talents with others with similar aspirations. A successful attempt was proof of mastery of a certain level of magic.

There was little doubt in Khyber's mind that Shadea and the other two were sufficiently talented to create a triagenel that could imprison, if not completely incapacitate, even as gifted a magic wielder as Grianne Ohmsford. A combination of three strong magics was just too much for one, even if the one was immensely powerful. If Grianne and Pen returned through the Forbidding after the triagenel had been set in place, they would be caught in a deadly trap.

And she was the only one who could prevent it. Aside from the three who would create the triagenel, she was the only one who knew about it. If she died in the furnace, as they intended, the chances of the Ard Rhys and Pen making a successful return were narrowed to almost nothing.

She had been carried down several levels by them, the Druids taking the back stairs to avoid being seen, keeping to the little-used parts of the Keep. She hung limply over Traunt Rowan's broad shoulder, still pretending at unconsciousness, trying to devise a plan. The idea of challenging two powerful Druids at the same time was not a consideration. She had to wait until they had delivered her to the Gnome Hunters before she could act.

She did not have to wait long. They quickly reached the ground level of the Keep and took her into a room filled with racks of weapons and armor. She risked a quick look around and caught glimpses of heavy wooden benches scarred by blades and fire, boxes of cutting tools, and grinding machines clamped in place. Bits and pieces of metal lay scattered across the worn surfaces of the benches and stone floor, and the air smelled of oil and was thick with dust.

Traunt Rowan slid her off his shoulder and onto the floor and left her in a heap. She lay without moving, eyes closed.

"Wait here," Pyson Wence said to him and went out again.

Khyber waited until she heard the door close, then waited some more in the ensuing silence. She felt Traunt Rowan's eyes on her, as if he was waiting for her to move, to reveal her subterfuge to him. She forced herself to remain exactly as he had left her, limp and unmoving, eyes closed. She let her breathing slow, and she listened for his movements.

When, moments later, she heard him turn away from her, she risked a quick look. He was perusing the room, studying the racks of weapons and armor. She shifted her gaze just enough that she could glimpse the floor about her. She searched for a weapon she could use to protect herself. But there were no weapons to be found, nothing but scraps of metal, leavings from the workbenches. Traunt Rowan moved away a few steps, his hand reaching out to feel the flat of a broadsword. Her eyes skipped across the littered surface of the floor, scanning desperately through the debris. There were blades everywhere, all of them out of reach.

Then she caught sight of something that might prove useful. She eased an outflung arm carefully toward a rough piece of metal, its edge razor-sharp. She pulled the scrap into the palm of her hand and closed her fingers around it carefully.

It was not much of a weapon, but it would have to do.

Traunt Rowan glanced back at her suddenly, but she had her eyes closed again and her body limp. He studied her nevertheless, as if noticing that her position had changed. She held her breath, waiting.

Then the door opened, and Pyson Wence reappeared. Four Gnome Hunters followed him in, then moved over to where she lay, rolled her over, and secured her wrists and ankles with heavy cord. Lying limp and unmoving, she let them do as they wished without signaling that she knew what was happening. Their strong, wiry hands roamed across her body, turning her this way and that, causing a wave of revulsion to run through her. Her instincts screamed at her to fight back, to break free while she still had the chance, before she was trussed so tightly she could not. But she knew that would be a mistake. She clutched the jagged piece of metal in her hand, her only real chance of surviving this, and forced herself to stay quiet.

When they were done binding her, they tied a rag about her mouth, covering it so completely that she was forced to begin breathing through her nose.

The Gnomes stood up, looking back at Pyson Wence. The Druid spoke to them softly, then handed one the pouch that contained the Elfstones. "I don't like giving these up," he said to Traunt Rowan. "It seems such a waste."

"Getting caught with them would be a death sentence," the other replied. "Shadea is right. Better to be rid of them." He paused. "Can we trust these four to do what is needed and keep silent afterward?"

"They understand their orders."

"Then let's be done with it."

Pyson Wence said something further, and one of the four picked Khyber up off the floor, tossed her over his shoulder as if she were no more than a sack of grain, and followed the other three out the door and into the torchlit hallway beyond.

She knew where they were taking her. She knew what they intended to do with her once they got there.

It was all she could do to keep from screaming.

They went deep into the bowels of the Keep, along twisting passageways that grew increasingly narrow and steadily darker, down stairways thick with gloom and heavy with damp. Eventually there were no wall-mounted torches to brighten the way, and the Gnomes were forced to light and carry their own. Khyber heard the drip of water and could smell the minerals the water contained. The gloom was impenetrable after more than a few feet, even with the torchlight to chase it back. In the silence, the only sounds were the labored breathing of the Gnomes and the measured beat of their footfalls.

If she had been afraid before, she was terrified now.

But she fought down her terror because she knew that if she panicked she was finished. She could open her eyes without fear of being discovered and did so. It was too dark for her captors to see her eyes, and she was hanging head-down anyway, her face obscured by the cloak of the guard who bore her. She had gained a fresh measure of anonymity. She was little more than a dark lump. She wondered if the men knew who she was; she wondered if they cared. She tried to imagine what it must have taken to imbue them with such blind obedience. Soldiers did what they were told and did not ask questions, she supposed. It was something she understood but would never accept.

She maneuvered the scrap of metal between her fingers until she had a good grip on it and began to saw at her bonds. She did so slowly and carefully, trying her best to disguise her movements by keeping them small and the rest of her body still. It was harder than she had expected because a certain amount of force was required to make any progress with the cutting. She did not know how long she had to free herself. She felt as if she had no time at all. She wanted to hurry her efforts, to work harder, to throw caution to the winds, to just be free. But Ahren had taught her that haste was your worst enemy when you were threatened, that mistakes were too easily made and chances lost. Patience was what would save you. Every fiber in her body shrieked at her to hurry, to cut faster, but she held herself in check.

Be patient.

Trussed and helpless, on her way to her own death, she wanted to be anything but.

Time slipped away, precious and fluid. She could not hold it back. She worked the metal diligently, even though by then her own fingers were cut and bleeding from the effort and the metal shard dangerously slippery. She almost dropped it several times, and she was forced more than once to cease her efforts long enough to wipe clean the shard and her fingers. She smelled her blood, coppery and rank. She could smell her own fear, the sweat of her body. She found that she was crying and hadn't even been aware of it.

She sawed harder, working diligently against the stubborn bonds as her captors trudged on, dark and silent wraiths in the gloom. Burning pitch hissed and spit at the ends of the brands they carried, the flames glinting in the dark like eyes, throwing shadows everywhere. She would be seen, she kept thinking, if she kept this up much longer. She would be caught out.

The air was growing warmer.

Her eyes snapped up as if to discover the reason, even though she already knew it. They were getting close to the furnace and the fire pits that fed it.

The bonds that secured her wrists snapped, nearly falling away before she caught them in her fingers and held them in place. She was free. She flexed her hands, first one, then the other, careful of her movements. Her ankles were still bound, but there was no help for it. She couldn't wait any longer. She had to act now.

But what was she going to do?

Her eyes skittered everywhere, then stopped. The butt of her captor's long knife protruded from its sheath less than a foot away from where her head hung down.

Momentary panic set in. She had never killed anyone. She had never had to fight for her life, never been threatened with serious harm until these past few weeks. Ahren had taught her how to defend herself, but she had never tested her skills in a situation even remotely like this one. She was just a girl, really. She was barely grown.

But they were going to kill her.

She swallowed hard, the panic deepening, threatening to immobilize her. She shouldn't be here. This shouldn't be happening. If she hadn't been so stubborn about going with Ahren and Pen, if she hadn't insisted on the quest being made in the first place, if she hadn't taken the Elfstones from where they were kept hidden away . . .

Her concentration faltered, and the metal shard slipped from her fingers and fell to the passageway floor with an audible *ping*.

She reacted without thinking, snatching the long knife from its sheath and burying it deep in the back of the Gnome Hunter carrying her. She heard his gasp of dismay and felt his body lurch and then collapse beneath her. She went down with him, rolled clear, and came to rest against one wall, the knife still in her hands, yanked free of the dead man's body. She caught a glimpse of the other three Gnomes as they wheeled back to see what was happening, momentarily confused but already reaching for their weapons. Her legs were still bound, and she could not flee them. She was trapped.

She dropped the knife instantly and began weaving her hands to summon a protective magic.

Please!

The magic responded, and the torches flared and went out, leaving the passageway shrouded in darkness.

Instantly, she was moving, dragging herself along the wall and away from her captors, the long knife clutched in one hand. The Gnome Hunters cursed as they stumbled about in the dark, running up against each other and tripping over their dead companion. She rolled all the way across the passage, trying to get as far away from them as she could manage. She had only moments before they found her, whatever she did, and she had to free her legs before that happened.

Backed against the far wall, she reached down and began cutting frantically at the bonds that wrapped her ankles. The blade of the knife was sharper and more efficient than the metal shard and severed the ropes in seconds.

She was struggling to her feet when the first of them, close enough by that time to hear her movements, thrust his short sword blindly into the rock wall only inches from her head. She reacted instantly, driving her own blade deep into his chest. He roared in pain and fear and staggered away from her, the blade still buried in his body. Weaponless, she backed her way along the wall, hearing the stricken man's grunts and moans mix with the guttural whispers of the two who remained. They would fan out along both walls and come toward her until they found her. But they would be more cautious. She would not get a chance to catch them unawares again.

She kept moving away, trying to think what to do. She could flee, if she chose, but her instincts told her that, unarmed and unfamiliar with the corridors, it would be impossible to get far in the blackness. The Gnomes, more at home in the dark, would hunt her down.

She heard them moving toward her already, their boots and clothing soft rustles and scuffs in the silence.

She needed another magic, she thought. But she did not know killing magic, so whatever she tried, it would only buy her a little more time. Perhaps it would gain her another weapon, but could she use it after what had happened? The memory of her blade sinking into the Gnomes she had killed was fresh and sharp and made her shudder. She wasn't sure she could do that again. She wasn't sure she should even try.

But she must try something.

Tell me what I should do, Ahren!

He couldn't, of course—not even in her memories of all he had taught her—because nowhere in his instruction had he addressed such a situation. He had been teaching her basic elemental magic right up to the moment they had set out for the Lazareen. True, anticipating the dangers they would face, he had given her harder lessons on the way, but none of them seemed useful against furious Gnome Hunters stalking her in pitch-black caverns.

They were closing on her, the sounds of their approach more distinct. She had no time left.

Her back against the passageway wall, she turned toward them, lifted her hands, whispered into the darkness and used her fingers to guide the magic accordingly, then clapped her hands to her head. Instantly, the passageway was filled with blinding light, its brilliance equal to the intensity of the sun at midday. With her hands, Khyber shielded her eyes against the sudden glare, but the Gnomes were caught unprepared and left momentarily blinded. She charged right at them, dodged their groping hands and slashing blades and broke into the clear to race down the corridor in the direction of the furnace, the explosion of light behind her revealing the way.

The Gnomes were after her at once, heavy footfalls echoing thunderously, shouts and curses rising up. She ran faster. She had no plan but to get away from them, to reach the confluence of passageways at the furnace and disappear into them. Let them hunt for her then, if they wished. She would be much harder to find once they could no longer see her.

A wave of heat suddenly washed over her, surging out of the gloom ahead. Pale light flickered from far down at the end of the narrowing passageway, the glow of the pit fires rising into the furnace room. Her goal was in sight.

Then something slammed into her, low on her right side, spinning her around and filling her with a wash of pain and shock. A dagger jutted from the fleshy part of her side. It felt as if a red-hot poker had been jammed into her, but she couldn't afford to take time to stop and pull the dagger free. She ran on instead, fighting down her sudden sense of weakness, hardening her resolve to reach the furnace room. Behind her, the Gnome Hunters were running to catch up, grunting from the effort, their breathing quick and heavy.

She reached the furnace just ahead of them, breaking free of the darkness in a rush that carried her right up against the metal railing of the catwalk that encircled the pit. She caught herself just in time, so close to the fires that she felt her hair singe and her lungs burn. She pushed away hurriedly and began to stagger along the catwalk. The fire pit yawned to one side, a deep, glowing chasm within which the earth's exposed magma burned fiercely, the source of the Keep's underground heat. Even with the fires dampened and the vents to the chamber open wide, the heat was all but unbearable.

She searched frantically for a way out. Several doors were set in the chamber walls, and across the way a spiral staircase wound upward to another. All were closed. She hurried to the nearest and tried to open it. It refused to budge.

Behind her, the Gnome Hunters stumbled into the chamber and caught sight of her. They hesitated for a moment, then split apart, one circling one way about the catwalk, one circling the other, trapping her between them. She moved quickly to the second door and pulled on the handle. It was locked, as well. The heat from the furnace fires and the loss of blood from her wound were making her dizzy. She felt the sticky dampness of blood all down her back. Her strength was fading.

She was in danger of passing out.

Bracing herself against the chamber wall, she reached back and pulled the dagger free. The pain was excruciating, but she managed to keep from collapsing. She had to get out of there, had to get through one of these doors. Even as she thought of doing so, however, she saw that it was too late. They would see where she had gone and come after her. They would have no choice; they could not afford to let her get away. Telling their Druid masters that they had let her escape would cost them their lives. They had to know that. They would keep coming until either she was dead or they were.

She felt a moment of despair. There was no way out. She was no match for the Gnomes. She was barely able to move; her growing weakness was coupled now with light-headedness and a sense of dislocation.

But she was the only one who knew of the triagenel. She was the only one who could warn Pen and Grianne Ohmsford of the danger.

With an effort, she straightened. She had her magic. She had the dagger.

Don't let me fail.

She moved ahead as quickly as she could to the stairway that led up to the single closed door at its head, words and gestures forming tendrils of magic like invisible threads. As she reached the stairs, she pretended to stagger—a pretense that was only partially faked—stumbling and reaching out to catch herself. When she righted herself and moved on again, she left the dagger on the sixth step, at head height, point outward, tucked back against the riser where it wouldn't be seen right away by the Gnome approaching from behind, the one now closest to her. A dozen paces farther on, she turned to face him, her back to the wall, waiting as he crept toward her, his blades glinting wickedly in the glow of the fire pit.

Closer.

When he was even with the step on which the dagger rested, she snapped her hands sideways in a sharp motion that jerked taut the tendrils of magic she had surreptitiously woven and attached and sent the dagger flying off the step and into the Gnome's throat. The blow wasn't enough to kill him, but the shock of it caused him to stagger into the railing, dropping both weapons to clutch at the wound. She was on top of him instantly, snatching up his dagger and jamming it into his unprotected chest, then slamming her elbow against his face with such force that he toppled backwards over the railing and was gone.

She hung on the metal stanchion and stared down into the pit, gasping for breath. One left.

When she straightened, the final Gnome was crouched a dozen yards away, watching her. They stared at each other across the fire pit, measuring their chances. Having witnessed the fate of his companions, he was clearly in no hurry to rush things. He might try to wait her out, she thought. Blood loss and exhaustion would claim her eventually. All he had to do was be patient.

To force him to expose himself, she started toward the chamber doors again, looking as if she intended to make her escape. The Gnome hesitated, then reached for the quiver of javelins strapped to his back, intending to kill her without getting close enough to be killed in turn. She paused at the first of the doors she came to, watching as he freed the first of his darts and hefted it into throwing position. She moved to the railing and crouched down again, making herself as small a target as possible.

It will take magic to save me. Earth magic, elemental magic. A little more of what Ahren worked so hard to teach me.

She gritted her teeth against a fresh wave of pain and began working her hands in subtle motions, drawing on fire to save her. It was there in the pit, all she could ask for, enough to accomplish anything, enough to put an end to this.

If I can remember how to summon it.

Her concentration faltered momentarily as she allowed herself to be distracted by the Gnome's stealthy approach, but she refocused instantly. *Steady your efforts.* Her head swam. She could hear Ahren speaking to her, gently encouraging, guiding her movements and her thoughts, walking her through the exercise. It was only an exercise, after all. It was only a little test to see what she had learned.

Close enough to act, the Gnome came out of his crouch, javelin raised to throw, and she snapped her hands upward in response, a lifting motion that suggested the splashing of water from a basin. But it was fire she was summoning, and it exploded from the furnace in a sudden wave to engulf the Gnome. Her attacker screamed in terror as his clothing caught fire, then his skin, then everything around him. He beat at the flames frantically, dropping his weapons, staggering away from the railing, falling onto the catwalk and rolling over and over. But the magic-summoned fire would not go out, his body the fuel it had been seeking.

In seconds, he stopped moving completely, a blackened husk. The flames died out, and the fire disappeared.

Khyber Elessedil hung on the catwalk railing and closed her eyes.

SEVENTEEN

Rain, a blessing and a curse, fell in windblown sheets that draped the whole of the wetlands through which the Elves trudged. On the one hand, it kept the Federation airships grounded, lessening considerably the chances that their enemy would discover their intentions. No vessel could fly safely in such weather, not even the little three-man skiffs that both sides preferred for scouting missions and which normally were so reliable. On the other hand, it made foot passage through the northwest bottom country all but impossible. Their enemies might not be able to see them, but they, in turn, could barely see the noses in front of their faces.

Pied Sanderling, at the point of the scouting patrol he led, heard something move just ahead and signaled silently for a halt. The three men spread out behind him froze, weapons ready. Somewhere behind them, lost in the mist and rain, the rest of his makeshift army followed, strung out through the wetlands like a long snake, relying on him to act as its eyes. They had been on the march for the better part of three days with no sleep in the last two. The weather had turned foul the first day and hadn't improved since. It hadn't mattered as much in the beginning, when they were still in the hill country north, the ground rolling but solid beneath their feet. Then the rain provided concealment from those who hunted them. But the wetlands were a treacherous bog that swallowed men whole and through which passage was difficult under the best of circumstances. The decision to go that way had been based on Pied's certainty that the Federation's perception of them as little more than harmless remnants of a defeated Elven army had changed with their destruction of the enemy force sent to track them down and finish them off. The hunt for them now would be intensive. Moreover, it would come from the broader, less congested country west, which persuaded him to choose the more difficult eastern route for his own command.

He just hoped that the veteran scout Whyl, on whom he had relied in making that decision, knew what he was talking about when he had assured Pied that there was passage through. It was his country, and he knew it as well as anyone in the Elven command. But in such miserable weather, it was difficult to find your way out of your own backyard. If Whyl was even a little mistaken or had in any way misjudged . . .

He broke off thinking about it. Doubts would not help them. Whyl was with the patrol and had not seemed confused even in the face of the disorienting weather. Pied had to trust him. He had no one else.

"Captain," the veteran whispered, standing at his elbow and pointing ahead into the rain.

At first, the whole of the landscape was gray and rain-washed, earth and sky looking very much the same. Pied didn't see anything. But then a figure appeared, crouched and hesitant.

Troon.

She gave a quick wave of recognition and hurried up to greet them. She was small and compact with unusual gray eyes and impish features. Her clothing was sodden and muddied, and her short-cropped dark hair had flattened against her head like a helmet. She was the best of his Home Guard Trackers, his first choice even before Acrolace had gone down.

"We are almost through," she whispered as they clustered around her, breaking into a smile in response to theirs.

"You're sure?" Pied pressed. "No mistaking a skirmish line for the real thing?"

"No mistake. The Federation lines are less than half a mile away. They have surrounded the east plateau on three sides, laying siege to Droshen's Free-born, but as yet they haven't broken through. I couldn't tell about the condition of the airship fleet; I couldn't get close enough to make certain. But the Free-born still hold the high ground."

"Then they haven't gotten the *Dechtera* aloft again so they can use that weapon." Pied reached out and gripped her shoulder. "Good work. And you also, Whyl," he added, turning to the veteran scout. "We're where we want to be, thanks to you."

"What happens now?" Troon asked. Rain dripped off her face in steady rivulets.

Pied shook his head. He wasn't sure of that himself. "First, we bring up the army."

He sent one of the members of his patrol back with the news, then hunkered down to wait. He sat apart from the others, giving himself time and space to think things through. At such times he wished he had Drumundoon with him to act as a sounding board. But his aide was still gone, hopefully in Arborlon, breaking the news of the disaster on the Prekkendorran to Arling and seeking the reinforcements Pied had requested. He wondered how successful Drum had been. Under Kellen Elessedil, such a request would have been granted with barely a second thought. But the King was dead, and Arling was Queen. Arling might not be so eager to commit further Elven forces to a cause she had never believed in, particularly when the request was coming from him.

How things changed.

Once, he could have asked her for anything. He had been close to her in ways that he had never been close to anyone else. He had thought they would be together forever. But Arling had grander plans. When she married Kellen, he had been devastated but had understood her reasons. Marrying the King of the Elves offered a chance for advancement that only a fool would refuse, and Arling was no one's fool. She had loved Pied, but not well enough to pass up an opportunity of that sort. She was always ambitious that way; she was always smart about her choices. He thought that her marriage to Kellen had lacked the passion of her relationship with him, but he realized that his perception might be mostly the result of wishful thinking. She had left him to marry his cousin, the King, and that made any sort of reasonable perspective difficult.

But she did not abandon him entirely. She had remained his friend, arranging for him to be named Captain of the Home Guard, advancing his career immeasurably. It was a gesture he did not mistake for anything but what it was, but which he appreciated never-theless. Over the years, she had come to rely on his advice in diffi-cult situations, seeking it surreptitiously, making it clear that Kellen must never know. By doing so, she revealed the lack of confidence she had in her husband's judgment. It was an attitude Pied shared, though both were loyal to and served him as King. Arling never at-tempted subterfuge or manipulation of the sort that might threaten the throne, but she was not above blunting Kellen's more impulsive behavior or reshaping his more ill-conceived plans when it was clear he was courting disaster of one sort or another. In most of those ef-forts, Pied was her willing ally.

It was a strange relationship the three shared, the product of lives that were so closely intertwined that it was impossible to separate out the different threads. Each understood the personal role that had been allotted to them; each accepted the roles of the others. But the emotional entanglements made it difficult for Pied, if not for Arling or the King. He would have preferred a different ending to the story than the one that had been thrust upon him, but that had never seemed possible.

Until now. Now, he wondered if the ending might be changed. Would Arling see him in a different light now that Kellen was dead? Could she feel about him again as she once had? He could barely make himself think about that without cringing. It felt like a betrayal. Arling might see it that way, as well.

Who was responsible for the safety of the King if not the Cap-tain of the Home Guard?

Ti Auberen appeared out of the haze and crouched down next to him, his tall frame bending close as he brushed the rain from his eyes. "Captain, the army is closing ranks behind us. Another half hour and the rear guard will have caught up and we will be ready to move. What are your orders?"

He glanced up at the big man, his thoughts of Arling scattered into the mist. "Ask Troon to come over."

The Elven Tracker came at once in response to his summons and dropped down beside him. They had known each other for most of their lives, friends before they were Elven Hunters, before he was her commander.

She gave him another of those quick, engaging smiles, and he smiled back. It was their way of acknowledging the depth of the relationship. "We're going to have to break through the Federation lines to reach the Free-born on the heights," he said. "Is there a place we might do that?"

She considered. "Breaking through isn't the problem; it's gaining the heights. There is a gate in the Free-born fortifications that wards a drift down off the heights west. That gate offers us our best chance. But Federation soldiers surround it to prevent a breakout."

"They think Vaden Wick might run?"

"I don't know. Maybe they think he might attack."

Pied grinned. "It would be like him. Can you get past the Federation lines and inside the fortifications?"

She shrugged. "Can I try it at night?"

He nodded. He could tell from the glint in her eyes that she relished the challenge. "I want you to tell Vaden Wick we will make our breakthrough tomorrow at sunrise. It would help our effort if he was to create a diversion that would draw attention elsewhere and stand ready to throw open the gates when we reach them."

"Sunrise, tomorrow," she repeated.

"Don't take any unnecessary risks. If you can't get through, come back. We'll find another way."

She reached out impulsively and patted his cheek. "Worry for someone who needs it, Captain. I will get through."

She arched an admonishing eyebrow at him, grinned at his obvious discomfort, then rose and hurried away.

By nightfall, she was gone. She left without saying anything further to anyone, slipping from the Elven camp as if her departure were of no consequence. She was like that, a steady presence who never made much of the dangerous work she did. Pied sometimes wondered why she continued to risk herself after so many years, but he could never bring himself to ask her. He felt the reasons were hers, and she was entitled to keep them private. It was enough that she was there for the Home Guard every time he called on her.

Unable to settle in, he slept poorly that night. With Drum gone, he lacked reassurance that things were in any sort of order and kept wondering what he had overlooked. He awoke well before sunrise, stiff and unrested, still dressed in the clothes he had worn for the past three days, rose from his blankets into the chilly morning air,

buckled on his weapons, and walked down through the camp to find
a cup of hot ale. It had quit raining, though the air was thick with the
smell of damp and mist hung in gauzy blankets across the whole of
the wilderness. They would march forward the last half mile when
the false dawn began to brighten the eastern sky and would be at the
backs of the Federation soldiers by true dawn. It would require that
they travel in silence, and he had given the order the previous night
that everything was to be lashed down or muffled. Whyl and two
other scouts would go on ahead to prevent unexpected encounters.
If things worked as he hoped, he would catch the Federation just rising and be on them before they knew what was happening.

He found his Elven Hunters mostly awake or coming awake, as
anxious as he was to get on with the effort of breaching the Federation lines and rejoining the Free-born army. Activity marked the
whole of the camp, and everywhere he walked he was greeted with
whispers and nods. He returned the greetings, aware of what they
meant. The men and women had come to believe in themselves
again, and he must see that they did not lose that newly rediscovered
self-confidence through any failure of his.

At the first indication of a graying in the east, the Elven command set out. They were formed up in units of fifty, with a commander of senior rank assigned to each. Erris Crewer had his archers
deployed to either side of the regular units, both Elven Hunter and
Home Guard, a screen against whatever they might encounter. They
moved forward quickly, trusting to the scouts, who had gone on
ahead, making their way through the deep gloom like wraiths.

Elves knew how to stay hidden when it was needed; it was one of
the first things they were taught while growing up, a part of their
heritage from the Old World. That day, in their approach to the Federation, it served them well. Before the sun crested the horizon, they
had reached the rear of the Federation siege lines and were able to
see how the enemy was deployed and to analyze what they would
have to do to get past. It was a daunting task. The Federation forces
easily outnumbered them three to one, even there, at that position,
and without regard for reinforcements that might be dispatched
from other parts of the siege line once the Elves' presence was discovered. The Federation soldiers were settled in behind fortifications
that had been erected over the previous week, when the Elves were
driven off the western heights and the rest of the Free-born allies

were trapped east. An extended line of pack animals and horses was picketed farther back, blocking the Elven way forward and offering still another obstacle that they must get past.

Pied took a long moment to consider how to proceed, weighing the choice of a breakthrough at a single point in the Federation line versus a breakthrough at several. The former kept things more tightly controlled, and he opted for it. They would all get through together or they would not get through at all.

He put the most dependable and seasoned of his Elven Hunters in the vanguard with Ti Auberen in command, wedged Erris Crewer and his archers in behind them with swordsmen and spear bearers on the flanks, passed the signal back to be ready to make a run for it when the front ranks broke from cover, and settled back to wait for the dawn.

We'll need help to do this, he was thinking as he watched the gray horizon slowly brighten.

Then a Federation picket that they had thought safely turned away wandered back through the lines and stumbled on them. He was dead almost immediately, killed by one of the archers, but not before he had gotten off a warning shout that caused heads to turn.

Pied never hesitated. "Elessedil!" he shouted, and the Elves took up the cry.

They broke from the cover of the gloom and the mist and charged through the Federation camp. Pied had been right in his assessment of the situation: The Federation soldiers were just beginning to stir from their sleep, and the Elves were in their midst before most even knew what was happening. The night watch fought back bravely but was swiftly overrun, and the Elves went through the camp virtually unopposed.

The Federation soldiers who manned the fortifications were better prepared, however, and the battle to get past them was bitter and hot. Trapped against their own walls, they fought like demons, slowing the Elven rush sufficiently that for a moment it nearly stalled. Pied pushed his way to the forefront of the fighting, shouting at Ti Auberen to keep moving, to break through the lines. Home Guard warded him every step of the way, fighting to keep the enemy from getting close. From the center of the rush, Elven archers sent flurries of arrows down the siege lines, forcing the soldiers who manned them to duck for cover. In a concerted rush, the Elves slammed into the fortifications. Sandbags, earthworks, and wooden slats gave way under the crush, and the Elves were through and streaming across the flats separating the siege lines from the heights.

Ahead, the Free-born gates were barely visible, a massive barrier formed of iron-reinforced timbers set into walls that stood twenty feet high. There was activity on those walls; Pied could see the movement from the soldiers manning them as he raced across the grasslands.

But the gates were not opening to them.

For just a moment, Pied considered the possibility that Troon had not reached Vaden Wick. It had never occurred to him that she could fail.

At their backs, Federation soldiers were rallying, archers and javelin throwers trying to bring down the Elves from behind. Some among the pursued fell victim to the missiles, stricken and helpless and lost in the rush. Those in the Elven rear guard stopped to help where they could, but the press forward was intense and there was no time for hesitation. A knot of Federation soldiers swarmed onto the plains in a foolish chase that was brought up short when Erris Crewer wheeled his archers back long enough for them to use their longbows in a sustained volley that dropped the pursuers in their tracks.

Farther down the line, Federation horsemen were riding out to intercept the Elves, charging hard and closing the distance between them with alarming quickness. Pied saw that the horsemen would reach the Elves before the Elves reached the protection of the Free-born, even should the Free-born be aware of what was happening.

Why didn't they open the gates?

They were still a hundred yards from the walls when Pied shouted for Ti Auberen to form up ranks. The Elves wheeled into triangle formations and turned to face the approaching riders. Erris Crewer brought the archers into position at the rear, their ranks three deep, and the Elves prepared to stand and fight. Pied felt his heart sink. They could hold for a time, but in the end they would be overrun, caught out in the open with no place to hide and no one to stand with them.

He moved to the front triangle to stand with Auberen. Neither spoke. There was nothing to say.

Then, with the Federation riders almost on top of them and the

Elven archers already letting go with their first volleys, the gates of the Free-born defenses finally swung open and out rode the Red Cloaks, the horse unit of the Bordermen of Callahorn, successors to the fabled Border Legion. They burst through the opening in a wave of crimson and a cacophony of wild cries, charging hard for the Federation cavalry. Clad in heavy armor and wielding lances, they tore through the Federation riders as if they were so many straw men, breaking apart their ranks and shattering the attack. In only minutes, the entire Federation force was in flight, and the Red Cloaks owned the grasslands.

The Elves, meanwhile, were running for the gates once more, the cheers of the defenders urging them on. Pied ran with them, a surge of relief flooding through him. As he passed through the gates and behind the safety of the Free-born defenses, a hand reached out and grabbed his arm. Troon stood at his elbow, grinning broadly.

"You didn't think I got through, did you?" she shouted at him above the din of men and horses. "Admit it, you saw the gates were closed and you thought I'd failed." Her gray eyes danced with glee. "Didn't I tell you not to worry?"

Pied responded by giving her a hug and was surprised when she hugged him back, even more surprised to discover how good it felt.

He moved on, searching for Ti Auberen and Erris Crewer. They had to make arrangements for what would happen next. But his Lieutenants were nowhere to be found in the surge of ebullient soldiers coming in from the grasslands. He found himself carried along by the tide, swept uphill to the heights where the main body of the Free-born was settled. There was a general milling about as the newly arrived were sorted out—the healthy directed to campsites and the wounded taken away for treatment. Pied wandered through the crowd, wondering what had possessed him to hug Troon, something commanding officers did not do to soldiers, no matter the nature of the relationship. It wasn't really the propriety of the action that bothered him; it was the emotions it had stirred. He had known Troon since they were children, but he had never been attracted to her. She was a Tracker in his Home Guard command, the one on whom he could always rely. She was his childhood friend, someone he liked to be around and who made him smile.

But for a minute back there, he had felt like she might be something more.

He forced his thoughts to other things and walked on.

Not an hour later, as he was buckling on his weapons, he heard his name called. He'd had just enough time to find his command post, connect with Ti Auberen and Erris Crewer, wash himself from a basin of warm water, and change into fresh clothes. He looked up to see a powerfully built Dwarf with long black hair and a beard braided at the chin and just below both ears approach. Several others of similar size but less flamboyant looks flanked him, hard-eyed men wearing multiple blades and bearing scars on their hands and faces. There was not a smile to be found on any of them save for the leader, but he was smiling broadly enough for them all.

"Captain Sanderling!" he boomed, his voice deep and resonant, the sound of it strangely compelling, like that of a practiced orator. "I'm Vaden Wick, Captain. Glad you made it through. We have been anticipating your arrival ever since your Tracker informed us of your coming. Heard about your success against the Federation three days back. That was impressive. Others would simply have kept running."

"I thought about it," Pied said. He reached out to shake the other's hand.

"I doubt that. You haven't the look." Vaden Wick tugged on the braid below his right ear, casting quick glances about the Elven camp, his sharp eyes taking in everything. "We have a lot to talk about. Can we do it now?"

He walked Pied down to the Free-born fortifications at the southern edge of the east plateau, exchanging greetings with his soldiers on the way, seemingly relaxed and unconcerned about anything. He had that quality of being able to disconnect from the burden of leadership when out among those he commanded, lending a sense of confidence to everyone he passed.

But when they stopped at a watchtower that was hastily vacated for their use, he abruptly changed. "Captain, we have a problem, and I need your help in solving it." He looked out across the Prekkendorran to where the Federation lines were dark creases against the horizon to the south, wrapping east and west about the Free-born encampment like a snake. "We're trapped here, hemmed in on every side but the one where we don't wish to go. We can't allow that to last much longer. That big airship with the weapon that burned Kellen Elessedil and his fleet out of the skies was airborne yesterday, a practice run that took her just outside the rear lines but was clearly meant as a test of her fitness. Another day, maybe two, and they will come after us. When they do, we're finished."

He looked over at Pied. "We have to find a way to stop that airship. You fought against her and you know her better than any of us. You damaged her or she would have done a good deal more than destroy the Elven fleet. I need to know if there is some way we can disable her when she comes after us again."

Pied shook his head. "I was lucky, that last time. We were in a skiff, too small even to be a threat, but we got behind her and under her and used rail slings to damage the steering. My guess is they won't let that happen again. The next time she comes after us, she'll have armor up all over."

Vaden Wick nodded. "I would guess so, too. So we need something else. Another way to damage her. A way to stop her before she even gets to us."

Pied looked at him, realizing suddenly what he was saying. "You plan on going after her, don't you?"

"If I get the chance. But I have to know how to knock her down before we engage her again. We have our airships ready to go, once we find what her weakness is. You've fought her and lived to tell about it. I thought you might have some insight."

Pied looked off into the distance. If he had any insight, it was eluding him. He wanted to help, but the depth of his knowledge about the *Dechtera* and her weapon was tiny. Mostly, he knew what would happen once the big Federation ship was aloft. Was there a weakness that the Free-born could exploit when that happened? He tried to think of one and failed.

"You think we have today and maybe tomorrow," he repeated.

"At most."

Pied thought about it some more. "They seem to have only one of these weapons," he said. "One ship, one weapon."

"So far."

"A prototype."

Vaden Wick looked at him, waiting.

"Can they even build another?"

The Dwarf shrugged. "Seems that if they could, they would have by now."

Pied took a deep breath, an idea forming. "I think we need to get to her while she is still on the ground," he said. "We need to get to her and destroy her completely. Maybe they really can't build another."

"We've thought of that. But she sits right in the center of the Federation camp, ringed by all sorts of protective barriers and hundreds of Federation soldiers. Neither a ground attack nor an air strike would even get close."

Pied nodded. "Not if they see it coming," he said. "But maybe we can arrange it so they don't."

EIGHTEEN

Pied had been sleeping for several hours when he felt the hand gently shake him. He could tell from the light seeping through the tent flap that the sun had moved west, though it wasn't yet dusk.

He opened one eye and saw Drumundoon bending over him. At first, he thought he was dreaming. "Drum?"

His aide knelt, and Pied could see clearly his young face with its high forehead and deeply slanted eyes. "It's me, Captain," Drum assured him.

He experienced a sudden sinking feeling. "You didn't get through to Arborlon?"

"Oh, yes, Captain, I got through all right." Drum rubbed his fringe of black beard. "I got there much quicker than I expected. I see you got through, as well. Everyone is talking about it. You've accomplished the impossible, if I may say so."

Pied blinked, trying to clear the sleep from his mind. "You may not." He pushed himself up on one elbow. "Have you brought help?"

Drumundoon nodded. "Three warships, several sloops, and two companies of Elven Hunters. They landed a little over an hour ago on the Free-born airfield. More will follow. The Elven High Council was quick to act once they understood the gravity of the situation. Arling was less impressed, but she accepted that their consensus constituted an edict she could not afford to ignore."

Drum hesitated. "Now she wants to talk to you."

Pied pushed himself into a sitting position. "I would expect she does. But she will have to wait. I can't go back there until this is finished."

Drum pursed his lips. "You don't understand, Captain. She's here."

"Here?" Now Pied was fully awake. "She came back with you?"

"She wouldn't have it any other way. The Council tried to dissuade her. Bad enough that we've lost a King. Losing a Queen as well would be too much. I even suggested she would do better to wait. But you know Arling. Once she has her mind set on something, that's pretty much the end of the discussion. She said she was coming or the ships and men were staying."

Pied nodded. That was Arling. Stubborn, though in an entirely different way from Kellen. She thought matters through first before setting her mind. She considered all sides. The war on the Prekkendorran was not an undertaking she would ever willingly support. No matter what the attitude of the High Council, she would look for a way to extricate the Elves. To do that, she would want to get a first-hand look at how things stood. She was Queen now, and she knew how to rule like one.

Of course, she had come to see how things stood with him, too. He could already picture her reaction.

"Where is she?" he asked.

"Right outside the tent," his aide said. He paused while Pied absorbed that information, looking decidedly uncomfortable with having been the one to deliver it. "She is waiting for you to invite her inside. I told her I ought to wake you first."

She would have woken me differently, had she been given the chance, Pied thought. He could already see her angry face, hear her accusatory voice. He knew what was coming with the certainty that he knew his own name.

"Let's not keep her waiting," he said.

He stood up, straightened his clothes, and nodded. Drum gave him a sympathetic look and ducked back outside. Alone, Pied stood staring at the tent flap, trying to compose himself, to think through what he knew he had to say.

Then the flap stirred and parted, and she stepped through, golden light trailing off her gilt-edged dress, her pale amber skin, and her long blond hair. She was so beautiful that it took his breath away, just as it always did, leaving him wishing for things that he suddenly knew he would never have. The revelation left him shocked. Arling was a Queen; she was always meant to be a Queen. To think that he had ever thought there could be anything permanent between them was a fantasy he had indulged with not the slightest consideration for reality.

"Hello, Pied," she greeted, coming up and offering her hand.

He bent to kiss it, bowing deeply out of protocol and deference. "My lady."

She stared at him for a moment, saying nothing. Then she clasped her hands in front of her and lifted her chin slightly, a curiously commanding gesture. "What do you have to say for yourself, Pied?"

He shook his head. "Nothing."

"Nothing? I was hoping you could do better than that. I don't know why, though. Nothing?" She gave him a glacial stare. "When I heard what had happened to Kiris and Wencling, I would have killed you if you had been within striking distance. I would have done so without a second thought. My sons, Pied. You were given responsibility for them."

"I know," he said. "I failed you."

"You failed me. You failed them. You failed your King. And you failed yourself." She paused. "I am angry with you still. Furious. But not for the same reasons as before. Do you know why?"

He shook his head, feeling foolish and slow-witted.

"Because Drumundoon told me what you have apparently failed to tell anyone else. Not that he wanted to, but I see more things than I am given credit for. When he told me my sons and husband were dead and the Elven fleet was destroyed, I asked what had happened to you. He told me you were alive. He told me you had rallied the survivors and achieved a decisive victory against the Federation force sent to crush what remained of our scattered units. He was quite proud of you. He was quick to tell me that without your presence, the Federation might well have succeeded in destroying the entire army."

She paused, studying his face. "I asked him how it was that you were in command of the Elven army. If my husband and sons were dead, why you were still alive? I asked why, as Captain of the Home

Guard and protector of the King and his family, you hadn't died with them. How could that possibly be?"

He nodded. "So he told you Kellen dismissed me from his service just before he set out."

"For insisting that he was making a mistake in attacking the Federation, in misreading the signs of what was clearly a trap, but particularly for insisting that my sons should go with him. For recognizing that Kiris and Wencling were pawns in his stupid, stupid game, pieces to be moved about on a board by a father who was mostly concerned that they grow to be the same sort of man he was, even when it was clear to everyone else that this was a bad idea, that they would never be even remotely like he was."

She lifted a finger and pointed it at him. "But none of that changes the fact that my sons are dead because of you. You failed them because you failed to out-think Kellen, something that should never have happened. You knew his propensity for rash behavior, for ill-considered action. You knew what he was like. Yet you reacted to the moment without thinking it through. You spoke your mind when you should have known better, and you got yourself dismissed from his service. No, don't say anything! Nothing you say will help now. You were given responsibility for my sons! You let them die, Pied! You put them in a position from which they could not extricate themselves and then you put *yourself* in a position where you couldn't help them. It would have been better for you if you had died with them. At least then I might be able to forgive you. That can never happen now. I can never forgive you for this. Never!"

He stood flushed and humiliated before her, the weight of the responsibility she was attributing to him immense and crushing and somehow inescapable. He knew he had done the best he could, but she made him feel as if that was not enough.

"So now you are the hero of the Elven army and my sons are dead," she continued softly. "You have pretended to be Captain of the Home Guard when in truth you were relieved of your command days ago. Shame on you."

He took a deep breath. "I did what I thought I needed to do to save the army. I didn't choose to pretend at what I was; it was thrust upon me by circumstance and need. I don't ask you to forgive me, only to try to understand." He paused. "I will resign my position at once and let another take my place."

"Oh, I think not!" she snapped at him. "Resign so that you can have the entire Elven army begging for your return? Resign, so that you can escape yet another obligation and another duty?"

He stared at her in shock. "It was not my intention—"

"Be quiet!" she snapped. He flinched at the force of her words. She froze him with her glare, with the bitterness reflected in her eyes. "Don't say another word unless I ask for it. Not one word."

His center went so cold that it might have been midwinter on the Prekkendorran instead of summer. He held her gaze and waited.

"You have won the hearts of my Elven Hunters," she said in a voice that was barely above a whisper. "You have won them and now you shall see to it that you do not break them as you have broken mine. Vaden Wick tells me that a counterattack is planned for tonight. What is your part in it?"

"I will go into the Federation camp after darkness with a handful of my Home Guard and destroy the airship and its weapon."

Now it was her turn to stare. "Do you really think you can do this?"

He shook his head wearily. "I will do it or die trying."

"Fair enough," she said. "I will take that as a promise and hold you to it. But hear me. If you survive this, if you manage somehow to come back alive, if you are successful in your efforts to put an end to the threat of this weapon that killed my sons, I will put this entire business behind me. Neither of us will speak of it again. But your service to the throne is finished. You will resign your position as Captain of the Home Guard immediately. You may give any reason you wish so long as my name is not mentioned. You will pack your belongings and leave Arborlon. You may go anywhere within the Westland so long as I never have to see you again. Is that clear?"

He thought of their past, a wisp of a memory turned to frost in the coldness of her voice. "It is."

She held herself very still. "It could have been different for us, Pied. If you had saved my sons as you had sworn you would do, it could have been different."

He said nothing in response. There was nothing to say. She might even believe that what she said was true. But he didn't.

She studied his face a moment longer, then held out her hand for him to kiss, turned, and went back through the tent flap. He stared after her, trying to decide how much of what had just happened was deserved. In the end, he guessed, it didn't really matter.

Two hours later, he stood at the edge of the Free-born airfield looking out over the broad sweep of the Prekkendorran to where the fires of the Federation army were being lit against the growing darkness. Dusk had settled in, deep and gloomy on a night that promised clouds and mist. It was the weather Pied had hoped for, an unexpected gift. He was dressed in black, and Drumundoon was standing in front of him applying lampblack to his face.

"She has no right to blame you," his young aide repeated yet again, scowling.

Pied held himself still as Drum's fingers worked across his face. "She has every right."

"She should be grateful you lived. If you hadn't, she might have lost the whole of her army."

"She isn't looking at it that way."

"Well, she should. She needs to distance herself from her emotions. She needs to exercise better judgment."

"A mother can't always do that."

"A Queen can. And should."

There was no satisfying him on the subject. He refused to consider any alternative but the one that favored Pied. Drum was nothing if not loyal. He had known of the entire conversation and confronted Pied with the whole of it minutes after Arling's departure. He didn't seem bothered in the least by the fact that if he had been caught eavesdropping, he would very likely have been shipped home in shackles. What mattered to him was that the Queen had done Pied an injustice that should be set right, and Pied did not seem inclined to do anything about it.

There were reasons for that, though Pied didn't want to talk about them. He was sick at heart at what had happened to Kellen and his sons and dismayed by Arling's response, even though he understood it and did not fault her for it. Mostly, he was weary. When the mission was finished, he did not want to continue as commander of the Elven army. Nor did he want to go back to being Captain of the Home Guard. Even if Arling had asked him to do so, a response

he did not foresee, he would have refused. His sense of account-
ability for what had happened to Kellen and the boys weighed on
him as if a tree had fallen on his shoulders. Nothing would ever be
the same in his relationship with the Elessedils. He no longer belonged in the position of Captain of the Home Guard. He did not
even think he belonged in Arborlon.

Drum would never understand that. So there was no point in discussing it with him. It was better if Pied simply presented it as settled
and let time do the rest.

Drum stepped back, eyeing him critically. "You're done. As good
as I can make it."

"That will have to be good enough," Pied replied.

They stared at each other for a moment, and then Drumundoon
stuck out his hand. "Good luck to you, Captain. I'll be here when you
return."

Pied took his hand and clasped it tightly. "I count on that, Drum.
I really do."

He turned away and moved to where the *Wayford* was anchored,
signaling to the other dark-clad figures scattered about that they
were leaving. The Free-born ship was rigged for sailing and ready to
fly, her captain already in the pilot box, her crew of six at the lines
and anchor ropes. It was dark enough that they could lift off without
drawing attention. If they flew east, into the darkness, they wouldn't
be seen when they turned south. After that, it would be up to fate
and luck.

Pied climbed the rope ladder with the other twelve members of
his tiny force, taking quick note of the flits that were stacked on both
sides of the mainmast before turning to take a head count. As he did
so, he caught sight of Troon, black-faced and black-clad like the others, levering one leg over the ship's railing and pulling herself aboard.
Breaking off his count, he went over to her at once, took her firmly
by the arm, and drew her aside.

"What are you doing here?" he demanded, trying to keep his
anger in check.

She arched one eyebrow. "I think you can figure that out for
yourself, Captain. I decided I didn't want to be left behind."

"You've just finished one mission. You're not ready for another."

"I'm ready enough. I had time to sleep last night once I was inside the Free-born lines. I told you it wasn't that hard. I slept today, as well."

He shook his head. "I don't want you doing this."

"You left it up to the Home Guard to choose a dozen of us. I volunteered, and I was chosen. A Tracker might prove useful."

"Well, I'm overruling the vote. You're off."

She stood her ground. "Because you are afraid I might not be up to doing what's needed? Or because of something else?" She gave him a moment, then shrugged. "Anyhow, we're already under way."

Pied glanced around hurriedly. She was right. The *Wayford* was lifting off, anchor lines released, her sails catching the evening breezes, the ground falling away below. He watched in frustration as the Free-born camp disappeared into the gloom and the ship swung about to fly east, and then he looked back at her, scowling. "I don't like it that you're here. It's asking too much."

"Of you or of me?" She glanced into the rigging as if the answer lay there. "For my part, I gather I am asking less of you than some. I am only asking to come along and help in whatever way I can. I might not be getting many more chances to do that." She looked back at him. "We've been friends a long time, Pied. Friends are supposed to stand by each other in difficult times. It seems to me, given how things have turned out for you, that standing by you just now is mandatory."

He shook his head in exasperation. "Drum just can't keep quiet about things, can he?"

"It's the army. You know how it works. Word gets around. There aren't any secrets." She glanced down at her weapons belt, and then hitched up her pack on her shoulders. "I don't like flying. I need to sit down. I'll be ready when you are."

He let her go; it was pointless to carry the discussion further because there was no reason to chastise her. She was there because she wanted to be. She was risking her life for him and for her comrades. It was hard to find fault with that.

They flew east until they had reached the far end of the Prekkendorran, then turned south and flew across the flats to the low mountains that buttressed the east end of the Federation lines. Slipping down the far side of those mountains, they got several miles behind the Southlanders, then turned west. In another hour, maybe less, they would reach their destination. It would not yet be midnight.

He glanced over at the flits. They were little gnats compared to the big ships of the line. But gnats were pesky and difficult to swat. Big ships would have trouble getting close to the *Dechtera*. Flits might have a chance.

A small chance, he thought.

He moved over to the railing and settled down to wait.

It was nearing midnight when the *Wayford*, skimming the tops of trees and hills south of the Federation lines, landed beyond a screen of woods that offered some small concealment from discovery. North, the horizon was lit by the glow of the Federation campfires, a dull yellowish coloring of the night sky. Pied disembarked with his company and began unloading the flits, weapons, and spare crystals for the return trip. A single crystal powered each flit, and the crystal had enough stored power for about two hours of use. After that, the flier was on borrowed time. Two hours would be enough to get them there, even given the necessity of evasive maneuvers. The spare crystal would get them back again.

If there was any getting back to be done.

When the group was assembled and the gear was checked and strapped in place, Pied told them what they were going to do and how they were going to do it. Once aloft, they would not be able to speak to one another; they would have to react on instinct. Knowing what they had to do and how they were supposed to do it was the framework that would hold them together. Acting as a team was what would keep them alive.

No one had to be told what the odds were of them succeeding. No one needed to speak of it and no one did.

"Remember that no matter what happens to us, that ship and her weapon have to be destroyed," Pied finished. "If we fail, thousands of Free-born will die. Don't let that happen."

They strapped themselves into the flits, taking time with the fastenings and the lines, bunched together in the center of a clearing that gave them sufficient room to lift off. Then, one by one, led by Pied and Sersen, a Southlander who had volunteered because he knew the country, each flier opened the single parse tube containing the diapson crystal that powered the flits, and soared off into the night.

Shadows against a night sky both clouded and misty, they flew low to the ground in near blackness, the only light coming from ahead of them, where the Federation fires burned through the gloom. Barely able to keep one another in sight, they flew in as tight a formation as possible, following the lead of Sersen, who chose their path and kept them on track for their destination. Pied, locked away in a kaleidoscopic rush of wind and sweeping landscape, found he was surprisingly calm. He was going to his death, in all likelihood, and yet he was at peace. He wished he could hold on to the moment, could stay in it forever.

The fringes of the Federation camp came into view, and Sersen took them right, keeping them within the concealment of the dark, just out of view of the sentries stationed along the backside of the enemy army. The airfield lay farther down the line, cradled by a series of low hills occupied by hundreds of Federation soldiers. They would have to fly right down into the center of that cradle, and when they did so they would come under attack from every side.

Pied took a deep breath and watched the Federation fleet begin to take shape in the harsh glow of the fires that warded the airfield. He found the *Dechtera* at once; her huge bulk was unmistakable. The weapon was mounted on her foredeck, covered over with sailcloth. Dozens of Federation soldiers stood on her decks and on the ground surrounding her hull. Pied's stomach lurched as he made a quick count and realized that they would be outnumbered at least thirty to one. Even without the rail slings on the surrounding hills and the soldiers manning them, even without the Federation camp being so close that it would take only minutes for an organized response to any attack, the odds his little force faced were insurmountable.

We're not coming back from this, he thought suddenly. *Not a one of us.*

Then it was too late to think about anything. Sersen had started his dive toward the airfield, flattening himself to the framework of his flit, trying to make himself as small a target as possible. Pied did the same, dipping his wings so that his flit nosed downward, gathering speed. Out of the corner of his eye, he saw the others follow, one by one, a sweep of flits winging out of the darkness and into the light.

It took the Federation soldiers a moment to react, perhaps because they could not believe the audacity of what they were seeing. It was a moment too long. Before they could bring their weapons to bear, including the rail slings mounted on the decks of the airships and the grounds surrounding, Pied and his Elves were crashing into them like waves off the ocean against rocks. The Elves didn't bother with controlled landings; they simply used whatever buffers were at hand—soldiers, weapons, supplies, and ships alike—to slow them down. Pied had just enough time to see Sersen sweep through the center of the airfield and another flit slam right atop the *Dechtera's* main decking and the sentries who weren't fast enough to get off her in time, and then he was down as well.

He skipped across the airfield in a series of bone-jarring bounces toward the nearest railgun, sending men leaping from his path, including the two who were assigned to man the gun. He had his straps off before the flit had finished its skid, leapt to his feet, and raced for the weapon. He got to it before the Federation soldiers could recover, swung it around on them, the crank already drawn back, and released the sling. Metal fragments sliced through the night with a hissing sound that ended in the death cries of the men in their path. Pied cranked back the handle once more, dropped in another load, swung the weapon toward a different group, and fired again.

Atop the *Dechtera*, two of the Home Guard fought hand-to-hand against a dozen soldiers surrounding the shrouded weapon. They held their own for several minutes before disappearing under the weight of their attackers. At the periphery of his vision, Pied saw a Federation-manned rail sling blow apart a flit that was trying to land, flinging its rider against the side of an airship, broken and lifeless.

Too many of them, too few of us.

Pied reloaded the rail sling and swung it toward the *Dechtera*. Fixing on the remnants of the Federation defenders still aboard, he released the sling and cut them apart. He was bringing the railgun back around when the first dart caught him in the shoulder, knocking him back. A second buried itself in his thigh a moment later. He was too exposed, standing out in the open. Worse, he was too far from the target.

Ignoring the pain of his wounds, he bolted for the *Dechtera*, leaping onto her rope ladder and hauling himself aboard so quickly that he bumped into the last of the defenders, a man who was crouched behind the railing, trying to hide. Pied killed him with one swipe of his long knife and broke for the weapon forward. Arrows and darts whistled past his ears, invisible killers. Elves had commandeered two of the railguns on the next ship over and were firing at clumps of Federation soldiers trying to reach the *Dechtera* and Pied. Another of the Home Guard, small and quick enough that it might be Troon, raced toward the airship with burning brands that streamed sparks and fire like comet tails and flung them onto the big ship's decking where they burned, wild and fierce.

Pied reached the mysterious weapon and yanked off the sail-cloth. A ten-foot-long barrel connected to a broad rectangular box sat atop a swivel. Cranks jutted from the swivel, clearly meant for maneuvering the weapon into firing position. Strange rods bored holes into the sides and back of the box. Pied snatched up an iron bar from off the deck and began smashing the hinges of the box, the *ping* of arrows and darts ringing in his ears as they bounced all around him. Sersen appeared beside him, blood streaming from a head wound, picked up a second iron bar, and began hammering at the casing from the other side. Behind them, the Elves from the next ship over abandoned their positions and scrambled aboard the *Dechtera*, fighting their way through smoke and flames to the aft port and starboard rail slings, swinging the deadly weapons around to face the Federation soldiers rushing to stop them.

Pied glanced at the airfield. If there were other Elves still standing, he couldn't see them.

Then the hinges on the casing gave way, snapping apart. Pied flung the casing aside, stared momentarily at the array of diapson crystals settled in their shielded slots, and began smashing them.

"Shades!" he gasped as another arrow caught him high on his wounded shoulder.

Sersen lurched backwards, a javelin protruding from his chest. The Southlander tried to catch himself, was hit again, and went down in a heap, sprawled across the ruined weapon. Pied dropped to one knee, seeking cover, and was surprised when the movement caused him intense pain in his side. He glanced down and saw another arrow protruding. When had that happened? Fire and smoke were all around him now, and he started to crawl across the decking, searching for a way out of the inferno, then stopped.

A trio of tattered and bloody Federation soldiers emerged from the haze right in front of him, blades unsheathed. As they caught sight of him, they slowed, weapons lifting. Pied drew his own sword, bracing for their rush. He didn't have the strength to stop them; he was weak from loss of blood, and pain was slowing his movements. He tried to think of how he could disable all three, but his mind was sluggish and unresponsive.

He tightened his grip on his sword.

Then a compact, black-clad form leapt from the roiling smoke behind the advancing soldiers, short sword cutting down first one, then another, quick blows that took both out of the fight before they even knew what had happened. The third turned, and the attacker went straight at him, as well, feinting and dodging, forcing him to swing wildly and thereby lower his guard.

In seconds, all three lay dead.

Troon moved quickly to Pied and slung his arm over her shoulder. "Time to be going, Captain."

She hauled him across the deck of the burning ship to the starboard side, practically dragging him. The flit that had crashed earlier lay jammed against the railing, its frame twisted and bent. "That won't hold us both," he said. "Leave me."

She ignored him, pulling the flit around so that it faced the port side of the airship, then jerking open the diapson crystal housing and yanking out the depleted crystal. Reaching into her pack, she retrieved her spare and fitted it in place. How she still managed to have that pack after what she had been through was incomprehensible to Pied. "What of the others?"

She laid him across the frame, strapping him securely into place. "As far as I know, all gone."

Thick smoke and flames surrounded them, forming a wall that closed them away from everything that lay beyond, hiding them from view. Federation soldiers were shouting wildly from somewhere close, and they heard the sound of boots thudding across the ship's decking by the ruined weapon. Troon ignored them, concentrating on the task at hand, her hands steady and sure. When she was satisfied that he was held fast, she lay down on top of him, wrapping her arms around his chest and her legs around the back part of the frame.

"Ready, Captain?" she whispered.

"Ready."

"This won't be pleasant. Hold tight."

She opened the parse tube, pulled back on the rudders, and threw the throttle all the way forward. The flit shot ahead as if catapulted from a sling, burrowing a tunnel through the smoke and flames, and lifting off the deck to clear the jagged stanchions of the broken railing with just enough room to spare.

An instant later, they were soaring across the Federation airfield, shouts rising from the throats of those below, missiles whipping past them in swarms. Pied heard Troon grunt, and her grip on him tightened. He felt a stinging in his leg, then another on his neck. He closed his eyes, waiting to die. The flit jerked and twisted as it flew, a victim of its damaged frame, unable to fully right itself. But Troon held the controls steady and kept them flying, moving out of the light to gain the darkness beyond.

They flew on for what seemed like an impossibly long time, wrapped together on the flit, sweeping through the night on an erratic path, the flit repeatedly jerking as if stricken, its frame shuddering. Pied wanted to look back to see if there was any pursuit, but he lacked both strength and maneuverability. He settled instead for staying quiet and balanced, trying to help them stay aloft.

"Are they back there?" he asked finally, the wind whipping the words from his mouth as he spoke them.

She pressed close. "Somewhere, but they haven't found us yet."

He fought to stay awake, but that was growing increasingly difficult. His strength was failing, and he thought that if she hadn't lashed him to the frame, he would not have been able to hang on. He felt the dampness of his own blood all down his body, and the arrows and darts buried in his flesh burned and throbbed.

After he hadn't heard or felt anything from Troon for a long time, he said to her, "Are you all right?"

There was no response. She lay heavily atop him, unmoving.

"Troon?"

"Still here."

"You're hurt?"

"A little. Like you. But we'll get through."

"I think I'm hurt pretty bad."

"Don't say that."

"You should have left me."

"Couldn't do that, Captain."

"You should have saved yourself."

She didn't say anything for a long time, then she put her lips close to his ear and said, "Saving you is the same as saving myself." And then he thought he heard her say, so softly he couldn't be sure, "I love you, Pied."

There was light ahead of them now, a fuzzy ball against the black, dim but growing brighter, and he found himself staring at it, watching it grow. He was a deadweight atop the flit, and Troon was a deadweight atop him. The flit was no longer flying straight, but beginning to slide downward, to dip and sway like a leaf tumbling from a tree.

"Troon?"

No answer. Pied stared at the light ahead. It didn't seem to have a source, didn't seem to be coming from anywhere. It occurred to him that there wasn't any light at all, that the light was inside his head. It occurred to him that he was watching the approach of his own death.

Fascinated, he kept his gaze fixed as it became a huge glowing ball and then swallowed him.

NINETEEN

Sen Dunsidan was awake long before his guards came to rouse him, dressed and waiting by the time they did. A light sleeper in the best of circumstances, he heard the sounds of the battle being fought on the airfield from inside his tented compound at the center rear of the Federation encampment almost a mile away. At first, he thought the entire camp was under attack, and his sole thought was to reach his private airship and flee. But as he dressed, frightened and angry and confused, standing in the dark to keep from becoming a ready target, he realized that the tumult was much farther away than the site of his compound and that any danger to him was still remote.

Nevertheless, he was edgy and impatient by the time his aide called to him from outside the tent flap. "My lord?"

"What is it?" he snapped, unable to keep his voice from betraying him. "What's happening?"

"The airfield is under attack!"

He knew the truth at once then. He didn't even have to leave his tent. The Free-born had watched him test-fly the *Dechtera* the day before, had taken note of how she performed, and had decided to act on the results. Having already witnessed the devastation wrought to the Elven airfleet, they would not have held anything back in their efforts to destroy her this time. He cursed

himself for a fool, waiting one day too long, confident that he had
them hemmed in and helpless, waiting for the end. He should have
paid better attention to what had happened to the command
he had sent to finish off those Elves. He had thought them helpless, too.

Still, why was it that his army, the biggest and most powerful
army in the Four Lands, couldn't manage to keep the Free-born from
breaking through the siege lines and reaching the airfield, which was
miles away? Why was it that his soldiers couldn't manage to protect
a single airship?

He pushed through the tent flap into the night and saw the
huge blaze east, the flames rising up against the darkened horizon, an inferno. He felt a sinking feeling in his stomach, the last of
his hopes fading, his worst fears confirmed. The *Dechtera* was destroyed. His weapon was gone. His plans for a strike against the
Free-born on the morrow were ruined. He knew it as surely as he
knew his own name. He stood looking at the flickering glow of
the fire in stunned silence, his aide hanging back, his guards keeping well away from him until they knew what his reaction was going
to be.

He turned to his aide. "Find Etan Orek. Bring him to the airfield."

His aide hurried away, and he signaled to his guards to bring up
the carriage. Someone was going to pay for this.

It took them only minutes to reach the airfield, which was
filled with soldiers running in every direction, some of them cart-
ing off the bodies of the dead and wounded, some of them trying
to put out the flames of the fires that burned all across the field.
The biggest of the fires was fed by what remained of the charred
hulk of the *Dechtera*, a smoking, blackened ruin, as he had known
she would be. Several other airships were burning, as well, but it
didn't appear that they would be a total loss. Weapons lay scattered everywhere, and he could just barely identify twisted pieces
of flits.

Composing himself, putting in place his politician's look, the one
that masked his true feelings and left his features devoid of expression, he climbed from the carriage.

One of his field commanders came over, saluted, and started to
give his report, but Sen Dunsidan cut him short.

"How many of them were there?"

His commander blinked. "We think about a dozen."

"A dozen." He was filled with sudden rage. A mere dozen had done this. "They used flits?"

His commander nodded. "They flew in from the backside of the camp. A suicide mission. We got all of them but two, and we'll have those two, as well, before dawn. Elves, from what we can tell."

"Elves?" Another remnant of those he had presumed helpless and in flight. He shook his head. "Any movement on the Free-born lines?"

The other man shook his head. "Not as yet."

"There will be. Strengthen the siege lines and be ready for an attack. Without the *Dechtera* to keep them at bay, the Free-born will try to break out. I don't want that to happen. Do you understand me, Commander?"

"Yes, Prime Minister."

"In case you don't, pay close attention to this. I want the watch Captain who was on duty tonight relieved of his command. I want him sent to the very front of our lines. When the Free-born attack, I want to be certain that he is the first soldier they see." He paused, his hard gaze fixed on the other. "Make sure everyone knows the reason."

His commander swallowed hard. "Yes, Prime Minister."

"Get out of my sight."

When he was alone, save for his guards, he walked down through the airfield to examine the damage firsthand. White-haired, magisterial, a commanding presence, he drew attention from all quarters. He let himself be seen, because it was necessary for the army to know he had matters under control. But he did not attempt to interact with the soldiers; he could never be reached by such as them. His guards formed a protective phalanx about him, keeping everyone at bay, and those who looked at him did not try to do more.

He stopped to study the wreck of the *Dechtera*, catching sight of what remained of his precious weapon, a twisted hunk of blackened metal. It was all he could do to keep from screaming his rage aloud, but he was practiced at dispassion.

He was contemplating what he would do to those responsible for what had happened here tonight when Etan Orek appeared at his elbow. "My lord?" he ventured.

Sen Dunsidan glanced at him. "You see for yourself what has happened, Engineer Orek. You see how determined our enemies are." He shook his head. "Their job is made easier by the fact that I am surrounded by incompetents. You and I, we must carry so much of the load ourselves."

The little man nodded eagerly, happy to be included as one of the chosen. "My lord, you can always depend on me."

Sen Dunsidan glanced at the *Dechtera*. "There is no salvaging the weapon now. We must start again. How long will it take?"

Etan Orek grinned conspiratorially. "You told me to build other weapons, my lord. I have been doing so. Another is almost complete." He leaned close. "I have actually tested it. The crystals align as they should to generate the fire rope. It needs only to have the casing made."

Sen Dunsidan felt a flush of satisfaction. He put a hand on the other's shoulder. "You have done well, Engineer Orek. Once again, you have not disappointed me. If I had a dozen of you, this war would be over in a week."

The little man flushed with pride. "Thank you, my lord."

"How many days, then?"

"Oh, end of the week, my lord. The weapon awaits my attention in Arishaig. It needs only a few final touches and a new airship to bear it aloft."

"Then we must spirit you back to Arishaig without further delay. I will have you returned at once. Pack up your things and make ready. I will follow in a day or two with the airship that will bear the weapon." He gave the other a smile. "There will be a reward in this for you, Engineer. Your service to the Federation will not be forgotten."

Flanked by two of Sen Dunsidan's personal guards who were charged with keeping close watch over the little man until he was safely away, Etan Orek scurried off. Nothing must happen to him. Not now, not when he was so close to finishing a second weapon. Wouldn't that be a nice surprise for the Free-born, once it was finished? They believed the danger over and done with, having destroyed the *Dechtera*. They believed him to be in possession of only a single weapon, since only the one had been used against them. They would find out soon enough how badly mistaken they were.

He took a final look around, decided there was nothing more he could do that night, and went back to his carriage. He might even be able to sleep again, he thought. At least until morning, when the Free-born attack came. He was still certain it would. Vaden Wick would take advantage of the opportunity. He would rally his forces in an attempt to break through the siege lines, to reclaim the heights lost by the Elves, and to return the Prekkendorran to a no-man's-land.

He might even succeed. But it wouldn't matter. Not anymore. Not once Sen Dunsidan brought up the new weapon and burned them all to cinders.

He reached the carriage and climbed inside. He was comfortably settled in place before he noticed the shadowy figure seated across from him.

"Prime Minister," Iridia Eleri greeted in her soft, insidious voice.

He started violently, but managed to keep the gasp that rose in his throat from escaping. She was cloaked in black and so deep in the shadows of the carriage interior that she was all but invisible.

"I've been waiting for you."

Shades, he thought. He exhaled sharply. "Come to gloat?"

She lifted her head slightly. "I am your personal Druid adviser, Sen Dunsidan. It is not my place to gloat. It is my place to advise. I have come to do so tonight. My sense of things suggests that you need me to do so."

The coach lurched forward, the team of horses turning it back toward the main compound and his tent. He rubbed at his tired eyes, wishing she would simply disappear. "What sort of advice would you offer, Iridia?"

"You have lost your airship and your weapon because you wasted time on a target of no consequence," she said quietly. "Now you will replace them with a new weapon and a new ship. Perhaps you should take this opportunity to reconsider your strategy for winning the war on the Prekkendorran."

He studied her without speaking for a moment. Odd, how used to her strangeness he had gotten, to the peculiar way she made him feel. It bothered him still that he couldn't define what it was about her that was so troubling, but he had gotten past his queasiness and now found her simply irksome. "My strategy?"

"It is still your intention to attack the Free-born forces on the Prekkendorran, to decimate them and thereby gain your victory," she said softly. "You would waste your time on an effort that will prove meaningless. I have told you this before and you have ignored me. I am telling you again, except that this time I must warn you that you ignore me at your peril. You won't get many more chances at winning this war. If you persist in trying to win it here, on this battlefield, or on any battlefield where soldiers and weapons alone are all that are at stake, the odds will catch up to you."

He folded his arms across his chest defensively. "You want me to attack Arborlon? Is that it?"

"It is what will end the war, Prime Minister. Attack the home city of the Elves, cause damage to their homes and their institutions, take the lives of their young and old, of their sick and crippled, and you take away their heart. They will cede you your victory. They will cede you anything to get you off their doorstep. Battles fought and won far from home make no lasting impression. Lives lost mean nothing when those lives are taken in a distant place. But kill a few thousand Elves in front of the rest of the population, and it will impact them forever."

He sighed. "We have had this discussion. I told you I would do as you advised. But I will do so when I am ready, Iridia."

"Time slips away, Prime Minister." Her words were a snake's hiss in the darkness.

"Does it? Perhaps time works differently for you than for me." He leaned forward. "I don't know why you are so adamant about attacking Arborlon. Why not attack Tyrsis or Culhaven? Why not go after the Bordermen or the Dwarves? We've already smashed the Elves on the battlefield. They are no longer the strongest of the Free-born allies."

"It is the Elves who serve as inspiration for the others. It is the Elves who promise hope in the worst of situations. In spite of the death of Kellen Elessedil, they came back to defeat you in the hills north. They broke the back of your pursuit force. Why do you think it was the Elves who attacked here tonight? Because they will give their lives willingly when they must. The other Races take note. They look to the Elves to see how they, too, must be."

"Well, they can look to their ashes when I am through with them.

They can sift through those and see how much courage they can find to continue the fight!"

The coach rolled to a stop within the Prime Minister's encampment. As Sen Dunsidan reached for the latch on the door, Iridia reached out and grasped his wrist, her hand as cold as ice. "Arborlon is the key to everything—"

"Enough!" he shouted at her, snatching back his wrist, repulsed by the feel of her hand on his skin. He rubbed at his wrist furiously. "You forget your place, Iridia! You are my adviser, but that is all you are! Do not presume to try to think for me! Confine your comments to suggestions and let me make the decisions!"

He threw open the door to the carriage and stalked off into the night.

The Moric waited until he was out of sight then climbed from the coach, as well. It stood looking off in the direction the Prime Minister had taken, thinking that Sen Dunsidan was proving to be more obstinate than anticipated. At first it had seemed a simple thing to twist his thinking in the way that was necessary. Persuade him of the need to attack the Elves on their own ground, to fly to their home city and let them discover firsthand the consequences of a war against the Federation, and the rest would be simple.

But Sen Dunsidan was a politician, first and foremost, and he constantly shifted his position to take advantage of the most favorable winds. He had rethought the matter, it seemed, and found that the attack was perhaps not to his advantage after all. He hadn't said so, but the Moric could tell that his hesitation to act quickly and decisively was governed by his sense that in doing as his adviser had recommended he might be making a mistake. Perhaps it was the visit from Shadea a'Ru that had caused him to back away from his earlier position. Perhaps it was something else. It didn't matter to the Moric. What mattered was that his mind had to be changed back.

The Moric breathed in the human stench, the smell of the Federation camp and its occupants, and was revolted. It was eager to have the matter over and done with. It was anxious to break down the wall of the Forbidding so that its brethren could join it and the killing could begin. It never doubted that this would happen. Superior to humans in every way, it knew it would not fail in its efforts. It would find a way to trick Sen Dunsidan into doing its bidding, fly the fire weapon to Arborlon, turn it on the Ellcrys, and destroy the Forbidding. The Moric would do that because there was no one to stop it. No one even knew it was there, save Tael Riverine, who had sent it. By the time the truth was out, there would be no way back.

Unless the Moric made a serious mistake, which it was thinking it might have done. Perhaps its decision to depend on its ability to influence Sen Dunsidan was such a mistake.

It started walking toward the rear of the Prime Minister's camp, back toward the wetland bog it had discovered on the first night of its arrival from Arishaig. Sen Dunsidan thought it settled somewhere within the larger Federation camp, but the Moric wanted nothing to do with humankind and its mode of dwelling. It thought fondly of its home in the swamps of Brockenthrog Weir in the world of the Jarka Ruus, steamy and fetid and rich with the smell of carrion. This world was too sterile, too clean. That would change when the demonkind reclaimed it.

It was deep in thought, paying little attention to anything around it, when the dart buried itself in its neck.

The Moric slowed, feeling the sting of the poison as it seeped into its flesh. Was the poison meant to kill it or merely to put it to sleep? Already its attackers were separating themselves from the surrounding shadows, coming toward it with knives drawn, crouched and ready. Apparently, they were determined to make certain of its demise. Or more to the point, to make certain of Iridia Eleri's demise. She was the one they had come to kill.

The Moric swung slowly about, counting heads. Four in all, stocky and garbed in black cloaks. Dwarves, perhaps. Assassins, whatever their species. But they had misjudged their quarry. They had come to kill a human. What they had found, unfortunately for them, was a demon.

The Moric waited for them to get closer, revealing nothing of its resistance to the poison, of its ability to shrug it off as nothing more than an irritation. When the closest of them, knife extended, rushed in from behind to finish it, the Moric whipped around swiftly, took hold of the attacker's arm, and yanked it from its socket. The attacker screamed and fell writhing on the earth. The Moric left this one where it lay and moved on to the next, catching it as it hesitated just a moment too long. Fingers twisting tightly into the folds of its cloak, the Moric yanked it off its feet and snapped its neck with a crack that sounded like the breaking of a piece of deadwood. The other two showed courage—or perhaps only foolishness—in choosing not to flee, but to attack as a unit, coming at the Moric from two sides. A foolish, pathetic effort. The demon tore the face off the first and crushed the skull of the second, all so swiftly that the struggle was over almost before it had begun.

A quick glance around assured it that no more attackers lurked in the shadows, that four had been deemed sufficient for the job. It pulled the attacker with the ruined face to its feet. It was still alive, though barely, and the Moric licked the blood from what remained of its face. Sweet. It took a second lick, then snapped the man's neck and threw the carcass down. One by one, it went to each of them and finished the job.

Then it took a moment to identify their species. It was surprised to discover that they were Gnomes.

Gnomes. Who would send Gnomes to kill Iridia Eleri? The answer, of course, was obvious. Finding Iridia's presence at Arishaig and her service to Sen Dunsidan intolerable, Shadea a'Ru had decided to take a hand in matters. The men must have been good at what they did or the Ard Rhys wouldn't have sent them. Too bad for her she didn't realize that Iridia was long since dead and that what they were dealing with was something else entirely.

But Shadea was no fool. She would discover that her assassins had failed, and she would take a closer look at what was really going on. She was already suspicious of Iridia's relationship with the Prime Minister. She would figure out soon enough that something about it was not right. Then she would try again, perhaps coming to do the job herself. The Moric was not afraid of her, but it did not want to become involved in a Druid feud that had nothing to do with its purpose in being in this wretched world in the first place.

What it must do, it decided as it walked away from the dead men, was to put an end to this nonsense. Its disguise had served its purpose, but it was becoming a liability. Its efforts at reaching the Ellcrys and tearing down the Forbidding were running up against obstacles it could not afford to spend time overcoming. Sen Dunsidan was recalcitrant. Shadea a'Ru was vengeful. Everything that lived and breathed in the Four Lands was a potential danger to it. Time, especially, was its enemy.

Its mind made up, the Moric licked a dollop of blood from its fingers as it continued on to its place of sleep. It would have to do something to change things. It would have to do so soon.

TWENTY

When she regained consciousness, Khyber Elessedil was sprawled on the catwalk, her body aching and her clothing soaked with her own blood. She pulled herself into a sitting position, glancing quickly about to be certain that the Gnome Hunter was still dead, lying where she had left him. The furnace room was unbearably hot, the tips of the flames from the pit dancing at the edges of her vision, as if trying to climb out. She felt suddenly dizzy, weakened from loss of blood and fatigue, and took a moment to gather her strength. Then she tore the sleeve of her tunic away, folded it into a compress, slipped it under her clothing, and pressed it against the dagger wound. When she had it in place, she pulled her belt free and used it to bind the compress tightly in place.

The effort took everything she had. She sat staring at the dead man, thinking that she had to move, that staying put was dangerous. Sooner or later, someone would come looking. She did not want to be there when they did.

But where was it that she wanted to be?

It was a question she could not answer easily. She had two choices. She could find her way clear of the Keep and seek help on the outside or she could stay where she was and try to find her way to the chambers of the Ard Rhys. Whichever she did, she had to do something to help Pen and Grianne Ohmsford avoid the triagenel. If she failed, they would be snared and made prisoners and the whole effort to rescue the Ard Rhys would have been for nothing.

She tried to think it through. Getting out of the Keep seemed the safer choice. Put some distance between herself and the rebel Druids and their Gnome Hunter protectors. But what would she do then? What sort of help could she expect to find outside Paranor? There were no communities for miles, no settlements, nothing but the heavy woods that surrounded the Keep. She could not count on Kermadec and his Trolls or Tagwen to find her. She could not even count on them to get free of Stridegate. She had no idea what had become of the Ohmsfords senior; they could be anywhere. And they did not know she was at Paranor in any case.

She knew she could not depend on help from the outside. Staying where she was made better sense, given that she had to come back in any case. But staying inside was also extremely dangerous. Enemies surrounded her. She did not know her way around. Everything about the Keep was a potential trap. No matter how careful she was, sooner or later she would make a mistake.

Either way, she might be done in by her wound, which burned like fire. If she didn't bleed to death, she ran a good risk of infection. Her compress was already soaked through, sticking to her clothing and flesh both.

She closed her eyes against her dilemma, trying to think it through. She would stay, she decided finally. Getting safely out of the Keep risked as much as trying to remain hidden inside. There was no guarantee of any help no matter which way she went. She might as well stay where she could do some good.

How much time did she have? How long before Pen and the Ard Rhys would come back into Paranor? It couldn't happen too quickly; he would have to find her first, and they would have to make their way back to the point of entry. But did time pass in the world of the Forbidding at the same speed it did in the Four Lands? What if the Ard Rhys was still at the place where she had entered, and Pen found her right away? It was possible they might come back much more quickly than she imagined.

She exhaled sharply. Too many questions, and there were no answers to any of them. She would have to do the best she could and hope that was enough.

With both hands grasping the catwalk guardrail, she pulled herself to her feet. She tottered for a moment, leaned against the railing for support, and waited for her head to clear. She was still hanging there when she remembered the Elfstones. In the heat of the struggle, she had forgotten them. Her throat tightened. Traunt Rowan had given them to one of the Gnome Hunters, but which one? What if it was the one she had pushed into the furnace pit? Fighting back against the burn of her fear, she pushed away from the railing and staggered back around the catwalk toward the tunnel through which she had entered. She passed the blackened husk of the third Gnome, turning her face away, trying not to look at him. She could not bring herself to begin her search there.

Instead, she retraced her steps and went back into the darkened passageway until she found the first of the remaining two. In the near darkness, she searched him thoroughly, but she did not find the Stones. Her heart sank. Taking his long knife from his belt so that she would have a weapon, she groped her way over to the second man. *Please*, she prayed, her fingers rummaging frantically through his clothing. This time she found what she was looking for. A surge of relief washed through her as she shoved the pouch into her tunic. Whatever else happened, she could not afford to lose the talismans.

Retrieving one of the torches she had extinguished earlier, she used her magic to relight it, and then started back up the passageway toward the Keep. If she encountered anyone at this point, she knew she was in trouble. There was no place for her to hide and she was too weak to fight. She moved ahead at a steady but painfully slow pace, concentrating on putting one foot in front of the other, conscious that her strength was slowing ebbing away. She knew she would have to treat her injury soon if she was to keep going, but she could not afford to stop and do so until she was someplace safe.

At some point, she lost her way, but she pushed on anyway. Eventually, she reached a confluence of tunnels, brightly lit with the smokeless torches the Druids favored in the Keep proper, and she cast her own aside. A stairway led upward, and she hesitated. She wasn't ready to go back into Paranor's upper regions just yet. Instead, she took one of the passageways leading off the hub. After passing several doors that were locked, she found one that wasn't and slipped inside.

A pair of smokeless torches cast a dim glow over a vaulted ceiling and stone-block walls. She was in a storage room jammed high with casks of ale and wine, the oaken barrels ironbound and tipped on their sides in huge cradles. A carpet of dust lay over everything; the air was thick with it. The room had clearly not been entered in a long time. She found that she could not lock the door from the inside, but she did not think she had the strength to look for another. If no one had been here recently, her odds were pretty good that no one would come soon. She worked her way to the back of the room, into the deep shadows where she could not be seen by anyone entering, and collapsed on a wooden pallet used for storing barrel staves.

She closed her eyes, wanting badly to sleep. But she knew if she did, she might not wake up again. She needed to stop the bleeding. Her healing skills were rudimentary, but Ahren had given her a few basic lessons. She knew she had to cauterize the wound. It would have been better if she were outside the Keep where she could gather some healing herbs and leaves, but there was no help for it. She would have to make do with magic and luck alone. She knew it was going to be painful. She was not brave, and she did not want to do this. But she had no choice if she wanted to go on.

She stripped off her tunic and pulled away the compress, then drew a little of the wine from one of the barrels and used it to wash the wound. The wine burned, and she clenched her teeth. It was a start, but it wasn't enough. For the healing process to begin, she had to close the wound all the way. She sat back down on the pallet and summoned a small magic that would help to numb the area around the wound, applying the dancing bits of colored light with her fingertips in gentle strokes. When the pain began to lessen, she brought out the long knife she had taken from the Gnome Hunter and used her magic-conjured fire to heat the tip of the blade until it glowed.

Then she bit down on a small piece of wood she found in a pile of scraps, summoned an image of Ahren and Emberen and better times to distract her, and laid the flat of the knife against the wound.

The pain was enormous. Trying not to and failing, she screamed into the wood, into the silence, smelling her flesh as it burned and seared. She did not lose consciousness, although she thought it might have been better if she had. When she could stand it no longer, she took the knife away, tears streaming down her cheeks, fire coursing through her body. She summoned more of the numbing magic and applied it with small strokes to the cauterized area. It took her a long time to make a difference, but finally the pain decreased.

She looked down at her side and then quickly away again. At least the wound was closed and the bleeding stopped. She had done what she could.

She pulled her tunic back on, wrapped herself in her cloak, and lay down to sleep, the knife gripped tightly in one hand.

Bek stood at the controls of *Swift Sure,* easing the airship down the line of the Charnals toward the Dragons Teeth and Paranor. The sky was hazy and gray, the midday sun blocked by storm clouds that were building into thunderheads. He watched the approaching weather mostly out of habit; his thoughts were elsewhere. On the deck below the pilot box, Trefen Morys and Bellizen sat together, heads bent close as they conversed. Kermadec, his brother Atalan, and a handful of other Rock Trolls were scattered about the aft decking, wrapped in blankets and asleep. Tagwen was belowdecks, fighting airsickness yet again, apparently unable to come to terms with flight motion even with help from Rue, who had given him herbs and a drink to calm his stomach. Some people were like that; no matter how hard they tried or how hard others tried for them, they simply couldn't make the adjustment.

He glanced over his shoulder. Somewhere behind them, perhaps half a day out, the balance of Taupo Rough's Rock Trolls followed aboard the huge flat transports that Trolls favored for conveying their armies to a place of battle. Slow and cumbersome, they rarely got more than a few hundred feet off the ground. But Kermadec had insisted they would reach Paranor in time to be of help. His job, and the job of the small company he had brought with him, was to get inside the Keep and secure at least one of the gates. Bek wasn't sure that eight or nine Trolls could manage that against a fortress of Druids and Gnome Hunters, but he kept his thoughts to himself. He wasn't sure, after all, that he could do what he intended, either.

He was flying the ship alone at that point, something he enjoyed and was comfortable with. He liked the feeling of satisfaction it gave him to be able to control her all by himself. He liked the way she rose and fell beneath his feet in response to the air currents. He knew *Swift Sure* better than any ship he had ever flown, and he had been flying for more than twenty years, ever since his journey to Parkasia aboard the *Jerle Shannara,* where Redden Alt Mer had taught him his flight skills and Rue Meridian had caused him to fall in love.

If Tagwen was to be believed, "falling in love" appeared to have happened all over again with his son and the blind Rover girl, Cinnaminson. An improbable happening under any circumstance, it seemed particularly strange here. Pen, following in the steps of his father, had fallen in love on a dangerous expedition, at a place and a time when falling in love was not convenient. Of course, that was the way love worked. You couldn't control the where or the when.

So many similarities in their lives. Pen, too, was a flier, although he had learned to fly much earlier and was already as comfortable aboard an airship as his father. It was strange to think of Pen traveling down such a familiar road, but the comparisons were inescapable.

But the strong possibility that, like himself, Pen possessed a secret magic gave Bek pause. He had been wrestling with the idea since the moment he had realized in his efforts to track his son that he was able to do so only because Pen had the use of a magic that neither he nor Rue had known anything about. Still, he could not ignore what reason and common sense told him about his connection to his son and, consequently, what it suggested about the possibility of another similarity in their lives. Bek, too, had possessed magic when he had gone with the Druid Walker to Parkasia, and he hadn't known of it. It was only after they were well out over the Blue Divide and confronted with the barriers of Ice Henge and the Squirm that Walker had revealed the truth about who he really was and how the magic had been passed down to him.

He wondered when Pen had made his discovery. Had he known about it earlier and kept it secret from his parents? There was reason to think he might have done so, given his mother's antipathy toward magic and Bek's own reluctance to make use of it. It might also be that while Pen had known of it, he had not until recently fully explored its uses. It might be that he was still on a journey of discovery.

Of one thing Bek was quite certain. The King of the Silver River had chosen his son to make the journey into the Forbidding for a very specific reason, and it almost certainly had something to do with his heritage of the wishsong magic. The Faerie creature could have come to Bek to do what was needed, but he had gone to Pen instead. That meant that something about Pen made him the more appropriate candidate for going into the Forbidding and rescuing Grianne. A boy, barely grown. It was almost impossible to understand. But the King of the Silver River had come to Ohmsfords since the time of Shea and Flick in the days of Allanon, and had always done so with unerring instincts for what each of them was capable of achieving.

Now it was up to Bek and Rue to find a way to help their son fulfill the charge that had been given to him. History was repeating itself, another instance of a similarity in the lives of the Ohmsfords, and more particularly in the lives of a father and son.

Bek paused in his thinking. Would history repeat itself? Would it repeat in every particular? He had come back alive from the expedition he had embarked upon. Would Pen have the same good fortune?

He hated thinking about such a question, but he could not help himself. In part, it was a reflection of his own sense of responsibility for his son. He had been given the task of seeing that Pen got safely back through the Forbidding. If he failed to do that, he would have failed his son. It was a possibility he refused to consider.

"What are you thinking about?" Rue asked him.

She stepped up into the pilot box and stood beside him, her green eyes inquisitive. When she saw the look that came over his face, she leaned over and kissed him. "What's wrong? Can't you tell me?"

He nodded. "I was thinking about how much Pen depends on us, even though he doesn't know it."

"He is supposed to depend on us. He is our son."

"I don't want to fail him."

"You won't. Neither of us will."

They were silent a moment, watching the land slide away beneath the airship's hull, the heavy weather west continuing to advance. Waterbirds from out of the Malg Swamp screamed eerie cries as they sailed across the skies. Far below, a cluster of Forest Trolls emerged from the trees and stalked in a line across the hills leading up to the mountains east.

"Is Tagwen any better?" he asked.

She shook her head. "He just isn't meant for this."

"I guess not." He paused. "I'm worried about how much he really knows about getting into Paranor without being seen."

"You ought to be," she said. He gave her a sharp look. "I asked him about it, and he admitted that he hadn't been inside those secret tunnels in several years and that his memory of them was sketchy at best."

"So we can't rely on him."

She shook her head again.

"How about Trefen Morys and Bellizen? Do they know anything that might help?"

"I don't think so. They've only been a part of the order for a little over two years. They haven't had time to do much more than complete the lessons assigned them as novice Druids. They are loyal to your sister, but they haven't had the closeness with her that Tagwen has. They didn't even know there were secret tunnels."

He looked off into the distance. "So we have to depend on ourselves in this business."

She nodded. "Pretty much like always."

He didn't say anything to that.

When she awoke, Khyber Elessedil ached from head to foot, as if the cauterization had been applied across her entire body. She was not feverish, but she was disoriented and weak. She sat up, wishing she had something to eat or drink, and then remembered she was surrounded by wine and ale casks. She moved over to the closest barrel, opened the spigot, and took a long, satisfying drink of cool wine. She would have preferred water, but the wine would suffice.

She could do nothing about her hunger, though. She considered the possibility that there might be foodstuffs stored somewhere down in these cellar passageways, but she had no idea where they might be and no time to spend looking for them. She would have to get by on whatever she might scavenge along the way. What mattered just then was reaching the sleeping chamber of the Ard Rhys as quickly as possible.

Something, she realized, she did not know how to do.

It was bad enough that she did not have a clear idea of where she was so that she might have some sense of which direction to go. It was much worse that she had no idea how to reach her destination without being seen. She could find a way to disguise herself, she supposed, just as she had done when she had freed Pen. But that was risky and, besides, even if she got that far the sleeping chamber would be heavily guarded.

Trying to decide where to begin, she considered her alternatives for a moment, but the task was hopeless. Everything she thought about trying was too dangerous. Once they found the dead Gnome Hunters, they would be looking for her anyway. Perhaps they already were. She needed to disappear, to become invisible.

She pondered the idea. There were secret passageways in the walls of Paranor. Ahren had told her so once. The Keep was honeycombed with them. The Druids had used them to reach one another when they wished their conferences kept secret. The Ard Rhys had used them from time to time, as well, to slip from her chamber without being seen when need or discretion warranted it.

If she could find a way into those . . .

She would be lost all over again, she finished dismally.

Unless . . .

Her mind raced. Unless she had a way to keep from getting lost.

Her hand strayed to the pocket in her tunic where the Elfstones were tucked away. The Elfstones could keep her from getting lost. They could show her a way into the sleeping chamber, just as they had shown Ahren the way to Stridegate and the tanequil.

She was suddenly excited, the aches and pains and hunger forgotten. But then she remembered that use of magic as powerful as the Elfstones was likely to be detected by the very people she was trying to avoid. It was the reason she had tried so hard not to use the Stones on the journey into the Charnals. Using them in the Druid's Keep, right beneath their noses, would be madness. Besides, they thought the Elfstones destroyed, thrown into the furnace along with her body. Any release of the magic risked revealing that she was still alive.

Or did it?

If the Elfstones had been thrown into the furnace, would the intense heat and pressure destroy them? Would it serve to release the magic in doing so? No one knew, she suspected. There were no other Elfstones save the ones she carried, and little was known about their properties. It might well be that their destruction would unlock their magic in the same way as a user's summoning.

Anyway, what other choice did she have?

She wondered suddenly how long she had been asleep. Did they know yet that she had escaped? Or did they think her dead and the Elfstones dead with her?

She rose and left the storage room, slipping cautiously through the door, and went back down the passageways of the Keep toward the furnace chamber. She picked up a torch on the way to provide her with the light she needed. She was hurrying by then, anxious to discover if her idea had a chance of working. It all depended on how much time had passed and what had happened in the interim. She moved quietly, listening for voices, for sounds that would indicate the bodies of the dead men had been discovered, that her deception was unworkable. But the passageways were silent and empty, and when she reached the place where the first two Gnomes had died, she found their bodies untouched. Farther down, within the furnace room itself, she found the third, as well. No one had missed them yet. No one had come looking.

She still had a chance.

One by one, she dragged the dead men to the edge of the fire pit and shoved them in. It would not conceal the struggle or the shedding of blood, but it would make it harder for those who eventually came looking to determine exactly what had happened. It might give her a measure of time and distance from discovery. She had to hope so because it was all she had to work with.

Exhausted from her efforts, she sat down with her back against the railing and took out the Elfstones. She had to try to use them, even if the release of the magic alerted Shadea and the other rebel Druids. She had to hope that they would register the source of the magic as the furnace room and attribute its presence to the destruction of the Stones in the fire.

She shook her head. She wished she had a better way. But she was stuck with things as they were, and there was no point wishing for something she couldn't have.

She poured the Elfstones out of their pouch and into the palm of her hand, studying them a moment. Then she closed her fingers tightly about them, held up her hand, and summoned the magic.

It was easier this time than it had been before, perhaps because she was used to the process and more receptive to it. The familiar

warmth spread from her hand through her arm and into her body before looping back again. When she was infused with the magic of the
Stones, her thoughts centered on what she needed, seeking a way
into the secret passages of the Keep, a blue glow formed within her
fist and began to seep through the cracks of her fingers. Then,
abruptly, it shot from her hand in a thin, long streamer, penetrating
the fiery atmosphere of the furnace room, burrowing through stone
and darkness, illuminating the way forward.

She watched as her route revealed itself, a twisting of passages
and stairways, cutting through the walls of the Keep, winding
steadily upward until they ended at a wall that gave secret entry into
the sleeping chambers of the Ard Rhys. A strange glow leaked
through the seams of the hidden door, a suggestion of magic contained within the room.

Then the vision flared and was gone, the blue glow of the Elfstone magic disappeared, and the warmth within her faded away.
She sat again on the catwalk with her back to the railing, her memory of what she had been shown sharp and clear.

High in the north tower, several floors below the sleeping room
draped with the lethal netting of the triagenel, the Druid on watch in
the cold chamber for disturbances triggered by unauthorized uses of
magic noticed a spike on the otherwise smooth surface of the scrye
waters. He leaned forward as the ripples spread outward, wanting to
be certain of what he was seeing.

The source of the spike was the Druid's Keep.

He took a long moment to consider what that meant. Magic was
in frequent use at Paranor, so disturbances of that sort were not unusual. Still, the spike suggested a usage more powerful than the conjuring normally done. He should report it, he knew. But he also knew
that if he chose to do so, he must go before Shadea a'Ru, something
no one wanted to do these days.

He tried to think the matter through. It was possible that the
usage was one the Ard Rhys knew about. It was even possible that
the usage was hers. The Druid on watch did not want to intrude
where he was not welcome. Discretion was well advised where matters involving Paranor and the order were concerned—especially by

those who only served. Drawing attention to oneself was not wise. Others had disappeared from the Keep for much less.

Besides, what sort of magic could be called up within these walls that someone in authority did not know about?

He debated the matter only a moment more, then went back to his seat and resumed his watch.

TWENTY-ONE

Dawn was a faint glimmer in the east when Penderrin Ohmsford stirred from his sleep and peered from his shelter into the gray, hazy gloom of a new day. Mist clung to the land in deep pockets. Clouds obscured the sky, thick and dull blankets that formed a canopy from horizon to horizon and refused to reveal the sun. The air was windless and raw with unpleasant smells and the landscape wintry and bleak in the pale first light. The night's rain had ended, leaving dark stains on the bare earth and rocks.

The dragon was right where it had been the night before, stretched in front of his shelter like a wall.

Only now, it was sleeping.

Pen stared at it for a moment, not quite believing. Yes, the dragon was asleep, its eyelids closed, its huge, horn-encrusted snout resting comfortably on its wagon-wheel feet, a steady snoring issuing from its maw, and its nostrils flaring at regular intervals as it inhaled and exhaled.

He waited long moments to be certain, then carefully climbed to his feet, his cloak wrapped close and the darkwand gripped firmly in one hand. A corridor opened to his left, leading just past the dragon's outstretched head, passing wickedly close to those teeth and claws but offering a narrow avenue of escape. He just needed to be very quiet. And lucky.

He took a deep breath and stepped from his shelter into the thin dawn light.

Instantly, one scaly lid slipped open and the dragon's yellow eye stared at him.

He froze, his blood gone cold, waiting to see if maybe, just possibly, the eye might not register his presence and simply close again. But it fixed firmly on him and did not move. He watched it for long moments, debating if he should try to go farther, then backed slowly into his shelter and sat down again.

So much for that.

He sat looking out at the dragon for a long time. He was so hungry he could hear his stomach growl. His nerves were ragged, and his hopes for reaching his aunt fading fast. Somehow, he had to get past the monster. To spend another day trapped in those rocks was unacceptable.

He closed his eyes in despair. Didn't the dragon ever get hungry? Why didn't it leave and go off to find something to eat?

Of course, dragons might not have to eat all that often, he reasoned. Maybe they only ate once a week, like the moor cats in the Four Lands. Maybe it had just eaten before it found him. Maybe it would never want to eat anything again as long as it had him to entertain it.

"Get out of here!" he screamed in a rush of frustration.

The dragon didn't move. It didn't even blink.

But the runes on the darkwand began to dance wildly.

He stared at them in confusion and surprise. The dancing continued for a few seconds more, and then slowed. He furrowed his brow. His voice had disturbed them. They had become more active because he had shouted at the dragon.

He found himself thinking again about how the runes continued to glow even while he was asleep and paying no attention to the staff at all. He had thought at first that the runes only brightened when they were responding to his thoughts. But that didn't seem to be the case. Hadn't been the case ever. From the moment he had encountered the dragon, the runes had acted independently of anything he had done, keeping the monster transfixed and at bay.

Even while he was sleeping.

Why would they do that?

They would do it, he thought suddenly, because the darkwand

was sentient. The tanequil had given him a living piece of itself. That was what had enabled him to carve the runes without seeing what he was doing. That was what had transported him from the Four Lands into the Forbidding. It knew to use the runes to charm the dragon, to mesmerize it so that it would not attack Pen. Just as it knew to guide him to the Ard Rhys, it knew to protect him.

But why had the runes responded to his voice?

Shades!

Because it was a thing of magic and it would always respond to other magic. His magic. Not his little magic, his ability to read the actions and behavior of other creatures in an effort to communicate with them. Not the magic he had grown up with and kept secret even from his parents because he never thought it mattered. No, not that magic.

Another magic. The wishsong magic.

Like father, like son.

He could scarcely believe it. He had always understood there was a possibility of his inheriting such magic. But he had thought that possibility long past, faded with the passing of the years. He was too old. If it was going to happen, it would have happened earlier.

Yet it hadn't happened to his father, either, until he was a few years older than Pen was now. So it was possible that history was repeating itself. The blood heritage was a part of his past. But perhaps it was also a part of his future, its seeds locked deep inside him. He knew that his small communicative magic was born of it, even if it wasn't as powerful.

And now, for reasons he didn't understand, the wishsong had surfaced in him as it had surfaced twenty years earlier in his father. It had awakened in his voice and given him a way to connect to the magic of the darkwand.

Except, he thought excitedly, he *did* understand the reasons for its emergence. The darkwand had awakened the wishsong. His joining to the staff in the carving of its intricate web of runes had brought the magic to life.

He looked into the distance, thinking that he was being foolish, that he had no reason to believe any of his conclusions. He glanced down at the staff, at the softly glowing runes, their patterns changing endlessly, dancing hypnotically across the darkened, burnished wood. He had no proof that the wishsong's magic was what had stirred those runes or, even if it had, that he could implement it in any useful way.

But where was the harm in trying to find out?

He began to hum, soft and steady, shifting tones and pitches, trying anything and everything. He kept at it, not knowing exactly what he was doing, just testing to see if anything he tried would make a difference. The response from the runes was immediate. They throbbed and pulsed, the glow shifting from rune to rune and from row to row, skipping here and there as if a thing alive. Patterns formed and were replaced almost quicker than the eye could follow, a kaleidoscope of brilliant images.

The dragon lifted its head, fascinated.

Pen changed from humming to stringing together words, not singing any specific song, just phrases that seemed to go together, seeking ways to make the runes do other things. But the runes just kept shifting about as they chose with little regard to anything he did. They seemed to respond only to sound and not to specific words or meanings. Frustrated, unable to see how this was helping anything, he tightened his resolve, burrowed down inside himself, and gave a harder push to what he was doing.

Get away from me, he sang in a dozen different ways. *Go far, far away from me.*

Suddenly, there was a different response from the staff. Imprints of the runes literally jumped off the wood and into the air, glowing images that hung like fireflies against the sullen morning light. Still throbbing and pulsing, still shifting about in intricate patterns that kept the dragon mesmerized, the rune images danced about and then flew off into the morning mist. Line after line of glowing symbols broke free of the darkwand and winged away like birds taking flight.

The dragon sniffed at them as they passed, and then licked out at them with its long, mottled tongue, but it could not capture them. Frustrated, it heaved its bulk off the ground and rose on its hind legs, maw splitting wide, scaly lips drawing back to reveal blackened teeth. Hissing and spitting, it snapped wildly at the images as they flitted past. Pen shrank back against the rock of his shelter in terror, but managed to keep singing. The dragon ripped at the images with its forelegs, and then finally, screaming with frustration as they continued to elude it, it spread great leathery wings and took flight, chasing after them.

It happened so fast that Pen barely had time to register his sudden change of fortune before the dragon was gone, a dark speck in the distance, pursuing the still-glowing images. Seconds later, it disappeared completely.

Pen kept singing anyway, sending more flights of glowing runes in the same direction, worried that the dragon would decide to come back. When he finally thought it safe, he went silent. The images faded and the runes on the staff ceased their excited dance and resumed a soft, gentle pulsing against the dark surface of the wood. All about, silence hung deep and pervasive on the hazy morning air.

Pen exhaled sharply. What in the world had happened?

The truth was, he didn't know. Obviously he had tapped into the magic of the wishsong, successfully summoning it from where it lay dormant within him. Probably his link with the darkwand enabled him to do so, to bring the magic to life and to make use of it to save himself. But he had no idea what sort of magic he had conjured. He didn't know how to control it; he didn't really even understand how to use it. All he had managed to do was to make the darkwand's runes respond to him in a way that had lured the dragon away and given him a chance to be free. Beyond that, he hadn't learned a thing.

But that was good enough.

Wrapping his cloak close about him once more and gripping the darkwand firmly in one hand, he stepped out of his shelter and looked about. There was no sign of the dragon or anything else. The day was sullen and dark, and the air smelled of damp and rot. He needed to get out of that place; he needed to find Grianne Ohmsford and go home again.

Turning his thoughts to his aunt and mindful of how he had begun his search two days before, he held up the staff, pointed it south again, and watched the runes brighten.

Then, with a last cautious look skyward, he set out.

He walked all the rest of that day through country so bleak and so heavy with the promise of evil that he found himself constantly looking over his shoulder for what he imagined might be following. He took the trail leading up into the mountains, the passage he had chosen before the dragon trapped him, climbing steadily into the rocks through the morning, and then descending on the other side in the afternoon. The day stayed dreary, the mountain air of no better quality than what he had found below. The haziness of the landscape was deep and pervasive. Not much grew anywhere he passed through. Mostly, the terrain was marked by different striations of earth and rock, a blending of washed-out grays and blacks and browns.

It rained a little at midday. He cupped his hands to catch the precious liquid and licked the dampness from his palms. Other than that, he found only stagnant ponds and sediment-fouled trickles coming out of the rocks. Higher up, he encountered trees that bore a vivid crimson fruit, but he knew that bright colors in living things frequently indicated danger, and he passed the fruit by. He found a flock of crowlike birds eating berries from a bush, and though the berries looked unpleasant, he tried one anyway and found it edible. With an eye toward the crow-birds, which were squawking at him angrily, he ate the rest.

Weary from his ordeal of the past few days, drained of energy in a way he had not expected, he rested at the crest of the pass for a time before starting down. Some of that had to do with the stress and fear that his encounter with the dragon had created, but some had to do with his not eating or sleeping well. The land had a draining effect on him, its blasted, empty terrain unbearably depressing. How anything could live in that world escaped him. He guessed that what lived there was a match for the land. Certainly the dragon was. He found himself hoping that the dragon was the most dangerous creature he would come across, but what were the chances of that?

After his rest, he descended the far side of the mountains, following the long, winding thread of the pass toward a vast misted plain that stretched away as far as the eye could see. The plain looked devoid of life, but he knew better than to expect that it was. Mist clung to its surface, twisting and writhing through deep ravines and skirting broad plateaus that lifted out of the flats like beasts rising from sleep. Skeletal trees jutted from the plains like bones, and here and there black pools of water shimmered slickly.

He looked out across the plains in despair. Crossing those flats was not something he wanted to do.

But what choice did he have?

He had no idea how far he would have to travel to reach his aunt or what he would find when he did. She had been there a long time by then; anything could have happened to her. He took it on faith that she was still alive. He did not think the runes would direct him to her lifeless body. But she could be hurt or damaged mentally or emotionally. She could have been made a captive or forced to endure any number of other unpleasant things. If she required physical assistance to get back to the doorway of the Forbidding, how was he going to manage that? If she required medical help, what could he do to heal her? The more he thought about it, the more daunting the prospects seemed. Too much time had passed for everything to be unchanged in her life. Something would be wrong with her; something would have happened.

He was not looking forward to finding out what that was.

He trudged on, reached the bottom of the pass, and struck out across the plains toward the heavily misted horizon. The darkwand was taking him south and east, turning him slightly from his previous path. The way forward was swathed in encroaching darkness that lifted out of the east like a shroud ready to be laid over a corpse. The land felt and looked like that corpse, and Pen supposed that it would be appropriate to lay a shroud over it. He did not care to be out and about when that happened, however, and he began to look for somewhere to spend the night. The clumps of rocks he had relied upon for protection and shelter the past few nights were missing here. All that was available were promontories, deep ravines, and stands of stunted trees. He chose the latter, thinking that if he could find a suitable clump in which to nest, he could conceal himself from whatever might come hunting by night.

For what must have been the hundredth time, he wished he knew more about the land and its inhabitants, knowledge that might help keep him safe. But there was nothing he could do about his ignorance; he was there, and the only person likely to give him any sort of useful information was the person he was searching for.

The light darkened from misty gray to deep twilight. A fog settled in, a thickening of the mist that slowly shortened visibility to a dozen yards. Pen had been making his way toward a particularly thick stand of broad-limbed trees with branches so thoroughly intertwined it was difficult to tell where one tree stopped and another began. The canopy of limbs provided a shelter that might hide him while he sought to gain a little sleep. He questioned whether he could sleep at all given his uneasiness after the dragon experience, but he knew he had to try.

He entered the woods just as darkness was closing down, found a stand of wintry, gray-barked hardwoods that were virtually bereft of leaves, and settled down in a patch of heavy, coarse grass nestled between a pair of ancient trunks. Wrapped in his cloak, he put his back against one of the trunks and watched the onset of night steal away the last of the light.

When everything turned black, he listened to the ensuing hush. When the hush gave way to night sounds, he sat listening to those. When the sounds grew closer, a mix of clicks and huffs and low growls, he pressed harder against the tree trunk and brought the darkwand around in front of him for whatever protection it might offer.

And then the sounds evened out and smoothed over, surrounding him but not coming so close that he felt the need to move, and his eyes began to grow heavy, his breathing to deepen and slow, and finally, he slept.

When he awoke, dawn had broken in a wash of familiar hazy gray light, and the surface of the surrounding land was covered in layers of vapor that ebbed and flowed across the contours of the terrain like an ocean's waves across a rocky shore. He stared out into the all-but-invisible distance, to horizons that ended much nearer than they had the day before and revealed nothing of what they concealed, and he was immediately depressed.

He was hungry, as well, but there was nothing to eat or drink, or at least nothing on which he wished to take a chance. So he turned his efforts to stretching cramped limbs and aching muscles, to finding fresh ways to make the blood flow sufficiently that he could get to his feet and go on. He could barely tolerate the thought of it, his search beginning to take on the feel of an endless odyssey, one that might not have an attainable destination, but would simply lead him on until he was lost beyond recovery in a trackless wilderness.

He thought he might try to use his magic, to employ it to make contact with some of the vegetation or smaller creatures and see what he could learn. It was all well and good to give himself over to the directional dictates of the darkwand, but it would be better if he could feel that he had some small control over his own destiny. Just being able to know a little something more of the world through which he passed might help. He didn't yet have much confidence in his ability to get out of tight spots, and knowing that his magic could do more than make the darkwand's runes dance about would go a long ways toward changing that.

He rose finally and looked about, peering through the gloom, trying not to breathe in the fetid smells of the deadwood and dank earth. The sky was lower today, more heavily clouded, as if rain threatened, and the mix of clouds and mist gave the sense of a sky and earth become joined. The way forward seemed immeasurable, a thick wall of gray that lacked any sense of up or down or sideways. He peered into it with trepidation and repulsion, then reluctantly set out.

He walked for a time, but could not seem to get clear of the woods. He was certain they did not stretch far and that he had set out in the right direction. But trees continued to materialize through the wall of the mist, their tangled limbs linked weblike overhead.

Finally he stopped, directed his thoughts toward his aunt, and held out the staff.

Nothing.

At first, he couldn't believe it. Then he panicked. Had the magic of the darkwand ceased to respond to him? He shook his head. No, that couldn't be. He turned to his left and tried again. Still nothing. He wheeled back in the direction from which he had come and tried a third time. This time, the runes flashed brightly in response.

He had gotten turned completely around.

Still a little afraid and not wishing to chance getting lost again, he kept the staff raised and his thoughts fixed and began to retrace his steps. He moved ahead carefully, watching where he placed his feet, taking note of the location of the trees, trying to form some sense of direction, even as he relied on the darkwand's magic to keep him from wandering astray.

When he stepped from the woods finally, clear at last, he found himself in a stretch of heavy grasses and rotting logs interspersed with stagnant, scum-laced ponds. The smell was terrible. He wrinkled his nose and glanced about apprehensively, took a quick reading from the staff, and moved ahead.

He had gone only a short distance when he saw the bones. Gray and bare and broken, they lay scattered on a patch of bare earth. He stopped at once and stared at them. He did not know what kind of bones they were, but there were enough of them that he could tell that they came from more than one creature. From the number and their condition, he guessed they had been there for a long time.

He was in the middle of a feeding ground.

He looked about once more, suddenly aware of how quiet it was. *A good idea to move away from this place,* he thought.

Sliding left through the grasses, away from the bones, he walked as silently as he could toward another sparse copse of dead trees, trying to breathe evenly, to keep his head clear and his thoughts collected. *Don't panic,* he told himself. *Whatever feeds here isn't necessarily about.*

A high-pitched shriek stopped him in his tracks. A second responded to the first, and a third. They came from all sides, piercing and raw. A huge shape descended from the gloom, wings outstretched as it settled onto the log not twenty feet ahead of him. It was a vulturelike bird, its body as big as his own, its wingspan at least a dozen feet. He watched it land, wings folding against its back, its narrow head lowering.

When the head lifted a moment later, he saw that the bird had the face of a woman. But not any kind of woman he had ever seen. This woman had sharp, bony features, its mouth jutting and pinched in the manner of a beak and its eyes hard and birdlike. Its body and wings were covered with dark feathers, and its feet ended in huge, hooked talons that seemed too big for the rest of it.

Hunched so far over that it looked deformed, it sat on the log and watched him intently but made no move toward him. He held his ground a moment, then started to back away. But another shriek rose, and a second bird-woman swooped down right behind him, blocking his way. Then two more appeared, and two more after that, materializing out of the haze, wings flapping as they landed all about him, some on the ground, some on the limbs of trees. A dozen, at least, he saw, all watching him, gazes hard and fixed.

Harpies.

He swallowed hard. He knew what Harpies were; he had read stories of them in his father's histories of the Four Lands. Vicious and unpredictable creatures, Harpies had been exiled to the Forbidding along with the other dark things in the time of Faerie. If memory served him correctly, Harpies were flesh eaters that were said to have preyed on men and animals alike.

He glanced again at the talons of the one perched on the log in front of him and felt a fresh surge of panic. He needed to be somewhere else right away, but he didn't know how he could manage that, encircled as he was. Some of them had started to edge closer, making small cooing sounds. They seemed pleased. They sounded eager.

"Get away!" he shouted at them, waving his arms threateningly.

Instantly, the runes on the darkwand flared, brightening like bits of fire, dancing up and down the wood. The Harpies shrieked and flapped their leathery wings, and those advancing paused. Pen shouted at them some more and tried to move through them, but they quickly adjusted to keep him in place. He swung the staff at them. The runes danced even more wildly. The Harpies flinched but held their ground.

Pen felt an overwhelming sense of desperation. He had to find something more effective. He remembered the dragon then and how his use of the wishsong had sent the runes flying off into the distance, luring it away. Perhaps that would work with the Harpies, as well. He didn't have much control over how the magic worked, but it was all he could think of.

He began to sing boldly, as if he might force his way through his attackers by the sheer force of his voice. He sang snatches of phrases and bits and pieces of things that just came to him, hoping that something would work. It did. Rune images spun off the staff in a glowing swirl and soared skyward, forming bright, complex patterns against the dark ceiling of the clouds.

The Harpies watched as the images lifted into the sky but they did not follow.

Pen's desperation increased. He didn't know what more he could do. He kept singing, punctuating his increasingly frantic efforts with shouts and cries, looking for something that would drive the Harpies back. But, having seen that his magic was confined to pretty glowing images that danced and flew and did nothing more, the bird-women were advancing again. Their sharp eyes glittered in the dim light and their strange mouths worked slowly up and down, opening and closing hungrily.

Pen gripped the darkwand tightly in both hands and prepared to use it as a club. It was all he had left.

But just when it seemed that he was all out of chances, a dark shape appeared on the horizon, winging toward him, quickly growing larger and taking form. The dragon! It was tracking the rune images once more, following them to their source. How it had seen them from so far away, Pen couldn't know. But it was flying right for where the greatest number circled and danced against the clouds overhead.

Their bright, hard eyes fixed on Pen, the Harpies didn't see the dragon at first. Then the dragon screamed—there was no other word for it—and they swung about swiftly, necks craned, a fresh urgency in their posture. A few took flight immediately, but the rest hesitated, unwilling to abandon their prey.

Plummeting out of the sky with such swiftness that Pen, who had thought he might try to make a run for it, had no chance to do anything but stand and watch, the dragon dropped on them like a stone. It snatched up the Harpies the way a big cat might small birds, tearing them apart and casting them aside as fast as it could reach them. A few flew at the dragon with their wicked talons outstretched, but the beast simply crushed them in its huge jaws and flung them to the ground. The Harpies screamed and hissed and flapped their wings frantically, unable to escape.

One by one, the dragon killed them until only two were left, crawling about the blood-soaked earth and whimpering in despair. The dragon played with them, nudging them this way and that. Pen watched for as long as it took him to realize that he might be next, then slowly backed away. Rune images still danced and soared overhead, and fresh images leapt from the darkwand to whirl about the dragon like fireflies. If the dragon saw them, it gave no indication. For the moment, its attention was fixed on its new toys.

Pen reached the edge of the woods without the dragon taking notice and slipped into the trees. After he was well into them, he put the darkwand beneath his cloak, closed down his thoughts of his aunt, and waited for the runes to go dark.

Soaked in his own sweat, he pushed on, barely able to make himself move. He had thought the dragon safely gone. But it couldn't have been far away if it had seen the rune images. That should have made him happy, since it had saved his life, but it only made him further aware of how vulnerable he was. He might be saved for the moment, but he would remain in peril until he was out of the Forbidding and back in the Four Lands. Until then, his life span probably didn't measure the length of his arm. He had to find his aunt, and he had to find her quickly or his luck would be used up.

He kept walking, refusing to look back, heading in the general direction he knew he had to go. He kept the darkwand lowered and inactive, afraid to do anything that would bring the runes to life.

He was half a mile away before he could no longer hear the crunching of bones.

TWENTY-TWO

No matter how often she scowled at him, he just wouldn't stop talking about it.

"Such power, Straken Queen! Such incredible power! No one can match you—no one who is or ever was! I sensed you were special, I did, Grianne of the trees! When I first saw you from my hiding place and knew you for who you were, I knew, too, *what* you were! It was in your eyes and the way you carried yourself. It was in your voice when you first spoke to me. You awoke in a prison, sent by your enemies to be destroyed, and still you showed no fear! *That* is evidence of real power!"

She let him go on mostly because she didn't know how to shut him up. Weka Dart was a bundle of pent-up energy, bouncing off the cavern walls and skittering across the uneven floor, darting this way and that, rushing ahead and then wheeling back, a wild thing in search of an outlet. She didn't think he could help himself; that was just the way he was, a creature of ungovernable whims and uncontrollable urges. He had been like that on the journey to the Forbidding's version of the Hadeshorn, so his hyperactivity was not a surprise.

In any case, she was too tired to do much more than put one foot in front of the other and press on.

"How much farther?" she asked at one point.

"Not far, not far," he said, dashing back to take her hand, which she yanked away irritably. "The tunnels open onto the Pashanon just ahead, and then we will be back outside in the fresh air and light!"

It was all relative, she supposed, picturing the world that waited with its greasy air and its dingy skies. She would not know true fresh air and light again ever if she did not get back into her own world. She found herself thinking again of the boy who was coming to find her, the salvation she had been promised by the Warlock Lord. He seemed such an impossibility that she could not make herself accept that he was real. But if he wasn't, she was trapped there forever. So she kept alive a faint hope that somehow he would appear, whether that appearance was reflected accurately in the words of the promise or in some less easily discernible way. She just knew it had better happen soon because she was beginning to fail.

She took a moment to measure the truth of that statement and found it accurate. It was happening in subtle ways—ways she did not think she could reverse while trapped within the Forbidding. Her physical strength was eroded, the result of poor food and drink, a lack of sleep, and the debilitating struggles she had waged with Tael Riverine. But her emotional and psychological strengths had been drained, as well, and those in a more direct and damaging way. She had been forced to use the magic several times, and each time she had felt something change inside her. It was bad enough that she was forced to use it at all—worse still that she was forced to use it in such horrifying ways. Assimilating with the Furies had torn apart her psyche. Resisting the power of the conjure collar had all but broken her spirit.

But her confrontation with the Graumth had reduced her to a new level of despair, one so fraught with bad feelings that she was literally afraid of calling up the magic again. It was the way the wishsong had responded. She should have been thankful she still had command of it after all she had been through. She should have welcomed its appearance. But the strength of its response had terrified her. It had been not only greater than she had expected, but also virtually uncontrollable. It hadn't just surfaced on being summoned, ready to do her bidding. It had exploded out of her, so wild and destructive that she couldn't hold it back. She had lived with the wishsong for more than thirty years, and she had known before coming into the Forbidding what to expect from it. But that was changed. The magic had taken on a new feel, becoming something she didn't recognize. It was a strange creature living inside her, threatening her in ways that made her afraid for the first time in years.

What she feared most was that it had evolved because of where she was and that the unforeseen evolution was changing her into something that belonged more to the Forbidding than to her world.

Yet what could she do to stop it?

Weka Dart had probably done as much for her as he could. Debilitated or not, she was the one with the magic. If they were backed into a corner, she was the one who could keep them alive. She would have to put aside her concerns about using the magic. The hunt for them would continue, and it would not end until she was free of the Forbidding or she was dead.

They continued working cautiously through the tunnels below Kraal Reach, and it wasn't long until there was a brightening of the darkness ahead of them. Within minutes, they had reached a fissure in the mountain rock, one that opened into the clouded mistiness of the Pashanon.

They stood in silence for a moment, staring out onto a broad wetlands pocked by dozens of stagnant pools and vast stands of heavy grasses and thick scrub. The waters of the ponds nearest were covered in greenish slime and smelled of decay. Insects buzzed and chirped from every quarter, swarms of gnats and flies hovered above the surface of the ponds, and snakes slid soundlessly through the shadows.

The wetlands spread away for miles in all directions.

Grianne shook her head in dismay. "How do we get through this?"

Weka Dart looked over at her, eyes bright and teeth showing. "Follow me, Grianne of the wondrous magic, and I will show you."

Without pausing, he started out through the swamp. She followed with no small amount of misgiving, not certain she should trust his judgment, yet unwilling to be left behind. But the Ulk Bog seemed to know what he was doing. Even though the hazy light was pale and deceptive, he chose their path without hesitating. Now and then he would change course in midstride, turning another way. More than once he reversed himself entirely, muttering about obstacles that hadn't been there before, that didn't belong, that had appeared merely to vex him. When a snake crossed his path he simply reached down, snatched it up, and tossed it aside. He didn't seem afraid of them. He didn't seem to mind the clouds of insects either. He lapped at them with his tongue, hissed at them to clear his nostrils.

Disgusted by her surroundings, Grianne settled for putting her arm and the sleeve of her tunic across her mouth and nose and lowering her head as far as she could without losing sight of the Ulk Bog. The odor of death permeated the air; she could feel the decay worming its way into her breathing passages. She used a little of the wishsong's magic to keep it all at bay—not enough to give them away to anyone following, but enough to give her a measure of distance from the foulness. She cast quick glances all about as they went, searching for movement that might signal a pursuit. But nothing of that sort showed itself, and she began to wonder if perhaps chase had not yet been given. It seemed unlikely that the dead Goblins hadn't been discovered in a changing of the guard, but it was possible. It was possible, as well, that even if they had been discovered, the search for her was still being conducted inside the walls of Kraal Reach and hadn't yet extended to the Pashanon.

Of course, when it did, she would be tracked down pretty fast if she was still out in the open.

"Is there somewhere we can go to hide?" she asked Weka Dart at one point, hurrying to catch up with him as he slipped eel-like through the swamp.

He gave her an irritated glance, feral features screwed up with concentration, breathing quick and heavy. "A place to hide? Why would we hide, Straken Queen? If we are going to your world, we should go there at once."

She took a quick breath. She had forgotten that she had not told him of the boy, of the need for the boy to find her before she could go anywhere. "We might not be able to do that," she said.

He wheeled on her, his face contorted with fury. "What do you mean, *We might not be able to do that*? What are you saying, Grianne of the broken promises?"

She would not tolerate his insolence or his rebelliousness, not then and not with what was at stake. She snatched his tunic front and yanked him close.

"Don't question me, little Ulk Bog!" she hissed. "I didn't make you a promise about how this would happen. Or even that it would happen. I told you there was a chance I couldn't do anything to help either of us!"

He hissed back at her, then dropped his head and sulked. "I didn't mean anything by it. You just upset me. You frightened me. I thought you had a plan."

She released him. "I do, but it relies on help from my own world. Someone is coming to find me, someone who can get through the Forbidding without help from Tael Riverine. We have to wait until he appears. I don't know when that will be. But if it doesn't happen before we reach the Dragon Line, then we might have to hide for a while. Do you understand?"

He nodded sullenly. "I understand."

"Then think about where we might go to do that and stop being so suspicious!"

She kicked at him, and he started off again, skittering away through the grasses. There was no point in telling him everything. Certainly not that she was waiting for a mysterious boy, for something of which she could barely conceive, for a miracle. She hated having told him she would try to get him out of the Forbidding. She would not have done so if there had been any other way of securing his help. She had no idea if there was a way to free him. Or even if such freedom was a good idea. In fact, it probably wasn't. But she would have said or done anything to escape Tael Riverine and thwart his plan to make her the bearer of his spawn. She shuddered at the thought of that, determined that she would die before she would let herself be taken by him again.

They slogged on through the fading daylight, nightfall tracking them west until, sweeping slowly across the flats, it began to overtake them. They crossed out of the swamp and found dry ground beyond, a wintry plain in which the grasses were as dry as old bones, crackling beneath their feet as they stepped through them. Ahead the land stretched away, bleak and empty, crisscrossed by deep ravines and dotted by hummocks.

After a time, Weka Dart dropped back to walk beside her.

"I didn't mean what I said before." He looked at her with his sharp, restless eyes, and then glanced away quickly. "I know you keep your promises. I know you haven't lied to me. If anyone has lied . . ." He shook his head. "I can't help myself, you know. I have lied about everything all my life because that is how Ulk Bogs are. That is how we live. That is how we stay alive. We lie to keep others from gaining an advantage over us."

"I don't think lying does as much for you as you think," she replied. "Do you know what they say about lies? They say that lies have a way of coming back to haunt you."

He shrugged. "I just want you to know that I will change when you take me to your country. I won't lie anymore. Or, at least, I will try hard not to lie. I will be a good companion for you, Grianne of the kind eyes. I will help you do your work, whatever your work is. You will see that I am always there to do your bidding. Here, I would do the bidding of a Straken to stay alive. I would do it because I would have no choice. But it will not be like that with you. I will do your bidding because I want to. Because I respect you."

She sighed wearily. "You don't know me well enough to promise that, Weka Dart. I am not what you think. I have dark secrets in my life. I have a history that is every bit as bad as that of Tael Riverine. I might not be like the demon now, but I was once, not so long ago." She paused. "I might still be like him in some ways."

But the Ulk Bog shook his head stubbornly. "No, you are not like him. You could never be like him."

But I was like him, she thought, the weight of the admission infusing her with a sadness she could barely stand. *I could be like him again.*

Ahead, the flats turned rocky and were eroded by gullies and pocked by wormholes, the grasses and scrub disappearing entirely, the whole of the landscape changing abruptly to something Grianne hadn't seen before. Weka Dart, who was walking next to her but paying little attention to the land into which they were walking, suddenly caught sight of where they were going and drew up short, putting out his arm urgently.

"Wait, stay where you are!" he snapped.

He scanned the rocky flats, searching for something, then hissed sharply. "This wasn't here before!" he exclaimed. "This is new! They've migrated from somewhere else and set up their colony here! How long, I wonder? Very recent. Very."

She looked down at him. "What are you talking about?"

He gave her one of his frightening grins, the ones that showed all his needle-sharp teeth. "Asphinx! This flat is riddled with them."

"The snakes?"

His head cocked. "Do you know about them?"

She did. Asphinx had been exiled to the Forbidding with the other dark things of Faerie. Except for one that had been sealed in a crevice by the Stone King, Uhl Belk, in the caverns of the Hall of Kings to guard the Black Elfstone. Walker Boh, before he became a Druid, had been bitten while searching for the talisman, and his arm had turned to stone. The story was a part of Bek's histories of the Shannara kin, a story she remembered as crucial to what happened to Walker later in his transformation into Allanon's heir.

She glanced back at the flats. "How many are out there?"

He shrugged. "Thousands. Want to have a look?"

"No, I don't want to have a look. Can we get around them?"

He gestured left. "This way. Stay off the rocks and you won't have to deal with them. But watch your step anyway. If one bites you, you will make a nice statue for the birds to perch on."

They walked carefully around the colony, staying on the grassy fringe and keeping well back from where the rocks began. It took them a long time to get all the way to the other side, and by then darkness had settled in so thoroughly that it was difficult to see more than a dozen feet.

Weka Dart took a quick visual survey of their surroundings and nodded. "We'll camp over there, in that stand of wincies." He gestured toward a small grove of needled trees that looked like diseased pines. "Wincies give us some protection. Snakes don't like their scent, and flying things can't get through the screen of their branches without first landing, which they won't do at night. A good place for us to get some rest."

Grianne glanced back the way they had come, toward Kraal Reach. "Do you think they have begun to track us yet?"

"Oh, yes." Weka Dart sounded indifferent. "The Straken Lord will have found his guards and your discarded collar. He will have determined which way you have gone. He will have sent Hobstull and his minions to bring you back." His dark eyes glittered in the fading light. "His magic is very powerful, Grianne Ohmsford. Very powerful. But not so powerful as yours."

She knelt in front of the Ulk Bog. "Listen to me. I know you want me to take you out of the Forbidding, and I have promised I will try. But if Hobstull and whatever dark things he commands catch up to us, I want you to leave me to deal with them. I want you to find someplace to hide—and don't let them see you. Don't give yourself away." She paused. "They don't know about you yet, do they?"

He snorted. "Of course they know about me. Tael Riverine will have determined my presence as easily as he will have recognized your absence. Running and hiding will do me no good. I settled my fate by coming to you in the dungeons of Kraal Reach, Straken Queen. That is why it is so important that you take me with you. If I remain in the world of the Jarka Ruus, I am dead. Now, come."

She ignored the sinking feeling in her stomach and followed him to the trees he called wincies. They were tall, spidery hardwoods with long, thin, whiplike branches that interlaced and, at some points, knotted together. With Weka Dart leading, they slipped into their midst, ducking more than once to get through, wending their way into the center of the grove. The Ulk Bog made a quick check of their surroundings and determined them safe.

"Now you should sleep while I keep watch," he told her. "We must set out early, and you will need your strength. Go ahead. Sleep."

Too tired to argue, she lay down obediently. She closed her eyes, thinking to do little more than nap. Her mind was awash in doubts and fears, in worries of what they would have to do to stay alive another day. Images of her imprisonment and of the creatures that had threatened her paraded like specters. She felt the magic of the conjure collar even as she slept, ripping her apart, draining her strength, and filling her with pain.

She would never sleep again, she thought, and was asleep in seconds.

Her waking thoughts followed her into her sleep and became her dreams, dark and menacing. The Straken Lord tracked her down shadowy corridors, close behind but just out of sight. He carried in one hand the conjure collar with which he would bind her to him, its fastenings glittering like teeth. Other creatures from the Forbidding appeared in front of her, creatures of all sizes and shapes, their features not entirely distinct, but their intentions clear. Winged monsters clung to the ceiling overhead, with claws that gripped like iron, threatening to drop on top of her if she dared to slow. She ran from all of them, blindly and helplessly, with no destination in mind and no end in sight.

She came awake to the sound of howling wolves, and a terrified gasp escaped her lips.

"Hssstt!" Weka Dart whispered in her ear. He was crouched next to her in the darkness, a vague shape barely distinguishable from the night. "Demonwolves! They've found us!"

She tried to scramble to her feet, but he forced her down again, hissing, "No, no, don't move! Stay still! They don't know exactly where we are and we don't want to tell them. Let them come to us!"

She panicked. "But they'll—"

"They'll go the way I want them to go, Straken Queen. They'll go the way of dead things!"

She forced herself to remain calm while trying to sort through what he was talking about. He didn't seem panicked. He didn't even seem particularly worried. He stared past her east, toward Kraal Reach and the sound of the howling as it drew steadily louder, drawing nearer.

She realized suddenly that she was cold. She glanced down and saw that she was missing her cloak.

Weka Dart glanced over quickly. "They have your scent well and good. But they won't have you, Grianne of the wincie woods!"

The howls were very close, coming fast, and there were other sounds as well, shouts and cries of other creatures as they urged the demonwolves on. The pursuit was heated, a sense of expectancy reverberating in the wildness of its sounds.

Then suddenly, with a swiftness that turned her stomach to ice, everything changed. The howls turned to screams and growls filled with rage. The shouts and cries turned to shrieks filled with terror. The pitch rose and the rawness sharpened, and the night was alive with a cacophony that transcended anything Grianne Ohmsford had ever heard. Her pursuers were under attack themselves and fighting for their lives.

At her side, Weka Dart laughed aloud. "They've found what they were searching for, but not what they expected, Straken Queen! Listen to them! Too bad they weren't paying better attention to what they were doing! I think maybe they've encountered something with teeth sharper than their own!"

She stared at him, and then she remembered. *The Asphinx!*

Her pursuers had stumbled right into the center of the colony, and the snakes were striking at them. She listened anew to the sounds of the struggle, and the sounds told her everything. "You put my cloak out there in the middle of the snakes!" she exclaimed. "You knew!"

His grin was frightening. "I suspected. They came more quickly than I had thought they would. Your cloak was a lure to draw them away from us. The night is dark and visibility poor. Too bad for them."

The sounds were dying out, the growls and screams and shrieks turned to whimpers and moans, to gasps that carried even to where she crouched in the trees next to the Ulk Bog. She tried not to listen, but could not help herself. It was destruction of a sort with which she was familiar and from which she could not turn away.

Then everything went still, save for a single lengthy, ragged sob. And then even that was gone.

Weka Dart bent close. "Isn't the silence beautiful?" he whispered.

When it was light enough to do so, the dawn a faint tinge of pale gray brightness set low against the horizon to the east, they walked back to where the Asphinx colony waited. What Grianne Ohmsford saw left her stunned. Statues filled the flats, sculpted creatures posed in desperate positions of battle and flight. There were demonwolves and Goblins, dozens of each, their bodies and necks twisted, their limbs lifted and crooked, and their mouths open in soundless cries.

In their midst stood Hobstull, his lean body rigid, his narrow face taut, hands closed into fists in recognition of what was happening to him.

All had been turned to stone. Not a one had escaped.

"It happens so quickly when you are bitten repeatedly," Weka Dart ventured. "No waiting around for the inevitable. No false hope that you might somehow find a cure. You haven't got more than a minute before it's over. Better that way."

He walked to the edge of the field, picked up one end of a thin line, and reeled in Grianne's cloak, which had been tossed into the center of the killing field. Shaking it out carefully to make certain no snakes had hidden in its folds, he detached the line and handed the cloak back to her. "There, good as ever."

She took the cloak and stared at him, seeing him in an entirely new light, one that gave her pause.

"I prefer Hobstull as a statue," he declared, his smile wicked and challenging. "Don't you?" He dusted off his hands and looked east. "Time to be on our way. The light is good enough for travel. If others are coming, we don't want to be here to greet them."

He walked away, and Grianne followed. As she did so, she glanced back a final time, reminded suddenly of her past. The Ilse Witch had used snakes to dispose of her enemies. That had been a long time ago, and she was no longer that person. Or didn't want to be. But she had felt herself reverting in her battles with the Straken Lord and the Furies. She had felt the magic turning her dark and hard again. It wasn't so difficult to imagine that, whether she wished it or not, she might be changing into something she had thought safely left behind.

She mulled the possibility as they walked, wondering what she could do to prevent it. It was like trying to hold water in your fingers; you could capture the wetness, but the water itself slipped away. She was that water, and she was running swiftly through the cracks in her determination.

They walked several miles, far enough that she could no longer see the statues and the flats, far enough that she had begun to turn her thoughts again to their destination. She could already see the dark rise of the Dragon Line ahead of them.

Then Weka Dart slowed. "Someone is coming," he said.

She peered into the distance. At first, she didn't see anything. The haze and the gloom obscured everything, blending the features of the landscape together. But finally she saw movement. A solitary figure was coming toward them, cloaked and spectral against the still-dark horizon. She tried to make out its features and failed. She could tell only one thing about it.

It was carrying a staff that glowed like fire.

TWENTY-THREE

Surrounded by the dark, menacing forms of his black-clad guards, Sen Dunsidan stalked onto the airfield and crossed to where the *Zolomach* was anchored at the center of the cordoned-off flats south. Chains ringed the big airship, and dozens of Federation soldiers stood at watch. He had no reason to believe that the Free-born would even know of her yet, let alone think to mount an attack, but since the loss of the *Dechtera* and other recent events he wasn't taking any chances.

He stopped when still some distance off to admire the warship. The *Zolomach* was sleek and smooth, strong enough to withstand an attack by multiple enemy craft if she chose to fight and fast enough to outrun them if she chose not to. She was an improvement over the *Dechtera*, not so cumbersome and unresponsive, better suited to making the maneuvers necessary to bring her weapons into line, more able to adjust to the unexpected. She had not yet been put into service on the Prekkendorran though she had been tested and was ready to fly north.

Which she would do, he promised himself, as soon as Etan Orek confirmed that the casing for the fire launcher was complete and the weapon ready to be installed on the *Zolomach*'s foredeck. All that would happen by "sunrise tomorrow," the little engineer had promised him, and Sen Dunsidan intended to take him at his word.

He moved ahead again, reaching the airship and climbing

aboard to view the swivel base on which the fire launcher would be mounted. It was a simple metal platform that rotated on a bed of gears and bearings activated by a pair of release levers, the whole of the assembly able to swivel forty-five degrees to either side from dead forward. Its mobility was an improvement over the mechanism employed on the *Dechtera*, as well. There would be no mishaps when he sent her out. The *Zolomach* would finish the job the *Dechtera* had started.

"Prime Minister."

He turned to find the Captain of the airship saluting him, eager to make his report. "Captain. Is she ready?"

"Yes, my lord. She awaits only the emplacement of the weapon, and she is on her way."

"You've shielded the rudders and underside controls so that we won't have a repeat of the *Dechtera's* collapse?"

The Captain nodded. "It will take a good deal more than a rail sling to damage her steering this time."

Sen Dunsidan didn't miss a beat. "What would it take, exactly?"

The Captain hesitated. "Another airship would have to ram her from below. That would be very difficult."

The Prime Minister looked away a moment, considering. There was no preventing every possibility, of course. Still, the Captain's words made him uneasy. "Stores and weapons are all accounted for?"

"Loaded and tied down. We are ready, Prime Minister."

Sen Dunsidan looked back at him. "I want you to post men at the rails during battle to watch for the possibility of an underside attack on the steering. I want you to devise a method of alerting the pilot box of the danger of such an attack so that evasive action can be taken in time to prevent any damage. Use the remainder of the day to train a team of men to do that. Take the *Zolomach* aloft and practice." He paused. "There are to be no mistakes, Captain. Is that understood?"

A shade paler than before, seeing in Sen Dunsidan's eyes his fate should he fail to comply, the other man nodded wordlessly.

"Good. I will get back to you with departure orders this evening." He waved the other off. "Get on with it."

His guard following close on his heels, he climbed back down the ladder, walked to the *Zolomach's* stern to check the shielding, found it satisfactory, and strolled back out onto the airfield. Turning, he watched the airship's Captain summon his crew to quarters, his Lieutenants shouting out instructions, his men rushing to man their positions for lifting off. Within moments, the anchor ropes were released and the big warship was sailing off into the afternoon sky.

This time, he thought as he watched her fly into the depthless blue void, *I'll use the fire launcher on the Free-born until I can't see anything moving.*

His determination to crush the Free-born was fueled by an unpleasant turn of events. First, those ragtag Elves had crushed his pursuit force in the hills north of the Prekkendorran. Then there had been the midnight raid that resulted in the destruction of the *Dechtera* and her weapon. Less than two days ago, a counterstrike by Free-born forces under the command of Vaden Wick had smashed his siege lines and driven his Federation soldiers all the way back to their original defenses, putting them right where they had been weeks earlier before the successes against Kellen Elessedil and the Elves. Except that now, after collapsing the right flank of the Federation army during the counterattack, Wick had gained a foothold in the hills east, threatening an assault that would roll up the entire Federation line and drive the army back into the middle Southland.

That last reversal had determined for him his present course of action. Whatever else happened, he did not intend to suffer a defeat of the sort that would result if his defensive line collapsed and was overrun. The members of the Coalition Council were afraid of him, but only so long as he did not show himself to be vulnerable. If he demonstrated any noticeable weakness, they would move quickly to eliminate him. A defeat on the Prekkendorran would give them all the encouragement they needed. No one would support him if the army was thrown back, not after all his promises of imminent victory.

So, in spite of Iridia Eleri's insistence on attacking the Elves and Arborlon, he had decided to use the fire launcher on the Free-born lines first, breaking down their defenses and driving them off the Prekkendorran for good. There would be plenty of time after that to test Iridia's theories about the erosion of Elven morale.

Suddenly uneasy, he glanced around. Even the thought of Iridia's name made him nervous. In spite of the presence of his guards, he found himself looking over his shoulder constantly. He had never been comfortable with her, but after their confrontation three nights earlier, he was much less so. It was something about her eyes or her voice, something in the way she held herself whenever she saw him. Whatever it was, it left him wondering how wise it was to continue to keep her around. He might be better off to get rid of her and go back to the way things were before. He didn't trust Shadea, but at least with her, what you saw was what you got. With Iridia, he wasn't sure.

He started back across the airfield toward his carriage. Iridia had traveled back with him to Arishaig, but he had not seen much of her since. He should have been grateful. Instead he found himself wondering where she was.

Perhaps he should find out.

He reached his carriage and climbed inside, half expecting to find her waiting. But the carriage was empty. He sat motionless, thinking about what he should do next. He was impatient for the departure north, back to the Prekkendorran. He was anxious to watch the destruction of the Free-born, to know that his weapon would put an end to them once and for all. He would not feel comfortable until then, no matter how hard he tried to reassure himself that matters were progressing as well as could be expected.

He glanced out the carriage window. He was aware of the driver sitting atop his seat, waiting for instructions. Let him wait. He began thinking about Iridia again. If his instincts were telling him the truth—and they usually were—he should get rid of her as soon as he could find a way to do so without placing himself in danger.

But what would be the best way?

Then, all at once, he knew. He would give her back to Shadea. He would drug her, bind her, and transport her back to Paranor. Shadea would know what to do with her and would welcome the opportunity. There was no longer any question of allowing Iridia back into the Druid order. There was no chance that Shadea would attempt to repair their shattered friendship. Shadea would eliminate Iridia in the blink of an eye, and that would be that.

Satisfied with his plan, he signaled for the driver to take him over to the engineering buildings and Etan Orek.

He rode slouched down in his seat, pondering his plan. He would have to be very careful how he carried it out. Iridia was no fool. She could smell a trap in the way most Druids could; her magic gave her a sixth sense about treachery. She already knew he didn't trust her; he would have to find a way to seduce her into thinking that he did. Perhaps if he agreed to her plan to fly the *Zolomach* to Arborlon, she would let down her guard. It couldn't hurt to try, to tell her he had decided to do as she advised. He could even pretend he was taking her there; propose a toast after they were on board the airship and let the drug do the rest. She wouldn't know what was happening until it was too late. Then he could fly her to Paranor and leave her in the hands of the Druids, and he would never have to worry about her again.

Calmed, reassured that his plan would work, he relaxed for the rest of the ride and looked out at the buildings of the city, their walls golden with the deepening of the approaching sunset.

When the carriage reached the engineering compound, he climbed down, his guards clustered about him, and waited for Etan Orek to respond to his summons. He did not have to wait long. The little engineer appeared within moments and hurried forward to meet his benefactor, eyes bright with excitement, hands clasped, head lowering deferentially as he scurried up.

"My lord," he said as he bowed so low that Sen Dunsidan thought he might topple over.

"Good day to you, Engineer Orek," he replied. He held himself straight, using his size and the strength of his voice to dominate the other. "How do matters progress with the weapon?"

The deferential gaze lifted marginally. "It is finished, Prime Minister! The casing was completed last night, and this morning I installed the weapon's components. Everything is in order. I tested it and it worked perfectly."

Sen Dunsidan felt a surge of satisfaction. Things were coming together nicely. "The range and power of this weapon are similar to those of the other?"

"Oh, much better! The faceting and alignment of the crystals have enhanced the gathering and expulsion of the fire. Where the first weapon would have burned a hole through metal or wood or set sails afire, the second actually incinerates them. It will bring down an airship or explode a defensive wall with virtually no effort at all."

Sen Dunsidan was nodding with approval. "Once again, Engineer, well done. Have we others in the making?"

The little man beamed. "We do. Two more, in fact. I need time to finish them, but they will be ready within a few weeks. Is that soon enough?"

Nothing sooner than tomorrow was soon enough, but Sen Dunsidan knew better than to press the matter. Completion of one weapon was all he needed, and he had that.

"Yes, two weeks is fine," he replied.

"My lord," Etan Orek said softly, moving a step closer. "Before you leave for the airfield, I have something new to show you."

"Something new?"

"I have made a fresh discovery." The bright eyes darted restlessly, looking right and left. "I think you need to see it."

Sen Dunsidan was excited all over again. A new discovery? What could it be? He remembered when Etan Orek had come to him in his bedchamber with news of the discovery of the fire launcher. He remembered his pleasure at finding out what the launcher did. And now there was something else?

"What have you found?" he demanded. He inclined his leonine head slightly, keeping the conversation just between them. "Tell me."

But Etan Orek shook his head. "No, Prime Minister, I need to show you." He glanced around some more. "Alone. Like before. You don't want anyone else to see this right away. For now, this information should belong only to you."

Sen Dunsidan thought about that a moment. He had gone down that road before with the little engineer. During his first visit, Orek had insisted he come into the workroom alone to view the fire launcher, leaving his guards outside. He had proved he was no threat. Nothing had changed where that was concerned. It wouldn't hurt to indulge him. He glanced at the burly, black-clad soldiers surrounding him. He would station them right outside the door, just as he had done before, safely within call.

"Very well," he agreed. "Show me."

With Orek leading the way, they moved over to the building in which the little engineer had been confined for the past few weeks. Sen Dunsidan was impatient to discover what it was the other had stumbled across. Perhaps this time he had found a way to increase airship thrust through enhanced effectiveness in the placement of the diapson crystals. It was while working on employing combinations of crystals that he had made his discovery of the fire launcher. Perhaps something similar had happened here.

He brushed back his mane of white hair and walked a little faster.

Inside the building, they filed down a broad central corridor to the workroom assigned to Orek, the engineer leading, Sen Dunsidan just behind, and his bodyguards following in a knot. At the door to the room, Etan Orek turned to him expectantly.

Sen Dunsidan glanced back at his Captain of the Guard. "Wait here for me, just outside the door. Come if I call."

He felt foolish asking even that. The odds of the little engineer turning treacherous were almost nonexistent. After all, Etan Orek's elevation in the ranks of Sen Dunsidan's subordinates depended entirely on him.

He went through the door, which the little man closed carefully behind them, and stood looking at the workbenches and clutter. Everything was just as he remembered it. His gaze drifted across the scattering of projects and scraps to the back table and the long metal box that held the newest discovery. Without waiting for the other man, he walked quickly to where the sleek casing was stretched across a pair of workbenches. He ran his hands lovingly over the smooth metal, and then lifted the top to peek inside at the array of crystals and shields. So perfect! He smiled broadly, already imagining the destruction he would be witness to in the days ahead.

He turned back to his engineer. "What is it that you wanted to show me?"

Etan Orek smiled and pointed off to his right to another workbench. "There, Prime Minister."

Sen Dunsidan turned and looked. He didn't see what the other was pointing at. He walked forward a few steps and stopped, still not seeing.

"What is it I am supposed to be looking at?" he asked.

Then everything went dark.

When he regained consciousness, he was stripped naked and tied down so securely to one of the workbenches that he couldn't move at all. Pain washed through his limbs and body, and his throat burned as if it were on fire.

He tried to speak and found he couldn't.

Etan Orek appeared next to him and bent close. "Don't bother trying to say anything, Sen Dunsidan. I removed your vocal cords while you were unconscious."

Sen Dunsidan stared. Etan Orek was speaking, but it wasn't the engineer's voice he was hearing. It was a voice he had never heard before, a raw and whispery croak that seemed dredged up from the rough depths of a rock quarry. The eyes weren't right, either. They were Iridia's eyes. Or were they? They reminded him of eyes he had seen somewhere else, somewhere he had all but forgotten. Eyes that belonged to the Ilse Witch. Or to the Morgawr.

Suddenly, he was more afraid than he had ever been in his life. He was terrified. It wasn't Etan Orek he was looking at. It was someone or something else entirely. In spite of what he had been told, he tried to scream. He opened his mouth wide and screamed with everything he could muster. But no sound came forth—only a tiny bubbling and a spray of his own blood.

"You waste your energy," his captor whispered. "Better save what is left. You will need it." He smiled. "You have no idea what has happened to you, do you? No idea at all. Listen to me, then, for the time you have left. I am not Etan Orek, and I was not Iridia Eleri, either. I killed them both and took their skins to hide what I really am. I am something from another place, Prime Minister. I am what you and your foolish Druids released from the Forbidding when you sent your Ard Rhys there to be imprisoned. It was not your fault that you did so; how could you know what you were doing when we were so careful not to let you discover the truth?"

He glanced over his shoulder at the door, and then bent close again. "Your fate is your own doing, Prime Minister. You could have avoided this if you hadn't been so insistent on attacking the Prekkendorran. Had you done as I suggested and gone to Arborlon, you would have preserved your life for at least a little while longer."

Sen Dunsidan stared at the other in horror, the full impact of those words settling in. Desperate to free himself, he surged upward violently against his bonds, but he might as well have been wrestling against iron chains.

"It is time for you to die, Sen Dunsidan. I doubt that many will miss you. I have watched how you are received, and there is no love for you. There is only hatred and fear and a sense it would be better for everyone if you simply disappeared."

His captor moved to the head of the workbench, standing where Sen Dunsidan could not see what he was doing. His mind fought to accept what was happening, to make sense of his situation, but all he could think about was getting free. He jerked his head back and forth violently, hammering it up and down against the table, trying to draw the attention of his guards who waited for his call from just outside the doorway of the workroom. Why had he left them out there? Why had he been so confident that he was safe?

Fool!

Hands grasped his head and held it firmly in place. The hands were scaly and clawed, and he shuddered at their touch. A face bent close, a face like none he had ever seen.

"Hold still," the creature whispered. "Breathe deeply, and it will all go much easier for you."

It leaned forward slowly, still holding Sen Dunsidan's head firmly in place. The clawed fingers reached into the corners of his mouth and pried it open. Sen Dunsidan tried again to scream and again failed. The creature's face was dissolving as it lowered toward his own, and he felt something bitter and sharp fill his mouth and worm its way down his throat. It was like inhaling a steaming mist thick with the taste of iron and sulfur. He gagged, but the mist continued down his throat and into his body, working its way all through him.

When the pain started, he began to shriek soundlessly, over and over again. His body heaved and bucked and twisted in a futile effort to gain relief. Nothing helped. The invasion continued until the pain became unbearable.

He never knew if his heart or his sanity gave out first, but either way, it was the end of him.

It was well after sunset, the sky beginning to fill with stars, a quarter moon rising in the east and the lights of the city of Arishaig glittering in the distance, when the Prime Minister reached the airfield. Accompanied by his personal guard and a wagon with its bed covered in a canvas, he arrived in his carriage. The Captain of the *Zolomach* was waiting for him, his airship ready and his crew trained as ordered to prevent against attacks on the vessel's steering. All that was needed was the order to depart.

The Prime Minister strode over wordlessly, wrapped and hooded in a heavy travel cloak, his face concealed in shadow.

The Captain came to attention and saluted. "My lord."

"Ready, Captain?"

"Yes, my lord."

"The weapon is in the wagon. Carry it aboard and set it in place. Make sure it is properly tightened down and the swivel mechanism working as it should. Take as much time as you need. Our departure is at dawn. Any questions?"

His guards were already unloading the weapon from the wagon bed and setting it carefully on the ground. "No questions, my lord," the Captain replied. "We will be ready at dawn." He paused. "You will be sailing with us?"

"I will."

"Engineer Orek?"

"Engineer Orek will not be coming back with us. He met with an accident. A fire. His workroom and all of his projects and plans were destroyed. A terrible loss. He was careless, and it cost him dearly. A good lesson for us all. Let's remember it when we set sail tomorrow. We can't afford any mistakes on the Prekkendorran."

"No, Prime Minister, of course." The Captain didn't like the way the other's eyes glinted from within the hood. "There will be no mistakes."

"I will hold you to your word," the Moric advised from within the skin of Sen Dunsidan, and turned away.

TWENTY-FOUR

She had intended to close her eyes for only a few moments, but Khyber Elessedil knew she must have fallen asleep for much longer. When she woke her thinking was fuzzy and lethargic and her mouth dry. She was slumped down against the railing where she had taken the reading with the Elfstones some time earlier, and the Stones were still clutched in her hand. She looked around, trying to get her bearings, trying to clear her head, and slowly her memory returned.

The Ard Rhys. Penderrin.

She reached down and touched her wounded side gingerly. The bleeding had stopped, but the entire area burned and throbbed. She tried not to think about what that meant, and instead shoved the Elfstones back in her pocket. Then, using the railing for support, she hauled herself to her feet. She had no idea how much time had passed; inside the furnace room of the Druid's Keep, there was no change of daylight for night from which to tell. At least no one had discovered her. Perhaps, if she was lucky, no one even knew she had escaped.

But time was slipping away.

She closed her eyes and in her mind retraced the hidden passageway that led to the sleeping chambers of the Ard Rhys. She had to get there quickly if she was to find a way to help Pen and Grianne Ohmsford before they attempted their return from the Forbidding.

Whether by warning them or by damaging the triagenel, she must give them a chance to escape the Druids waiting for them.

She looked down at herself and saw rags and dirt and blood. She saw that her hands were shaking. It had taken almost all her energy to get so far. She didn't have much strength left, and there was still a long way to go. She wanted to go back to sleep, but she knew that if she did, she might not wake up.

She had to get out of there. She had to keep moving.

She looked around the room. Her journey began at the door at the top of the stone stairway behind her. She took a deep breath, tottered from the pit railing to the steps, and began to climb, leaning against the wall on her left as she did so. Climbing made her feel even dizzier, and she was constantly in danger of losing her balance. She stopped at one point and shut her eyes, trying to muster her strength. But closing her eyes just made her feel worse, so she opened them quickly and forced herself to continue on.

At the door, she pulled downward on the handle, but it wouldn't move. The door was locked.

She paused a moment, then summoned a small bit of her magic to force the lock. A little pressure, carefully applied, would release it from the catch. She heard it open with a sharp *snick*, pulled down on the handle again to be sure, and was through.

The passageway beyond was dark and musty and narrow. She had to go back out to retrieve a pair of torches from the hallway leading into the furnace room, one to light the way, one to serve as a backup. It took an enormous effort just to do that, and she began to wonder how in the world she was going to muster enough strength to make the climb into the Keep. She wished she had some food and water, but there would be nothing to eat or drink inside these walls.

She lit the first of the torches with her magic and started ahead.

The passageway wound through a series of short, disjoined segments that ended at a stairway. The stairway took her upward in a series of switchbacks for several hundred steps to a door. The door opened, and a second passageway continued from there. At first, there were no choices to be made about which way to go; there were only forward and back. But when she had successfully navigated the second passageway and climbed another set of stairs to a third passageway, things changed. That passageway and those that followed branched out repeatedly, and the stairways she passed led both upward and downward. She still knew where she was meant to go, but she had to stop and think about it more than once.

When finally she reached a branch in the maze of corridors about which she was uncertain, the temptation to use the Elfstones was almost overpowering. She was afraid that if she didn't and made the wrong choice, she would become hopelessly lost. Her feverish mind made her frightened of doing so, eroding what little confidence remained to her, and for a moment she was sure that she was about to make a mistake. But she forced herself to stay calm, gave herself a moment to think, and resisted the impulse to act in haste. When she started walking again, she felt that she was going the right way.

Soon enough, the first of her two torches sputtered out. If the second one gave out as well, she would be left in blackness. By then, she was deep inside the upper reaches of Paranor, passing doors in the walls whose seams were outlined by light from the other side. She had no idea what rooms these secret doors opened into and did not care to find out. The passageways branched off in dozens of directions at each level she passed through. It was a disquieting discovery. Paranor's walls, like her occupants, were rife with secrets.

She stopped several times to rest, to give her head a few moments to clear and her fever and pain time to diminish. Her body ached, and she was so tired that she half believed she might simply collapse at some point.

She wished she knew more about healing magic. She had used what little she did know to cleanse her body of infection and to restore some of her rapidly diminishing strength. But it was hard going. Her injuries were eroding both her strength and her concentration. Determination and adrenaline would get her only so far. If she didn't reach her destination soon, she would not reach it at all.

Time dragged on, and she continued through the darkness, the smoky light of the torch illuminating her way. She felt as if she were entombed, buried in the earth beneath tons of rock. The blackness of the passageways and stairwells never changed. Her torch was all she had for light. In her head, she was seeing movement and hearing noises everywhere.

I can do this, she kept telling herself.

She encountered the first strands of Druid magic not long after the passageway narrowed so far that there was only room for a single person to pass through. She detected them at once, the skills that Ahren Elessedil had imparted warning her they were in place. But in fact the strands were just that: bits and pieces of webbing that had been severed and were hanging loose and forgotten, remnants of some more elaborate magic from an earlier time. She was careful to study them only with her senses; touching them might still serve to alert the one who had placed them. She could not yet tell who that was.

She discovered soon enough that more than one set of magic users had left imprints in those wormholes. One had visited more recently than the other and had severed the other's earlier efforts all along the route she was following. That suggested that the second user was Shadea or one of her minions, while the earlier was Grianne Ohmsford. If magic had been used to transport the Ard Rhys into the Forbidding from her sleeping chamber, that was the way it would have happened. To reach her victim undetected, Shadea would have broken down the protective barriers Grianne had installed.

Khyber moved ahead cautiously, keeping close watch for traps, but it appeared that Shadea's efforts to reach the Ard Rhys had been her sole concern. None of the earlier snares and warning webs had been reset.

Khyber slowed further as she realized she was getting close to her goal. The last part of the Elfstones' vision was playing itself out in her mind, and she knew that the corridor she was following would twist and turn through the Keep's walls a bit more before ending just ahead at the secret door leading into the sleeping chamber. She breathed a long sigh of relief, grateful to have reached her destination, even if she wasn't sure yet what she was going to do about it.

Then she sensed the clipps.

She stopped at once, holding herself perfectly still as she sought out their hiding places. Clipps were little bits of reactive magic that magic users embedded in walls and floors and, sometimes, even in ceilings to give warning of intruders. They were not as powerful or as difficult to bypass as strands of webbing, but they were effective enough. She could tell they had been placed quite recently, a new form of magic layered over the old. Apparently Shadea had decided to protect this approach to the sleeping chamber as well.

She would have to remove or disable the clipps, and that would take time she didn't have. But there was no help for it.

On hands and knees she edged forward and, one by one, began searching them out.

Bek Ohmsford crouched at the edge of the forest abutting the rocky promontory on which Paranor rested, studying its steep walls through the screen of trees and scrub. The walls were cleft in a dozen visible places and many dozens more beyond his plane of view. Any of them could be the secret entrance they were looking for, but they all looked pretty much the same.

He glanced over at Tagwen, who knelt next to him, his bearded face screwed up in a knot of indecision. "Any idea which one it is?" he asked softly.

The Dwarf sighed. "It was only once she took me there, and it was several years ago. I wasn't really paying much attention to the location." He shook his head. "But there was something about it . . ."

He trailed off, lips compressing into a tight line. "I know it was right around here."

Bek wasn't sure Tagwen knew anything at all, that he hadn't forgotten everything. But he didn't have much else to work with. Rue, the young Druids, and the Rock Trolls were all crouched farther back in the trees, hiding until they were summoned to go in. They had arrived at dawn, and after anchoring *Swift Sure* in a place of deep concealment they had made their way in through the shadowed forest to Paranor. The day was gray and hazy, and mist snaked through the trees in long trailers, giving the woods an otherworldly feel that threatened to make them lose their way. But it was Pen who was in the other world and in need of finding.

"I don't think this is exactly right," Tagwen said after a moment's further thought. "Let's try left a bit."

They moved silently through the trees, Bek determined to give the Dwarf whatever leeway he needed to find the entrance. As a last resort, he might try his own magic, although that was a stretch at best. His magic couldn't locate hidden entrances. It might track traces of magic, but there was little chance that such could be found down there. Worse, if the Keep was protected by Druid magic, his own use might give them away. It was an untenable situation at best, and unless they found the entry quickly, it was only going to get worse.

"This looks familiar," Tagwen was saying, muttering to himself as he worked his way through the heavy undergrowth.

It looks familiar because it is familiar, Bek was thinking. They had been that way less than half an hour ago. He exhaled softly. How much longer could he afford to let Tagwen wander about?

"Wait!" The Dwarf grabbed his arm tightly. "This is it! This is the way in!"

He pointed at a rift in the cliff wall that was barely visible through a heavy screen of undergrowth, just a slantwise break in the rocks. "Through that opening?" Bek asked.

"No, through the wall next to it!" Tagwen grinned. "That was why I couldn't find it! I kept thinking it had to be a split in the rocks, but the entrance is through a section of the rock that swings open when you do something to it!"

Bek stared. "Do something to it?"

"Yes, you have to touch it in a certain way. That was exactly what the Ard Rhys did when she opened it!"

He looked so pleased that Bek could not bring himself to point out that without knowing where and how Grianne touched the rock, they were no better off than they had been. Thinking about what to do to find where it was, he glanced at the section of rock where the entrance was concealed.

Then he had a sudden flash of inspiration and got to his feet hurriedly. "Wait here," he said.

He crept forward, keeping to the shadows and the concealment of the tree branches until he was at the cliff wall. Looking back at the Dwarf, he pointed to the section of the wall he thought the other had indicated, and received a firm nod. Turning back again, he worked his way forward through the undergrowth to where the wall blocked his way.

Carefully, he ran his hands over the rock, using just a shading of the wishsong's magic to test for Grianne's presence. His connection to her was so strong that any usage in the immediate past would reveal where she had touched the stone. Because she came and went secretly from the Keep all the time, he thought it reasonable to expect that she had come and gone that way at least once.

He was right. He found her invisible fingerprints on the stone right away. Placing his own fingers over the four places where he sensed Grianne, he tried different combinations of touching, one right after the other, little presses against the rock.

On his ninth try, the concealed door swung open and the entrance was revealed.

He looked back at Tagwen, who was already moving from his hiding place to fetch the others. Bek stayed where he was in the opening, waiting impatiently. No one else had seen him find the entrance, of that he was fairly sure. The cliff wall hid him from the Keep above and from any within it. Nor did there seem to be any protective measures in place below the Keep. He had detected no foreign magic at the entrance, just the lingering presence of the magic used by his sister. He suspected that while the walls of Paranor were carefully warded, the rock on which it rested was not. It was likely that no one other than Grianne and Tagwen even knew about this entrance.

Tagwen was back quickly with Rue, the young Druids, and the Rock Trolls. All of them bristled with weapons and protective leathers, and the Trolls wore chain mail. No one thought they would escape what lay ahead without a fight. Bek herded them through the opening quickly, found torches stacked against one wall, waited long enough for Kermadec to light several using flint and tinder, then touched the rock facing of the secret door a second time in the same combination as before and ducked inside as it swung silently shut.

They moved into the tunnels quickly, Tagwen in the lead with one of the torches, Atalan bringing up the rear with the other. Bek stayed close to Tagwen, worried that he might lose his way if he was left to his own devices. But the passageway burrowed straight ahead until it reached a stairway leading up. They climbed the stairs cautiously, and even the footsteps of the ponderous Rock Trolls were barely audible in the silence.

But as they ascended, the silence was slowly replaced by a deep thrumming sound, and the air grew steadily warmer. Bek unsheathed his long knife and held it ready.

At the head of the stairs, they came up against a huge, ironbound wooden door that looked to have been in place for centuries. When Tagwen pulled down on the handle, though, the door swung open easily.

They stood inside Paranor's furnace room, a cavernous chamber with a pit at its center that opened down into the earth's core. Fire-light flickered within the pit walls, thrown from the burning magma deep within. The slow ooze and bubbling of the magma accounted for the thrumming sound. A walkway ringed by an iron railing encircled the pit. Conduits for the heat given off by the fire looked like black wormholes in the stone ceiling.

Bek looked around quickly. The chamber was empty. They had to act quickly.

He turned to the others. "This is what I think we should do. Rue and I will go with Tagwen to find the sleeping chamber of the Ard Rhys and set up watch for her return. Kermadec, you and your men will go with Trefen Morys and Bellizen and wait for the rest of your army to arrive." He paused. "I don't know what to tell you to do after that, whether you should lie in wait or come right through the gates. We won't have any way to communicate with each other. You won't know how things are going with us."

Kermadec nodded, his impassive face crimson in the light from the pit. "It doesn't matter, Bek Ohmsford. Our course is decided. The Trolls owe something to Shadea and her Druids for what they did to us at Taupo Rough. I don't think we will bother waiting on anything. I think we will do what Atalan has already suggested—pull the walls down about their ears. We will force the gates and take the Keep. Then we will come in search of you."

"That won't be easy," Bek pointed out. "The Druids will fight back."

Kermadec laughed softly. "Some of them will fight, but most of them will do what they have wanted to do all along—let Shadea and her bunch of vipers suffer the fate they deserve."

He came forward and put his hand on Bek's shoulder. "Yours is the task that matters most. If we can reach you in time to be of help, that will make any sacrifice worthwhile." He squeezed gently. "We've come a long way to reach this point, Bek Ohmsford. Your son will have come even farther, once he returns. And the Ard Rhys farther still. Let's make certain that our efforts are not wasted. Let's put things back where they belong."

"Let's do that!" Bek said. He put his own hand over the Troll's. "Good luck to you, Kermadec."

The Maturen stepped back. "And to you."

In a knot of huge bodies, the Rock Trolls trundled away along the catwalk, following the smaller forms of Trefen Morys and Bellizen. When they had disappeared into the dark mouth of the passageway, Bek turned to Tagwen once more.

"I guess we're ready," he said. "Where are the secret passageways that lead to my sister's sleeping chamber?"

Tagwen stared at him with a stricken look. "I have no idea. She never showed me." He glanced helplessly at Rue and back again to Bek. "Can't you find them with your magic?"

Rue Meridian rolled her eyes.

Shadea a'Ru sat at a desk in her new quarters, which were not far down the hallway from the sleeping chamber she had abandoned when she and Traunt Rowan and Pyson Wence had set the triagenel in place. At the sound of the knock on her door, she looked up guardedly.

Who is it? she started to ask, and then simply said, "Come."

The door opened and Traunt Rowan stepped through. "We may have a new problem, Shadea."

She stared at him in a way that suggested she did not want to hear about it. He met her gaze squarely. He had always been better able to do so than the others. "What sort of problem?" she said.

He stood deferentially to one side, knowing his place. "The Gnome Hunters we sent to dispose of the Elessedil girl have disappeared. All of them. Without a trace."

She turned in her chair to face him. "And the girl?"

"Disappeared, as well. The Elfstones, too. We wouldn't have found out at all except that Pyson went back to check with the man he had chosen to lead the squad. He couldn't be found. Further inquiries revealed that the entire squad was gone. It's impossible at this point to say what's happened. Pyson is conducting a search of the Keep, combing all of its passageways and courtyards, every inch. He enlisted more than a hundred of his Gnome Hunters to help."

She thought it through. "But there is no sign of the girl?" She paused. "Has there been any unexplained usage of magic within these walls?"

"Nothing that's been reported."

"Go up to the cold room and see if there has been any disturbance of the scrye waters. Anything at all. Especially here at Paranor.
Anything. Make sure you speak with everyone who has kept watch
for the last twenty-four hours." Her finger came up, pointing at him.
"Don't let them lie to you."

She got to her feet. "If that girl escaped, she might try to go back
to the sleeping chamber."

But Traunt Rowan was already shaking his head. "No, I've been
there already. I stood outside the door and checked to see if the triagenel was still in place. It was. It has not been disturbed in any way.
If she's alive, I don't think that is where she is."

"Perhaps she's gone to Arborlon for help. But how did she escape
a squad of Gnome Hunters when she was bound and gagged? She
doesn't have the magic for that! She's just a girl!"

"Well, maybe she didn't escape. Maybe there's another explanation."

She looked at him as if he were an idiot. "If the Gnomes are missing, she's escaped. But we can deal with that." She gestured toward
the door. "Go. See what the watch in the cold room has to say. Then
come tell me."

He went out the door without a word. She stood looking after
him a moment, considering what she should do. She would check
the triagenel herself, of course. She would not rely on him. Her own
magic was the more powerful and the more capable; it would give
a more sensitive reading. In any case, she no longer cared to rely
on anyone else in matters of importance—even her confederates.
Maybe especially her confederates. They hadn't shown her anything
yet that suggested she should rely on them.

Nor had anyone else, she reminded herself, thinking suddenly of
Iridia.

She paused a moment to ponder the disappearance of the assassins she had dispatched to Arishaig to dispose of the sorceress.
Those Gnomes had vanished as well, which would suggest that they
had failed. Iridia was dangerous, the most capable of those who had
conspired with her to lock Grianne Ohmsford within the Forbidding, but the men sent to kill her should have been equal to the task.

She shook her head. Sooner or later, she would have to deal with
Iridia herself. Perhaps Sen Dunsidan, too. It might be better if she rid

herself of both of them. Let the Federation choose a new Prime Minister. She would take her chances. Sen Dunsidan was becoming more trouble than he was worth.

For the moment, however, she needed to find out if the Elessedil girl was still inside Paranor's walls.

Pulling her dark robes close about her, she went out the door and down the hall toward the Ard Rhys's sleeping chambers.

It took Khyber a while to figure out how to disable the clipps, but in the end she managed. She did so by masking them with her own magic, a small covering that closed down their ability to read the presence of intruders in the passageway and left them useless. The magic she used was small, but sufficiently strong to last for several days. That should be long enough, she decided. It would have to be.

She fell asleep again after that, not meaning to, unable to help herself; she was so exhausted that just resting her eyes for a moment was sufficient to send her off. She awoke feeling a little better, although her wound still throbbed and her face felt hot and tight. She couldn't risk using any further magic to heal herself, couldn't risk anything that might give her away unless it had to do with helping Pen and Grianne, and so she did her best to turn her thoughts away from the pain and to the task at hand.

She slipped the rest of the way down the passage, checking carefully as she went for traps, and reached the doorway at the end. She saw the faint glow of the triagenel's magic as it seeped through the cracks in the doorway from the chamber beyond, a wicked green light that cut through the darkness like a razor's edge. She crouched down in the gloom and studied the doorway for a moment, then inched forward until she was close enough to touch the light seeping through. She kept herself from doing so; some magic could convey disturbances even from something as minuscule as the brush of fingertips. Sitting to one side of the doorway, she tried to plan her next actions.

Warning Pen and the Ard Rhys after they had reentered Paranor would do no good. The trap would be sprung by then, and they would be prisoners. She could try to help them, but she knew she lacked the kind of magic that could break them free. Whatever she was going to do, she had to do it before they attempted their return.

Which meant that she couldn't afford to wait since she didn't know how long she had. Which meant that she had to do something soon.

But what?

The only real magic she possessed was the Elfstones. But if she used them, she would give herself away in a heartbeat. She would be captured anew, and Shadea a'Ru and her allies would simply rebuild the triagenel. Besides, the Elfstones could only serve two purposes— to discover what was hidden and to defend against enemy magic. Neither usage seemed right for what was needed.

She leaned back against the passage wall, thinking. She was still thinking when she heard a noise in the darkness behind her. The hair at the back of her neck prickled and her throat tightened in fear.

Someone was coming.

TWENTY-FIVE

Willing herself to disappear, Khyber pressed back against the rough wall of the darkened passage. She had nowhere to run or to hide, nowhere at all to go. She was trapped, and unless whoever or whatever approached changed direction quickly, she would be caught out. She tried to remember how far back down the passage diverged, but she couldn't. The sounds continued to advance toward her. There was no mistaking the inevitable.

She reached into her tunic and brought out the Elfstones. If Shadea or one of the other Druids had found her, she would have to fight. If magic was used, the Elfstones would give her some protection.

Then a shadowy form appeared from out of the gloom, squat and heavy, too small to be anything other than a Gnome or a Dwarf. One of the Hunters she had feared would come searching, she thought in despair. The Elfstones would do her no good against him. She would have to rely on the long knife she had used to cauterize her wound. She tucked the Stones away swiftly and brought it out.

Not a dozen feet away, the approaching figure paused. Two more figures, cloaked and hooded and much larger than the first, appeared as well. Dizziness washed through her, triggered by the sudden surge of adrenaline that the new threat brought. She could not fight all three. She did not think she could fight one. She was weak and feverish and holding herself together through sheer determination.

Could she use magic to mask her presence? It was a possibility, and she grasped at it as she would a lifeline. Using magic was dangerous, but she was all out of choices.

She brought up her hands in front of her and was beginning to conjure a masking spell when a familiar voice said, "Khyber Elessedil, is that you?"

She was so astonished that she stopped what she was doing and stared at the speaker, realizing as she did so that the light from the triagenel magic was giving him a clear view of her silhouette. "Tagwen?" she whispered in disbelief.

He hurried forward, knelt in front of her, and took her hands in his own. "Shades, Elven girl! We didn't know what had become of you! I must say, I thought the worst more than once. But here you are." He reached out impulsively and hugged her. "Look, I've brought help!" He gestured to the two figures that had joined him. "These are Pen's parents, Bek and Rue."

The older couple knelt as well, and whispered greetings were quickly exchanged in the greenish cast of the magic's light. "How did you find me?" Khyber asked.

"By accident," Bek said, keeping his voice low. "We came looking for my sister's sleeping chamber so that we would be here when she and Pen came through the Forbidding."

Quickly, he explained how Rue and he had escaped the Druids and the Keep more than a week earlier, then flown north aboard *Swift Sure* in search of Pen and his companions, not realizing that Pen was already a prisoner. After finding Tagwen and the others at Stridegate and learning what had become of their son, they had flown back again, determined to rescue him.

"Is Kermadec with you?" she asked excitedly.

"Somewhere in the Keep with Atalan and a few others," Tagwen answered. "The rest of the Trolls of Taupo Rough are following us. They might not be more than a day out. Then we'll see how Shadea and those other weasels handle things."

"We'll need their help," Khyber said. She explained what had befallen after her successful attempt at freeing Pen and helping him to enter the Forbidding. "But Shadea and her allies have constructed a triagenel in the sleeping chamber. If we can't disable it in some way, it will trap Pen and the Ard Rhys the moment they come back through the Forbidding. I've been trying to think of something to do, but I haven't had much luck."

Rue Meridian, who had been listening silently in the background, moved forward and put her hand on Khyber's forehead. "You're burning up, Khyber. We have to do something about that or we're going to lose you." She glanced at the seams of greenish light leaking from the secret door and said, "Let's move you back down the passageway a little."

Khyber was too weak to put up much of a protest. She allowed herself to be stretched out on the passage floor while Rue opened her soiled tunic and began working on the wound. From a sealed pouch, she produced a salve. She spread it on the wound, then rebound the wound with fresh cloth from her own pack. Rue's fingers were cool and soft, and Khyber closed her eyes in momentary relief. The pain began to lessen and the ache subsided.

"Drink this," Rue ordered.

She gave Khyber a bitter-tasting liquid and some water to wash it down. Khyber drank it all, after telling her, "I haven't had anything to eat or drink in a long time."

"You need better care than we can give you here," Rue replied, holding Khyber's face in her hands and looking into her eyes. "You have some infection in you; that wound needs to be reopened and cleaned out. But that will have to wait."

She looked at Bek. "That's the best I can do for her right now."

Her husband nodded. "Tell me about the triagenel, Khyber."

She did so, sitting up again and explaining how it worked. "I still have the Elfstones, but I don't know how I can use them to help."

Bek thought a moment. "Is the strength of the triagenel uniform? Is it the same everywhere or does it vary from strand to strand?"

"There will be some variation in the strands. The building of each by the three magic users necessarily involves some ebb and flow." She hesitated. "At least, that was what Uncle Ahren told me. The more skilled the users, the more uniform the magic. But even with the most accomplished users, there would be weaknesses."

"Ahren would have known." Bek looked toward the concealed

door and the thin shafts of green light leaking through the cracks. "How is the triagenel attached? Your description makes it seem like a net. Does it hang from the ceiling?"

Khyber nodded. "It does. It is gathered at the corners of the room so that when the magic is triggered, it collapses about its victims and seals them away. It happens very fast, too fast for anyone to avoid, even if they are warned immediately."

"What triggers the magic?"

"What do you mean?"

"What does it take to cause the triagenel to collapse?"

"A human presence in the room. Any human presence."

"But not the presence of another magic?"

She hesitated. "What are you thinking?"

Bek leaned forward slightly, brow furrowed. "What if you and I were to weaken a few of the strands that make up the triagenel? Would that give a magic user as powerful as my sister a way of breaking through the net once it collapsed on her?"

Khyber hesitated, thinking. "I don't think the triagenel can heal itself, so yes, I suppose if enough strands were weakened, a captive could break free. But how in the world are you going to do that, Bek? If you go into that room, the magic will be triggered and the triagenel will collapse on you."

"I'm not talking about going into the room. What I want to try requires using two different forms of magic, one yours, one mine. That's why I asked if the presence of another magic would trigger its release. Will it?"

She considered the question, and then shook her head. "I don't think so. I think only the presence of a flesh-and-blood body will do that."

"Then this might work. We don't need much of our own magic to get the job done, and if we're lucky, we won't be detected. The magic of the triagenel is pretty strong, you said?" She nodded. "Then perhaps it will help mask our own."

"What are you thinking about doing?" Rue said as Tagwen pressed close.

Bek sat back on his heels. "What if Khyber were to use the Elfstones to search out weaknesses in the triagenel? The Elfstones are seeking-stones; they should be able to do that. If she can pinpoint, oh, maybe a dozen, I think I can use the wishsong to weaken them further—enough so that any sort of force applied to them after the net collapses will break them apart."

Rue shook her head doubtfully. "That's very delicate work, isn't it? If you weaken even one of those strands too much, it will break through before you want it to. If that happens, won't Shadea detect it? In fact, won't she detect any kind of interference with the triagenel?"

Seeing the possibilities, Khyber leaned forward. "Maybe not. Yes, if Bek breaks one of the strands, that creates a flaw in the netting and anyone looking for it will know right away. But a weakening might not be detected so easily; over time the net erodes anyway. The magic slowly fails and the triagenel has to be rebuilt. So an erosion of the sort Bek is suggesting probably wouldn't draw attention."

The four looked at each other. "Is there another way?" Tagwen asked bluntly.

No one said anything. They all knew the answer.

The Dwarf grunted. "You better get started."

Much farther down and deeper into the bowels of the Keep, Kermadec and his Trolls crept through the passageways of the lower levels, following the cautious lead of Trefen Morys and Bellizen. Seeking to reach Paranor's north walls, they had worked their way steadily upward from the furnace chamber. Kermadec's plan was to get close enough to the outermost of those walls that he could take control of one of the smaller gates, one that would not be heavily manned.

Kermadec knew something that neither Shadea nor her Gnome Hunters knew. There were too many gates for all of them to be guarded all the time, and many of the smaller gates had been permanently sealed over the years to prevent a surprise breach. But the Maturen had unsealed one of them long ago to give the Ard Rhys a means of leaving the castle secretly without having to go all the way down to the furnace chamber and the tunnels below. When he visited, she slipped from the Keep through that gate, to the meeting places outside Paranor's walls they had prearranged over the years.

That unsealed lesser gate was their best chance of breaching Paranor's defenses. It was small, nothing more than a single door. It would not permit a massive rush, but if enough Trolls sneaked through before they were discovered, they could mass within the walls and take one of the main gates. In Kermadec's view, that was how Paranor would fall.

But reaching the north wall undetected, not to mention the gate in question, would have been difficult for any one person, let alone ten. It had become clear early on that some sort of search was under way within the Keep. Twice they had narrowly avoided being discovered, the first time because they had heard the search party approaching and doubled back to another corridor and the second because they were warier after the first.

So they were proceeding much more cautiously, keeping to seldom-used passageways and back stairs, tactics that were slowing them down considerably. It had taken them several hours to get that far, what with hiding and doubling back, and it was beginning to look as if even getting to where they wanted to go was in doubt.

But Trefen Morys seemed to know his way about Paranor even better than Kermadec, and under his guidance they worked their way forward, slowly getting closer.

Then, just when it seemed they would make it safely through the search parties, they slipped from a side corridor into a main passageway and ran right into one. A group of five Gnome Hunters rounded a corner right in front of them and came to an uncertain stop. Trefen Morys tried to bluff their way past, hailing the Gnomes, pretending that everything was as it should be. But the Gnomes were on guard, and they knew that Trolls were forbidden entry into the Keep. Before Kermadec or the other Trolls could stop them, the Gnomes had given the alarm.

Atalan was on top of them quickly, and three were dead before they could defend themselves. The remaining two fled, and Kermadec called his brother back so that they could do the same.

"Where can we go?" he shouted at Trefen Morys as they ran down the corridor toward a stairway leading up.

They rounded the corner of the stairway and were immediately in a second fight, this one with a much larger party. The Gnomes drove the Trolls and the young Druids backwards into the corridor, calling for reinforcements as they did so. Bigger and stronger, and with a great deal more to lose, the Trolls fought back and, after a concerted rush, broke through the Gnome crush and charged up the stairway to the next floor.

"Keep going!" Trefen Morys shouted, pointing to the next set of stairs. "Two more floors!"

They did as he directed, rushing ahead heedlessly, trusting that he knew what he was doing. At the top of the third set of stairs, he reached out and grabbed Kermadec's arm, pointing to a wide set of double doors.

"In there!"

The entire party rushed into a cavernous meeting room filled with chairs and tables stacked all about, the ceiling high and dark with shadows, the room brightened only by a pair of narrow windows on their left.

The young Druid went straight to the windows and released the catch on the nearest. "Go outside," he told them as they rushed up to him. His breath came in short gasps, and there was blood on one arm. "Follow the ledge to the third set of windows. Inside the room beyond, you will find a door that opens onto a narrow stairway. It leads directly down two flights to the base of the north wall. You will know where your gate is once you get there."

"You're not coming with us?" Kermadec asked, realizing what the young Druid had decided.

Trefen Morys shook his head. "We're of no further use to you, Bellizen and I. We're not fighters; we'll just hold you back. Maybe we can do something from up here. Another distraction, perhaps." He stretched out his hand. "Don't fail us, Kermadec. Don't fail our mistress. She isn't the monster they try to make her seem. She has done much good with the order. We need her back."

The Maturen gripped his hand tightly. "Get out of this room, Trefen. If they find you somewhere else, they might think you are just another pair of Druids."

"They're coming," Bellizen hissed from where she kept watch at the door.

"Keep safe," Trefen Morys said. He released the big Troll's hand and hurried over to stand next to her.

Kermadec climbed through the window without another word, the other Trolls following, and disappeared onto the ledge.

With Rue Meridian and Tagwen keeping watch from just down the darkened passageway, Bek Ohmsford and Khyber Elessedil placed themselves, one on each side of the hidden door, keeping clear of the greenish glow that seeped from the sleeping chamber, staying back from the opening itself. They were going to have to use their magic in entirely new ways. Bek, in particular, was going to test himself as he never had. The wishsong was a powerful magic, and he had never spent much time trying to master it. Now he was going to attempt something that even a practiced user would have thought twice about.

But he had no choice if he wanted to save his sister and his son.

"Are you ready?" he asked the Elven girl.

She nodded, and he released the catch that held the door in place. The door swung slowly toward her.

Beyond, the sleeping chamber was bathed in a deep greenish glow. A complex webbing was strung all across the ceiling, thousands of strands of magic carefully joined together, the whole of it secured at the corners and center.

Placing herself to one side, staying carefully out of the magic's steady glow as it flooded the passageway, Khyber brought out the Elfstones. Cradling them in the palm of her hand, she stared at the triagenel, concentrating on what she wanted revealed. She had never seen a triagenel; she had only heard about them. So it was difficult for her to know exactly what to look for. She relied on the Elfstones to respond to her need, and they did. Within seconds, they flared to life, their blue glow spreading all through the chamber, bathing the triagenel in a new brightness. At perhaps twenty-five or thirty places, the webbing burned faintly crimson, mostly where the strands connected to one another.

"Those red spots are the weaknesses," Khyber whispered.

Bek took a long moment to study them, and then whispered back, "Good work, Khyber. Now hold the Elfstone magic steady."

He called up the wishsong in a soft, barely audible hum. Building it slowly, he honed it to a cutting edge, a trick he had learned twenty years earlier from Grianne. When he had the edge sharp enough, he eased it up to the ceiling to where the brightest of the crimson spots could be found and began to cut. He was slow and careful, weakening each strand just a little at a time. Relying on his magic to give him a sense of its strength, he would cut the strand as deeply as he felt he could, and then move on to the next. The process took him a little longer each time, his concentration faltering; his strength was still not back after the injuries suffered in the escape from Paranor two weeks earlier.

"Hurry," Khyber whispered, the word evidence that her own efforts were beginning to fail.

He continued until he had cut into ten strands. It was tedious, demanding work. His eyes watered and his body cramped, but it was his mind that screamed for release. Still, he was afraid to stop, afraid that starting up again would be too dangerous, that it risked discovery through the sheer repetitiveness of the magical activity. Too much of anything would be noticed in a place like Paranor, especially with the scrye waters able to detect any usage of magic at all.

Bek cut two more strands, making his tally an even dozen. When he had finished with the twelfth, he was too tired to go on. He withdrew the cutting edge of his magic and let the wishsong go still. He closed his eyes wearily and leaned back against the passageway wall. "That's all I can do," he whispered to Khyber.

She exhaled sharply, and when he opened his eyes again, the Elfstones had gone dark. She was slumped down across from him, her fingers closed tightly about the talismans. "Do you think it was enough? Will it break apart for your sister and Pen? I couldn't tell. I couldn't feel the weakening at all. All I could do was make out the places where it might give way."

He shook his head. "I don't know."

He reached over from behind the open door and pushed against it. The door closed softly, and the latch caught. They were left in darkness again save for where greenish light leaked through the cracks, blade-thin and knife-sharp. In the ensuing silence, they stared at each other wordlessly, wondering if they had done enough.

Shadea a'Ru had finished rechecking the strength and positioning of the triagenel and was on her way back down the hall when Traunt Rowan reappeared from the cold chamber. She noticed for the first time how much he had aged over the past few weeks. His strong face was lined and gray, the way he held himself was less confident and erect. He had been the most dependable of her allies, the strongest-minded if not the strongest wielder of magic, and she was dismayed that he had not held up better. It pointed up again a truth she regretted.

In the end, she was the only one she could depend on. In the end, she was in the battle alone.

"You were right to have me check the scrye waters," he announced perfunctorily. "The Druid on watch said there was a noticeable disturbance perhaps eight or ten hours ago, one that clearly indicated the presence of a powerful magic. He said he failed to report it because he thought it was Druid magic. The truth is he was afraid he would stumble into something he shouldn't know about and pay the price for doing so."

"What does that mean?"

His laugh was bitter. "It means our decision to keep everyone guessing about who is expendable is having unavoidable consequences. We have created a climate of fear, Shadea, in which no one wants to risk drawing attention. Better to keep silent than to make a mistake and become another unfortunate example."

She glared at him, then looked away. He was right, of course. What was the purpose in getting mad at him for pointing out something she already knew? She had the Druids well in line and working to complete their tasks, but they were frightened and uncertain. Her early, unexplained dismissals had made them that way. Now she was in danger of losing them all.

She was no better than Grianne Ohmsford.

But that would change, she promised herself. She would make it change.

She looked back at him. "What was the source of the disturbance?"

"The furnace chamber, where we sent the Elven girl to be killed. I think we must assume she is still alive. Pyson sent an armed unit to search that whole area. They found evidence of blood, but nothing else."

Shadea shook her head. "What is she up to? What does she think she can accomplish?" Her hard gaze fixed on him. "I want her found, Traunt. I want her found and killed. I don't care how it's done or who knows. We have to put an end to this business."

He nodded wordlessly. There was nothing for him to say.

They walked back down the hall toward her chamber. "I received word from our spies in Arishaig," he said quietly. "Iridia has disappeared."

She looked over in surprise. "How long ago?"

"Several days, at least. She simply vanished. Sen Dunsidan doesn't seem bothered, though. That leads me to believe he may have had something to do with it."

She nodded, thinking that Sen Dunsidan couldn't have gotten rid of Iridia on the best day of his life. It was far more likely that her Gnome assassins had been more successful than she had believed, even if they hadn't gotten word back to her yet.

They reached her door. "Find that girl," she repeated, turning to face him. "And anyone else she might have brought with her into Paranor. Tell Pyson to have his Gnome Hunters sweep the Keep again—every passageway, every room."

She paused. "And double the guard on the sleeping chamber. I have a feeling that Grianne Ohmsford is about to reappear. I want to be sure we are ready for her when she does."

She saw the stricken look on his face and smiled. "What's the trouble? Don't you think we are a match for her? We dispatched her once; we can do so again. Only this time, I intend to make sure she won't ever come back."

She turned away. "I need to rest. Wake me when something happens." She glanced back at him. "And make sure that something happens soon."

He was still standing there in the hallway when she closed the door.

Bek was sitting next to Khyber in the darkened passageway off the sleeping chamber of the Ard Rhys. They had slept for several hours, and now Tagwen and Rue were sleeping. Bek wasn't sure how much time had passed. Not that it mattered; there was nothing they could do but wait. He found himself wondering how long that might be. They couldn't wait indefinitely. Sooner or later, someone would find them. They would need food and drink, as well, although they had brought a little of each with them into the Keep. He guessed that the waiting would end either when Grianne and Pen reappeared out of the Forbidding or Paranor fell to Kermadec and his Trolls.

He wondered about the chances of the latter. The Trolls were formidable, but no one had taken Paranor since it had been betrayed to the Warlock Lord in the time of Jerle Shannara. The Druids were a powerful order, even if dissatisfied with their leadership and their present situation. Their command of magic gave them an edge that no one else possessed. Bek hoped that Kermadec was right when he said that most of them would not support Shadea a'Ru, but he had a feeling that if faced with an assault on Paranor, they might.

But he couldn't do anything about that. He could only do something about the things he had control over.

He leaned close to Khyber. "There is something I have to tell you," he whispered. "About Pen and the staff."

She glanced up. "The darkwand?"

He nodded. "The King of the Silver River came to me in a fever dream while I was flying north in search of Pen. In that dream, he told me that demons from the Forbidding had manipulated Shadea and her Druid allies. Their purpose in helping Shadea had nothing to do with getting their hands on Grianne; their purpose was to release a demon into our world. That demon's mission is to destroy the Ellcrys and tear down the Forbidding."

He felt her fingers dig into his arm. "Let me finish. Pen can stop this from happening. He can send the demon back through the Forbidding. The purpose of the darkwand is not only to bring Grianne out, but also to send the demon back. But Pen has to find it first. It is a changeling, and it will be in disguise."

"What if it reaches Arborlon before Pen gets back?" She looked at him as if she wasn't sure she wanted to hear the answer.

He shook his head. "The Elves guard the Ellcrys day and night. Arborlon has defenses to keep anything from getting close. We have to hope that's enough. There's only so much we can do."

He put his hand over hers. "Now, listen to me. I don't know what will happen once Grianne and Pen reappear in the Four Lands. We are all at risk. But whatever happens, you and Pen have only one concern. You have to find that demon. Escape back through the secret passageway and get outside Paranor's walls. Then go after it. Take *Swift Sure*. Use the Elfstones to track it down and then send it back into the Forbidding."

He paused. "Pen doesn't know about any of this. You might have to be the one to tell him, if Rue and I can't. If so, make sure he understands what he is supposed to do. He can't worry about us or about what happens here. You know the way out; you have to make certain he uses it."

She stared at him doubtfully. "He won't want to leave you. I don't know if he will listen to me."

Bek took her hands and held them. "He will listen to reason. You will find the words."

He wished he had something more to offer. But what he had just given her was the best he had.

TWENTY-SIX

On the wide night-shadowed plains of the Pashanon, Grianne Ohmsford stared in shock as the approaching figure
came into the light and its features were revealed.

It was a boy.

At first, she thought she must be mistaken, even though she had
been told the boy would come for her, even though she had been
looking for him all this time. It was the unexpectedness of his appearance that gave her pause, the way he simply materialized out
of the receding night, the ease with which he had found her in the
middle of nowhere. But it was more than that. She had just left a
killing field, a slaughterhouse of the Forbidding's creatures turned to
stone. She thought the figure must be something come out of that
madness. She thought she was seeing a ghost.

"Shades," she whispered, and stopped walking altogether.

At her side, Weka Dart growled. "What is it, Straken? Who is
this creature?"

The boy approached as if there were no hurry, as if he had all the
time in the world. He looked haggard and beaten down. He looked
to her, she thought suddenly, as she must look to him. His clothing
was ragged and his face dirty and careworn. He walked in a way that
suggested his journey had been long and hard, and indeed, if he had
come from her world, from the world of the Four Lands, it must have

been. Though he was clearly young, everything about him was dark and weathered.

Except for the odd staff he carried, which was made of a wood that was polished and smooth and glowed red with bits of fire.

He walked right up to her and stopped. "Hello, Aunt Grianne."

It was Penderrin. Of all the boys she might have imagined, he was the last. She couldn't say why, but he was. Maybe it was because he was Bek's son, and it would never have occurred to her that Pen would come for her rather than Bek. Maybe it was just her certainty that if a boy was indeed coming, he would be extraordinary, and Pen was not. He was just an average boy. He lacked his father's magic; he lacked his mother's experience. She had met him only a couple of times, and while he was goodhearted and interested in her, he had never seemed special.

Yet there he was, come to her from a place no one else could have come, there when no one else was.

"Penderrin," she whispered.

She stepped forward, placed her hands on his shoulders, and looked into his eyes to make sure. Then she hugged him to her, holding on to him with a mix of disbelief and gratitude. He was the one; just the fact of his being there was confirmation of what the shade of the Warlock Lord had foretold. She felt his arms come around her as well, and he hugged her back. In that instant, they were bonded in a way that could only have happened under the circumstances of that improbable meeting. Whatever befell her, she would never feel the same way about him again.

She released him and stepped back. "How did you find me? How did you get here?"

He smiled faintly. "It might take a while to explain that." He held up the glowing staff. "This is what brought me and what will take us both back, once we return to the place I came in at. The runes carved in its surface glow brighter when it gets nearer to you. I just followed their lead."

She shook her head in disbelief. "I had no idea it could be you. I was told that a boy would come for me, but I never thought it would be Bek's son." She gave him another hug. There were tears in her eyes, and she wiped them away quickly. "I am so grateful to you."

Weka Dart was standing off to one side, a mix of emotions mirrored in his feral features, suspicion fighting with curiosity and hope. She glanced at him, and then turned Pen about to face him. "This is Weka Dart, Pen. He is an Ulk Bog, a creature of the Forbidding. He calls this the world of the Jarka Ruus—the banished ones. What you should know is that he is my friend. He, alone, of all the creatures I have encountered, has tried to help me. Without him, I would be . . ."

She trailed off. "I don't know where I would be," she finished quietly.

Weka Dart beamed. "I am honored to have served the Straken Queen," he announced, and bowed deeply. He looked up again quickly. "If you are her savior, then perhaps you will be mine, as well. I wish to continue to protect Grianne of the kind heart and powerful magic. I have pledged myself to do so for as long as she needs me. Can you help me? Are you a Straken, too?"

"No," Grianne said quickly. "Pen is family. He is not a Straken, Weka Dart. He comes only to take me home again."

"And take me, too?" the Ulk Bog pressed.

"What do you mean?" Pen asked, and then looked at Grianne. "What is he talking about?"

"Leave it alone for now. I have to know more about what you are doing here. I don't understand why you've come instead of your father. Is he all right? He hasn't been harmed, has he?"

She listened then as he told her everything that had happened since Tagwen had appeared in Patch Run to seek his father's help. He told her of the little company that had come together in Emberen to start the quest for the tanequil. She learned of the death of Ahren Elessedil and of the dark creatures that had been enlisted by Shadea to hunt Pen down. He told her of the fate of the *Skatelow* and the Rovers who crewed her and of star-crossed Cinnaminson's transformation into one of the aeriads. He told her of brave Kermadec and his Rock Trolls. He told her of the tanequil, of its dual nature and of the shaping of the darkwand. By listening, she came to understand how desperate the struggle had been to reach her and how much had been sacrificed so that Pen could find a way to bring her back into the Four Lands.

"I would have thought my father a better choice for this, too," he finished. "But the King of the Silver River said that I was the one who was needed. I guess it was because my magic allowed me to communicate with the tanequil. Perhaps my father's couldn't do that. I don't know. I only know that I had to come looking for you, that it was important that I try, even if I really didn't think I could succeed."

Grianne smiled in spite of herself. "Perhaps the King of the Silver River saw something in you that you didn't see in yourself, Penderrin Ohmsford, because here you are, whether you believed it could happen or not."

He smiled back. "I'm glad I found you, Aunt Grianne."

Weka Dart was dancing around again, looking agitated, his craggy features twisting and knotting. "We should leave this place," he whined anxiously. He glanced back in the direction of the Asphinx colony and the stone statues. "It is dangerous to remain here."

Grianne nodded. "He is right, Pen. We can continue talking while we travel. We must go as quickly as possible to the doorway out of the Forbidding. Time slips away."

They began retracing Pen's steps, walking west toward the receding darkness, the dim gray brightening of the dawn at their backs. The vast sweep of the Pashanon stretched away before them, its stunted, broken landscape empty of movement. Far distant still to the north, the Dragon Line lifted in stark relief against the horizon. The sky remained clouded and the air hazy as the daylight brightened only marginally the world of the Jarka Ruus.

"I am very sorry to hear about Ahren Elessedil," she said to Pen after a time. "He was the best of my Druids, the one I could always depend upon. It proved to be so here, at the end, too. But I will miss him."

In truth, she felt as if her heart would break. Only losing Bek could hurt worse. Ahren had been with her since the formation of the Third Druid Order, the linchpin she had relied upon time and time again. He had committed to her during their return to the Four Lands from Parkasia, and she had come to respect him deeply. She looked off into the distance, took a deep breath, and exhaled wearily.

"I am sorry about your father and mother, too," she continued, glancing over at him. "It isn't fair that they should have been brought into this. It isn't fair that any of you should have—Tagwen, Kermadec, the Rover girl, any who tried to help. I won't forget. I will try to make things right again, as much as I can."

"It was their choice," Pen said. "Just as it was mine. We all wanted to help."

She shook her head dismissively. "Shadea," she said softly. "I should have done what Kermadec told me to do a long time ago; I should have rid myself of her. I should have rid myself of them all. Pyson Wence, Terek Molt, Iridia. Even Traunt Rowan. I am the most disappointed in him. I never thought he would turn against me, no matter how bad things got. I let my judgment be clouded. A bad thing for an Ard Rhys to do."

She was silent for a moment. "How many of my Druids stand with Shadea and those others, Pen?" she asked. "Do you know?"

He shook his head. "Some, I guess. She is Ard Rhys now. The Druids all answer to her. But I don't know how loyal they are." He paused. "When I was a prisoner, she was away in Arishaig. She has an alliance with the Prime Minister."

"Sen Dunsidan," she whispered. "Another viper. I would expect him to be involved somehow. Shadea would not act without some sort of outside support, and Sen Dunsidan has always hated me."

With reason, she thought. As the Ilse Witch, she had made his life nightmarish. But he had allied himself with the Morgawr and tried to have her killed. So she had reason to hate him, too. Yet she had forgiven him his maliciousness and thought he had done the same. Clearly, she had shown poor judgment there, as well.

"Are there any I can count upon within the order to support me?"

Pen shook his head. "I don't know of any. No one came to help me but Khyber."

She dropped the matter, and they walked in silence for a time. It was wrong of her to ask such things of Pen. He had no way of knowing the answers. Since her disappearance, his time had been spent in flight. The machinations of those at Paranor and elsewhere would not have been his concern; his concern would have been in trying to stay alive. Her answers to questions of that kind would have to wait until she was back in the Four Lands. Then it would be up to her to find them quickly.

Weka Dart was back to skittering about, crisscrossing the land ahead, dashing first this way and then that, chattering to himself, anxious to get where they were going. But she had a feeling about that. Something Pen had said when the Ulk Bog had mentioned him as being savior not only to her but also to him nagged at her.

"Weka Dart!" she called.

He came racing over, eyes bright with excitement. "I am here, Straken Queen."

"No sign of further pursuit?" she asked. "No sign of Tael Riverine or his creatures?"

The Ulk Bog grinned wickedly. "He won't have learned of Hobstull's new employment as a resting post for birds quite yet," he said. "It will take time for word to reach him. Too much time for him to do anything about it. We will be well away and out of his reach by then."

"Run on ahead a distance and see if the land is clear that way. I want to turn north soon toward the mountains."

He glanced in that direction. "Nothing lies there. What is the point of wasting my time . . . ?"

"Don't argue, little man!" she snapped. "Remember your promise to serve and protect."

He was gone without another word, a dark spot rapidly disappearing into the haze. She felt bad about snapping at him, but he responded better when she did, and she needed to talk with Pen alone.

"A word, Pen," she said to him when Weka Dart was safely away. "I made a promise to the Ulk Bog in return for his help in getting free of the Straken Lord's prisons. I'll explain about that later. My promise was that I would do what I could to get him out of the Forbidding and into the Four Lands. He wants to come with us."

Pen gave her an anxious look. "I thought that was what he meant. But I don't think we can do it. The darkwand will take only you and me out of the Forbidding. It will not allow anyone else to go with us. The King of the Silver River told me so."

She had suspected as much. Creatures consigned to the Forbidding by Faerie magic could not be set free without a disruption of the wall that separated the two worlds. The darkwand was not created for that purpose. It was created for putting things back the way they were meant to be.

"I'll have to tell him," she said quietly, already wondering how she was going to do that. "I can't let him think he still has a chance of getting out when I know he doesn't."

They walked on, the boy keeping pace with her, his head lowered, his staff serving as a walking stick, its runes glowing softly in the dusky light.

Her thoughts stayed with Weka Dart. He was so convinced that she could do anything, that her Straken powers were omnipotent. He had already made up his mind that she would be able to break him free of the Forbidding and bring him back into the Four Lands. She had warned him not to expect too much, but after the encounter with the Graumth, he had ceased believing there was anything to worry about.

Now she was going to have to disappoint him in the way she had disappointed so many others—by not being able to do enough, by being less able than he needed her to be. She felt shackled by her inability, by her weakness, by her humanity. It was almost better not to have any power than to have a lot. Having a lot always created expectations, and somewhere along the way those expectations would not be met because that was the way the world worked.

"Do you remember when you asked me once if I had any of my father's magic?" Pen asked her suddenly.

She glanced over at him, happy for the distraction. "I remember."

"I told you I hadn't. But that wasn't entirely true. I hadn't any of the wishsong's magic. But I had another kind. It was such a small magic that I didn't think it worth mentioning. It allowed me to sense what animals and plants and birds were thinking or why they were acting as they were. I didn't think it was worth anything. I never even told my parents about it. Especially my mother, who is afraid of the Ohmsford magic."

Grianne nodded. "I know. She is right to be afraid."

He sighed. "Well, now I think maybe my magic does come from the wishsong. It changed when I took the limb from the tanequil and shaped it into the darkwand. It changed when I began to bond with the darkwand so that it responded to me. I found I could make it do things by humming and singing, in the way of the wishsong."

"It came late to your father, too," she said. "He was older than you before he discovered he had use of it. Walker let him see by giving him the Sword of Shannara and telling him he would have to use it. That bonding triggered a surfacing. Just as with you."

"I sense it changing still. I think I am just beginning to understand what's there."

"There is a history of that in our family. It happened with Jair Ohmsford. Do you know the story? His sister had full use of the wishsong, the first of the Ohmsfords to have it. Jair, the brother, had a magic that gave the appearance of being wishsong magic, but was only illusion. Except that some years after their quest to destroy the Ildatch, he discovered that it had evolved and he had the same use of it as she had, even though it had started out as something else."

She gave him a questioning look. "What's bothering you?"

He ran his fingers through his shock of reddish hair, tangling it further. "I just thought that since it is my connection with the dark-wand that allows us to cross through the Forbidding, maybe there is still a chance for Weka Dart to come with us. If my magic is still changing, if I don't know what it will do yet, it might turn out that it can help."

He looked over at her. "So maybe you should wait to tell him. Until we're sure, I mean."

She stared at him for a moment, surprised. "I don't know if that's such a good idea, Pen," she said finally.

He looked off in the direction the Ulk Bog had gone. "I just don't think anyone should have to stay here if they don't want to. I know he is a descendant of one of those consigned to the Forbidding. But that was a long time ago. Things can change. He doesn't seem so bad to me."

She smiled to herself. She liked the way he wanted to help Weka Dart, even without knowing anything about him. It spoke volumes about the kind of boy he was, and it made her feel still closer to him. She was glad he was like that. She hoped she would get a chance later to tell her brother so.

"He isn't so bad," she said finally.

She tried to tell herself that was so, that being imprisoned in the demon world did not necessarily indicate that the Ulk Bog was beyond redemption. No one was beyond redemption, after all. Wasn't she proof of that?

Then a scream, a mix of shriek and roar, blew past them like a windstorm, and Pen's dragon dropped out of the sky and settled to the ground directly in front of them.

High in the towers of Paranor, Trefen Morys turned another corner on another passageway, Bellizen at his heels, and looked for a way out. They had been running ever since they had helped Kermadec escape through the windows of the meeting chamber. Surrounded by Gnome Hunters, they had been lucky to get away themselves. They'd been able to climb up through the heating vents and crawl down the shaft to another room before the Gnomes could discover what they had done.

But the hunt had gone on, and their time and space were running out. The Gnomes knew they were trapped on the upper levels of the Keep, and had blocked all the passageways down. All that was left to the young Druids were the towers above, and even those were being closed off, one by one.

"In here!" he hissed at Bellizen, pulling her through an open door into a storage room filled with Druid cloaks and soft slippers.

The sounds of pursuit already drawing near, he shut the door quietly behind them. He slid the locking bolt into place and looked around wearily. It was just another in an endless series of rooms into which they had fled and tried to hide. This one had a connecting door that led to a second room, and after determining there was no other way out of the one they were in, he took Bellizen with him into the second and locked its door, as well.

The room was tiny, a chamber he had never seen before. It had no other door than the one they had come through. A single narrow window was set in the far wall. When he crossed to open it, he found himself peering out at the north wall and the woods beyond. They were five stories up, and the wall dropped straight down.

He looked at Bellizen, who stood waiting for his assessment. "They might not think to look here."

But they already had. He could hear them at the door of the first chamber, trying to break through. Eventually, they would. Then they would break through the second door.

He scanned the room from wall to wall, from floor to ceiling, and then looked out through the window again to see if he had missed anything. But there was no help to be found anywhere.

They were trapped.

Bellizen read it in his eyes and nodded. He walked back to her. "I won't let them take me," he said. "I know what will happen if they do."

She nodded, her pale, round face calm, her gaze clear and steady. "I won't let them take me, either."

"But they will take us," he said. "There's too many of them. We'll be overwhelmed."

She gave him a small smile. "Not if we don't wait around for that to happen."

She reached for his hands and led him over to the window. She looked out into the afternoon, and then stepped up onto the windowsill. "Come up with me, Trefen."

He did so, deliberately keeping his eyes on her face, refusing to look down. He stood with her in the opening, holding her hands, feeling the cool wind blow over him in a soothing wash.

In the room beyond, the door began to splinter and break.

"It's only a short jump," she said. "It won't take long."

"I wish we could be here when our mistress returns," he said. "I would like her to know how much she means to us."

"Someone will tell her," she replied. She glanced back at the door to their room. "Are you ready?"

"I think so," he said.

He took a deep breath. They waited quietly, listening to the sounds without, to the breaking down of the door in the far chamber and then to the thudding of booted feet as the Gnomes rushed to the door that led into their room.

"It helps that you are with me," he said softly.

Bellizen gave him a small smile.

Then a horn sounded, its wail deep and ominous, reverberating off the walls and through the rooms of the Keep. Shouts rose from below, and abruptly Paranor came alive in a new and terrible way.

Outside their door, the Gnomes turned and ran, abandoning their efforts. Trefen Morys and Bellizen stared at each other in disbe-

lief, and then they looked out the window where the sounds of activity were loudest.

Thousands of Rock Trolls were striding out of the trees, armored
giants forming up battle lines at the gates to the fortress of the
Druids.

TWENTY-SEVEN

Grianne Ohmsford took a quick step back as the dragon settled into place on the flats, its wings folding against its huge, scaly body. Steam rose off its back in clouds, and she could feel the heat of it from fifty feet away. The dragon flexed and undulated from head to tail, the spikes that ridged its back shivering like great stalks of grass blown in a wind. It coughed once and then exhaled a huge gout of fire and smoke.

An eerie silence settled over the landscape, and it felt to her in that instant as if everything living had disappeared from the earth save the dragon, the boy, and herself.

Then the head swung toward her and the maw parted to reveal rows of blackened teeth. The stench of its breath sent her backwards another few steps. Its yellow eyes narrowed and fixed on her.

Except they weren't fixed on her, she realized suddenly. They were fixed on Pen, who was standing next to her.

"It's the darkwand," he said quietly. "It's fascinated by the glowing runes."

He was right. The dragon had settled down into a comfortable crouch and was staring intently at the staff. The runes carved into its surface were pulsating with hypnotic consistency in the gray mistiness of the afternoon.

"It's been following me ever since I arrived," Pen said.

She blinked at him. "You've encountered it before?"

"Twice." He looked chagrined. "The first time was after I had walked into the passes leading down from the heights where I came into the Forbidding. I fell asleep, and it was there when I awoke, staring at me. Or at the staff. I couldn't get rid of it at first, but finally I did. I thought I was done with it, but yesterday it reappeared here on the flats while I was trying to reach you. It came to my rescue, actually."

"Your rescue?" She couldn't hide her disbelief.

"I was trying to find somewhere to spend the night and I wandered into a nest of Harpies. They wouldn't let me out again. They were going to eat me. But the dragon reappeared and ate them, instead."

He saw the look on her face and shook his head. "It doesn't have any interest in me. It doesn't care about me one way or the other. It's the runes." He glanced over at the dragon, which was watching them contentedly. "Something about watching the glow of the runes makes it happy. Or fascinates it. I don't know, Aunt Grianne. I just know that I can't get rid of it."

"Well, you managed to do so twice now," she pointed out.

"It was the wishsong magic," he said. "It surfaced after my bonding with the darkwand, but it was the dragon's appearance that gave me a reason to test it. I didn't know if the magic would work, but I was desperate. So I tried it out. I used it to send images of the runes off into the distance, like a lure. The dragon went after them, and I escaped."

He paused for a moment, frowning. "The second time it was too busy eating the Harpies to pay much attention to me. I just slipped away. But I guess it came looking for me."

"I guess it did." She looked at the monster, at its huge bulk and great, hooked claws and muscular body. She stared into its yellowed eyes and found them glazed and unfocused. A dragon mesmerized by bits of light—she would never have believed it. "Can you get rid of it now?"

"I don't know. I can try."

He began to hum softly, connecting with the wishsong, and as he did so the runes of the darkwand danced in response, growing brighter and more active as the music increased. Soon their glow was racing across the length of the staff in ever-changing and increasingly complex patterns. She glanced at the dragon. It was staring at the staff, satisfaction and delight mirrored in its lidded eyes. It was sitting up straight, head bent forward, as still as if it had been carved from stone.

Then the runes began to cast their images into the air, a kaleidoscope of fire bits whirling this way and that. The images spun and wove together, leaving tiny trails of light in the wake of their passing. The dragon's jaws widened, and its breath came in grunts and snorts. Claws dug into the earth, and its tail coiled and uncoiled rhythmically. The images danced toward it, closing on it like tiny fireflies, then leapt away into the sky, speeding off into the horizon, a long line of them, beckoning with their comet light.

But the dragon didn't move. It sat watching them intently for a moment, then turned back to Pen and the staff once more.

Pen kept at it a few moments longer then gave up. "It's not working," he said, breaking off with a tired gasp. "I don't understand. Before, it would have flown after the images. Now it's only watching them."

Grianne studied the dragon a moment. "It's learned that flying after the images doesn't do it any good. The images don't last. It's figured out that the source is the staff and that staying close to the staff is the best way to keep the images coming." She shook her head. "It's a brute, but it isn't stupid."

They stared at the dragon in silence. The dragon stared back. In Pen's hand, the darkwand continued to glow and its runes to dance and pulse.

"What are we going to do?" Pen asked finally.

Grianne didn't know. She could use the wishsong's magic, but she was afraid of the reaction she would trigger. If she didn't kill the dragon, it would be on them in a heartbeat. Even if she did kill it, using so much magic would draw the Straken Lord to them like a beacon of firelight in darkest night. Either result would be horrendous.

She was beginning to think she wasn't going to be given a choice in the matter when a strange, barking cough sounded from somewhere in the distance, off toward the Dragon Line. It was rough and made her think of scraping metal and of old saws cutting green wood. She flinched in spite of herself.

But the dragon sat up immediately, head swinging away from the darkwand and its glowing runes, eyes peering out toward the sound.

Several minutes passed, and no one moved. Then the sound came again, farther away this time and more to the east. The dragon's head swung toward it, lifting alertly. It huffed, and steam poured out of its nostrils. When the sound came a third time, the dragon roared with such ferocity that Grianne and Pen dropped to their knees in shock.

Seconds later, the monster was airborne, winging away in the direction of the sound, flying off without a backwards glance.

"What happened?" Pen breathed in confusion.

Grianne shook her head. "I don't know, but let's not stand around talking about it." She glanced over. "Can you do something to quiet those runes? Can you stop them from glowing? If it comes back, I don't want the staff to help it find us."

"I'll try," he said. He slipped off his cloak and wrapped it carefully about the darkwand so that the glow of the runes was hidden. "There," he said, satisfied.

They began walking again, heading toward the mountains, changing direction just enough that they were moving more north than west. More than once, Grianne peered off into the distance in the direction the dragon had taken, but there was no sign of it. No more than a mile ahead were hills that would offer them better cover. If they hurried, they would reach the hills before the dragon decided to come looking for them.

She wondered how far it was to where they could try to get back through the Forbidding. She glanced skyward. Night was approaching.

"Pen, why do the runes continue to glow even when you're not using the wishsong?"

He shrugged. "They just do. They were glowing that first morning when I woke and the dragon was sitting there. They respond to me in a way that doesn't involve me telling them what to do. I'm not even sure how much control I have over them. Not much, I think."

Odd, she thought. The magic of the wishsong did not have a history of independent response. It came only when summoned and did only what it was asked to do. Its behavior here must have something to do with Pen's bonding with the darkwand, with the melding of two magics. In some way, the wishsong had developed the ability to activate itself, to respond to the boy's needs even when the boy wasn't aware of exactly what they were.

Her magic, she thought, though far more powerful than his, had never been able to do that.

They had walked until they were almost into the hills when Weka Dart reappeared, arms flailing excitedly as he sprang out from behind a stand of heavy brush.

"Did you see? Did you see?" He jumped up and down and cackled as if gone mad. "It was completely fooled! I told you I would protect you, Straken Queen! I could see what would happen if I did not act, and so I used my brain and tricked it!"

She realized he was talking about the dragon. "What did you do, Weka Dart? What was that sound?"

He shrieked with laughter. "A mating call! What better way to get its attention than to give it something more important to think about than the two of you!"

"You know how to give a dragon mating call?"

"I was Catcher for Tael Riverine a long time! I learned how to give many kinds of calls! I would have been a poor Catcher otherwise, and I was the best that ever was! Did you like it? You had no idea what it was, did you? Did it make you wonder if maybe something was dying? That's how dragons sound when they're in love!"

He danced about wildly, and then started away. "Hurry, come, come! We have to reach the Dragon Line by nightfall! We need to keep moving!" He wheeled back a moment. "It was good that I was close by and watching out for you, wasn't it? I saved you both!"

Then he was off again, racing into the distance, a small, crook-limbed blur against the haze.

Grianne stared after him and thought in despair, *There must be a way.*

When the battle horns sounded, Kermadec was crouched in the shadow of a half-wall atop the gatehouse where Atalan and the other Rock Trolls were hiding. He hesitated only long enough to make certain he was not mistaken about what was happening, then leapt from his place of concealment to the floor below and raced for the gatehouse door.

After leaving Trefen Morys and Bellizen, the Trolls had made it down from the parapets and found their way to the base of the north wall and the gate that Grianne had always kept open for meetings.

But the gate was closed and sealed, and Kermadec could tell at a glance that it would take too much effort and make entirely too much noise to force it. Someone had taken a good deal of time and trouble to make certain that it would not be used again. More than likely it had been discovered by Shadea and her allies after they had dispatched the Ard Rhys into the Forbidding and assumed control of the Keep. Shadea would have been quick to recognize its significance.

So for the better part of two hours, the Trolls had hidden in the gatehouse next to it, a less-than-satisfactory location given what they were now faced with doing, but one that was unlikely to be visited anytime soon. But, with the gate of choice stoutly sealed, Kermadec and his Trolls would have to breach another gate. Since the next closest gate was some distance from where they hid, there was every possibility that they would be spotted long before they reached it.

There was nothing they could do about that. The only way the Trolls were going to take Paranor was by breaching the Druid defenses from the inside. That meant seizing and holding a gate long enough for the Trolls outside the walls to get inside.

Kermadec burst through the gatehouse door. All around him, the fortress of the Druids was erupting in a frenzy of wild shouts and charging men.

"They've arrived," he informed the other Trolls, putting his back to the door and facing them across the tiny, shadow-streaked room.

Atalan's face was a mask of excitement. "Now we'll see how strong these walls really are!" he hissed. "Let's go!"

"Not yet." His brother blocked his way. "Give it a moment more. Let them get to the walls and settle in place. Let them all be looking at what threatens from without so they won't be looking at us. Then we'll take them."

Atalan came right up against him. "Why wait, brother? Confusion serves us better than it serves them. Delay is for cowards and weaklings. We should take them now!"

Kermadec held his ground, his gaze steady. "You are too impatient, Atalan. You rush to do everything too quickly."

Atalan spit. "If I am too impatient, you are too cautious. You delay everything too long. Move more quickly, and we might have better success. Are we here to help the Ard Rhys or not?"

"Don't push too hard on me," Kermadec said softly. "And do not question my commitment to the Ard Rhys. It is not your place to do so."

"Shhh," Barek hissed at them. He was standing at the shuttered window, keeping watch as dozens of Gnome Hunters charged past on their way to the parapets. "You'll be heard if you keep this up!"

The brothers faced each other a moment longer, then Atalan turned away with a shrug. "You are Maturen, Kermadec. You are leader. The responsibility for what happens here is yours. Who am I to question you?"

He slouched back to the far wall and slumped down, staring at nothing. Seething with anger and embarrassment, Kermadec turned back to the door and ignored him.

It was dark by the time Grianne and Pen began the climb into the Dragon Line. Shadows thrown by the skeletal trees and distant peaks draped the land. West, the light was fading from gray to black, and the twilight hush that marked the transition from day to night was retiring the creatures of one and bringing out the creatures of the other. Sounds faded as if swallowed beneath the surface of an endless sea, and the world became a place for the quick and the dead.

Grianne's eyes roamed the landscape on a ceaseless scour, alert for things that might be hunting them. The boy walked quietly beside her. They had not seen Weka Dart since he had departed, but she felt certain he was close, watching their progress, ready to save them once more should the need arise. Or save himself, perhaps. She knew enough of the Ulk Bog to appreciate that whatever his good intentions, he would always look after himself first.

Still, it seemed petty of her to think of him that way after he had lured off the dragon. She wished she could form a better opinion of the Ulk Bog, but she was too familiar with how he managed to get through life to do so.

It seemed only moments later that Weka Dart appeared out of the black, materializing so suddenly that she almost struck out at him.

"Straken!" he hissed at her in a clear tone of reprimand. "You cannot continue in the dark! Too many things hunt at night, and even I cannot see them all! We must stop and wait for morning!"

She was anxious to reach their destination and get out of the For-bidding for good. But the urgency in his voice gave her pause. "Is it really so dangerous? We are almost there."

"You are not as close as you think. This is a different pass than the one you took down. Best not to repeat your steps when Tael Riverine is looking for you. No, Grianne of the powerful magic, you must stop now. You and the boy. Rest here. Wait for dawn."

So they did, taking shelter in a cluster of boulders that gave them protection on three sides and provided an overhang as well. They would take turns keeping watch, they agreed. When first light ap-peared, they would set out again. The remainder of the journey would take only a couple of hours.

Then, Grianne told herself once again, she would be free.

"Weka Dart," she said after they had settled into the rocks. She could barely see him in the hazy darkness, a dim shadow hunched down to one side. Only his eyes gleamed, watchful and steady. "I have something to tell you."

She heard Pen exhale in anticipation of what was coming. She ran her fingers through her hair, pushing it back from her face, won-dering how to put what she must say into words, and then deciding she should just say it.

"Penderrin tells me that the darkwand will not take you out of the Forbidding. It will only take him and me. No one else."

Weka Dart snorted. "He is mistaken. Or if not mistaken, he un-derestimates the power of your magic. You can find a way to take me even if the staff does not wish it."

She sighed. "I don't think so. This is old magic, older than I am, and more powerful. The wall of the Forbidding cannot be broken by ordinary means. That is why it was so difficult for Tael Riverine to get his demon into the Four Lands. He had to work a switch to make that happen. You told me so yourself."

"Perhaps you can switch the Moric back again in exchange for me," he said brightly.

His enthusiasm was frustrating. "No, I can't. I don't know how. I don't even know how this staff works. It responds to Pen, not to me. What matters is that the Faerie creature who told Pen about the staff was very explicit—it cannot bring anyone out of the Forbidding but us."

Weka Dart was on his feet in an instant, arms pinwheeling. "But

you promised! You said you would take me with you if I got you out
of Tael Riverine's prisons! You said you would! Did you lie? Is it true
that all Strakens lie? Even you?"

She held up her hands. "I told you that I would do what I could
to help you but that I didn't even know if I could help myself! That
was what I said. It was the truth, not a lie. If Pen hadn't come with the
staff, I couldn't escape the Forbidding, either. I would be trapped
here, as well."

"Now you won't be, will you?" he shrieked.

"No."

"But I will! I will!"

"Not if we can—"

"You lied, you lied, you lied!"

Spitting at Penderrin, as if the situation were his fault, the Ulk
Bog rushed out of the shelter, screaming invectives at both of them,
and then disappeared into the night. But he was back again within
minutes, trudging out of the inky black and flinging himself down
where he had been sitting before. For a long time, he didn't say anything. Grianne waited.

"Who will protect you from dragons, Grianne of the broken
promises?" he whispered finally.

He said it with such sadness that it made her throat tighten in response. "There are no dragons in my world," she answered.

"No dragons?" His head lifted from the cradle of his arms. "Well,
who will protect you from the Furies, then? Or the giants, and ogres
and Graumths? Who will warn you of their coming? Who will keep
you from stumbling into their lairs?"

"There are no Furies, ogres, giants, or Graumths. All of those are
here. They were all sent here in the time of Faerie, when the Forbidding was created." She paused. "My world is nothing like yours, little
Ulk Bog. It is a very different kind of place."

"Are there Ulk Bogs like me?"

"No. There are no Faerie kind at all, save Elves."

"I hate Elves," he muttered. "Elves enslaved the Jarka Ruus."

"Weka Dart," she said quietly. "We will try to take you with us, just
as I promised. I will keep my word. I just want you to know that I may
not be able to break you free. I may not have the power to do that."

He was silent a long time. "No Ulk Bogs?"

"No."

He squirmed around in the dark, shifting positions, trying first one, then another, so restless that she thought there was something wrong with him. "Are you all right?"

"I might not come with you after all," he said suddenly. "I might stay here. Your world sounds boring. It sounds as if there is nothing to do. I might be better off staying right where I am."

She stared at him. "I thought you said you couldn't do that. I thought you said Tael Riverine would kill you if you stayed."

"He might take me back, now that Hobstull is dead." Weka Dart's voice was small and contemplative. "He will need a new Catcher."

"No!" she said at once. "The Straken Lord will have you killed, Weka Dart! He will find out what you have done and that will be the end of you!"

"He might not. He might think me too valuable now."

She wanted to shake him so hard his teeth rattled. "If this is a threat meant to get back at me for telling you the truth, for telling you what I thought you had a right to know, then it is a poor one! Don't be such a fool! You cannot talk about going back to Tael River-ine! Going back is suicide!"

"Or maybe I will go west, where I said I wanted to go when we met." He shrugged. "Maybe I will go to Huka Flats and find a place where I will be accepted."

She didn't know what to say. She wanted him to quit talking the way he was. She wanted to tell him that they would find a way to get him out of the Forbidding. She wanted him to wait until they knew for sure what was going to happen when they used the darkwand. But Weka Dart was already sifting his expectations in his mind, re-thinking his life and his plans for the future, accepting better than she, perhaps, the realities.

"Don't decide anything tonight," she said to him. "Wait until we have a chance to test the staff. Will you do that?"

He was silent for a long time. "I will sleep on it, Straken Queen. I will give it the thought it deserves."

"I wouldn't ask for more than that," she said.

"I would be a good Catcher for you. Is there was anything to catch over there? Or to protect you from? There must be some-thing."

"There are enemies," she assured him. "There are always enemies."

She watched him lie down and curl into a ball. "I will keep you
safe from your enemies," he said softly. "I will protect you."

"I know."

She sat staring out into the night, her thoughts dark and threatening, pushing back her weariness. She should be able to do more
for him than what she believed she could. She should be able to help
him. But she didn't know where to start. She didn't know how to do
what was needed. She felt weak and impotent.

"I will be there for you," he whispered.

Then he said nothing more.

She awoke with the dawn, the silvery tinge of its breaking a
faint blush on the eastern horizon. The sky was overcast and the
clouds thick and roiling across the Pashanon. A storm was building
to the southwest, and there was a screen of rain where it swept eastward out of Huka Flats.

She looked around. Pen was sound asleep at her side, the darkwand cradled in his arms. Weka Dart was nowhere to be found. She
took a moment to scan the countryside, but didn't see him. Apparently, he had left early to scout the pass.

She roused Pen, and after eating the remainder of the roots Weka
Dart had provided for their evening meal, they set off. She felt an urgency about doing so, a need to reach their destination quickly. She
was aware of how fragile she was. Still unhealed from her experiences at the hands of Tael Riverine, her strength came mostly from
the knowledge that she was close to being free of him for good. If
she could escape the Forbidding, as well, she might recover herself.
If she could put enough distance between herself and what had been
done to her, she might be able to shore up her uncertain psyche. The
memories would never leave her but, perhaps, she could take the
edge off them. She was holding herself together mostly through
cobbled-together bits and pieces of determination, stubbornness,
and pride. She was still Ard Rhys, but to become anything like whole
again, she must regain her hold on the position as well as the title.

She looked around with haunted eyes. The oppressiveness of the
world of the Jarka Ruus closed about her. Another day in the Forbid-

ding, and she could not say for certain that she would not give way to the madness that had threatened to claim her ever since her arrival. Time was growing increasingly short for her. She could listen to the sound of its passing in the beating of her heart.

They climbed steadily into the pass, frequently looking back over their shoulders to the plains, which were disappearing in the sweep of the storm. But there appeared to be no pursuit and no indication of anything dangerous coming their way.

And there was still no sign of Weka Dart.

It was nearing midday when they gained the forested heights of the Dragon Line and began to head west, toward the place where they had entered the Forbidding. The day had gone very dark as the storm clouds continued to roll eastward. The wind had picked up, and the first sprinkles of rain blew into their faces. Not wanting to be caught in the storm, they pressed on. Grianne chose their path; her sense of where she was stronger now. The boy walked silently beside her, the staff covered and out of sight.

In the distance, thunder rumbled in long, rolling peals and lightning flashed on the plains.

Then, quite unexpectedly, they emerged from the trees into a clearing, and Grianne recognized it as the place they had been searching for. She took Pen's arm and nodded to him without speaking. The boy grinned, a disarming response that made her smile, as well. It was almost over.

She looked around for Weka Dart, but still he wasn't there.

Pen saw the look on her face. "Where is he, Aunt Grianne? I thought he would be waiting for us."

She took a long moment to study the trees, to peer through the gloom not only of the day but also of her own realization of what had happened.

"He isn't coming," she said.

The boy stared at her. "Why wouldn't he come? Doesn't he want to get out of here?"

She shook her head. "I don't know. I'm not sure he knows. I think he's afraid. Of failing to get out, if the darkwand won't take him. Of getting out and finding it isn't what he expects. Maybe something else altogether."

Penderrin looked away. "I wouldn't stay here if I were him. I would take the chance that there might be something better."

She took a deep breath. She could use her magic to try to find the Ulk Bog. He might be close still, waiting to see if they would look for him. He might be testing her. But she knew in her heart that he wasn't, that he was far away, that he had put her behind him. She would be someone he had known and helped, someone he could brag about. But she would be only a memory.

Would he try to go back to Tael Riverine and become his Catcher once more? Would he take the chance that the Straken Lord either did not know of his participation in her escape or would forgive him for it? With the Ulk Bog, it was impossible to tell.

Weka Dart.

She spoke his name in her mind, conjuring up images of him that she thought she would carry with her to the grave.

"We have to go," she told Pen abruptly. "We can't wait on him. Use the staff."

The boy brought out the darkwand and set it butt-downward against the earth, his hands wrapped around its carved surface. The runes were glowing softly, pulsing bright red in the darkness of the midday storm.

"Place your hands with mine," he said.

She started to do so, and then stopped. "Pen, listen to me. They will be waiting for us when we come through—Shadea a'Ru and those who have allied themselves with her. They will have figured out where you went and be prepared for the possibility that you might get back again and bring me with you. They will know where to look for us. They will attack the moment they see us. They will try to put an end to both of us. So I want you to be ready. I want you to get behind me and stay there until you have a chance to get clear. Any chance. As soon as you see one, you are to take it. Don't wait for me. Don't even think about me. Just run and keep running. Do you understand?"

He nodded, but looked uncertain.

She put her hands on his shoulders. "You showed great courage in coming here to save me. I don't know anyone else who could have done what you did, except perhaps your father. I owe it to him to do for you what you have done for me. I want you safe and sound when this business is finished, Penderrin. Tell me you will do as I have asked."

He nodded again, more firmly this time. "I will, Aunt Grianne."
She took her hands from his shoulders. "Are you ready?"
He took a deep breath. "I am."
"Then let's go home."
She wrapped her hands on the staff and held tight.

TWENTY-EIGHT

The transition happened quickly. The runes began to glow more intensely, gaining strength from her touch. Grianne blinked against the sudden brightness, and then felt a kind of shifting in the space she occupied. The grayness of the Forbidding grew slowly darker, as if the storm had caught up to them and they were about to be engulfed. All that took place in seconds, barely giving her time enough to register what was transpiring. She glanced over at Pen, who held on to the darkwand from the other side, his eyes closed.

But she did not close hers. She wanted to see what was going to happen to her.

Even so, she did not. The runes suddenly burst into fiery brightness, and it appeared as if the staff itself was aflame. It was all she could do to keep holding on to it, to persuade herself that the fire was an illusion. The glow grew steadily, cocooning her away, shutting off her surroundings, from the world of the Jarka Ruus, from everything but the staff and herself and Pen.

Then everything was gone, and she was fighting for air as a massive fist closed about her body, crushing her, squeezing the air from her lungs with relentless pressure. She fought back against it, struggling to breathe, to stay alive. *Something has gone wrong*, she thought in desperation. *Something isn't right.*

Then the light dimmed, the runes darkened, and she was standing once more in the familiar surroundings of her sleeping chamber, returned safe and whole to Paranor. She still had a death grip on the staff, but the runes had gone dark.

She exhaled sharply in relief.

In the next instant, the triagenel collapsed about her.

She knew what it was immediately. She had caught a glimpse of the magic's glow in the few seconds it took for her passage out of the Forbidding to become complete, but had failed to recognize its significance until it was too late. The glow disappeared as the triagenel dropped into place, becoming an invisible presence that hemmed her in on all sides, an unbreakable cage.

"Don't move, Penderrin," she said to him.

He stood across from her, still smiling happily at having escaped the Forbidding. The smile faded slowly, and he looked around in surprise.

"We're caught in a triagenel," she informed him. A quick sweep of her hand illuminated the strands of their prison. "I told you they would be waiting. But I didn't foresee this."

"What is it?"

"A very powerful form of magic. It takes three magic users to create it, a combination of their skills to bring it to life."

But the glow was not uniform, she saw. In some places it was very nearly dark. In a properly constructed triagenel, the magic should be equally distributed. "There's something wrong here," she murmured. "See?"

She pointed at a couple of the weaker spots, at the obvious darknesses, and as she did so the door to the concealed passageway on the far side of the chamber swung inward and her brother's face appeared in the opening. "Grianne?"

"Bek!" she exclaimed in shock. "How in the world . . . ?"

"Listen to me," he interrupted, cutting her short. "I've used the wishsong to weaken several of the triagenel's strands. I think you can break free, if you try."

"Close the door!" she said.

He did so, and she pushed Pen down on the floor and stood over him. "Cover your head. Don't look up until I tell you."

She would not have much time. Shadea and the others would be coming. Perhaps they were already just outside. She would have to hurry. She was afraid of the wishsong after what had happened inside the Forbidding, but she had no other choice. She was going to have to use it anyway when she faced Shadea.

So she summoned the magic boldly, and when it surfaced she formed it into razor-sharp edges that would cut and sever and then sent them screaming into the weakened places in the net. The wishsong spun and ripped through the netting, overcoming momentary resistance from the enabling magic and slicing through strands until the cage sagged like soft rope. She kept at it, working at first one place and then another, and when she had the entire structure sufficiently weakened, she attacked it with such force that the triagenel disintegrated, and she blew out the entire north wall of the sleeping chamber. Stone blocks and debris exploded outward, and a huge cloud of dust mushroomed through the room.

Grianne covered her face, waited for the dust to settle, and then pulled Pen back to his feet. "Bek!" she shouted.

Her brother burst into the room with Rue Meridian, Tagwen, and an Elven girl she took to be Khyber Elessedil right behind. There was a quick exchange of grateful hugs between Pen and his parents and Khyber. Only Bek hugged her. Grianne saw dismay and shock reflected in their faces when they looked at her. She could even see pity.

"I'm all right," she said to them.

Her brother shook his head. "You are not all right. Shadea a'Ru and all those others who betrayed you will pay for this. We will hunt them down. We will find out everything. But we have something else we have to talk about now, something that won't wait. A demon was set free when you were taken. It's still here, and it's trying to break down the Forbidding."

"I know of this," she said.

"I thought as much. What you don't know is that the only way to stop it is for Pen to find it and use the darkwand to return it, just as he used the staff to return you."

"Penderrin has to do this?" she asked in surprise.

"The King of the Silver River said he must. Only the darkwand can complete the transfer from one world to the other, and only Pen can command the magic. I have to take him with us to find the demon."

In the hallway outside the sleeping chamber door, there was new activity, the sound of running and of shouts.

"They're coming," she said to the others. She brought up her hands, summoned her magic once more, and sealed the door from the inside. "That will hold them for a few minutes, no more." She turned back to Bek. "Take the others and go. You found your way here through the secret passageways—can you find your way back again?"

He nodded. "Between us, Tagwen and I can manage."

"I'm not coming," the Dwarf declared almost belligerently. "I belong here with the Ard Rhys."

Grianne moved over to him quickly and knelt. "Yes, you do. But you must leave anyway. All of you must. There's nothing you can do for me by staying. I have to face Shadea and the others alone. I am the one who can deal with them best. Only Bek might be able to help, but his place is with Pen, finding that demon and dispatching it. Listen to me." She gripped the Dwarf's shoulders tightly. "I've seen the inside of the Forbidding, Tagwen. It is a horror beyond anything you can imagine. If the creatures that live there were to be set free in this world, it would be the end of us all. You have to stop that from happening. Whatever becomes of me, you have to stop that."

She held his gaze. Finally, he gave her a small nod, his bearded face twisted into an unhappy knot. "I will do this because you ask it," he said quietly. "But not willingly."

She turned at once to Pen. "This won't be easy. You won't know what you have to do until you find the demon. Perhaps you will have to find a way to get it to touch the staff. Perhaps it will take more. I wish I could tell you something helpful, but you know as much as I do about how it works. Trust your instincts, Pen. They won't betray you."

The boy nodded. "I don't want to leave you, either."

She smiled. "I'll see you again. Just go. Do what you must. Do what is needed." She looked around. "All of you. Go, now."

They did so, one by one, disappearing through the door into the secret passageway, glancing back at her as they did, a mix of reluctance and dismay mirrored on their faces. Bek was the last to depart.

"Don't let anything happen to you," he said. "It's taken too much

out of us getting you back to bear the thought of losing you again."
He paused. "I love you, Grianne."

Then he pulled the door shut behind him and was gone, his
words still echoing in her mind.

I love you, too, she thought.

She turned back to the sleeping chamber and looked at the
sealed door. She had come a long way to face what awaited her on
the other side. She had fought hard for a chance to put things right.
But all of a sudden, she was unsure if she could do so.

How odd, she thought.

On the floor in front of her, the last strands of the ruined triagenel were slowly dissolving as their magic leached away. She stared
for a moment, then caught sight of herself in the mirror and saw
what Bek and the others had seen: a ghost, a tattered imitation of
herself.

She walked to the closet on the other side of the room, opened
it, and took out one of the robes hanging there, clean and sleekly
black. She draped it around her shoulders and fastened it in place
with the clasp she had fashioned in the shape of the Eilt Druin, the
Druid chain of office, the symbol of their order.

Her enemies would see her this last time, she told herself, as she
meant for them to see her. As leader. As Ard Rhys.

She fingered the clasp, tracing the raised image of a hand holding forth a burning torch. The meaning of the Elfish words came
back to her. THROUGH KNOWLEDGE, POWER.

Perhaps. This day, she would see.

Then she crossed the room and swept the air in front of the
chamber door with one hand to remove the magic that sealed it.
Tightening her resolve, she flung open the door.

Shadea a'Ru stood on the battlements of Paranor's north wall
with Traunt Rowan and looked down at the army of Rock Trolls
amassed before the gates. On hearing of this new threat, she had
come at once, determined that she would deal with it herself, that
she would not leave it up to her less-than-reliable allies. But having seen for herself how many Trolls were gathered—in excess of a
thousand—she was unsure of what to do.

"Have they made any sort of demand?" she asked Traunt Rowan.

He shook his head. "Not a word out of any of them. They simply walked out of the trees and formed up in ranks and haven't moved or said anything since."

"This must have something to do with Kermadec," she said quietly. "Those Trolls bear the banner of Taupo Rough. They wouldn't be here if it wasn't for him. Are you sure you left him safely behind at Stridegate? After all, that girl managed to find a way onto one of the ships."

"He was on the ground with the others when we lifted off. He was trapped by thousands of Urdas. Even if he got past them, he would have had to walk out. It would have taken days." Traunt Rowan shook his head, and then gestured toward the Troll army. "Maybe they've come looking for him. Maybe they think he's here."

She considered the possibility. "Maybe."

But that suggestion didn't feel right. A few might come, but not an entire army. It was something else, something much more dangerous. She glanced at the lower walls, where the Gnome Hunters were hiding behind the battlements. They could hold against an attack if the Trolls did not get past the walls. But there were too few of them to withstand an assault if the attackers broke through.

She had already ordered that the gates be reinforced. There was nothing more she could think of to do at that point. She would let the Trolls stand out there all day if that was what they wanted to do. If they were still standing there the next day, she might consider using her magic to disperse them. But that would require an enormous drain on her reserves, a last resort when all else failed. She would need a good reason to commit herself to such an action.

She was considering the possibility of sending word to the Eastland Gnomes that they needed reinforcements when Pyson Wence came flying down the stairs from the north tower, his black robes billowing wildly, his sharp features stricken.

"The triagenel has collapsed!" he shouted to them.

She's back, Shadea thought instantly.

"You're sure about this?" she snapped, exchanging a quick glance with Traunt Rowan.

Pyson Wence sneered, trying to hide the fear in his eyes. "Do you think me a fool? The magic's gone dark. What else could it mean?"

She ignored the taunt, brushing past him as she moved quickly toward the tower stairs, her strong features hard and set. "Let's finish this," she said softly.

They went up the stairs in a rush. Already, Shadea felt the magic building inside her in anticipation of the battle ahead. She smiled fiercely. This time there would be no mistakes.

They had gained the head of the stairs and were turning down the hallway leading to the sleeping chamber when its north wall blew apart.

Deep in the hidden passageways in the walls of the Keep, the Ohmsfords, Khyber Elessedil, and a grumbling Tagwen descended toward the furnace room. In a somber mood, the group moved ahead in silence.

"I don't like it that we left her back there alone," the Dwarf repeated over and over again.

"You know we couldn't stay, Tagwen," Rue Meridian said finally. "You know she wouldn't let us."

"There are too many of them for her to have a chance."

Rue shook her head. "I wouldn't wager against her, whatever the odds."

Tagwen went silent for a time as the little band continued through the darkness using a small light provided by Khyber's elemental magic as a beacon. They could not tell what was happening behind them. The stone-block walls were thick and massive and muffled all sounds from the other side. The chambers of the Druid's Keep were tombs, and they kept their secrets well.

"We could still go back," Tagwen muttered under his breath. "It isn't too late."

Bek wheeled back on him furiously. "Stop it, Tagwen! None of the rest of us likes this any better than you do! How do you think I feel about leaving her? She's my sister! But if the Forbidding comes down, it really won't make any difference what happens to Grianne, will it?"

"Bek," Rue admonished softly.

Tagwen went crimson with shame at the rebuke, his lips compressing into a tight line. He tried to say something in response, but failed. Trembling, he pushed past Bek and went on alone.

It was Pen who went after him, hurrying to catch up as he wandered blindly ahead into the darkness. "Wait, Tagwen!"

When he was even with the Dwarf, Pen slowed and walked at his side. They were descending a stairway that was broad enough for two to pass together, so the boy was able to stay on his shoulder.

"He didn't mean it, Tagwen. He just thinks like you do; he's afraid he will lose her."

Tagwen didn't say anything.

"We all want to go back and help her," Pen continued. "We are all afraid for her. I saw what sort of place the Forbidding is. I saw what she had to survive for all those weeks. She has been though a lot more than you think. I don't even know it all; she wouldn't talk about it with me. But I sensed it, anyway."

"All the more reason we should be back there helping her," Tagwen said furiously. "She's not strong enough to face Shadea and those others. She'll try to stand up to them, to reclaim the order, but she might not have the strength to do it."

Pen nodded. "I know. But if we're not there, Tagwen, she doesn't have to worry about us getting hurt. She only has to worry about herself. I think that's all she can manage just now. She sent us away to find the demon, but she sent us away to keep us safe, too."

He paused. "And if something bad does happen to her, we won't be there to see it happen. I think she wants that, too."

The Dwarf looked over at him, but made no response.

Kermadec had been waiting for the right moment, and when he heard the explosion from high in the north tower, he knew it had arrived. He took his little band of Rock Trolls from the gatehouse in which they had been hiding and moved toward the main gates securing the north wall. They advanced at a trot, bunched close together for protection, prepared to fight their way through any resistance. But they were lucky. The Gnome Hunters guarding the Keep were all on the walls or at the gates themselves, and the corridors between were empty.

The Trolls got to within fifty feet of the north gates before the Gnome Hunters standing guard at the huge crossbar securing the gates caught sight of them and shouted a warning to those on the walls. Kermadec responded by ordering his Trolls to charge. They rushed the Gnomes at the gates and fought their way through them. A hail of arrows and darts rained down from the walls, but once the Trolls were past the defenders and up against the gates, the men on the walls couldn't see them anymore.

"Atalan!" Kermadec shouted to his brother. "Take the others! Watch our backs!"

With Barek to aid him, he turned to the crossbar. It was too heavy for even a dozen men to lift and had to be rolled in and out of a series of iron clasps by a pulley system. With attackers coming at Atalan and the remaining Trolls from every direction, Kermadec and Barek heaved against the levers that engaged the pulleys and began to slide the crossbar free.

Shouts turned to screams of rage and fear as the Gnomes realized what was happening, and they flung themselves on the Trolls heedlessly. Atalan's small line held for a moment, and then broke apart under the rush. Dozens of Gnome Hunters converged on Kermadec and Barek. The latter fought to protect his Maturen, but was overwhelmed. Kermadec threw aside the Gnomes who reached him, still leaning into the pulley levers. The crossbar grated slowly out of its metal fastenings, the pulley wheels squealing from the strain.

"Atalan!" Kermadec shouted again as his attackers tore him away from the levers.

His brother reached him instantly, hammering aside the Gnomes who sought to bar his way, roaring the Taupo Rough battle cry, which was instantly taken up by the Trolls without. The gates sagged inward as Kermadec's soldiers outside pressed up against them. The crossbar was drawn halfway out by then, a single fastening securing it on its farthest end. Gnome Hunters clinging to him, Atalan threw himself against the levers and the crossbar slid all the way free.

An instant later, the gates heaved open behind the crush of armored giants pressing inward, and the Trolls of Taupo Rough poured through. The remaining defenders held their ground for a moment longer, then broke and ran, looking for somewhere farther inside the Keep to regroup.

Kermadec waited just long enough to be certain that entry into Paranor was secure, then broke free of the others and began to climb the stairs to the north tower.

Although his brother didn't see him, Atalan was right behind.

TWENTY-NINE

When Shadea a'Ru reached the sleeping chamber door and pushed her way through the knot of Gnome Hunters that surrounded it, the first thing she recognized was that the door was magic-sealed.

"She's free!" she hissed at Traunt Rowan and Pyson Wence as they came up next to her.

"Free? Of the triagenel?" The Gnome looked stricken. "That's impossible! No one can break out of a triagenel!"

Traunt Rowan smiled faintly, almost as if he had expected as much. "Perhaps we failed to build it properly."

Shadea didn't know and didn't care. What mattered was that their worst enemy was no longer a captive in any sense. She would have to be dealt with in a more direct and immediate manner or they were all finished.

She motioned for the Gnome Hunters to move behind her, thinking to put some space between all of them and the closed door. "To my left," she told Pyson, pulling Traunt Rowan to her right. "When she comes through that door, burn her. Don't hesitate. Don't think about it. Just do it. We'll catch her from three sides. Even Grianne Ohmsford isn't impervious to Druid magic!"

They backed away, Shadea all the way across the hall to the far wall, where she pressed her back up against the stone and summoned her magic to her fingertips. She glanced left and right to the other two, standing perhaps twenty feet away on either side in the middle of the hallway. The Gnome Hunters were crouched behind them, swords drawn, arrows noched into bows.

Thirty, perhaps forty strong, they waited.

Then the door flew open, banging hard against the wall, and a specter emerged, a black and impenetrable wraith backlit by light that poured through a ragged hole in the sleeping chamber wall. Its robes billowed out from its slender form, and light from the flameless hallway lamps reflected off the shiny surface of a clasp fashioned in the shape of the Eilt Druin, a hand holding forth a burning torch.

For a second, in spite of their combined resolve, no one among those who obeyed Shadea a'Ru moved. The sight of the ghostly form froze even the sorceress herself.

But then Shadea broke free of her momentary shock and sent Druid Fire streaking into the black-cloaked form, burning it to ash. Fire from the other two Druids followed on the heels of her own, disintegrating even the ash. Shouts of encouragement rose from the Gnome Hunters, who leapt up and down in response to the destruction.

Then silence settled over the hallway, and everyone went still again. Shadea moved out to the center of the corridor, peering cautiously through the haze.

"I am not where you thought me to be," Grianne Ohmsford said from somewhere off to the right.

All three rebel Druids froze where they were, staring at nothing but wall and smoke and ash as they tried to find her.

"You are not my equal, Shadea," Grianne continued quietly. "You never were. You never will be. You are banished from the order and from these walls. All of you are. If you leave now, I will let you live. I have seen enough of killing and vengeance and do not wish to see more. You deserve much worse than banishment, but if you go now, that will be the end of it. You have my word."

A dozen responses went through Shadea a'Ru's mind, all of them pointless. "I don't think banishment will suit me," she said finally. "And it remains to be seen if I am your equal or not. Show yourself, and let's find out."

But Grianne Ohmsford stayed invisible, speaking out of shadows and smoke. "Do you have any idea of what you have done? Do you have any idea at all? You sought to confine me to the Forbidding. To do so, you enlisted the aid of demons. One demon, in particular. You never stopped to consider why that demon would want to help you. You never thought that it might be using you as you were using it. What you did, Shadea—what all of you did—was to release a demon into this world by imprisoning me in the Forbidding. That demon remains free. It has a purpose in coming here. It seeks to destroy the wall of the Forbidding and set free all the demons it contains."

What nonsense, Shadea thought at once. "Where is your proof of that, Grianne?" she snapped angrily. "Do you think us fools to believe such lies?"

"I think you fools not to. You have set free a changeling, Shadea. You have set free a creature that can disguise itself as anything or anyone. It will have already assumed the identity of another and begun seeking ways to destroy the Ellcrys. If we don't stop it, it will succeed."

"We? You would enlist us? Even as we are banished?" Shadea straightened to her full height. "Come out of hiding and persuade us better, Grianne."

But even as she spoke, she was thinking of Iridia. Iridia, who had not seemed herself in that last encounter and who had gone to Sen Dunsidan to be his adviser when Shadea would have bet anything against that happening. Iridia, who had subsequently disappeared completely.

Could it be?

In an impulsive response to a possibility she could not bring herself to face, and disregarding her own safety, Shadea sent a scattering of illumination specks all across the facing of the wall fronting the bedchamber, trying to uncover Grianne's hiding place. The glittering specks coated everything, leaving a clear outline of what lay concealed within the shadows and smoke.

Grianne Ohmsford was nowhere to be found.

"Show yourself, you coward!" Shadea screamed in fury.

"Turn around."

Shadea stiffened, and then did so. Grianne Ohmsford stood a few yards away against the wall behind Shadea and to the right. She mirrored the wraith that had appeared in the doorway, cloaked and hooded in black, the Eilt Druin clasp at her throat. Her face and hands were pale and ravaged. She looked beaten and tired; she did not look up to a confrontation. Shadea took her measure and recognized the truth. The demon business and the offer of banishment were all a bluff.

"You don't look well, Grianne," she said. "You look as if a strong breeze might topple you. I don't imagine it was very pleasant inside the Forbidding, was it?"

Her enemy said nothing, but those strange blue eyes never left her own. They were watching her, waiting to see which way she would go. Whatever else Grianne was, she wasn't a fool.

"I think you have come to Paranor for the last time," Shadea continued softly. "I think you have just wasted your one chance at escaping with your life."

"Don't mistake what you see," the other whispered. "Take my offer. Go now. Banishment is not the worst of what can happen to you."

"I'll burn your eyes out first," Shadea responded.

"Shadea, wait!" Traunt Rowan stepped forward, hands stretched out in a gesture of supplication. "Enough of this. It's over. We've lost. Don't you see?"

"Be silent!" she hissed.

"To what end? The time for silence is past. Look at what's before us. Anyone who can survive the Forbidding and come back alive to the Four Lands and then break free of a triagenel is no one I care to challenge. If she can do all she has done to get back here and confront us like this, she has magic and luck beyond anything we possess."

He looked at Grianne. "I told you once that you should resign for the good of the order. I have not changed my mind about that. I still think you should. I still think you are too divisive to ever bring the order together in the way that will serve the greater good. I took sides against you because of it. Maybe I was wrong to do so, but I was not wrong about you."

He shook his head. "You must make your own decision. I have made mine. I accept this offer. I accept banishment. I've had enough."

He gave Shadea a hard, searching look, and she returned it with enough venom to poison a city. But he would not look away, and he did not blink. "Do the right thing, Shadea. Give it up."

He turned away from her and stalked down the hall, brushing aside a cluster of Gnomes that barred his way.

Shadea stared after him in disbelief, and then screamed in rage. "Traitor!"

She sent an explosion of Druid Fire into his back, white-hot and corrosive. The force of the blow lifted him off his feet and flung him against the far wall, where he slid to the floor, a lifeless, burning wreck.

In the next instant, Pyson Wence attacked Grianne Ohmsford.

Kermadec had climbed almost two flights into the Keep before he realized Atalan was following him. He wheeled back instantly. "What are you doing?" he shouted at his brother in dismay. "Go back and wait with the others!"

Atalan kept coming and shoved past him as if he weren't there. "Go back yourself, brother."

Kermadec reached for him angrily and then stopped himself. Getting into a fight with his brother would serve no useful purpose. If Atalan wanted to come, it was because he wanted to help. What was the point in being angry with that?

The point, he knew, was that he was afraid for Atalan. But he also knew that their relationship was well beyond a time and place where he could do anything about that.

He forced his concerns aside, caught up with Atalan, and without looking at him said, "We'll go back together when this business is finished and done with."

They passed knots of Druids who stood looking at them in surprise, books and scrolls cradled in their hands, dark robes gathered close. A few recognized him and nodded. They didn't seem to know what was happening. One or two moved quickly away when they realized he had been in a fight, and he shouted after them to go to the Assembly and stay there. He assumed that most of them would; he was still convinced that they would not fight for Shadea if they were not threatened themselves.

The hallways came and went as the two Rock Trolls raced ahead. Only once did they encounter anything resembling resistance, and that was an unexpected run-in with a knot of Gnome Hunters who fled the moment they saw what they were up against. Kermadec had not been inside the Keep in years, but he remembered it well from his time as Captain of the Druid Guard, and he found his way without difficulty. Almost all of the Gnomes were on the walls, fighting to hold against the onslaught of Rock Trolls pouring through the north gates.

As they neared the upper reaches of the north tower, Kermadec grew increasingly uneasy. He did not like the Keep's empty feeling. He did not like the unusual quiet. His battle instincts were finely tuned from years of fighting, and he knew better than to ignore them. There was an edge to his anticipation this time that was unusual. He had the strange sensation of wanting to hurry and at the same time needing to slow down. Perhaps it was the nature of the mission or what was at stake. Perhaps it was the place and time. He could not explain it. But he did not slow. His concerns must be for his mistress. She had come back to them, he believed. She had escaped the Forbidding. The explosion in the north tower told him Penderrin had succeeded. She was there, and he knew in his heart that she needed him.

As he neared the upper hallway and the sleeping chamber of the Ard Rhys, the sounds of a desperate struggle convinced him that he was right.

Grianne Ohmsford was caught off guard by Pyson Wense's attack. She had assumed that any attack would begin with Shadea, to whom the others clearly looked. On coming out of the sleeping chamber and using the false image to distract the Druids, she had placed herself in a position where she could best defend herself against the sorceress. She had not forgotten about Pyson or Traunt Rowan, but she had focused her attention principally on Shadea.

But Shadea's unexpected attack on Traunt Rowan had surprised her, and for just a moment she had taken her attention away from the Gnome. Perhaps he had been watching for that. His attack came just as she realized the danger, but she was too slow to deflect it entirely. The Druid Fire slammed into her, nearly shattering her defenses. It scorched her hair and the skin of her face, and if not for the protective magic already in place, including that woven through her Druid robes, she would have been incinerated.

Even so, the force of the attack knocked her off her feet and sent her sprawling down the hall, tangled in her black robes. Furious at herself for her inattention and desperate to regain control of the situation, she sprang up again, but a second explosion immediately knocked her down once more. Pyson was moving toward her by then, leveling a steady barrage of incendiary magic, trying to keep her down long enough to finish her. She rolled and twisted, using the wall to lever herself back to her knees, and launched her own Druid Fire in response. But her efforts were weak and unsustained, and the Gnome kept advancing.

Then Shadea wheeled back, and Grianne was forced to turn her attention to the new threat, lashing out at the sorceress before she had a chance to join the attack. Shadea screamed in fury as the magic of the wishsong knocked her backwards. But Shadea was physically much stronger than Grianne and was quick to regain her balance. Within seconds, Grianne was under attack from two sides.

Just as it seemed that she had exposed herself too quickly and would pay the price for her impatience, Kermadec came charging down the hallway with a second Troll right behind, slamming into a cluster of Gnome Hunters that tried to slow him, scattering the gnarled figures as if they were made of paper. Roaring with a ferociousness that froze the blood, the big Troll went right at Shadea.

But Shadea a'Ru had fought on the Prekkendorran and was no stranger to hand-to-hand combat. Moreover, she was very nearly as strong as the Troll. She met his rush with a howl as ferocious as his own, slipped his grasp, and let his momentum carry him into the wall. Then she wheeled back on him, able to bring her magic to bear now, and sent the Druid Fire burning into him.

Just as she did so, the second Troll came at her, as well. "Kermadec!" he roared in what seemed more a battle cry than a warning.

Down went Shadea a'Ru and the second Troll in a tangled, thrashing knot, rolling over and over on the stone floor. Kermadec was struggling to rise, but Pyson Wence joined the attack and searing Druid Fire slammed Kermadec back against the wall, knocking the breath out of him and leaving his thick hide steaming from the heat. The Gnome struck at him again and again, shouting for his Hunters to move in and finish him.

But Pyson made the same mistake now with Grianne that she had made earlier with him. He forgot about her. She surged to her feet in a white-hot fury, summoned the power of the wishsong, and struck out at him with every ounce of strength she could manage. Sensing his danger, the Gnome turned from Kermadec toward her just in time to receive the full brunt of the attack. She had a glimpse of his terrified face as he fought to protect himself. For just a second, his defenses held. Then they fell apart, and Pyson Wence simply exploded.

So damaged by the Gnome Druid's attack that flames were licking at the burned places on his body, Kermadec was trying to get up again. "Atalan!" he called desperately.

Shadea a'Ru broke free of Kermadec's brother, wheeled away, and went into a crouch. When she came out of it, she was holding a long knife at waist level. Atalan came at her fearlessly, his massive arms reaching out to crush her, but she sidestepped him easily in a practiced, fluid movement and drove the knife hilt-deep into his chest. Atalan sagged from the blow and dropped to his knees, gasping.

Shadea kicked his body aside and turned back to Grianne. Hands lifting, she attacked anew, sending a hail of Druid Fire into her enemy. Grianne was able to fight off the attack, but only barely. The force of it knocked her backwards once more, and she struggled to keep her feet as she sought to defend herself, trying in vain to mount a counterattack.

She felt her defenses crumbling. She felt the heat of the Druid Fire beginning to break through.

Suddenly, out of the corner of her eye, she saw Kermadec, his great body bloodied and steaming, lurch to his feet. One hand grasped a spear he had taken from one of his Gnome attackers. Bracing himself against the wall, he gripped the spear in one huge fist, set himself, and heaved it at Shadea.

Too late the sorceress realized the danger. She wheeled to protect herself, but the spear caught her in the chest and drove her back against the wall, the force of the throw pinning her fast. Her body jerked and her head snapped back. Her eyes went wide with shock and disbelief. She screamed and flailed, trying to break free. She sprayed Druid Fire everywhere. But the blow was fatal, and a moment later she collapsed and did not move again.

The remaining Gnome Hunters were already in flight, disappearing down the hallway as fast as they could manage. Grianne stood alone among the wounded and the dead. She lowered her hands, dispersed the magic she had summoned to defend herself, and stared at Shadea a'Ru. The sorceress was staring back at her, eyes blank and unseeing, face twisted in a death mask. Grianne looked away, sickened, then walked quickly over to Kermadec. The big Rock Troll slid down the wall into a sitting position, his chin sunk on his chest. Blood and burned patches were everywhere on his massive body.

She knelt before him and gently raised his head. "Kermadec?" she whispered. "Can you hear me?"

His eyes opened and fixed on her. "Mistress," he replied, his voice thin and reedy. "I told you they were vipers."

She bent forward and kissed his face, and then cradled him against her and whispered, "You great bear."

THIRTY

Pen Ohmsford, his parents, Khyber Elessedil, and Tagwen descended through the corridors of Paranor to the furnace room, then back down along the hidden passageway that led to the outside world. They encountered no one on their way. The silence of the Druid's Keep was deep and pervasive and gave the false impression that it was deserted save for them.

But once they were outside, they heard the sounds of the battle being fought at the north wall, and although they hadn't seen the Trolls arrive, they could pretty well guess at what was happening.

"That will give Shadea something else to think about!" Tagwen grunted, a smile on his bearded face. "Kermadec won't rest until he has the Ard Rhys safely out of there!"

That knowledge seemed to give him some sense of peace, and he quit muttering about how he should be back in the north tower trying to help her. Pen was grateful for that because, given that he was the only one sympathetic enough to permit it, most of the muttering was being done in his ear. While he appreciated Tagwen's concern for his mistress, he was struggling with his own problems.

Pen was beginning to contemplate in some detail the task that lay ahead of him. He had thought he would be safely out of danger once he returned to Paranor with his aunt, so the news that he must go off and find a changeling demon and confront it with the darkwand had come as an unpleasant surprise. Once again, he was being asked to do something without being told exactly how he was supposed to do it. Only this time, he was being asked to confront a very dangerous creature. It was one thing to go into the Forbidding and bring back the Ard Rhys, who was ready and willing to come. It was another to force a demon to go back into a place it did not wish to go.

At least he had his parents to help him. And Khyber, as well. They were much more self-possessed and experienced than he was. His father and Khyber had the use of magic, as well. That should give them an edge once they found the demon. Still, it was his responsibility to use the darkwand to return the demon to the Forbidding, and no amount of reassurance could disguise the fact that he didn't know how to do that.

As they moved away from the base of the cliffs on which Paranor rested, slipping quickly and quietly into the forest toward *Swift Sure*, Pen found himself wondering what demons were like. He hadn't really seen any in the Forbidding, unless you counted Weka Dart, and he didn't. The Ulk Bog didn't seem like a demon to him; he envisioned demons as being something much more fearsome and threatening.

In any case, he didn't know what he was going to do once he met a real one, but he thought it might be a good idea to figure out something before the moment arrived.

They passed through the trees to the clearing where *Swift Sure* was tethered, climbed up the rope ladder, and set about releasing the anchor ropes. His parents did most of the work, his mother taking the helm and his father working the lines. In minutes they were airborne, lifting away from the woods, rising swiftly into the air. He stood with Tagwen and Khyber at the railing and looked down on Paranor. The north wall of the Druid's Keep was under attack by huge numbers of Rock Trolls, their size and build unmistakable from any height. The Trolls were spread out all along the wall, but the greatest number were bunched together at the gates, and from the surge pushing inward it seemed clear that the gates had been taken.

Then *Swift Sure* was moving away too rapidly for them to follow the action below any further, and Bek was calling out to Khyber as he moved toward the ship's bow. The trio moved away from the railing in response and joined the elder Ohmsford in front of the fore-mast.

"Will you use the Elfstones now?" he asked Khyber.

"What am I looking for?" She already had the Stones out and was holding them in the palm of her hand. "I don't know what a demon looks like. I don't know what sort of creature I ought to tell the Stones to find."

Perplexed by the problem, they stared at each other in silence for a moment. None of them, after all, had ever seen a demon or had any clear idea of what one looked like. If they didn't know what they were looking for, how were they supposed to find it?

Then Pen said, "Try holding on to the staff, Khyber. It helped me find Grianne in the Forbidding. If its purpose now is to find the demon, it might help you here."

He handed her the darkwand, which she took from him and held out in front of her in one hand while gripping the Elfstones in the other, summoning their magic. The moments crept by. Nothing happened.

"It isn't working," she said, a hint of panic in her dark eyes.

Pen took the staff back from her. "I guess it only responds to me. Let me try. If it showed me how to find Grianne, it should show me how to find the demon, as well."

He gripped the darkwand and turned his thoughts to the demon and the Forbidding. Instantly, the runes began to brighten all up and down the length of the staff, their glow soft at first and then building in intensity. When they began to dance off the staff like fireflies, Pen said quickly, "Now, Khyber! Put your hand over mine and use the Elfstones!"

She did so, gripping the staff with her left hand and lifting her right fist to call forth the magic. The response was immediate. The Elfstones brightened like blue fire, their light flooding from between her fingers in brilliant shards and exploding away toward the southwest. The light showed miles and miles of plains and hills, green expanses of grasslands and farms, then tightened to a point where a single airship sailed steadily west across the landscape. The craft was huge, a great warship, its decks thick with the black-and-silver uniforms of the Federation but stripped of any visible weapons. The vision tightened and settled on one man, an imposing patriarch with flowing white hair and a strong, imperious face, who stood in the pilot box as if to oversee its workings, his arms folded across his chest as he stared off into the distance where the thick forests of the Westland spread away from the broad, gleaming surface of a sunlit lake.

Seconds later, the image flared once and went dark, and the magic faded.

"Sen Dunsidan," Tagwen declared, loathing in his voice. Then he realized the implications of what that meant. "Shades!" he breathed, his face going pale.

"You're sure about this?" Bek asked, putting a hand on the Dwarf's broad shoulder.

Tagwen nodded firmly. "There's no mistaking him. He's come to Paranor enough times that I should know. Prime Minister of the Federation, but a snake of the first order. I would have been willing to bet everything I own that he was Shadea's ally in sending the Ard Rhys into the Forbidding. He's always hated her, ever since she manipulated him as the Ilse Witch. She made it up to him, but he never forgave her. He isn't the type to forgive anyone."

"But now he's the demon?" Rue interrupted. "What's going on?"

Bek shook his head. "The demon crossed over when Grianne was sent into the Forbidding. It must have taken another form right away. It probably switched identities more than once. Now it pretends to be Sen Dunsidan. A good choice; it gives the demon tremendous power."

"It's going into the Westland," Khyber said. "That lake was the Myrian and those forests the Tirfing. It must think it's found a way to destroy the Ellcrys."

Bek nodded. "Flying west below Callahorn, away from the Prekkendorran and the normal routes of travel. It's trying to sneak in from below. It knows it will be seen eventually, but perhaps not right away. It must have a plan for what it will do when the Elves intercept it. Negotiation first, perhaps, then force if all else fails. That warship looks formidable, even if it doesn't seem to be carrying any weapons. There must be something aboard that will allow the demon to destroy the Ellcrys."

"The Elves will never let it get close enough to threaten the tree," Khyber insisted.

"Not if they know it is a demon. But as Sen Dunsidan, it will get closer than it would otherwise. At any rate, we have to stop it. If we fly all night, we should intercept it by dawn."

"I might remind you," said Rue Meridian, who had come up quietly behind them while they were discussing what to do, "that we don't have any weapons on this ship except for a pair of rail slings. How are we supposed to intercept anything?"

Pen's father didn't seem to have an answer to that, saying that he would think about it.

Bek went back with Rue into the pilot box, leaving Pen with Khyber and Tagwen. Unable to get past his susceptibility to airsickness even on the calmest of days, the Dwarf was already starting to look a little green, and after grunting something about taking a nap he disappeared below. Pen talked with Khyber for a time, catching up on what had happened to her after he had gone into the Forbidding and telling her in turn what he had seen there. When they were finished with that, neither one wanted to talk about much of anything. They were exhausted from their struggles and in need of nourishment and rest. Khyber left to find something for them to eat, and Pen moved over to the bow and settled in.

Looking out over the countryside, he thought anew about what he was going to do when they found that warship and its demon commander. He was aware of how uncertain things were becoming once again, and the particulars of his own role in what lay ahead were the most nebulous of all. He had survived the Forbidding and a good deal more, but that didn't make him feel any better about his chances. He wished he had some idea of how the darkwand would work on the demon, but there was no one to tell him and no way for him to find out until the moment he was using it. He wasn't very reassured.

He found himself thinking about his aunt. Events at Paranor were in all likelihood already over. She had either regained control of the Druid order or she was dead. He didn't want to think like that, but he knew it was true. Thinking of what they had left her to face made him sick at heart. She seemed so frail and so vulnerable that he couldn't conceive of her surviving a battle with the rebel Druids. He told himself that she had survived in the Forbidding, so she might find a way to survive at Paranor. It would have been better, though, if they could have stayed to help. It would have been better if she weren't so alone.

Khyber returned with food and drink, and after Pen had consumed both, he went below and slept. His sleep was deep and untroubled until sometime around midnight, when he dreamed of a dark presence enfolding him so tightly that he couldn't breathe, and he woke sweating with fear.

After that, he didn't sleep at all.

It was two hours past dawn when the Moric saw the other airship approaching. By then, the Zolomach had turned north along the silver ribbon of the Mermidon and was approaching the Valley of Rhenn on a day that was bright and clear and warm. The Moric didn't care what kind of day it was; it only cared that it was to be the last day it would have to spend in an unpleasant world. It hated the brightness and the smells. It hated the humans it was forced to live among. It was worse aboard this airship, where it was in proximity to them all the time and could not escape to its sewer refuge. Worse still, it had assumed the identity of a human who was never left alone for more than a few moments, even when sleeping.

It couldn't change the conditions of this world quickly enough.

But time was running out on the Moric. In spite of its success in avoiding detection by Elven airships, the atmosphere aboard this vessel was poisonous. Two days earlier, the Free-born army had overrun the Federation defensive lines on the Prekkendorran and sent that once seemingly invincible force fleeing back into the deep Southland in a reprise of what the Federation had done to the Elves some days earlier. Matters had turned about completely, and there was no changing them back. All attempts at rallying the remnants of the battered Southland army had failed, and the war, after decades of indecision, had turned decisively in favor of the allied Free-born. The Coalition Council was furious with Sen Dunsidan and had summoned him to appear before it, but the Moric was no fool. It knew, as Sen Dunsidan would have known, what that summoning meant.

So it simply ignored the Council, boarded the Zolomach, and set sail for Arborlon. Its own plans were settled and in no way affected by anything that had happened on the Prekkendorran. Those aboard ship knew of their army's defeat, but had been assured that what they were doing would carry the war to the Elves and turn things around. They accepted that because they were soldiers and because they had no choice. No one wanted to question Sen Dunsidan, even when he was in disfavor with the Coalition Council. Sen Dunsidan had come back before; there was no reason to think he would not come back again.

They had been forced to travel cautiously, choosing a route that would keep them from being spotted by Free-born airships and would get them close enough to Arborlon and the Ellcrys that the Moric could implement its plan to get closer still. In a way, the defeat of the Federation army on the Prekkendorran had made its task easier. When finally intercepted by the Elves, the demon would say, in its guise as Sen Dunsidan, that it had come to discuss a plan for peace, to accede to conditions that would assure that the war would not resume. It would ask permission to fly to Arborlon to speak to the Elven High Council. It would give assurances that no treachery was intended and offer hostages as a show of good faith. It would demand that they let it remain aboard the *Zolomach* because, in the face of so many of the enemy, no right-thinking commander would leave the only protection available. The Elves would accept his condition. The Federation ship would display no weapons and pose no visible threat. They would feel confident that they could deal with anything the Prime Minister might attempt.

If persuasion failed to win them over, then the demon would use the fire launcher, which was concealed inside what appeared to be a storage cabin on the foredeck. In the event of an attack, the front section of the cabin could be dropped away and the weapon armed and fired in seconds. The Elven airships would be burned out of the sky before they knew what was happening, and the *Zolomach* would continue on its way. Once within range of the Ellcrys, a single direct hit was all it would take. It would be over before the Elves had a chance to do anything to stop it. In spite of having the fire launcher, the *Zolomach* would be destroyed and its crew killed in reprisal, but the demon would escape because it would shed Sen Dunsidan's skin and take a new form. In the chaos, it would slip over the side of the ship. Once it was on the ground, they would never find it.

But now an unfamiliar airship was approaching, and they were still too far away from Arborlon for it to be an Elven vessel. It was flying alone, as well, which suggested it had another purpose. The demon watched it grow larger, closing steadily, in no apparent hurry and with no indication that it meant any harm.

"Captain?" the demon said to the tall man on his right. "What ship is this?"

The *Zolomach's* Captain, who had been studying the vessel through his spyglass, shook his head. "No ship I know. Not a ship of the line. Not a warship." He looked again. "Wait. Her insignia is of a burning torch on a field of black." He trailed off. "She's a Druid ship."

The Moric stiffened. Shadea a'Ru? Come looking for him out here? The idea seemed preposterous. "Who's aboard her? Tell me what you see."

The Captain put the spyglass up again and studied the ship. "Two Druids standing at the bow. A pilot. Someone else. A boy, it looks like."

"Let me see."

The demon took the spyglass from the Captain and scanned the decks of the approaching airship. It was just as the Captain had said—four figures were visible on deck and no one else. No railguns were mounted, and no other weapons were to be seen. The demon lowered the spyglass and made a quick scan of the decks of the *Zolomach,* reassured by the presence of Federation soldiers at every turn. There was no reason to be worried.

Still, it was uneasy. What was a Druid airship doing way out there by itself? It was not there by chance. The encounter was not a coincidence.

"They're signaling to us," the Captain advised.

The demon glanced over at him in confusion. "Signaling?"

The Captain pointed to the line of pennants being raised along the other ship's foremast. "They wish to come aboard and speak with you. See the pennant with the silver and black on it? That's your pennant, Prime Minister. They must know you are aboard."

The demon's first impulse was to turn on the approaching airship and attack it at once. But the demon was trapped inside Sen Dunsidan's skin, and an unprovoked aggression against an ally would not be well received by the officers and men who crewed the ship. Worse, it might result in a battle they could not win. Although the Druid airship was not armed, the Druids themselves were formidable. If they were to damage the *Zolomach* and force another delay, it might prove fatal to the demon's plans to reach the Ellcrys.

White-hot fury fed the Moric's sense of frustration, but it kept calm outwardly. It would have to deal with the situation in a diplomatic way. "Move alongside them and ask what they wish to speak to us about," he ordered.

The Captain raised his own line of pennants, then maneuvered the *Zolomach* until she was close by her counterpart. The Druids stood at the railing, black-cloaked and hooded. The Moric glanced at the name carved into the ship's bow. *SWIFT SURE.*

"Sen Dunsidan!" shouted one of the Druids, the taller of the two, a woman by the sound of her voice. She kept her hood raised. "Shadea a'Ru sends greetings."

The Moric felt a twinge of panic. If Shadea had sent this ship and these Druids, then nothing good could come of it. After all, the Ard Rhys had already tried to kill it once. There was nothing to say that she was not about to try to do so again.

But then the demon remembered that it was no longer in the guise of Iridia Eleri, and it was the sorceress whom Shadea had sent assassins to kill. Sen Dunsidan was Shadea's ally. So far as the demon knew, nothing had happened to change that.

It calmed itself. "What does Shadea wish of me?" it shouted back in Sen Dunsidan's deep, resonant voice. "How can I be of service to the Ard Rhys?"

"She wishes to be of service to you," the speaker replied. "She wishes to present you with a gift that will be of use in negotiating with the Elves. She knows of the disaster on the Prekkendorran and wishes to mitigate the consequences. May I come over and present it?"

The Moric had no use for such a gift, but it understood that it could not afford to cast aside the offer out of hand. To do so would look suspicious. Worse, it would suggest that its motives in coming to the Westland were not peaceful. Shadea had allied herself and the Druids with Sen Dunsidan and the Federation. It made sense that she would want to aid the Prime Minister in his efforts at resolving the Federation dispute with the Free-born. She was as much at risk in this business as he was. The Moric wondered fleetingly how she had found out about where Sen Dunsidan was going and why, but it assumed she had spies at Arishaig who told her everything.

The Moric steeled itself. It would have to suppress its impulses and act as Sen Dunsidan would. This would only take a few minutes, and then it could be on its way. Better to placate the Druids than to irritate them.

"Let them board, Captain," it said to the *Zolomach's* commander. "But watch them closely in the event this is something other than what it seems."

The Captain nodded wordlessly, and the Moric climbed down from the pilot box and walked over to the railing to await its visitors.

It won't work, Pen kept thinking. *It will never work.*

But it did. He could scarcely believe it when the *Zolomach's* Captain ran up the line of signal pennants that invited the Druids aboard. He had been convinced that permission would be refused and they would be turned away without a second thought. But his father, who had conceived of the plan during the night and worked the details through carefully with his mother, had assured them all that the demon would relent. In its guise as Sen Dunsidan, it would be forced to do what Sen Dunsidan would do. It might want to turn them away, but it would realize that to do so would create suspicion and risk disruption of its efforts to reach the Ellcrys. Its overriding goal was to reach Arborlon as quickly as possible, Bek reminded them. It would do whatever was necessary to make that happen.

Under his father's steady hand, *Swift Sure* eased closer to the *Zolomach,* and lines were thrown from the latter to the former and secured by Pen to the anchor stanchions so that the two vessels were joined. Pen glanced up and down at the soldiers lining the other ship's railings and tried to reassure himself that they didn't matter, that the plan would work out as his father intended. His mother and Khyber, cloaked in the Druid robes his mother had stolen from Paranor and stowed aboard some weeks earlier, stood together at the bow, waiting patiently. They kept their hoods up and their features concealed. Sen Dunsidan didn't know any of them by sight save Tagwen, who was hiding belowdecks, but it didn't hurt to be cautious.

As he finished tying off the lines, Pen went over in his mind one last time the details of what was about to happen. If they were mistaken in any way about how the darkwand would react or if his aunt had guessed wrong about what he needed to do or, worst of all, if the King of the Silver River had deceived his father in his fever dream, then none of them were likely to return from the *Zolomach* alive. But it was mostly up to him to make the plan succeed, and it was his own judgment that was likely to determine how things turned out.

His mother and Khyber were moving along the railing toward the ramp that had been lowered from the *Zolomach* to allow them to board. Unbidden, he fell into step behind them, carrying the dark-wand in his right hand, the almost black, rune-carved surface gleaming in the sunlight. He sensed Sen Dunsidan's gaze—his demon's gaze—drawn to it. Cold and dead as deep winter, those blue eyes flared with sudden interest, and Pen felt a chill run up and down his spine.

Fighting down his repulsion and fear, he took a deep, steadying breath and stepped up onto the ramp behind his mother and Khyber as they walked slowly across to the other vessel. His father stood silently in the pilot box, showing no particular interest in the proceedings, a mercenary paid to do his job. But he would have already summoned the magic of the wishsong and be holding it at his fingertips. He would be watching carefully for any sign of treachery.

Pen paused to glance down. Below, the countryside spread away in a broad tapestry of mixed greens and mottled browns. They were several hundred feet in the air, suspended above the world with no place to run. Trapped, if things went wrong. But things would not go wrong, he told himself. He tightened his resolve and moved quickly off the ramp and onto the *Zolomach's* decks.

Federation soldiers and crew surrounded him, crowding in until there was nowhere left to stand. Seeing what was happening, Khyber lowered her hood to reveal her Elven features, glanced disdainfully at the men, made a quick warding motion with one hand, and watched in satisfaction as they fell backwards like stalks of grass in a heavy wind. Only the demon was left untouched. It smiled Sen Dunsidan's smile, gave Khyber a small nod of approval, and came forward until it was only steps away.

The smile froze. "We have not yet met."

Khyber bowed. "I am a servant to my mistress, Shadea a'Ru, the true Ard Rhys. My name is of no consequence. Shadea sends greetings and asks that you accept her gift of this staff. She would have come herself, but her presence at Paranor is required while matters remain so unsettled within the order. She sends my sister and myself in her place to offer reassurances of her commitment to the Federation. The staff is a demonstration of her support for your alliance."

She gestured dramatically past Rue, who was still cloaked and hooded, to where Pen waited with the darkwand. As prearranged, Pen lifted the staff and held it out so that it could be clearly seen.

"The staff," Khyber said to the demon, whose eyes were riveted on it, "has a special use."

She nodded to Pen, who turned his thoughts to the Forbidding and the creatures that lived within it. At once, his connection with the staff took hold and the runes blazed to life, a crimson glow that was blinding even in the bright morning sunshine. He saw that glow mirrored in the demon's gaze, hot and intense.

Khyber stepped close to the demon so that only it could hear. "The staff gives the holder the ability to command the attention of all who come into its presence. You can see that this is so. It also gives the holder small insights into the thinking of those with whom he negotiates, a window on their attitudes and concerns. It can be useful in knowing how best to persuade."

By now, images of the runes were dancing off the staff in wild patterns that flitted in the air all about Pen. The Federation soldiers and crew muttered excitedly. The demon blinked and its eyes took on a new look, one both hungry and anticipatory. It wanted the staff; it needed to possess it.

"Will you accept my mistress's gift?" Khyber pressed gently.

Sen Dunsidan's anxious features tightened, and the demon's eyes glittered. "I would be honored to accept it."

Khyber looked once more at Pen, who came forward obediently, eyes lowered as much out of fear for what was about to happen as for the demon itself. When he got to within three feet, he stretched out his arm and canted the glowing staff toward the demon. The demon reached for it, and then, for just a second, hesitated. Pen felt his heart stop.

Then Sen Dunsidan's face broke into a broad smile and his fingers closed about the staff.

From the moment it saw the staff, the demon knew it had to possess it. It was not a rational craving. It was a compulsion that defied explanation and transcended reason. It was so overpowering that the demon barely heard what the Druid was saying as she explained the staff's uses. And when the boy held the staff forth and the runes carved into its burnished surface flared with hypnotic brilliance, the demon was lost. The staff must be claimed. The demon was its rightful owner and must possess it. Nothing else mattered. Not the destruction of the Ellcrys. Not its plans to bring down the Forbidding. Nothing.

Even so, it hesitated for just a second when the staff was extended, a glimmer of suspicion aroused by recognition of the intensity of its inexplicable attraction.

But it took the staff anyway, and the moment it did so it realized it had made a mistake. The runes blazed like tiny flames as the demon's hand closed about the carved wood, and another kind of fire exploded through the demon in response. It was a fire of possession, of transference and of magic, a fire meant to cleanse and to purify. The demon felt it instantly, and tried to pull away. But its fingers would not release. They had taken on a separate existence, and no matter how hard it tried to loosen its grip, it could not.

It screamed then, a sound that rent the air and caused even the most hardened of the Federation soldiers to shrink away. It threw back its head and shrieked its defiance and fury. Some among the crew, the Captain included, came racing to its aid. The demon lashed out in response, its claws splitting the concealing skin of the human fingers, slashing and tearing at them until they fell bleeding on the deck of the airship.

The boy still gripped the other end of the darkwand, eyes wide and staring. He knew something of what was happening, the demon saw. Enraged, it snatched at him, trying to draw him close. But the boy ducked away, and one of the Druid women shouted at him to let go of the staff. They understood what was happening, as well, the demon realized. It stumbled toward them, its limbs leaden and unresponsive, filled with the fire of the magic, throbbing with the molten heat of its workings. The boy backed away, stubbornly keeping hold of the staff, and finally the taller of the women flung herself atop him, dragged him to the deck, pried loose his fingers from the staff, and pulled him clear.

Instantly, the light of the staff bloomed until the demon was enveloped by its glow. It fought furiously to free itself, slamming the staff against the deck, twisting and flailing futilely. The skin of the human Dunsidan split wide and the clothes of the human Dunsidan ripped and tore. Both fell away, leaving it fully revealed. Gasps and sharp hisses issued from the mouths of all who saw what it was, and there was a rush of booted feet on the wooden decks as men fled in all directions. The demon would have given chase, if it could have. It would have ripped their throats out. It would have drunk their blood. But it was consumed by its struggle with the staff and could do nothing but thrash and scream its hatred of them.

Then the light closed about it completely, and the world it had sought to subvert, together with the inhabitants it had come to despise, disappeared. The demon felt a crushing pressure on its chest and fought to breathe. It felt a shifting in time and place and realized in horror what was happening. It was going back into the Forbidding, back into the prison from which it had escaped. It was being returned to the world of the Jarka Ruus, a victim of the staff's magic, and there was nothing it could do to prevent it from happening.

It fought anyway, shrieking and spitting and thrashing, an insane thing, right up until the moment it blacked out.

Aboard the *Zolomach*, Federation soldiers and crew alike stared in shocked silence at the space Sen Dunsidan—or whatever had played at being Sen Dunsidan—had occupied only seconds before. Nothing remained but blood and shredded clothing and pieces of skin. None of them knew what had happened, and most didn't care to find out. All they wanted to know was whether there was any risk that the thing that had been the Prime Minister of the Federation was coming back.

Khyber swept the air in front of her with a sparkle of elemental magic to gain their attention, black Druid robes billowing out. "Back away!" she shouted at them, moving forward threateningly, occupying the space directly in front of what remained of Sen Dunsidan. She glanced down at those remains, and then up at dozens of frozen stares. "You didn't want him for a leader anyway, did you?"

Rue Meridian was hugging Pen, her face fierce. "What were you thinking, Penderrin?" she whispered. "It would have taken you with it if I hadn't broken your grip on the staff!"

Pen was white-faced, both from the pressure of his mother's grip and the realization of how narrow his escape had been. He took a deep breath. "I wasn't sure what would happen if I let go."

She hugged him tighter still. "Well, whatever the reason, you hung on too long to suit me. You scared me to death!"

"I wonder if it worked," he said softly.

"You wonder if what worked?"

"Something I tried, right there at the end. The staff and I were joined. We were communicating. I was telling it things. I was trying to make it understand me." He drew back and looked at her. "That was what I was doing, when I was hanging on, before you made me let go."

"Trying to tell the darkwand something?"

He smiled and nodded. "But I don't know if it understood."

It took a while for the Moric to regain consciousness after its struggle to resist being sent back into the Forbidding. As a result, it did not see the bright images projected into the air by the runes of the darkwand as it pulsated with light on the barren ground next to it. It did not see those images rise skyward to form intricate patterns that danced across the sullen clouds. By the time the demon stirred, the images had faded and the fire had gone out of the runes.

The Moric sat up slowly, knowing at once from the taste of the air and the smell of the earth that it was back inside its prison. It stared down at the staff, the once-gleaming surface become dusty and scarred. The runes had gone dark and the magic had disappeared. It was just a length of wood, a useless thing.

When it became aware of the shadow looming over it and looked up to find the dragon, the demon had to stifle a gasp. A huge, scaly, armored monster, it was easily the biggest the demon had ever seen. Freezing in place, the demon tried to figure out what to do, casting about in vain for a way to escape. The dragon was studying it intently, its lidded yellow eyes gleaming with a strange fascination.

And then it saw that the dragon wasn't looking at it, but at the staff that lay at its feet. The demon snatched up the staff and held it out to the beast, offering it eagerly. But the dragon didn't move. It was waiting for something. The demon laid the staff close by one of its huge, clawed feet and started to move away. But the dragon hissed at it in warning, freezing it in place.

The Moric turned back slowly, not knowing what to do, unable to determine what it was the dragon wanted.

The dragon, in no hurry, waited for the demon to figure it out.

THIRTY-ONE

The day was drenched in sunlight, and from high in the air where she rode aboard the Druid airship *Bremen*, Grianne Ohmsford could see the countryside for fifty miles in all directions. Huge, cottony clouds floated against the western horizon far out on the flats of the Streleheim, distant and remote, a soft promise of good weather. The airship sailed north on the first day of its expedition, and the woman who had once been Ard Rhys of the Third Druid Order was at peace.

She had known for a long time what she would do, she supposed. She had known from before she had come back through the Forbidding what must happen. The order would never heal while she was Ard Rhys, no matter how much she wanted to make it well, no matter how hard she tried to mend its wounds. The past is always with us, and more so with her than with most. She had accepted that she would never be free of that past.

She could chart the important phases of her life: as a child of six hiding in the cellar of her home with her baby brother while her parents were slaughtered in the rooms above; as a young girl subverted by the Morgawr into believing that the Druid Walker Boh had been responsible; as the Ilse Witch working to destroy Walker until a chance meeting with the brother she had thought dead revealed the truth; and as Ard Rhys of the Third Druid Order struggling to find a way to gain acceptance as a force for good within the Four Lands.

She could see the path her life had taken and comprehend the reasons for all that she had done. But she could never explain it satisfactorily to anyone else. She could try, but most would dismiss her words as clever attempts at self-justification or worse.

She understood the truth of things. Some would always see her as the Ilse Witch, and would worry that beneath the surface of the image she projected, a monster lurked. That would never change; the roots of mistrust had grown too deep. Traunt Rowan had been right about that. Had he been more patient and less foolish, he would have lived to see her admit it.

She glanced back at the pilot box, where one of Kermadec's Rock Trolls stood at the helm. Kermadec himself was seated on a box below the side wall, deep in conversation with Penderrin. She wondered what they were talking about. Even in the short time since the big Troll's recovery from the battle in the north tower, the two had grown close. After returning the Moric to the Forbidding, the boy had come back to Paranor with his parents and had remained to help her restore some semblance of order to the Druid's Keep. His parents had stayed, too, for a little while. But they had grown uncomfortable, as they always did with Paranor, and—seeing that she had matters well enough in hand, and missing their home and their old life—they had decided to go home to Patch Run.

But Pen had stayed on, his friendships with Kermadec, Tagwen, and Khyber Elessedil influencing his decision at least in part. All were aware of the transition Grianne was working; all were anxious to help her see it through. Pen could do no less, he told his parents. Bek understood; Rue accepted. They made him promise he would not stay past the end of the month. They wished Grianne and the others well, said good-bye, and flew *Swift Sure* home. Grianne never told them all of what she intended, although she would have liked to tell Bek. But it was best if she didn't, she told herself. It would be easier on them if they didn't know.

She had dissolved the order and dismissed those still in her service. As Ard Rhys, she had the power to do this, and there was no one who would question her now. She gave Paranor into the keeping of Khyber, Bellizen, and Trefen Morys. When the time was right and when they had found a way to do so, they would re-form the order. A handful of others who had remained loyal were invited to stay, as well. But she charged the three she trusted most with spearheading the task of carrying on, the ones she believed would work the hardest. All three had asked her to reconsider. All had pleaded inexperience and limited skills. They were not equal to the task. Others could do better.

But there were no others she could rely on, and there were covenants to monitor, a part of the agreement that she had forged with the Federation and the Free-born. Her young successors would struggle at first, but they would learn from their mistakes and they would grow from their experiences. They would survive, protected as they were by Paranor and their magic, by the mystique of the Druids, and by their own perseverance and determination. She had thought this through carefully after talking with each. It was the right choice.

In the end, persuaded that she would not accept their refusals, they had acquiesced. They would select those men and women who would make up the next generation of Druids at Paranor. Perhaps, in time, the governments and peoples of the Four Lands would come to accept them as a good and necessary force for the furtherance of peace and cooperation among the Races. Certainly, they would have a better chance of achieving that goal than Grianne did.

Just then the Elves and the Federation were in the difficult process of putting themselves back together. Arling Elessedil would serve as Queen regent until her eldest daughter grew to adulthood and assumed the throne. There was a rumor she would remarry and seek to put a son on the throne instead, that she would never permit her daughters to follow in the footsteps of their father and grandfather. She was a strong-willed, at times intractable woman, and she did not look back fondly on her marriage to Kellen Elessedil. With the war on the Prekkendorran ended, she was seeking ways to assure that madness of the sort he had displayed as King would never happen again. She would never achieve that goal, of course. Perhaps she knew that. But it did not stop her from trying.

Battered and disheartened by their defeat on the Prekkendorran, the Federation had withdrawn its armies, ceding to Callahorn and its people the lands to which it had laid claim during the war. After more than thirty years, the Southlanders had lost their taste for fighting a war that had netted them nothing. Sen Dunsidan was dead, and a new Prime Minister ruled the Coalition Council—a man who did not favor expansion as a goal and war as a means to an end. His people appeared to agree. There were those on both sides who believed that the war should be fought to the bitter end, those who would never accept any resolution short of victory on the battlefield, but they represented a small minority. A peace accord was swiftly brokered.

The threat presented by the deadly fire launcher was blunted, at least for the time being. As a condition to the peace she had brokered between the Federation and the Free-born, Grianne had won a single concession: There would be no further use of diapson crystals in the making of weapons. Diapson crystals would be used to power airships, and that would be all. The last fire launcher had been destroyed. The man who had invented it had disappeared and was believed dead, and his plans for building other weapons had been lost in a fire along with his models and designs. She had made certain of those things. She had assured herself that the matter was settled.

Her price for winning the agreement and assistance of all parties in enforcing covenants regarding the future use of diapson crystals was her promise to relinquish her place as head of the Druid order. Those who sought that did not know she had already made the decision to step down. It did not hurt to let them believe they had been responsible for persuading her. They were as frightened of her as they were of any weapon, and the bargain was easily struck.

She could not know if the bargain would be kept, but for the moment, at least, there was a fresh outlook in the governing bodies of the Races and a chance that common sense might prevail. Her successors would do their best to see that it did. Tagwen would serve as their adviser. Kermadec, who had re-formed the Druid Guard from among his own people, would see that they were protected. It was as much as anyone could hope for. It was the best she could do.

"Aunt Grianne?"

Penderrin stood at her elbow. She gave him a quick smile, her reflections and musings scattering like dust motes. "It's a beautiful day, Pen. Perhaps that is a good omen."

He smiled back guardedly. "Do you really think you can do something to help?" he asked. "Do you think there is a chance you can get her back?"

"I think maybe there is. Don't you?"

He bit his lip. "I think that if anyone can do it, you can."

"That is high praise, coming from a boy who found his way into the Forbidding and back again." She paused. "Perhaps when we get there, you will discover that you don't really need me after all, that you can do this by yourself."

She saw the unsettled look that crossed his face. "No," he said. "I've seen what's down there, how she's bound by the tree roots with the others. I don't think I would be strong enough to free her on my own."

They were flying to Stridegate and the island of the tanequil, where they would attempt to reclaim Cinnaminson. She thought that perhaps she had made the decision to do so even before coming out of the Forbidding, that she knew even then that she owed the boy that much. She understood from what he had told her how much the girl meant to him and how hard it had been to give up trying to free her and come looking for Grianne instead. That sort of sacrifice deserved more than a simple thank-you. She had waited until things were settled with the order and the treaties between the Federation and Free-born signed before acting. She had waited until his parents had returned home. It wasn't that she didn't think they would support their son's efforts to free Cinnaminson; indeed, they would want to help. But making the attempt was something she had decided she must do with Pen alone, for reasons she had kept to herself. Only Kermadec and his Trolls were invited to come along.

She put a hand on Pen's shoulder. "You are a lot stronger than you think," she said. "I want you to remember that. Don't make the mistake of underestimating what you can do."

He shrugged. "I'm not very strong, really." He hesitated. "I think that you are wonderful for doing this. I won't ever forget, even if we don't get her back."

She almost hugged him, but couldn't bring herself to do so. She had been distanced from others for too long, and although she might feel affection toward them, she was not comfortable with demonstrating it. She still saw herself as an outcast, as someone who didn't really belong anywhere and would never be close to anyone. Worse, she saw herself as dangerous, more so since the events that had taken place inside the Forbidding. The workings of the wishsong's magic when she had transformed herself into a Fury and when she had destroyed the Graumth had left her shaken. For the first time since she was a child, she was uncertain of the magic. Something about it was changed—perhaps still changing—and she was not sure how well she could control it.

She looked off into the horizon. "Strength comes to us through belief and determination, Pen. The trick is in recognizing how to use it."

"You've done that better than I have," he said quietly.

She glanced over at him and smiled.

How I wish that were true.

The grave diggers arrived around midday on their way south, and the old man invited them to eat with him. He set out ale and cheese and bread and sat with the three men around an old wooden table that occupied one corner of the porch and looked out over the fields of wheat he farmed as his family had farmed them for five generations.

"How is it up there?" he asked, after food and drink were consumed and the men were smoking.

The stocky one shook his head. "Bad. A lot of bodies. We did the best we could, along with the others. But they'll be finding the bones of those we missed for years."

"At least it's over," the old man said.

The tall one shook his head in reproof. "Should have been over years ago. Didn't accomplish anything, did it? Years and years gone and nothing's changed. Except a lot of good men are dead."

"And women," the stocky one added.

The tall one grunted. "Treaty with the Free-born gives us just exactly what we had before the war started. The only good thing that's come of all this is we have a new Prime Minister. Maybe he won't be as stupid as Sen Dunsidan was."

He looked at the old man. "Did you hear what happened with that one?"

The old man shook his head.

"I heard it from one of the soldiers on the *Zolomach.* He was there and saw it all. They were flying Dunsidan to Arborlon, maybe to make peace, maybe not. There's some debate. They had that weapon aboard, the one that shot down the Elven King and his whole fleet. Anyway, some Druids intercepted the ship. One of them had a staff with markings that glowed like fire. Soldier who told me this said Sen Dunsidan couldn't take his eyes off it. The Druids offered it to him, but when he took it, he changed into some sort of monster. Split right out of his skin, like a snake, then disappeared. No one's seen him since."

"Druid magic at work there," the stocky one declared softly. "More of it later, too, if you ask me. The *Zolomach* sailed back to Arishaig, was there maybe a day, caught fire, and burned to her keel. Everything destroyed. Took that weapon with her."

"A fire took the place where they built that weapon and the plans for it, too," the tall one said. "Nothing left but ash and smoke. You're right about those Druids. They were involved in it. Happened right after the witch reappeared. They thought she was gone, but she won't ever be gone, that one. Not her. What is it they called her before she was Ard Rhys? Ilse Witch. She comes back and all this happens? Not by chance, I don't think."

"Doesn't matter what you or I think," the third man said. "What matters is that the war is over, and we can get on with living our lives. There's been enough madness. I lost a brother and two cousins out there on the Prekkendorran. Everyone lost someone. For what? Tell me that. For what?"

"For Sen Dunsidan and his kind," the stocky man declared. "For the politicians and their stupid schemes." He took a long pull on his ale. "This is good," he said to the old man, smiling. "Good enough to help me forget the smell of all those dead men. Can I trouble you for another glass?"

When they were gone, the old man went back into the house, pulled aside the rug to the storm cellar, and let the two Elves out. They'd been in hiding down there for several weeks, too damaged at first to do much more than sleep and eat, and then too weak to travel. He'd nursed them as best he could, using the remedies and skills he had acquired from his mother when she was still alive and working the fields with him. The man was the worse of the two, shot through with arrows and cut with blades in a dozen places. But the woman wasn't much better. He'd helped them because they were hurt and that was the kind of man he was. The war on the Prekkendorran was not his war and not his concern. No Federation war ever had been.

"They're gone," he said as the two climbed back into the light.

Pied Sanderling glanced around, and then reached back for

Troon's hand. The day was clouded, but warm and calm, and it felt good to come back into the light. The old man brought them up whenever it was safe to do so, but that hadn't been often until now. They all knew before the treaty what would happen if they were caught out.

"Did you hear what they said?" the old man asked them.

Pied nodded. He was thinking of those who had gone with him into the Federation camp. He was thinking that their efforts had been worth something after all. The tide of war might have turned on the destruction of the *Dechtera* and her deadly weapon. Twenty-four hours later, Vaden Wick had broken the siege, counterattacked, and driven the Federation off the heights. In the end, the Free-born had prevailed.

Now, it seemed, any danger of fresh weapons of the sort the *Dechtera* had carried was ended, as well. If the Druids had intervened, the chances were good that whatever remained of those weapons had been hunted down and destroyed.

"Sit, and I'll bring you a glass of ale," the old man offered.

He had saved their lives. He had cared for and protected them while they recovered. He had asked nothing about them, nothing from them. He had been kind to them in a place and time when some would have wished them dead and worked to make the wish a reality. They were Elves and enemy soldiers. The old man didn't seem to care.

They took chairs at the table while the old man brought the glasses and set them down. When he left to feed the animals in the barn, Pied looked at Troon. "I guess it's finally over."

She nodded. They were mirror images of each other, their faces cut and bruised, their limbs bandaged, and their bodies so sore that every movement hurt. But they were alive, which was more than they could say about any of the others who had gone with them that night. They would have been dead, too, if not for the old man. He had been burning off a field he had partially cleared, the fire still bright even after darkness fell, and they had homed in on that beacon. The old man had seen the flit come down, found them in the wreckage, and taken them in. He had thrown what remained of the flit into the fire, and then lied to the Federation soldiers who came looking the next morning. Neither of them knew why. Maybe he was just like that. Maybe, like the grave diggers, he'd had enough of war.

"We can go home now," he said to her.

She gave him a bitter smile. "To Arborlon? Where Arling is Queen?"

She was reminding him that he was forbidden to return to Arborlon, that Arling had dismissed him from her service.

They stared at each other wordlessly.

"Let's not go home," she said finally. She held his gaze. "Let's go somewhere else. They think we are dead. Let's leave it that way. Have you anyone waiting for you?"

He thought about Drum for a moment and shook his head. "No."

"Nor I." She took a quick breath and exhaled sharply. "Let's start over. Let's make a new home."

He studied her face, appreciating the straightforward, uncomplicated way it revealed her. With Troon, there was never any question about what she was feeling. Certainly, there wasn't any question there. She was in love with him. She had told him that night on the flit. She had told him any number of times since. The revelation had surprised him, but pleased him, too. Eventually, while they recovered from their wounds, he realized he was in love with her, too.

She reached out for his hands and took them in her own. "I want to spend the rest of my life with you. But I don't want to do it in a place that reminds me of the past. I want to do it where we can start over again and leave behind what we've known. Do you love me enough to do that?"

He smiled. "You know I do."

They smiled at each other across the table, sharing feelings that shouldn't be put into words because words would only get in the way.

They set the *Bremen* down in the gardens that fronted the bridge to the island of the tanequil, anchoring her well back, but safely within walking distance. Stridegate's ruins were empty and still on an afternoon filled with sunshine and blue sky. They had flown into the Inkrim that morning, sailing out of night's departing darkness into dawn's bright promise, the boy and she standing together at the bow and looking down at the world. They had not spoken a word, lost in their separate thoughts. She thought she could probably guess at his but that he could not possibly know hers.

The Urdas were not in evidence on that visit, but Kermadec and his Trolls kept careful watch for them, even after they were anchored and on the ground. Urdas would not enter the ruins, it was said. They would not come into any place they considered sacred. Kermadec was taking no chances, and sent scouts in all directions with instructions to make sure.

Grianne turned to him. "Keep watch for us, Old Bear," she said with a smile. "This won't take long."

He shook his great, impassive face in disagreement. "I wish you would let this wait for a while longer, Mistress. You have been through too much already. If there is a confrontation down there—"

"There will be no confrontation," she said quickly, putting a reassuring hand on his armored wrist. She glanced over to where Penderrin stood at the bridgehead, looking over at the island. "This isn't to be an encounter of that sort."

She took her hand away. "You were the best of them all," she told him. "No one was more faithful or gave more to me when it was needed. I will never forget that."

He looked away. "You should go now, so that you can be back before dark." There was resignation in his eyes. He knew. "Go, Mistress."

She nodded and turned away, walking over to join the boy. He glanced at her as she came up beside him, but said nothing. "Are you ready?" she asked.

He shook his head. "I don't know. What if the tanequil won't let us cross?"

"Why don't we see?"

She walked out onto the bridge, the boy following, and called up the magic of the wishsong, humming softly to let it build, working on the message she wanted it to convey. She stopped perhaps a quarter of the way across until she had it just right, then released the magic into the afternoon silence and let it drift downward into the ravine. She gave it the whole of what she thought was needed, taking her time, content to be patient if patience was what was required.

It was not. A response came almost immediately, a shifting of heavy roots within the earth, a rustle of leaves and grasses, a whisper

of wind. Voices, soft and lilting, that only she could hear. She understood what it meant.

"Come, Pen," she said.

They crossed untroubled to the other side of the bridge and
walked to the trail that had led the boy into the ravine weeks earlier
in his search for Cinnaminson. The island forest was deep and still,
the air cooler, the light diffuse, and the earth dappled with layered
shadows. She watched Pen cast about, eyes shifting left and right,
searching. He was looking for the aeriads, but she already knew they
would not come. Nothing would come to them now. Everything was
waiting.

They found the trailhead and stopped. The path wound downward in a steep descent that gradually faded into a mix of mist and
shadows. It was so dark within the ravine that they could not see the
bottom. It was the sort of place she had entered many times. It was a
mirror of her heart.

She turned to him. "You are to wait here for me, Pen. I will do
this best if I am alone. I know what is needed. I will bring Cinnaminson back to you."

He studied her face carefully, unable to keep the hope from his
eyes. "I know you will try, Aunt Grianne."

She reached out impulsively and hugged the boy. It was something she had seldom done, and it felt awkward, but the boy was
quick to hug her back, and that made her feel better about it.

"Be careful," he whispered.

She broke away, moving slowly down the trail toward the shadows.

"Thank you," he called after her. "For doing this."

She gave him a small wave in response, but did not look back.

The afternoon eased toward evening, and the light shifted and
began to fade. Pen stood until he grew tired, then sat with his back
against an ancient trunk, staring down into the ravine, keeping
watch. He listened for sounds he did not care to think of too carefully, but no sounds came. Silence cloaked the ravine and the forest
and, for all he knew, the entire world. He watched patterns of light
and shadows form and re-form, slow-moving kaleidoscopic images
against the earth. He smelled the scents released into air by the for-

est and the things that lived there. He rubbed the blunted tips of his damaged fingers and remembered how they had gotten that way. He remembered what it had felt like to become joined to the tanequil through the carving of the runes. He remembered night in the island forest and his terrifying encounter with Aphasia Wye.

Mostly, he remembered Cinnaminson. He could picture her face and the way she smiled. He could remember the way she moved. He could hear her voice. She was there, alive and well within his mind, and it made him want to cry for his loss.

But he smiled instead. He knew she was coming back to him. He believed in his aunt Grianne. He had faith in her magic and her skills, in her promise that she would find a way. He loved Cinnaminson, although he had never loved a girl before and had no frame of reference from which to draw a comparison. But love seemed to him to be a state of mind peculiar to each, and there was no set standard by which you could measure its strength. He knew what he felt for Cinnaminson, and if the difference between what he felt when he had her with him and when he did not was an accurate measure, then he could not imagine how love could be any stronger.

Time slipped away, and at last, when no one had appeared and darkness had begun to close about, he found himself wondering what he would do if his aunt failed and Cinnaminson didn't come back to him.

He dozed then, made sleepy-eyed by the warmth and brightness of the late afternoon sun slanting down through breaks in the branches of the trees. He did not fall deeply asleep, but hovered at the edge of wakefulness, arms about his drawn-up knees, head sunk on his chest.

Eyes closed, he drifted.

Then something stirred him awake—a whisper of sound, a hint of movement, a sense of presence—and he looked up to find Cinnaminson standing before him. She was more ghost than flesh and blood, pale and thin and disheveled in her tattered clothes. He got to his feet slowly and stood looking at her, afraid that he was mistaken, that he might be hallucinating.

"It's me, Pen," she said, tears welling in her eyes.

He didn't rush to her, didn't grasp her and hold her close, although he wanted to do that, to make certain of her. Instead, he walked up to her as if time didn't matter. He took her hands and held them, studying her face, the spray of freckles and the milky eyes. The musty smell of earth and damp emanated from her body, and tendrils of root ends still clung to her arms.

He reached out and touched her face.

"I'm all right," she said. She touched his face. "I missed you. Even when I was one of them and thought I couldn't possibly be happier, I remembered you and missed you. I don't think that ever would have stopped."

She put her arms around him and held on to him as if she was afraid she would be taken away again, and he could feel her crying against his shoulder. He started to speak, then gave it up and just hugged her, closing his eyes and losing himself in the warmth of her body.

"Who was it who came down for me?" she asked him finally, her voice muffled. She lifted her head from his shoulder put her mouth close to his ear. "I don't understand it," she whispered. "Why did she do it? Why did she trade herself for me?"

Pen thought his heart would stop.

In the air above them, the aeriads hummed and sang and danced on the breeze, invisible and soundless. Heedless of time's passage, they played in the soft glow of the sunset's red and gold and the evening's deep indigo. They were spirits unfettered by the restrictions of the human body and the limitations of the human existence. They were sisters and friends, and the whole of the world was their playground.

One strayed momentarily, the newest of them, looking down on the young couple that stood at the edge of the ravine and spoke in soft, comforting tones, their heads bent close. The girl was telling the boy about her, and the boy was trying to understand. She knew it would be hard, that he might never come to terms with what she had done for the girl. But she had done it for herself, too—to give herself a new life, to set herself on a different path, to be reborn. She had known what she would do almost from the time the boy had spoken of the girl's transformation and of her joy at what she had experienced. She had wanted that for herself. That the boy and the girl would make a better life together than apart was incentive to take the chance. Offer herself for the girl, a woman not so young, but deeply talented and magically enhanced, a creature Mother Tanequil could not help but covet.

The trade was simple; the change of places was done in a heartbeat and a small balance to things was set in place.

Come, sister, the others called to her.

She lingered a moment longer, thinking of what she had given up and finding she had no regrets. There was nothing of her old life that was so precious to her, nothing so compelling as even the first few moments of this new one. Too many years of struggle and travail, of heartbreaking loss and backbreaking responsibility, of failure, ruin, and death had marked the path of her life. She would never escape from it in human form. She knew that; she accepted it. But as a creature of the air she had left it all behind, a part of another life.

She watched the boy and the girl turn away and start back through the woods toward the stone bridge. Maybe they would find in their lives something of what she had failed to find in hers. She had already found something precious in her new form, something she had not known since she was six years old and living still in the house of her parents with her baby brother.

She had found freedom.

ABOUT THE AUTHOR

TERRY BROOKS is the *New York Times* bestselling author of more than twenty books, including *The Sword of Shannara*, The Voyage of the *Jerle Shannara* trilogy: *Ilse Witch*, *Antrax*, and *Morgawr*, the High Druid of Shannara trilogy, which includes *Jarka Ruus* and *Tanequil*, the non-fiction book *Sometimes the Magic Works: Lessons from a Writing Life*, and the novel based upon the screenplay and story by George Lucas, *Star Wars®*: Episode I *The Phantom Menace™*. His novels *Running with the Demon* and *A Knight of the Word* were selected by the Rocky Mountain News as two of the best science fiction/fantasy novels of the twentieth century.

The author was a practicing attorney for many years but now writes full-time. He lives with his wife, Judine, in the Pacific Northwest and Hawaii.

About the Type

This book was set in Weiss, a typeface designed by a German artist, Emil Rudolf Weiss (1875–1942). The designs of the roman and italic were completed in 1928 and 1931 respectively. The Weiss types are rich, well-balanced, and even in color, and they reflect the subtle skill of a fine calligrapher.